"Did you just arrive in Norcastle?" she asked pointedly. He could tell she was fishing.

"I came in on the bus last night."

"Were people shooting at you before you came to town?"

"Nope. Is this how you welcome newcomers?"

"Hardly. I'd lose my job for sure. I will find out who did this, Mr. Stone."

"Oh, that's easy. I already know who wants me dead." He grunted as he slipped his arms in a chambray shirt, stained with dirt from many hours on the job.

"Well, do tell. I can't help you if you're withholding information."

"The Spencers."

Sylvie let out a laugh. Such a loud, robust sound for a little lady. Ian pictured the chief of police issuing orders in the same tone. People would take notice of her, although she'd had his attention long before she opened her mouth to speak.

HOLIDAY
MOUNTAIN RESCUE

KATY LEE
&
HOPE WHITE

Previously published as *High Speed Holiday*
and *Christmas Undercover*

LOVE INSPIRED
INSPIRATIONAL ROMANCE

LOVE INSPIRED®
INSPIRATIONAL ROMANCE

ISBN-13: 978-1-335-23092-8

Holiday Mountain Rescue

Copyright © 2020 by Harlequin Books S.A.

High Speed Holiday
First published in 2016. This edition published in 2020.
Copyright © 2016 by Katherine Lee

Christmas Undercover
First published in 2015. This edition published in 2020.
Copyright © 2015 by Pat White

This edition published by arrangement with Harlequin Books S.A.

For questions and comments about the quality of this book,
please contact us at CustomerService@Harlequin.com.

Love Inspired
22 Adelaide St. West, 40th Floor
Toronto, Ontario M5H 4E3, Canada
www.Harlequin.com

Printed in U.S.A.

Katy Lee writes suspenseful romances that thrill and inspire. She believes every story should stir and satisfy the reader—from the edge of their seat. A native New Englander, Katy loves to knit warm, woolly things. She enjoys traveling the side roads and exploring the locals' hideaways. A homeschooling mom of three competitive swimmers, Katy often writes from the stands while cheering them on. Visit Katy at katyleebooks.com.

Books by Katy Lee

Love Inspired Suspense

Warning Signs
Grave Danger
Sunken Treasure
Permanent Vacancy
Amish Country Undercover
Amish Sanctuary

Roads to Danger

Silent Night Pursuit
Blindsided
High Speed Holiday

Visit the Author Profile page
at Harlequin.com for more titles.

HIGH SPEED HOLIDAY

Katy Lee

You intended to harm me,
but God intended it for good to accomplish
what is now being done, the saving of many lives.
—*Genesis* 50:20

To my dad, John. I love that you are my biggest fan.
And I love you.

Acknowledgments

I am so grateful for my editors
at Harlequin Love Inspired Suspense
for their help and insights in making the
Roads to Danger series come alive. Thank you,
Emily Rodmell, Shana Asaro and Giselle Regas.
Your enthusiasm made all the difference.

ONE

Was a cop ever really off duty?

Chief of Police Sylvie Laurent didn't think so. She freed her hands from her wool gloves and pocketed them in her winter police coat.

Then she unclipped her gun holster.

Trouble never waited for her to clock in, and it wasn't about to start now.

Even when it posed as a good-looking man sporting a golden tan.

"You're not in Kansas anymore," she mumbled aloud, heading the stranger's way. Or, with his bronze skin maybe she should say Cali.

He appeared like a black sheep against a sea of snow white—the snow-covered grounds of Spencer Speedway, as well as the paled complexions of the townspeople he pushed through. It would be months before any of them glowed a golden bronze like that, maybe not ever.

So, who was he? And why was he here?

A group of local children with cotton candy frozen to their cold faces cut in front of her, innocent to the possible threat at the annual Jingle Bell Jam celebration. The Christmas event put on by the Spencer family for longer than Sylvie could remember wasn't a tourist at-traction. It was something the Spencers offered to their employees every year to start off the holiday festivities. That included pretty much everyone in Norcastle, New Hampshire, but it did *not* include this guy.

A horn from the racetrack blew. Sylvie kept walking, even though she knew she was expected down in the pits. The small 1940s reproduction cars called Legends were set to compete on the track in ten minutes. Sets of snow tires strapped under the carriages of the tiny vehicles would give the crowd some excitement as the teen division of drivers raced to the finish line in the annual Legends snow race. Her son would be among them—and expect her to be on the sidelines.

Duty calls. Sorry, Jaxon.

The stranger's eyes met hers, chilling her with their hold. There was something about their ice-blue color that was so familiar. With one blink, he took them away and dismissed her.

Bad move, mister.

Sylvie picked up her steps to cut him off, but three teenage boys stepped in front of the guy, blocking her path. Just a few feet from making contact, she ran into one of the boys, knocking something to the ground. A glance down and her plans changed in an instant.

A can of beer lay in the snow.

She picked it up. "Belong to you?" she asked one of the teens, noticing his bulkier-than-normal parka. A closer look at all three boys, the same age as her fourteen-year-old son, and she noticed they were all smugglers today.

Sylvie took her last look at the black sheep's retreat-ing back and decided he would have to wait.

"Unless you boys want to be cuffed and stuffed in the backseat of my cruiser, I suggest you hand over the alcohol you have in your pockets."

Bret Dolan, the son of Norcastle's mayor, flicked his straight, dirty blond bangs from his eyes and lifted a defiant chin to Sylvie.

Like father, like son.

"I don't know what you're talking about," the boy spouted. "That's not ours. That was already on the ground. We just have a couple sodas." The boy lifted a cola out of his pocket. "See?"

Sylvie reached inside her navy blue uniform coat. "Shall I call your parents, Bret, for the show when I search you? I'm game for an audience." Sylvie took out her cell phone. She checked the bars and saw none, but she didn't let on about the lack of coverage, which was spotty in these mountains on most days.

On a huff, the Dolan kid reached into his other pocket and withdrew a can of beer. He jammed it over to Sylvie.

"Crack it open and pour it out," she instructed without touching it.

"Really? You can't be serious." Bret's distaste for the whole event became even more evident as each of the boys followed suit with the same task, their lifted spirits at getting away with something doused right along with the six-pack of beer now on the snow around them.

"I'm very serious. I care for your safety, Bret, even if you don't see that right now."

"You don't care for me. You just hate alcohol because your mother drank herself to death when you got knocked up."

The horn from the racetrack blew again, but its penetrating sound paled in comparison to the pulsing of blood pumping behind Sylvie's ears at Bret's remark. She bit back a lethal response. She was sure the boy was only repeating what he'd heard his father say. "Why aren't you racing today, Bret? You should be out there."

"Mind your business," the boy spouted off. Again his dad's words. She let Bret's disrespect go…for now.

"The next time I catch you, I take you in," Sylvie said. She looked Bret in the eyes, holding his attention on her. "Tell your mom I said hi."

He blinked a few times. Then he sent her a scathing look as his friends dragged him away.

She hoped someday he would see that she cared for his safety, his and his mom's. She prayed it would be soon. For now, though, she had a stranger to find.

Sylvie hit the button to her radio on her shoulder. "Preston, Buzz, Chief here. I know you're at the track. Be on the lookout for an adult male in his early thirties, shaggy black hair and black leather coat, about six feet in height. Not from around here. Just want to make sure he's not about to cause any problems."

"10-4, Chief" came a response from one of her lieutenants.

Scanning the crowds in the grandstand and still finding no sign of the black sheep, she entered through the fence marked Authorized Personnel and sought out the number eleven coupe her son drove. He weaved his tiny yellow car in a wavy line with the other racers, who were warming up their reflexes for the start of the race. The yellow flags waved, but as soon as the lead car approached the starting line, it would be go time.

She hadn't missed it after all.

As a single parent with a full-time job there was a lot she missed in her son's life. It caused a wedge.

She sighed at the growing distance between her and her son and thanked God that Jaxon was behind the wheel today and not smuggling alcohol with Bret and his gang.

Thank You, Lord, for watching out for him when I can't. Just as You watched out for me fourteen years ago. You never left me to raise him alone.

Unlike Jaxon's birth father.

Unlike everyone else in her family.

The starting horn blared. The green flags waved like crazy. The crowds behind her in the towering grandstand cheered. The race was on.

Sylvie watched her son take the lead from the number eight car. His tiny vehicle roared as its motorcycle engine was pushed to the max. She fisted a hand in the air. "Go, Jaxon!"

Her son had been racing cars since he was six, starting with little go-karts. It wasn't a cheap sport, by any means, but Sylvie worked extra shifts to give him something he could be proud of and work toward, something that kept him off the streets. She hadn't been too excited about him following in his birth father's footsteps, but she lived in a racing town and it was hard to steer Jaxon in other directions. Her brother was out in the world following circuit after circuit, racing on tracks in strange and exotic locales now. She'd barely heard from him since Mom had died.

Jaxon lost the lead, and Sylvie snapped out of her reverie, especially when his wheels swerved off to the left.

What was he doing? Sylvie rushed forward a few steps, but knew she couldn't get any closer to the track to find out. She scanned the area for Roni Spencer Rhodes, her son's trainer and owner of the racetrack. Would Roni know if something was wrong?

Sylvie spotted her friend in a white down coat and matching hat and scarf, her long red hair whipped a bit in the cold wind. She wore a headset that had to be connected to Jaxon. Sylvie headed Roni's way, but as she approached, she noticed out of the corner of her eye someone else approaching Roni.

The stranger!

He had no business being behind the fence.

His ice-blue eyes targeting Roni dead-on said otherwise.

The race became immediately forgotten. Sylvie reached for her weapon. "Stop right there!" She raised her voice to be heard over the motors.

The unidentified man came to an abrupt halt.

Sylvie took three determined steps, her hand curled around her gun's handle. A bang from the track echoed through the valley, bouncing off the surrounding White Mountains and back again.

The man flew forward at her and fell to his knees. Sylvie withdrew her gun and took aim. The crowds in the grandstand inhaled and shouted at the same time. Had they all seen her draw her weapon?

Or was something else going down on the track that claimed their attention?

A quick glance showed a mass of cars piling up and flipping. Number eleven's wheels were overturned.

Jaxon!

Sylvie wanted to run to him but the stranger now lay facedown on the snow, blood spatter around him, stark in its rich contrast of dark on light, like the man himself.

He was injured.

But how?

Torn between him and her son, Sylvie holstered her weapon and dropped to the stranger's side. A hole in the arm of his leather coat showed where an object had entered his body. Something flying off the track?

She inspected at a closer range.

No. A bullet.

Sylvie took in the perimeter in short, jerky perusals for a shooter in the area.

No time. She had to first take care of the victim.

She lifted the man under his arms and dragged him behind a snow pile. A groan told her he was conscious.

"Sir, I'm Chief Sylvie Laurent. Can you tell me your name?" she yelled over the ensuing chaos around her.

"Ian Stone," the man groaned and moved to turn.

"Stay still, Mr. Stone. I'm calling for help." Sylvie reached for her radio.

"No!" The man raised his good hand. "No help." He pushed himself to his knees. Blood seeped from his left shoulder, his other hand stretched across his wide chest to staunch the flow.

"Ian, I need to get you to the hospital. And you need to stay down. The shooter is still out there."

He shook away from her grasp. "Help the drivers. Not me." He stood up and mumbled, "I should have known they would take me out. I should have known this was too good to be true." He half ran, half staggered to the fence exit. The alarmed crowd of spectators behind it swallowed him whole.

A war waged in Sylvie. She had to go after him. What if he bled out and died? She couldn't have a murder in Norcastle. And a murder it would be. She knew a gunshot when she saw one. The crash had muffled the sound, and the mountains…

Sylvie looked to the lofty peaks overlooking the race-track.

The mountains were hiding a killer. The marksman could be out there somewhere on Mount Randolph. He could go after Ian Stone again.

Sylvie hit her radio to call her team, but all emergency personnel were flooding the track to help the drivers, the kids.

The place she needed to be, too.

Jaxon.

Sylvie zeroed in on her son being lifted from his car, awake but limping, his pale blond hair that matched her own shielded his eyes, but he was talking. Her heart lodged in her throat as she watched him enter one of the ambulances opened and ready to whisk him off to the hospital. The police and paramedics had everything under control, and he was in good hands.

Sylvie stepped in the direction Ian Stone had staggered off in, the direction she was needed most.

Her conflicted steps turned to a full, determined run.

She'd known Ian Stone was trouble the second she'd laid eyes on him.

But apparently, someone else did, too.

Ian slammed the door of the studio apartment he'd rented the day before. Carrying a pharmacy bag, he put it between his teeth as he tore off his coat and dropped it to the wood floor of the old factory mill, now turned into living quarters. The brick building was one of many along the river in this old New England mill town—a place he supposedly had been born in thirty years ago, but hadn't known existed until two weeks ago.

The bullet hole in his arm said someone wasn't happy about him finding out.

Pain from his shoulder seared like an unrelenting burn. Of course it had to be his already injured arm. Two weeks ago he'd had surgery on his shoulder for a bad rotator cuff, an injury he'd had for years but left unrepaired for lack of funds. Working construction these past two years for Alex Sarno had finally given him enough to check himself into a hospital for the procedure.

But how would he pay for a gunshot wound?

The Spencer money perhaps? And not because he'd taken a bullet on their property. According to the guy who'd shown up in his hospital room after the surgery, their money was also his money.

All these years he had an inheritance to claim and never knew.

Thirty years ago, a car was pushed over the side of a mountain. The crash left two very rich parents dead and their three children orphans. Except when the smoke cleared and the blaze was extinguished, only two children were accounted for. Little eighteen-month-old Luke Spencer's body had never been recovered.

Instead, he grew up across the country in a cabin in the Washington mountains, playing the unwanted son to Phil and Cecilia Stone.

Ian bit hard as he ripped off his green T-shirt, the words Sarno Construction scrawled across the front. His wound seeped blood, but not at an alarming rate. He would live to collect his inheritance and soon the T-shirts would read Sarno and Stone. Alex had already offered him a partnership. The idea of being a business owner was more than a dream come true. Things like this didn't happen to Ian Stone, or Ian the Idiot as his father called him too many times to count.

But he wasn't Ian Stone, if he believed the guy in his hospital room. He was the missing sibling, Luke Spencer.

Judging by the poor welcome home, however, his brother and sister didn't want to share the wealth. But would they take another shot at him to see they didn't have to?

Ian bounded around the sofa bed and pulled the blinds closed just in case. With his teeth he ripped the package of cleansing wipes open.

A bang on his door jerked him alert.

"Now's not a good time!" he shouted. He hoped it was just the landlady, Mrs. Wilson or Wilton, or whatever. A busybody was what she was. So many questions. *Where are you from, Mr. Stone? Do you have family in Norcastle, Mr. Stone? Perhaps I know them. What are their names?*

"But at least she didn't shoot me," he muttered, then seethed when the alcohol splashed over his wound.

The door knocked again, harder.

"Go away!" he yelled, biting through the pain.

"Ian Stone, this is Police Chief Sylvie Laurent. I need you to open this door."

The cop from the track? The one with the eyes. Great. "I did nothing wrong. Leave me alone!"

"Sir, I didn't say you did anything wrong. But you were shot right in front of me. It's my job to make sure you live. Open this door, or I will call for backup and do this the hard way."

Backup? That's all he needed, people in uniform taking sides. They'd probably arrest him for extortion. Ian figured he could play the victim to the little slip of a woman they called chief. The fact that she was the chief stumped him.

She shouldn't be too hard to get rid of.

Ian opened the door ajar. "I'm fine, Officer, really. I can take care—"

The door banged in on him with a force that sent him backward. She jammed a thumb over her shoulder as she pushed past him. Dark blotches of blood drops lay stark against the snow behind her. "You're dripping. You are not fine. Now take a seat," she commanded, pointing to the stool at the breakfast bar.

The cop washed her hands, ignoring the fact that Ian remained standing. She removed a pair of latex gloves from a compartment on her belt. "Sit," she said and slapped them on.

He obeyed and she quickly cleaned his wound and prodded around for the bullet.

Her ministrations killed, but Ian wasn't about to let on in the presence of this small, but tough, woman. While on the stool, their eye levels matched.

Green.

He smiled.

"I'm sorry I'm hurting you," she said without glancing up from his wound.

"Hurting? Nah, not at all. I could stay here all day." He leaned closer to her face, zeroing in on her almond-shaped eyes. "They've got to be jade."

"What does?" she asked absently.

"Your eyes. They're the inspiration of epic poems. Marlowe, Yeats, Ovid. I'm not sure any of the greats would do them justice. When I saw you at the track, I thought it was a trick of the sun, but it wasn't. Has anyone ever told you how beautiful they are?"

A startled look from under long curved lashes came his way. Her eyes narrowed. "Has anyone ever told you, you are a glutton for pain?" She pushed her finger through his wound.

Ian yelled out and bit down under her digging. He moaned and gagged and stopped breathing as she continued, succumbing under her thumb to being a puddle of feebleness.

Her gloved fingers removed the bullet and she held it up to him with a brilliant smile of victory. "Got it."

The slug blurred in front of him and he gagged again. "I think I'm going to pass out." He'd still yet to breathe.

"It's possible. You also need stitches to stop the bleeding." She put the bullet in a small plastic bag she took from another belt compartment and reached for the bandages. "I need to take you to the hospital."

"No." Ian straightened, swallowing the bile rising in his throat. "You obviously know what you're doing. Just do what you have to do and stitch me up."

She applied butterfly bandages to pull the holes closed, but shook her head. "Sir, these won't hold. You need to let me take you."

"You gonna pay for it?"

She stilled her hand. "You don't want help because of finances?"

"More like lack of them."

"You don't need to worry about that."

"You obviously never had to enter a hospital without a way to pay for your visit."

The chief frowned.

He'd upset her. The idea of hurting her made him feel like a creep. "I'm sorry. I shouldn't have said that."

"We all have our stories, but I can tell you the hospital will not turn you away, no matter what yours is. Trust me. Let me bring you. It's only about a thirty-minute ride."

"Thanks, but you can save the gas."

"I have to go there anyway. That crash at the track? My son was in it. He's probably already flipping out that I'm not there."

Ian studied the officer's face for what she wasn't saying. He detected a glimpse of fear, and suddenly she wasn't just a cop. She was a mom. "Was he badly hurt?" Ian asked.

Her eyelids closed on a sigh. "No, I thank the Lord that he walked away. Barely, but he walked." She re-opened them and got back to work on his arm. "So you see, I do need to get over there. We're all each of us has."

"No dad in the picture?" He felt odd asking, as if it was any of his business.

"Not needed." Her answer was even stranger.

But then Ian thought of his own old man, and understood her statement perfectly. "The man who raised me died recently. I hadn't seen him in ten years. Not needed. I get it."

"So, you'll let me take you?"

"I have a feeling that's not really a question."

"It's not, and every second that goes by is making my son feel abandoned."

"Way to tack on the guilt. Fine. For your son's sake. Let me grab another shirt, then my coat…what's left of it."

Sylvie taped the gauze in place and he reached for his duffel bag, his clothes still jammed inside, unpacked.

"Did you just arrive in Norcastle?" she asked pointedly, obviously fishing.

"I came in on the bus yesterday."

"Were people shooting at you before you came to town?"

"Nope. Is this how your town welcomes newcomers?"

"Hardly. I'd lose my job for sure. Any idea who did this?"

"Yup." He grunted as he slipped his arms into a chambray shirt, stained with dirt from many hours on the job.

"Well, do tell. I can't help you if you're withholding information."

"The Spencers."

Sylvie let out a laugh. Such a loud, robust sound for one so small. Ian pictured the chief of police issuing orders in the same tone. People would take notice of her, although she'd had his attention long before she opened her mouth to speak. Still, he didn't like her laughing at him, and that's what her reaction felt like.

"What's so funny, Chief?"

"You are. Roni and her brother Wade are not trying to kill you. You're completely wrong about that. Why would you think they want you dead?"

He snatched his MP3 player and headphones from the bag and stuffed them in his front blue jeans pocket. "Because they have something that belongs to me, and they don't want to give it up."

"Well, I don't believe they'd put a bullet in your arm, no matter what they have of yours, but I do plan to find who did pull the trigger. There hasn't been a premeditated murder in Norcastle in thirty years, and I want to keep it that way." She opened the door and scanned the area before telling Ian to follow her to her cruiser.

"Who was the unfortunate victim, then?" Ian asked—as if he didn't know.

Sylvie opened the passenger-side door for him, then came around the front of the car. Once behind the wheel, she replied, "Actually, it was Bobby and Meredith Spencer. Wade and Roni's parents."

And mine.

Ian faced front, revealing nothing to the local PD. He couldn't be sure the police could be trusted. After all, his parents were murdered, pushed over the side of that mountain in their car, and the police thirty years ago called the crash an accident.

Had the police been a part of the crime?

Did they know why he had been taken from the scene?

Ian peered out from the corner of his eye at Sylvie. It was too soon to tell her.

He looked to her eyes again. Long lashes curled like a perfect Pacific Ocean wave. He didn't believe them to be fake. She wasn't wearing a swipe of makeup. Perfect, creamy skin, a hint of blush from the cold. She looked like a porcelain doll, so pale compared to his baked skin.

"You hanging in there, Stone?" she asked, giving her attention to him for a brief moment while she drove. "You look a little…off. Not feeling light-headed, are you?"

"Just a bit," he said, but had to wonder if it was more from her presence than the loss of blood. He cleared his throat and scanned the mountains out his window. "I'm just not feeling the love in this town."

"You'll be safe with me, Ian. I promise I won't let another shot find its mark. It'll be me before it will be you."

TWO

The emergency room buzzed with standing room only. Sylvie bypassed it and led Ian up to the front counter. "Good evening, Liz. I've got a GSW in the arm. Any way you can get him in? He's bandaged well and the bullet is out, but he still needs stitches."

"Anything for you, Chief." The front-desk nurse pushed a clipboard over to Sylvie.

"Can you also tell me where Jaxon is?"

"Curtain three."

"Great, you'll find us waiting in there. Stay close and follow," she said to Ian.

They passed by the waiting room and a familiar redhead jumped up from her chair and rushed their way. "Sylvie, hold up!"

"Walk with us, Roni," Sylvie said without halting her steps. Her friend joined them down the hall. "How's Jaxon?"

"He's a champ, but what took you so long getting here?"

"Roni, meet Ian. Ian, Roni Spencer."

"I know who Veronica Spencer is," Ian said, his voice hard and condemning. Did the man still think Roni tried to kill him? She was watching the track when everything went down. She couldn't have shot him.

"Have we met?" Roni replied.

"No, we haven't," Ian clipped.

"But you know me. Are you a fan?"

"Figures you would think so, but no. I don't follow racing."

Sylvie leaned into Ian. "You're barking up the wrong tree, Mr. Stone. Watch it."

"It's all right, Sylvie," Roni assured, but her normally bright smile dulled. However, Sylvie quickly noticed a mischievous glint spark up in the woman's ice-blue eyes. Her friend never got offended, even when the joke was on her. She just angled those ice crystals on the other person and gave it back tenfold. A quick glance Ian's way, and Sylvie noticed his eye color had the same hue. That's where she'd seen it. Wade and Roni had the same eyes. Interesting that Ian's eyes matched the Spencers'. Before Sylvie could speculate further, Roni said, "I'm sure your Ian will smarten up soon enough. It won't take too long for him to realize what the town revolves around."

"I assume we're talking about you again?" Ian shot back.

"Ian!" Sylvie nearly grabbed his injured arm and threw him behind a curtain—any curtain would do. "She was talking about racing. Now knock it off. Roni is not your enemy. And, Roni—" Sylvie leveled her eyes on her friend "—he is not *my* Ian."

Roni pursed her lips. "Good, because you could do so much better. He reminds me of all the locusts claiming to be our long-lost baby brother lately. We got another one this week. Now that word is getting out that

Luke didn't die in the car crash, strange men are coming out of the woodwork. Don't they know we will have them tested?"

"Right," Ian said with a smirk, "because you can't let a penny of your money go to a locust."

"All right, that's it." Sylvie made a grab for Ian's good arm and twisted it up his back. He didn't fight her as she pushed him toward curtain three. "Get in there before I throw you out the front door and let whoever shot you have another go at it." That part she whispered, but not softly enough because her son immediately spoke from behind the curtain.

"Shot?" Jaxon said.

Sylvie opened the curtain to shush him. Anxiety she'd held at bay since the accident lifted from her shoulders at the healthy sight of him. She shoved Ian inside and turned back to Roni to see if she'd heard, but her friend only said, "He's cute, and a worthy opponent, but watch yourself." Sylvie wanted to set the record straight. She was in no way interested in Ian Stone. In anyone for that matter. But she knew her friend would never stop hoping she would find someone someday, like Roni had found her handsome FBI agent, Ethan Rhodes.

Sylvie yanked the curtain closed with a rattle to the metal rings above. "Sit in that chair and fill this out." She passed over the clipboard and went to her son's bedside to hug him, relieved he let her embrace him. After a few moments of assurance that he was alive and well she pulled back and picked up his chart to read. "How you feeling? Anything broken? Has the doctor seen you yet?"

"Leg snapped. I'm getting a boot. Who is he?" Jaxon asked, peering around Sylvie.

"He's someone I brought in for stitches."

"Because he got shot?"

"Yes, but's that's between us. Don't go repeating that. I'm keeping him with me until I know more details." Sylvie turned to see Ian hadn't even clicked the pen to write his name. "The doctor won't be able to see you until that's filled out, Mr. Stone."

Ian barely looked at the forms. "I told you I didn't need this. I shouldn't have come here."

"Just why *did* you come to Norcastle? Especially if you don't follow racing."

"Is it a crime to want to see a mountain town in New England at Christmastime?"

"No, but you don't fit the profile of a tourist, most know how to dress appropriately for the harsh winters. It snows practically every night up here. Did you even pack a hat and gloves? A scarf? I'd say you're a California man. Am I right?"

"I'm impressed."

"I don't care if you're impressed." She nodded at the clipboard. "Just write it."

Ian stared at the information sheet and clicked the pen. He clicked it again and again. Five more times at a rapid rate before he sent the clipboard clattering to the floor and jumped to his feet. He was out the curtain in an instant.

But he wasn't faster than Chief Sylvie.

She had an arm wrapped securely around his neck and had him back behind the curtain and in his chair before anyone saw the takedown.

"Man, you thought you were going to escape my

mom?" Jaxon said with a wry smile. "I could have told you not to bother. She's got some moves."

Ian cleared his throat and mumbled aloud, "'And though she be but little, she is fierce.'" He ran his fingers through his hair to right it back into its unkempt style. He straightened up in his chair. "How about a warning next time, Chief?"

"It wouldn't change anything. She'd still win." Jaxon smirked.

"Thanks a lot, kid," Ian said, chagrined.

"Was that Shakespeare?" Jaxon asked. "That quote about my mom being little but fierce?"

"Yeah, *Midsummer Night's Dream*."

"I'll have to read it."

"Here." Ian reached into his pocket and withdrew the MP3 player. "I have the audiobook on here. You can listen to it."

Sylvie picked the clipboard up and held it out to Ian again. "If this is about money, I already told you not to worry. It'll get worked out."

Ian stared at the floor. "It's not about the money. At least not all of it."

"Then explain. What was that outburst for?"

He hesitated, but then blurted out, "I can't read, okay?" His gaze lifted to her.

"Whoa," Jaxon said, but Sylvie warned her son with a shake of her head before he could say more.

"You should have just said so," she said to Ian.

"I try to avoid being ridiculed whenever possible." He looked away. "I have dyslexia. Words and letters make no sense to me. They're all one big wavy line, moving around the page."

"We won't ridicule, right, Jaxon?" Sylvie said.

"No, man. I get enough of that at school to know it stinks." Jaxon reached for the clipboard. "I can help you fill it out."

Sylvie's heart swelled with pride to see her son jump in to help a complete stranger with no judgment. But she did wonder what her son meant by experiencing enough ridicule at school. He hadn't mentioned anything to her before about it. And it couldn't be for his academics. The boy excelled in every subject.

Sylvie's cell beeped with one of her lieutenants calling her. "Excuse me for a second," she told the boys, but they didn't seem to notice she'd said anything. The two were laughing about something Ian said was a ridiculous question on the sheet. She walked behind the curtain. "Preston, I'm glad you're calling. I have a nonresident who's been shot today. I need to get a report going."

"A GSW? Drug related?"

Sylvie glanced at the closed curtain. "Possibly. The victim hasn't given me much to go on, other than blaming it on the Spencers. I'm thinking he's hard up for money, maybe owes someone. They retaliated by pulling the trigger. Anyway, I have the bullet. I'm bringing it in. I'll need you to run ballistics."

"Got it."

"So, you called me. What do you need?"

"Nothing so full of grandeur. Just that I think I'm right about Smitty and Reggie. I found a business card for an ecologist specializing in salt contamination in Smitty's desk. You know I think Officer Smith has been instigating the picketers over at the salt shed. He wants Reggie back as chief." A recent wave of protesters had sprouted up in town, vocalizing their disapproval about the state of the shed that stored the season's road salt.

"Reggie is retired from the force and doesn't want to come back. Trust me. I'll talk to the people over at the shed. I realize they're worried about contamination of the river, but this is going to have to wait until I get home. Maybe even after Christmas. My son is injured."

"Is Jaxon all right? I heard that he was going to be okay."

"He is. But his leg is broken."

"Should I come down?"

"Thanks, Preston, that's nice of you to offer, but I need you holding down the fort."

I should be back in Norcastle in a few hours."

"What about Smitty and Reggie?"

"Like I said, Reggie is retired and Smitty will be up for retirement this year. I'm not worried that they want my job. They've been on the force for over thirty years, and I think I have shown them they can pass the baton. My probation period will be up in two months, and the town council will approve my position as permanent. I need you to stop worrying and just follow my orders."

Preston huffed. "Right. Hold down the fort. It's all you think I'm good for. I know others who would disagree."

The line went dead. Great, another ego she would have to console.

After Christmas.

Sylvie turned on her heel and plowed right into Ian's wide, very hard chest. The guy did some manual labor for sure.

"Is everything all right?" he asked. His piercing gaze saw too much…and sent a tingle up her spine.

The effect baffled her.

"Yeah, of course. Why wouldn't it be?" Her voice squeaked.

Her voice *never* squeaked.

She gave orders like a drill sergeant. Deep, loud, so there was no mistaking the fact that she was in charge. She snatched the clipboard from his hand.

Ian Stone
Construction worker for Sarno Construction
Pasadena, CA.

"Pasadena, huh? I thought money was an issue for you."

"It's temporary. I live in a trailer on the construction site my boss is working on. We're building a development. Homes that I will never sleep one night in. I just build them and move on."

She eyed him over the clipboard. Maybe Ian Stone was moving on to other ventures. Like setting up shop in Norcastle to sell drugs.

If that was the case, he would quickly learn he'd picked the wrong town to target.

And the wrong cop to dupe.

"I don't need a shadow," Ian stated against Sylvie's plan for security detail. He pulled on his coat slowly. "I just need a ride back to my apartment."

She glanced her son's way. "The doctor wants you to stay the night. Do you mind if I leave for a while to bring Ian to the station? I want to keep an eye on him to make sure no other bullets find their way into him. You okay with me leaving, Jax?"

"No, but since when does that matter?"

"Jaxon, we made a pact. Remember? I accepted the chief position, but only because we understood the sacrifices would be on both of us. A team."

Jaxon shrugged. "Yeah, I know what we said. It's just…"

"Just what?"

Jaxon avoided his mother's questioning gaze. "Never mind. It's nothing. Just go. I'm tired anyway. I'm just going to go to sleep."

Sylvie hesitated at her son's brush-off. Ian thought her frown expressed a bit of sadness about something going on between the two of them. But she quickly snapped back to her stoic self and patted Jaxon's good leg. Whatever it was wouldn't be hashed out tonight. "Okay, kiddo, they're getting a room ready for you. I'll be back as soon as I can."

Sylvie turned to Ian. "Stay by me." She took the lead and Ian gave a single wave to her son.

"Bye, Ian."

"Take care of my player, kid. It's my window to the world."

At the exit they stepped out into the freezing night. Sylvie held an arm up to survey the parking lot. "Looks clear."

Ian stifled a laugh at the absurdity of the situation. *She* was protecting *him*?

If nothing else, Ian had to think Sylvie took her job seriously. He had to figure his previous concern to trust her had been unwarranted.

Still his lips remained sealed.

But so did hers. Something weighed on her mind, if her chewed-up lower lip was any indication.

It wasn't until they made it to the interstate that Sylvie broke the void. "All right, I want to know why you're in town, and I want the truth. Are you here to sell drugs?"

Now he did laugh. "What? Drugs?"

"I want to help you, Ian. Please let me."

He sobered. How many times in his life had he hoped to hear those very words? Hearing them now put him in uncharted waters. What would happen if he accepted the offer?

He decided to trust her and find out.

"No drugs. But I am here for my cut."

"Cut of what? Somebody owe you something?"

The vast blackness of the New Hampshire night shrouded and protected him. His shoulder hurt, but not only from the bullet hole. A memory that predated any surgical procedure to fix the injury caused by an abusive father flowed vivid and clear. No money in the world would ease that pain. "Nobody owes Ian Stone anything. But Luke Spencer has an inheritance coming to him."

Sylvie slammed on the brakes, screeching the car to a halt on the side of the highway. She jammed the car into Park. "Are you telling me you think you're the long-lost missing Spencer sibling, Luke Spencer?"

"Not think. Know."

"You heard Roni. They've had a slew of men staking the claim. They *will* run tests."

"Already done and passed."

Sylvie's dashboard lights illuminated her shocked face to an eerie version of her sweet, good-natured self. "Do you have any idea how much pain Wade and Roni have been through? The possibility of finding their

missing brother has been a light at the end of a horrifying tunnel."

"Meaning they'll be highly disappointed they get
me? That obvious?" He tried to sound indifferent and
shrug it off, but deep down it hurt because he knew
they would be right. He wasn't Spencer material. He
was an illiterate drifter. Not a racing star like his sister
or a United States Army captain like his brother. And
he couldn't forget the grandfather in the CIA. The family was full of overachievers.

"Well, maybe if you had been a little nicer, they
would be more accepting," Sylvie said.

"And maybe if they hadn't tried to take me out, I
would be nicer."

"I already told you the Spencers are not trying to
k—" Sylvie's words were cut off as headlights from
behind neared the cruiser. The car slowed as it came
up alongside the driver's side. Sylvie rolled down her
window and waved them by.

An unmistakable silhouette appeared out the car's
window.

"Gun!" Ian yelled and pulled her down with him as
a bullet whizzed through the car and smashed out the
passenger-side window. The car sped up and screeched
away.

"Are you okay?" Sylvie yelled.

"I'm fine. You?"

"Fine." She jammed her cruiser into Drive. "Hold
on. I'm not letting this car out of my sight." She radioed for backup to be ready for the shooter heading into
Norcastle.

"You'll never catch him," Ian said as she sped up.

"Thanks for the vote of confidence, but they don't

hand out chief of police badges to just anyone. I did have to prove my ability, even if some people don't think I did." She mumbled the last remark.

"I'm sure you're a fine cop, but that is a paid assassin up there. When there are millions of dollars on the line, people will pay out big for an experienced hitman to make a problem go away. Those types of professionals generally don't let themselves get caught."

"So you're back to calling out the Spencers as shooters? They would never be involved in anything so devious."

"Then what about their CIA grandfather? I'm sure he's got at least a handful of assassins on speed dial."

Sylvie did a double take. "How do you know about him? That's top secret information. The Spencers don't tell anyone about their grandfather's job."

"Michael told me himself." The use of their gramps's name silenced her. "Michael Ackerman, some head honcho at the CIA, showed up in my hospital room two weeks ago. I went in for surgery on my shoulder for a torn rotator cuff. I woke up to find him sitting in the chair beside the bed. Apparently, he found me just as lacking as you do. It appears with all this shooting, he's now wishing he'd never found me and is trying to get rid of me. If I were you, I'd think twice about going after one of his hired guns."

"News flash for you. I'm the chief of police. That means I go, no questions asked." Sylvie radioed for her officers to be aware that the perpetrator was a possible assassin, and to proceed with caution.

But the woman didn't heed her own advice. She continued to take to the road like a bolt of lightning.

"Your son's not the only one who races cars, I see."

"This is the only kind of racing I do now, but there was a day…" She trailed off and said no more.

The vehicle ahead took the exit off the highway, before reaching Norcastle.

Sylvie banged her steering wheel. "He must've figured I would set up a blockade in town." She took the exit, too.

"So we're going after him with no backup?"

Sylvie glanced his way. "You're a smart man, Ian Stone. Or should I call you Luke Spencer? You may have dyslexia, but you can read a situation just fine."

"It's Ian, and you're right. This has insanity written all over it."

THREE

"Preston, this guy's heading up to Mount Randolph. How fast can you get a team up there? Charney Road's about to end. After that, snowmobiles will be needed. He's in an all-terrain Jeep. He'll get a lot farther than I will."

"I'm on it, Chief, but I was already en route to the town line. It could be a while before I get to the garage and load up the sleds."

"Smitty, are you reading this?" Sylvie asked, hoping Officer Ed Smith was on the transmission.

"10-4. I'm less than a mile away from the garage. You'll have your sleds in fifteen, little miss."

"Roger that."

"Boyfriend?" Ian asked when Sylvie pushed her car's tires to grab the snow. Her gunman's taillights were long gone, but not his tire tracks.

"Who? Smitty?"

"You seem…close."

"Smitty's old enough to be my father…and filled the role for a lot longer than my real one did. Or at least, he used to."

"Used to? When did he stop?"

"When I applied for the former chief's position."

"Not supportive of his little miss?"

"Just not as supportive as he was for Reggie Porter. Reggie had been on the force for thirty years. He was qualified, but…"

"But?"

"But nothing. I took the test and got the majority of the town council's vote. End of story. They had their reasons for choosing me, and everyone's just going to have to get used to it. It's been two years, almost, and I'm a good cop."

"Something tells me you're as stoic as one of Virgil's duty-bound soldiers in his stories."

"I see you make good use of your audiobooks."

"For someone dyslexic they're an answer to prayer."

"You pray?"

"Everyone prays. Whether they admit it or not, there comes a moment where everyone calls out for help."

Sylvie had to agree. She remembered her moment like it was yesterday, even though it was fifteen years ago.

"The Jeep's off to the right, hidden behind those pines. Your lights just reflected off the red taillights."

"I see it. Good eye." Sylvie pulled to the left. "Stay down," she instructed and radioed her location. Using her door as a shield, she crouched low, her gun drawn and held at the ready.

The cold night wind whipped around her and through the empty tree branches.

"Come out with your hands up!" she commanded.

No response.

Sylvie glanced into her cruiser at Ian. Slowly, he shook his head. It was as though he'd read her mind and knew what she was about to do. Again, the man may have trouble with his letters, but that was it.

She made her move and stepped out from behind her door. Ian mumbled his dislike under his breath. Then she heard his boots crunch on the snow. She swung around and pointed back at the car.

He did the same to her.

Seriously? Did he think she was a rookie?

What did she expect? Guys liked the idea of her being a cop for about ten minutes. Just until she had to do her job and go into the danger.

Sylvie turned her back on him and approached the Jeep. She breached the pines and came up on the rear of the vehicle. With one hand, she grabbed her flashlight and shined the beam into the rear window. Through the back driver's side door, she peered inside.

No signs of life were evident.

"There're snowmobile tracks out here," Ian whispered loudly from the other side of the trees. "Whoever he is, he's long gone."

"Well, his Jeep won't be here when he returns. I'll have it processed for prints before the morning."

"Get away from the car."

Sylvie shined the light in the direction of Ian. "Excuse me? You keep forgetting this is what I do. I go in when *you* can't. I definitely don't take orders from you. I may have to protect you with my life, but the oath ends there."

"Get…away…from…the car!"

Ian's tone had Sylvie questioning her decision to approach the vehicle in the first place. Did he know something?

Slowly, she stepped back through the pines. His arms

were around her so fast, lifting her frame off the ground and across the road. She barely had time to fight back with anything more than a few twists of her body when a flash of light lit the sky above and an explosion rushed at her from behind.

A painful ringing filled her head. It took her a few seconds to realize she was on the ground with Ian over her. His head of hair brushed her neck. Her gun and flashlight were gone to places unknown, her ears pierced with the effects of the blast.

Her lungs emptied in the toss. They burned with a need for air that Ian's weight didn't allow for replenishing.

Sylvie banged a fist on his back. "Can't—" she pushed out in a squeak "—breathe."

Ian moaned, but didn't move quickly enough for her. She banged three more times before his head lifted with a dazed look of confusion.

Had he lost consciousness? She couldn't assess him until she could breathe.

Ian snapped to and rolled off her, allowing air to enter her body. Heat roared at her from the fire across the road, fighting her for the oxygen. She heaved over in spasms.

"Easy. Slow it down. Breathe into your nose, not your mouth." Ian's soothing commands and his hand on her back told her he'd returned to her side.

But what about him? He'd taken the brunt of the blast. Was he burned?

Sylvie followed his directions but willed her lungs to fill enough for her to help.

"Let me check you out," she said on a breathy whisper.

"Just a little singed. The coat's trashed. I can feel

wind on my back, and it actually feels good. I probably won't need a haircut for a while, either." He laughed, but she didn't think she'd heard such nervousness in him before.

"Just humor me and turn around."

"Fine, but I may not be decent." More nervousness threaded through his voice. He was scared.

But then so was she.

"The trees took the brunt."

Sylvie glanced at the flaming pine trees with the burning car behind them. The trees had saved their lives.

But Ian had saved hers by telling her to get away from the car in the first place.

"How did you know?" Her voice cracked.

She touched his obliterated jacket pieces, pulling them away from his body. His shirt stuck to him. He grunted when she lifted it.

"You're burned, but I don't think anything more than second degree in a couple spots. It'll feel like a bad sunburn."

"Thanks, Doc." Ian rolled and lay in the snow, gritting his teeth against the cold, but it seemed welcoming at the same time.

"You still haven't told me how you knew."

"Just a feeling of impending doom. I'm attuned to stuff like that."

"From experience?"

"You could say that. You face it enough times and you start to live on the balls of your feet, ready to spring into action or retreat, whatever comes first. Besides, it looked like a setup. Like I was supposed to find that car. Me. Not you. Regardless of your oath and duty you didn't sign up for this." He lifted up from the snow and leaned in close. "Leave me here. Go home to your son. I would never forgive myself if he lost you because of me."

"Because you're not worth me doing my job?"

Cruisers' lights and sirens blared off in the distance as they stared at each other.

"You shouldn't have come looking for me at my apartment."

"And find you washed up on the riverbank instead? I don't think so. Someone wants you six feet under, Mr. Stone. They're going to have to go through me first."

"You see the flames, right? The Spencers are your friends but with me around they won't think twice about leaving your son an orphan."

Cars rushed in and squeaked to a stop around them. As glad as she was to have their help, they could use this scene against her, especially if Preston was right in his thinking and somebody wanted her off the job. "Can you not tell them I approached the vehicle alone?"

Ian eyed her quizzically. "Aren't you the chief?"

"Yes, but I still have two more months on my probationary period and someone on the force may be looking for any slipup to stack against me. Please."

"Only if I get a sled."

"No way. You're going into protective custody. I can't allow you to go up the mountain with us."

"And I can't allow you to put yourself in danger for me."

"It's my job, Ian."

"Not for long if I tell them you approached the car without backup."

"That's blackmail. I can arrest you, you know."

Ian shrugged. "I'm always ready to spring into action, whatever that might be. In this case it will be your choice how this all goes down. So, what's your decision, Chief? Do I get a sled or do your weekends open up?"

"You could be killed," she said quietly.

"And so could you. Don't make me responsible for leaving your son alone in this world. I have to look myself in the mirror every day. You should know about mirrors more than anyone. You've made sacrifices to give Jaxon a good life."

His reference to her circumstances as a pregnant teen silenced her. He'd obviously done the math. However, she didn't feel his judgment like so many others. Just his understanding. She did what she had to do to look herself in the mirror every day. She couldn't take that from Ian.

"Chief!" Smitty fell to his knees beside her. His wisps of balding hair fell in his face. "Are you hurt?"

"No. I'm fine. Ian has lost his coat. Did you bring the winter gear? He'll need a set."

"A full set? Is he going up the mountain?" Smitty glanced Ian's way in confusion. Caution took over. "Who are you?"

"He says he's Lu—"

"I'm Ian Stone." Ian glared at Sylvie as he cut her off. "Just call me Ian, and everyone stays safe."

Sylvie realized the ramifications of having this knowledge. If someone was trying to kill Ian before Roni and Wade learned he was alive, they could come after her, too.

Protecting Ian was one thing, but as a single mother, making herself a target was not a road she could afford to go down.

* * *

"Ian's going up because he thinks he can ID the shooter," Sylvie told her men.

Ian nodded at her decision to allow him to stick by her. He really had no intention of getting her fired if she didn't comply, but he did intend to keep her alive. And to do that, he couldn't stay behind.

Sylvie jumped to her feet with rapid orders spilling from her lips. Her team responded on her command. When no one squabbled over her decision, Ian could tell they respected her as their leader.

One half of the team stayed to process the scene and wait for the fire department, while the other prepped the sleds and geared up.

As Ian pulled on his second glove and stamped his feet in the too-tight boots given to him, Sylvie pushed a helmet at his chest.

"Don't make me regret this, Ian. And make sure you stay alive." She climbed on her sled. "We ride!" Three of her officers fell in behind her. Ian straddled his sled and started the engine. He revved the gas by turning the handle and after getting acquainted with his machine, saluted Sylvie to let her know he was good to go.

She took off at a breakneck speed. She'd hinted at racing cars as a retired pastime, but obviously snowmobiling hadn't been given up. Ian had trouble keeping up with her and her team. He had one officer behind him, pressing in on his tail. The guy didn't like lagging behind, judging by the way he pressed close. Ian gave his sled more gas and leaned in.

Still the officer hedged in.

The officers' helmets had radios installed in them so they could talk with each other, but no one had given him one. Yelling at the guy to back off did nothing. Ian couldn't even hear himself over the engines.

But he *could* feel the officer practically breathing down his neck. Ian's sled was already pushed to the max. What more did the guy want? Any faster and Ian would be on top of the officer in front of him. He pushed on, but finally couldn't take it.

Ian flashed his headlight to get someone's attention.

Only not one person ahead or behind responded with a word or hand signal. Not even a brake light to show they'd slowed down.

Was it a scare tactic done by the police? Was Sylvie in on this?

Ian's snowmobile jerked and skidded from an impact from behind. He'd been hit. He righted his machine, but knew the officer had struck him with his sled. This just went from annoying to…calculated.

But Sylvie couldn't be involved. Her oath of duty to serve and protect drove her every decision. The cop behind him was working alone…or perhaps was working for someone else.

The Spencers.

Their wealthy reach exceeded the local PD. They must have people bought and paid for in every back pocket of their designer jeans.

Ian craned his neck to catch a glimpse of the guy so determined to push him off course.

For what?

Was the shooter waiting for him nearby? Maybe this officer just had to roll Ian's sled off the path and let the killer finish what he was sent here to do.

Get rid of Luke Spencer.

Ian jammed the back of his sled out in a fishtail to

push his pursuer off. He stood to his feet on the sled and ramped up the engine to catch up with the officers in the lead. His engine screamed at the assault. He cranked the handle harder, popping the front end of the sled up and back down with a thud.

His teeth jarred with the impact, then clenched as the machine blasted up the mountain. A quick glance over his shoulder and he found his tail gone. Ian drove on and quickly caught up with the other four officers.

The number stumped him. There had been three officers and the chief when they set out, and still there were three officers and the chief.

Then who had been trying to run him off the path?

Ian pushed on to reach the group. Something told him the guy they were pursuing had been behind him the whole time.

The assassin had made the tracks for them to follow, then circled back around to nab his assignment. But where were the tracks leading the police?

Trap. The word lodged in Ian's throat. He shouted it to no avail. They would never hear his warning before whatever awaited them made its appearance. With no radio, all he could do was race headfirst with them into a trap that Sylvie would fall into before anyone else.

Ian had to stop her. She was experienced, but in the dark mountain night, with only the lights on their sleds, her vision was limited to a few feet. Just enough to keep an eye on the tracks leading them to…where?

A dead end?

Sweat poured down Ian's back into his suit. His burns were nothing compared to the painful fear gripping his lungs in a vise. Sylvie didn't deserve this. *He* was the one who'd brought this danger to her town.

He was the one they wanted, and they didn't mind killing a few cops to achieve their goal.

It wouldn't even look like murder. It would look like a horrible snowmobile accident that took the lives of four brave officers in hot pursuit. This guy was a skilled mastermind killer.

Ian pushed on, but realized he would need to leave the path and cut them off ahead. It would be the only way to stop them.

Ian peered into the darkness for an alternate path. When one off to his left came into view, he took it and brought his sled up and around a steep pass. At a point he had to stand and lean forward to prevent his sled from falling backward. Overturning it now would be catastrophic.

Finally, his path rejoined the other one, but Sylvie had already flown by.

Ian was able to pull out and cut the officers off.

Two collided at the shock of seeing him, not able to brake fast enough. The third officer pulled off to the side.

Ian whipped off his helmet. "It's a trap! The guy tried to take me out down the mountain. One of you, radio to stop her."

"Her radio's not working!" the one who had pulled off shouted. "We've been trying to get ahold of her."

Ian didn't wait for any instructions. He had to get Sylvie. He pushed his sled back into Drive and screamed it up the mountain.

Quickly, she came into view…but so did the end of the road. Ian's light took in all that surrounded her from this far back. But she would only see what was directly in front of her. What she was meant to see.

The tracks.

Tracks that were about to come to an end without warning—straight off the side of the mountain.

FOUR

Sylvie cranked her throttle to give her engine the gas it needed to continue its steep ascent. She tried her radio again.

No response. She risked a glance over her shoulder to catch her team's headlights. At least one kept up.

She slowed to allow the rest to do so and quickly the one sled pulled up alongside her. A gloved hand reached over and grabbed her hand.

"What are you doing?" she yelled inside her helmet. She didn't expect an answer. But suddenly the man pulled her hard and she lost her grip on the snowmobile. His assault didn't let up and before she could fight back, she found herself draped over his sled and veering in another direction.

The ride came to an abrupt end and Sylvie pushed off into the three-foot-deep snow, landing on her back.

The driver's hand lifted her up. Sylvie ripped away from him to go after her sled.

Only she couldn't see it. She also couldn't hear it.

She tore off her helmet and looked back at the man who'd removed her from her ride. She stepped up to his sled and hit the red kill switch. The machine shut down instantly. "Take the helmet off."

He did as he was told.

Ian's face appeared beneath the great unveiling.

"I should have left you behind," Sylvie said.

"Because I saved your life again?"

"How did you save my life?"

"Do you see your sled around? No, you don't. That's because it was a trap. You were following tracks that led you off the side of the mountain."

Sylvie whipped around to search the darkness for her snowmobile. Even if it had crashed and the head-light had gone out she would have seen evidence of it around. A dark abyss less than ten feet away could only be what swallowed it, and it would have taken her right along with it if…

"We weren't the ones doing the chasing," Ian said. "He tried to get me away from the pack a little ways back there."

She pivoted back. "While sending the cops to their deaths?"

"Looks that way. You should get as far away from me as you can before it's too late for you and your men. Go now. Leave me here. I beg of you."

"Be serious. I'm not leaving you up here. You'd die before morning, whether killed by this guy or the ele-ments." Sylvie needed to do what their enemy wouldn't expect. Did he know these mountains? If she went left, she would pick up the McKeeny Pass and could cut down into inhabited land. There was also an emergency supply cabin at the beginning of the pass. But if she started on her way, it would be for the duration.

"You up for a ride?"

"I don't think this is a good time for an adventure."

"It's not a good time to die, either. I'm thinking our guy will be expecting us to double back. He'll be waiting to spring another trap for you. Christmas is two days away. I mean to be sitting around a tree sipping eggnog, and I'd like to do that without all the paperwork your death would heap on my desk. I'd also like to be alive to pick my son up from the hospital in the morning."

"So what's your plan?"

"I know another way down. We have to go across the McKeeny Pass. The ridge runs along for a few miles, then it descends to safety. You can trust me. I've driven these trails many times, but there's a chance we'll run out of gas and will need to walk the rest of the way. Are you too hurt for that?"

"I'm fine. Hop on."

"Wait, I need to tell my men."

As if on cue, the three of them cleared the slope. "Chief? Are you all right?"

"Karl!" Sylvie approached them. "We're not going down the way we came up. It's too risky for Ian. I'm taking him across the pass. Are you guys able to get back down?"

"We lost a sled, but we'll double up."

"Us too. I need you off this mountain as fast as possible. We're dealing with a psychopath who doesn't care if he takes you out in the process."

"Should we call Reggie?"

The name Reggie froze Sylvie's chest faster than the freezing temperature "No. There's no need to call him in. Let him enjoy his retirement."

"But—"

"No *but*s. Do not, I repeat, do not call Reginald Porter. We will catch this guy on our own. Now go."

Her men followed her orders, but she could tell they were hoping to call in the man who had been next in line for the chief position. She still had a lot to prove to her team. Sylvie hoped catching this guy and keeping Ian safe would be what it took to earn her rightful place as chief in their eyes. But even if it didn't, it wouldn't change the fact that she was still in charge.

Ian held on to Sylvie's waist as she pushed the snowmobile through deep snow. He kept an eye out behind him every few seconds to be sure they didn't have unwanted company. Two hours of riding at a slow twenty miles an hour, Ian worried they weren't putting enough distance between them and his would-be assassin. The guy knew how to use these treacherous drops to his advantage. Ian peered over the side of the ridge to his right. One push and they would be bouncing over jagged rocks all the way down. In addition to speed, he questioned Sylvie's choice of path.

The snowmobile slowed even more until it drifted to an idling stop. Sylvie hopped off and indicated a small cabin down the hill about a hundred feet. The snowdrifts covered the door to about a foot from the top.

Sylvie's short legs disappeared in the heavy snow as she made tracks to the building. She pushed through, breaking trail with all her strength.

Ian joined her and reached the door to help her scoop the drifts away in a flying flurry. The door opened inward with ease and a cold woodstove in the center of the one-room cabin greeted them.

Sylvie lifted the visor of her helmet. The fact that

she didn't remove it completely told him this was a quick stop. He lifted his own as she went to a cabinet in search of something.

"Do you use this place a lot?"

"No, but I know it's stocked with things we might need to keep going." She lifted two pairs of snowshoes from a rack.

"We're hoofing it from here?"

"This is heavy snow and not compacted down. It's causing the sled to use more gas than normal to get us through. I almost thought we wouldn't make it here at all."

"There's no gas here?"

She slammed a cabinet door then opened another. "Not that I can find. I'll make a note to have it stocked." Sylvie looped ropes over her shoulder. "When I was younger the McKeeny Pass was a place I would come to, to silence the world."

"Silence? Those sleds are the loudest things I've ever heard, and I work in construction."

She moved on to a drawer. "I guess the motor never bothered me, but I know there are people who hate it. Same thing with the racetrack."

"And yet that's not a part of your life anymore."

"Things change. Times change. Responsibilities change."

"Right, and your responsibilities dictate your days now, including protecting me. It doesn't matter how much you hate them."

"Hate is an emotion, and in this job there's no room for emotions. I make the best decisions I can with what is given to me."

"I've got news for you. I haven't been given to you,

so you don't need to view me as one of your responsibilities to handle."

The whiny pine of a snowmobile drifted from the east.

"You're wrong. You're in my jurisdiction. I am responsible for what happens to you." She pushed the snowshoes into his arms. "Now let's move. That sled is getting closer."

Sylvie whipped her right-hand glove off and retrieved her gun from her holster. The .45 Glock consumed her small hand as she readied it to shoot. He closed the door as she led the way back to the sled. He dropped the snowshoes into the storage under the seat and waited for her to climb on.

"You're driving. I'm riding shotgun. Just follow the pass until it ends. If we make it that far, we'll stop and I'll give you directions from there. Pray that we do." With that she dropped her visor and communication ended.

Ian climbed on and started the engine. The gas gauge indicated less than a quarter tank. He closed his eyes and said a prayer to the only Father he'd ever had. The only Father who cared about him and promised blessings beyond Ian's imagination. Even when Ian didn't deserve them.

Ian hit the gas and moved across the pass as fast as the machine could get through the treacherous level of snow. He felt Sylvie grab hold of his waist with one hand and felt where she held her gun tucked against his back. But that meant her glove was still off. Her hand had to be freezing with the frigid cold and no covering, even held protectively between them. Would she be able to pull the trigger?

He pushed on so she wouldn't have to.

The only consolation was the assassin would be having just as much trouble getting through the elements as them.

The sled's high beam flickered and dimmed. The motor strained. The end of the road neared for them whether the pass came to an end or not.

Out of the corner of Ian's left eye, he saw movement come at them. His pursuer had found a faster way up here to cut them off. Ian yanked the sled to his left to cut in front of the other rider.

He gave the sled the last surge of gas to power them ahead. The motor screamed and the assassin's headlight came up on the right side. One shove over and Ian might be able to end this right now. But that risked sending them over the edge right along with him. Still, Ian had to lose the guy, but maybe breaking away wasn't the answer.

He let off the gas and pressed the brake controls, not enough to stop completely, but to slow down enough that the two sleds rode side by side. The two drivers looked at each other, their visors hiding their identities. Ian reached his right hand out as Sylvie's gun appeared over his shoulder aimed at the other rider. The hitman reached for the gun as Ian reached for the guy's kill switch.

The round red button that Sylvie had used on his own sled before depressed easily and shut down the machine, lights and all, in an instant. In the same moment, Ian kicked his foot out and sent the sled into a flip. The driver went flying over his handle controls and landed in the snow ahead of them.

Ian's machine puttered by him as the guy reached for

them. *Please God, just a little farther to give us some space.* Ian managed to squeeze out enough gas for another few hundred feet. He moved the vehicle down to the left behind some trees and he and Sylvie made fast work strapping on their snowshoes.

They lifted their visors to talk. No need to whisper since the assassin's motor was back in full swing and would be coming up on them real soon.

"Do you know where we are?"

"Yes, but we have to keep moving. There's a home nearby."

"Someone lives up here on this mountain?"

Sylvie didn't reply and Ian took that as a sign to keep moving. They hoofed it for what could only be another mile. The sound of the motor ceased, which meant the guy either gave up his chase or was following on foot. Snow fell down on them, first a few light spattering flakes, but quickly Ian's visor required swipe after swipe. His fingers numbed quickly even in his gloves. A look to his left and he saw Sylvie still held the gun, her hand exposed. He reached for the gun and had to pry it from her hand. Not because she fought him, but because it had frozen to her skin. He took his own glove off and pushed her small hand into it. His would be warmer than the one in her pocket.

Ian pushed up her visor and witnessed pain on her face. She fought it with her every breath and averted her gaze to his right. A glance that way and he saw a rustling in some snow-covered shrubs.

A bear, perhaps? Great. If the killer and the snowstorm weren't enough, now they would have a preying animal on their heels.

Ian lifted the gun in his hand and took aim at a creature barreling at them full force. The animal bounced up and out of the snow, flying through a blinding flurry of whiteness. The rapidly falling snow made it impossible to tell what kind of animal had set their sights on them.

Ian could do only one thing.

As he pressed the trigger to unload the bullet, Sylvie steamrolled herself directly at him, sending them both sinking into the snow.

Ian quickly rolled over to protect her from the approaching threat. Figures the woman would want to protect the animal. "Do your responsibilities extend to protecting the creatures in your jurisdiction, too?"

The animal landed hard on Ian's back, putting its whole weight on him and not giving an inch.

Sylvie glanced over Ian's shoulder, her eyes wide.

"Is it a bear?" Ian asked low and controlled. Sweat beaded up on his forehead.

A giggle erupted from Sylvie, and Ian realized it was the first time he'd heard her laugh. It was the first lightheartedness he'd seen her express. Never would he think it would come out in a time of danger.

"Well, what is it?" he demanded.

She reached a hand up and lifted his visor. "It's Promise." Her lips curled with mischief.

"Promise? Promise what? Now's not the time to be making deals, Sylvie. Just tell me what kind of animal is on my back. Is it a mountain lion?"

"She just told you," a deep male voice spoke from above them. He sounded mad and lethal. Had his killer caught up to them? "Promise is my service dog, and you nearly killed her. That doesn't make us friends, just so you know."

Ian squinted into Sylvie's almond-shaped eyes. He

knew them to be green, but without light all he could see was the glistening tears of laughter in them. "What's so funny?"

"Ian, meet Wade Spencer." She lifted her head and chinked her helmet against his. She moved her lips in a bare whisper. "Your brother."

FIVE

Stockings hung with embroidered names from the Spencer family's fireplace mantle, some old and worn, many new. Sylvie watched Ian study the long row before he gave his attention back to rubbing her pained fingers near the flame.

"I don't need you to do this," she said. "I can warm my own hands."

Ian rubbed on, glancing over his shoulder. She followed his gaze and saw they were alone. "Why did you bring me here?" he demanded. "They are the enemy. They're the ones behind ordering the kill."

"I wouldn't have brought you here if I believed that. They are good people."

His hands pressed harder. "Good people with money. That Christmas tree has to be pushing twenty feet." Ian jabbed his head in the direction of the elaborate holiday spruce reaching to the high ceiling of the Spencers' ten-thousand-square-foot home. He nodded to the long row of stockings. "Who are all these people? Do they all live here?"

"No." Sylvie pointed to the first two stockings in the line. "Wade and Lacey are married. She's expecting their first baby any day now. In fact I think she's over-due. But soon there'll be another stocking beside theirs."

Sylvie couldn't contain the excitement about the new arrival. She was so happy for Wade and prayed his new baby would bring healing to him just as Jaxon had done for her so many years ago. She wasn't the same person she was before, all because of a new life.

She pointed to the next stockings in line. "Roni is married to Ethan. They do live here. Ethan was an FBI agent and the FBI called him in to help with an un-dercover case for a few weeks. But Roni still has his stocking out, so maybe he'll be home for Christmas. Then there's Cora, who used to be the Spencers' maid, but she married their uncle Clay, making her official family, not that she wasn't already. She's lived here for forty years, long before their parents were murdered."

"My parents, too," he pointed out under his breath.

"Right, sorry." Sylvie moved down the stocking line. "Magdalena is a woman Roni freed from a human traf-ficker last spring. She lives here permanently now and also goes by the name Maddie. She helps Roni run a refuge here for women who've been trafficked, which leads to the next two names. Angela and Sarah were brought here after their captor was arrested. They're in protective custody while he's being prosecuted for his crimes."

"Will they stay here forever?"

"For however long they need to. If that's forever, then it's forever. Many of these girls feel they can't go home. Roni gives them a fresh start if they want it. She had a third girl who returned to her captor over the summer. It was hard for Roni to accept, but…well, it's just the girls are so broken, some of them don't know any other life, or don't feel worthy of a better one."

"I thought Roni ran a racing school. That's what her website says."

"I thought you couldn't read."

"My boss read it to me. He's the one who convinced me to come back here and accept my inheritance. I wasn't going to. I should have listened to my gut telling me this was a bad idea."

"This is the guy you work for in construction?"

"Alex Sarno of Sarno Construction, soon to be Sarno and Stone. He's promised to make me a partner in the business when I get back."

"But first you need to get your hands on the Spencer dough, is that it? Did he promise you this partnership before or after you told him the news of your birth family?"

"Does it matter?"

"Maybe, maybe not."

"I say not. Alex took a chance on me when no one else would. He's watched me struggle and has helped me rise above my circumstances. He took me to church with him. It's because of him that I know God wants more for me than to be an illiterate lackey for the rest of my life."

"That sounds great and all, but money does strange things to people. Makes them act differently. Selfishly."

"You think Alex is after my money?"

"You don't even have it yet, and the man already offered you a part in his business. Did he name a price, or is he eagerly waiting to find out what you stand to gain from the Spencers?"

Wade cleared his throat from the doorway. He stood

there with Promise beside him, his hand in her fur at her head. "Stand to gain from us? I already don't like you for shooting at my dog. If it wasn't for Sylvie's quick reflexes, Promise wouldn't be here keeping me calm. But maybe I should be kicking you out of here anyway."

The golden Labrador retriever pressed her head deeper into Wade's palm.

"Wade has post-traumatic stress disorder," Sylvie said. "Promise is his service dog. She helps with his daily activities that his memories impair. You see, he's also had circumstances he's struggled with over the years. In fact, he turned his back on all you see around you for the life of a soldier. He knew money never fixed anything."

"Never." Wade stepped farther into the room, but the man's hard-edged tone had disappeared. He must have sensed Sylvie was helping Ian to understand something and Wade respected her to know her business. She felt safe from having to answer the question of who Ian was…for now. He was an army captain, however, and would want to be briefed about why they were out in the storm and running from someone.

She didn't know Wade well enough to know when he would require the knowledge, though. Roni was the closer friend, and even Sylvie's relationship with his sister hadn't come easy. Sylvie grew up downtown. Her family worked for the Spencers, and friendships between the kids would never have happened in polite society.

But polite society wasn't the natural way of things. Kids didn't care about the rules of social classes. They wanted to play, and on one of Sylvie's hikes up the mountain to the McKeeny Pass, she came into contact with a very rebellious Roni Spencer on her snowmobile. The teenager gained a friend she could break all the rules with. She taught Sylvie to ride the sled as well as the race cars. She even introduced her to the handsome racer, Greg Santos.

The charismatic man quickly took notice of the blond-haired, green-eyed nobody who worked the concession stand at the track, and quickly took advantage of her.

Sylvie had fallen hard. She couldn't believe Greg Santos would pick her over all the pretty, wealthier girls. Looking back, she had to think the other girls wouldn't have him because they knew something she didn't.

It wasn't long before she understood and found herself alone and pregnant. Sylvie's days of playing came to a screeching halt. From then on, playing consisted of baby rattles, stuffed bunnies and lullabies.

Something Wade would soon be enjoying, as well.

"How's Lacey? Is she here?" Sylvie strayed to safer conversation.

"I left her in town at Clay's. I don't want her on the mountain in case she goes into labor. The snow's getting worse by the minute."

"I'm sorry I took you from her, but we appreciate you coming out to meet us."

"With Ethan away undercover, I had to. Your team came straight to Clay's and told me you would be coming out on the other side of the pass onto our land. I didn't want Roni out there searching for you, although she would have gone, no questions asked. Who is this guy you're running from?" Wade asked the question to Ian.

Just as she'd thought. Wade wouldn't wait for answers.

But would Ian give them? The anger in his eyes said things could get ugly, especially since Ian believed Wade and Roni were behind the order to kill.

Ian looked to Sylvie, his lips tight. "I would like to know that, too, but at the moment, I'm in the dark."

So he was playing it safe. Smart man.

"Where you from?" Wade asked.

Ian replied, "California now. Washington State originally."

"What's your last name?"

"Stone. Ian Stone."

"Stone… Stone." Wade squinted as he looked to be contemplating something. "You have family around here?"

Ian pressed his lips even tighter. It had to be killing him not to say who he really was. "Somewhere." He locked gazes with Sylvie, and she offered a sad smile. Why didn't he just tell the truth? This could all be out in the open and dealt with tonight.

She decided to offer a lead in for Ian if he wanted to take it. "Wade, Roni told me earlier today that you had another man notify you about possibly being your brother, Luke. How'd that end up?"

Wade shrugged. "Just like the last one. We served him his walking papers. I thought he might need a little more persuasion of the full-contact kind to take his leave, but he saw reason by the end." Wade raised his fist. "Meet Reason."

All right, so maybe things wouldn't be all dealt with tonight as she'd thought. Still, the time would come when Ian would have to tell his birth family who he was. In the meantime, she just needed to do her job.

"We don't know who's after Ian. He thinks it's a hired gun to take him out."

"Did you upset someone you shouldn't have?" Wade asked. "Someone in the mob, perhaps?"

"CIA."

"That'll do it. I might be able to help. I have family in the CIA."

"I don't want your help," Ian responded forcefully.

Wade raised a hand in surrender. "Your choice. If you change your mind just let me know."

Roni swept into the room with a tray of snacks. She placed it on the square coffee table and flipped her fiery red hair, exposing the burn scars on her neck left over from the car crash.

Sylvie caught Ian staring at the raised skin in mute silence.

"What are you looking at?" Roni stepped toward Ian, her head lifted to show the scars. "Didn't your mother ever teach you manners?"

"Roni, don't start," Wade said. "You're just instigating a fight. You're used to people staring at your scars and have never put anyone on the spot before. Give the guy a break. He's being hunted down."

"I'm not surprised someone wants to kill him. He's rude."

Wade smirked at his sister. "Sounds like someone else I know. The two of you should get along great. Ian, help yourself to the food."

Ian curled his upper lip. "If she made it, I'd rather eat my shoelaces."

Wade nodded. "No truer words have ever been spoken. Just wait until you eat it."

Roni gasped and spun to face her brother. "Thanks a lot, Wade. I thought you were on my side."

"Why do you think I live in town? Since Cora married Uncle Clay, the cooking up here has gone downhill."

Roni pouted. "That's not why you live down the hill, and you know it. You don't live up here because—"

"Enough, Roni." The warning glare Wade sent his sister had everyone dropping their gazes to anything but the direction of the conversation. It had Promise burrowing her furry head into Wade's thigh and hand again.

Ian searched Sylvie's face for the answer to what had just deflated the room's atmosphere. She assured him with a slight smile that she would tell him later. It was good for Ian to see that his siblings suffered from the crash just as much as he did. They weren't the bad guys.

"You can stay here, Ian. You'll be safe." Wade brought the subject back on task. "The glass is all bulletproof. And the food really is not that bad. Especially when Magdalena cooks."

"I have my own apartment in town. At one of the old mills."

Sylvie put a hand on his forearm. "Actually, staying here's not a bad idea. I can't find this guy and protect you at the same time. You saw how that turned out tonight."

"You are not leaving me here," Ian practically growled at the idea.

"Not big enough for you?" Roni taunted.

"Not with you here," Ian responded.

Wade shook his head. "What is up with you two? Do you know each other?"

"We just met today," Roni said.

"Call it hate at first sight," Ian added.

Roni stuck out her tongue. "The feeling's mutual." She said it, but the sparkle in her eyes said she was having the time of her life sparring with him.

Sylvie puffed out an exasperated release of air. "Well, you two can have at it all night long while I get to work." To Ian she said, "Stay here. I'll be in touch in the morning."

"I'm going with you."

"Then it's a jail cell for you. That's the only way I'll know you're safe while I do my job."

"You need me to find this guy. He's a professional and won't show his face unless I show mine."

"I don't use civilians as bait."

A text beeped on Wade's phone. He read it and said, "This train is leaving the station. Lacey asked for pickles before I left. She's getting antsy. Am I bringing you two back to town?"

Sylvie warred within herself. All it would take was one wrong move to lose her job. Her probationary period was nearly completed, but it wasn't over yet.

A murder she could have prevented could end her future in an instant.

But where would Ian be the safest? With her in town, or up on this secluded mountain with Roni?

One look at Roni's scheming glare directed at Ian answered that question. Sylvie didn't think Roni was behind the murder attempts, but there was definitely animosity, and they could do each other harm up here alone.

"On second thought—" Sylvie grabbed Ian with her thawed hand "—he better come with me. A jail cell might be the safest place for him after all."

"You didn't even say goodbye to Wade. Pushing your brother and sister away won't help you," Sylvie said, as Ian noticed her cruiser in its parking spot in front of the station. Her men must have delivered it back. Snow covered the top by a few inches.

But where were the rest of the cars?

Ian scoffed at her words and brushed past her to reach the police station entrance first.

Sylvie's hand shot out to stop him. "You need to stay with me, Ian. I can't protect you if you go on ahead like that."

Now he really scoffed. "You're a foot shorter than me. You must see how ridiculous that looks."

"No, all I see is your dead body if I slip up."

The town's police station sported neon green trim around the top portion of the old building. It appeared to be an old car dealership from the 1940s, its art deco style still intact. Hard to take any of the Norcastle police seriously when they were holed up in this retrofitted building.

"Is there no one here? Who's watching this place?" he asked.

"Just the dispatcher. My team is still out," Sylvie said, shutting the door on the frigid night. "Carla, any word on tonight's events?" she asked a woman who sat at the front desk among a lighted switchboard and computer screen with a map of the area at her fingertips. She seemed to be in her sixties, brown hair cut short to the neck. So, Sylvie wasn't the only woman in the department.

"No, honey. But with the snow covering the guy's tracks, they're running out of options. I told them you called to tell me you made it to the Spencers' and were coming in. They'll wait for your direction from here."

"Did Preston join them?"

"Preston's still handling the Jeep that exploded. Trying to find its owner."

"He'll have a hard time. That thing is toast," Ian cut in.

Carla eyed Ian with a raised eyebrow. "Is this our victim?"

Sylvie entered an office with a large viewing window, likely the old car manager's office—now the office for the chief of police. "Ian Stone, meet Carla Brown," Sylvie hollered from her office. "She's been Norcastle's dispatcher since her late husband was chief two chiefs ago. And yes, Carla, Ian is our victim. I'm keeping an eye on him so no more bullets find their way into him. Any messages I should read first?" Sylvie lifted a stack of paper slips from her meticulous desk and flipped through them, tossing them one by one into the trash.

"Jaxon would say his." Carla cackled. "He called to say goodnight and wanted you to know he was sorry. I do love talking to that boy of yours. I should say young man now. He's growing up."

"Yeah, times are changing." Sylvie frowned through the glass. "Too fast."

"I know all about change. And I've learned to embrace it. Speaking of change, one of those messages is from you know who. He called with a few choice words about his wife leaving him. He's having a hard time accepting it, and I think he's figured out you know where she is."

Ian watched Sylvie bite her lower lip as she read the message. Her whole demeanor sagged. He wondered who you know who was.

Sylvie dropped the note to the desk. "Well, Carla, why don't you go on home? You don't need to hang around here while I answer these. Thank you for holding down the fort during tonight's escapade."

"Are you kidding? That was the most excitement I've seen since the shoot-out at the Spencers' last spring."

"Shoot-out?" Ian tuned in to the conversation. "Why was there a shoot-out at the Spencers'?"

"It had something to do with the men who kidnapped Roni. She escaped and they came after her," Carla offered as she retrieved her keys from the red pleather pocketbook on her scattered desk. She tightened her scarf and pulled the zipper of her coat up to her chin. "Those Spencers, I tell you, they're always being targeted for something. Such a shame. They're such nice people. Well, good night, all. Ian, nice to meet you. Stick by the chief's side and you'll be all right. She'll catch that guy after you. She won't sleep until she does."

The door closed on a gust of bitterly cold wind, and Ian turned back to the office window. He caught Sylvie studying one of the messages on the slips of paper. Her face darkened and she looked as if she were deep in thought.

"Is everything all right?" He stepped to her office doorway. She looked up as though she'd just remembered he was there.

"Um, yeah, everything's fine. Just a call from someone who used to work here. He wants to meet with me."

"And this worries you?"

"Worries? No. Yes. Maybe. Reggie Porter worked for the department for over thirty years. In fact, he worked here as a rookie the night the car carrying you and your family was pushed off the road."

Ian lifted his head. "Would he talk to me about it?"

"Are you going to tell him who you are?"

"Should I?"

"Why are you asking me?"

"Because if you don't trust him, I don't."

She paused. "I thank you for the vote of confidence, especially having only met me twelve hours ago, but yes, you can trust Reggie. Some days I wish the town council had awarded him the chief position instead of me."

"Why didn't they?" Ian stepped deeper into her space and dropped down onto the two-seater sofa. Sylvie dropped into her own chair and leaned back. She fit perfectly, as tiny as she was. She belonged in this room, and he had to think the council recognized this, too.

"Reggie had a heart attack, but that's between you and me. My men don't know about it. Reggie didn't want them knowing. He made up an excuse that he was taking the wife on an adventure in Europe, but really went to cardiac rehab. I guess he wanted to go out of his career with the guys seeing him still larger than life. I respect that, but…"

"But the guys think you stole the chief position from him."

Sylvie gave a sad smile and nodded. "Especially Smitty. I love the man. Have since I stepped into his church with my belly out to here." She modeled her pregnant belly with her arms extended as if she was trying to hug a snowman.

Ian chuckled. "I can't imagine you being that big."

"Oh, imagine it, buddy. There was no hiding a nine-pound baby."

"Nine pounds."

"And six ounces. You can't forget those six ounces."

"I wouldn't dream of taking away your thunder. Brag away, Mama."

She flashed him a beautiful smile. A row of perfect white teeth in a cherublike face. Her almond-shaped eyes crinkled at their edges. Her blond ponytail swung over her shoulder and rested there as she reached to toss the last of her messages on her desk.

"Who was Carla talking about? The man not happy about his wife leaving him."

Sylvie sized him up.

"You've trusted me with Reggie's heart condition. You must know I won't go blabbing," he assured her. It wasn't any of his business, but there was something inspiring about learning all that she handled in a day. Essentially keeping everyone safe.

"No town likes to admit they have domestic violence issues," she said. "They want to keep the persona of quaint little town, but even picturesque villages have their troubles. Let's just say I helped a woman escape hers."

"So you do know where she is."

"Of course. I brought her there." She smiled her bright smile of victory.

"Do you think Carla's right? Do you think the husband knows you know?"

"Doesn't matter. I will go to my grave with the location."

"What if he retaliates and comes after you?"

She barked with laughter. "Let him try. I won't need anyone pressing charges to arrest him then."

"Does Norcastle have any more of these domestic violence cases?"

Sylvie dropped her head to her chair with sadness in her eyes. He took that as a yes.

Ian not only saw all she handled in a day, but also how the situations she couldn't change affected her.

"I grew up in an abusive home, Sylvie. Don't be so hard on yourself. Some people are really good at keeping the law at bay."

Sylvie locked on his gaze. The anguish he saw in her green pools didn't bring him comfort but he knew she wanted to fix his problem, too.

"It's done," he said. "But promise me you'll never give up going after the bad guys."

A liquid smile blossomed on her face. "Never."

"I wish I had a Chief Sylvie Laurent growing up." Ian took in her smile and thought about how stunning she looked relaxed against her chair. "But with all these guns aimed at me, I'm glad I have you in my life now."

"Speaking of which, you ready for your jail cell?" She unlatched her keys from her belt and swung the ring around her finger. Her face deadpanned.

"I think you're enjoying this too much. I hate to break it to you but I'm not going in your jail cell, at least not willingly."

She snapped her fingers with a dimpled smile. "Oh, fine, but that means I'm putting you to work." Sylvie stood and approached a filing cabinet. She rummaged through the top drawer and pulled out a paper roll. She unraveled it and draped it across her desk. A terrain map of a mountain lay before them.

"Is this the mountain we were on tonight?"

"Mount Randolph. Yes. It's also the mountain I think your gunshot came from. I'm thinking he's holed up here somewhere. He's spent some time on the mountain and knows the terrain enough to take out half my police department."

"Including the chief."

"I'm not any more important than my men."

"Jaxon would disagree."

Sylvie flashed him a heated glare from her hunched-over position. All sweetness gone. She jammed a pencil into her silky hair behind her ear and straightened. "You don't need to concern yourself with my son. We have a deal, a pact, which goes way back. He understands the dangers of my job. I don't shield things from him."

"He's still a fourteen-year-old boy with a single parent. Where's his father?"

"Again, none of your concern."

"No, but if you weren't around, would Jaxon's old man be back in the picture?"

Sylvie dropped her gaze to the map and pored over it with her full attention.

"Something tells me it wouldn't be a good thing." Ian pushed the conversation on, wondering more than ever who the man in Sylvie's life had been…and what would make him leave her and his son behind. The man must be insane.

Sylvie kept her head down and removed her pencil to circle a place on the map. "One more word out of your mouth, Ian, and I won't give you the choice about the jail cell."

"Just answer the question. Would you want Jaxon's father to be back in the boy's life?"

She threw the pencil down and came around the desk.

Ian stayed firm in his position, even when she grabbed his good arm and yanked it behind him. The woman had some muscle. He didn't doubt she could handle her own, but just as the incident on the mountain tonight proved, mistakes happened.

"Who's watching out for you, Sylvie?"

She paused in shoving him out the door. "I don't need anyone watching out for me." She jammed a hand into his back to make him move. They exited her office and walked across the hall to a metal door with a single window at the top. She opened it and pushed him inside. "Say hello to your room for the night."

She slammed the door, and he called out, "All this because you don't want to admit you haven't planned for Jaxon's future if something happens to you?"

He stepped up to the tiny window and watched her return to her desk to study the map. Her lower lip became something to bite on while she tapped her finger on the paper. She wrote something down on it, then took a picture with her phone. Ian figured she was working out a theory.

A movement off to the back of the department caught Ian's eye. The small window on the cell door blurred at the edges, so he couldn't get a clear view of what moved. But he didn't need to see who it was to know someone else was in the building, and they were keeping themselves hidden from view.

"Sylvie!" Ian yelled to warn her, not sure if he could be heard beyond the metal door. His room was probably soundproof.

The next second a gunshot blasted out in the bull pen and the window to Sylvie's office shattered into a million pieces.

Ian ducked out of instinct, but when he looked to her office again, she was gone.

The lights throughout the building shut down in a blink. Pitch blackness descended in the station. Even without the lights, it was obvious what was happening.

His would-be killer had returned. And there would be no kill switch to get them out of this one.

SIX

Sylvie's heart jumped in her chest, her breathing shallowed to quick gasps. She crouched low under her desk in the pitch black, fumbling for her gun at her belt. Sliding a round into the chamber, she debated her next move.

Get to the radio and call for backup. She could kick herself for not putting her individual shoulder radio back on when she returned.

And for putting Ian in the holding cell.

Did he know she hadn't locked him inside? She'd figured he would try the doorknob after she left and would show his annoyingly handsome face in her office any second.

Oh, how she wished he had. Then he would be next to her and she could protect him. How would she get to him in the dark with glass pieces to crawl over without alerting their shooter to her still being alive?

She had Ian to thank for that. If he hadn't called out her name in such a panicked pitch, she wouldn't have dropped to the floor. She would have been blown across her office before hitting the floor dead.

She had to get to him. She'd put him in there with

no place to run. The shooter wasn't walking out of here without his mission accomplished this time. All he had to do was open the door and shoot Ian. A quick shot at close range. Job done. Ian was trapped…and she'd trapped him.

Sylvie reached her hand up to her cell phone. She'd placed it on her desk when she'd taken a picture of the drop-off on the map. The one she and her team had nearly plummeted over.

Quickly, she texted a message to Preston. Shooter at the station. Help.

She hit Send.

Please God, let there be coverage. Let this go through.

She couldn't wait for backup. She gingerly crawled out from her desk and patted the floor as she went. Two more steps and she exited her office for the wide open bull pen. She crawled two more steps and heard a loud crunch of glass beneath her knee.

A gunshot banged through the office and flew by her head just as she managed to fling her body to her left.

Sylvie's chest constricted. Her pulse tripped, then tripled in time. The bullet had come within an inch of her head.

A beep sounded from across the room. A phone lit up from one of the officers' desks. The light gave a quick shadowed depiction of the bull pen. A dark figure of a person appeared by Carla's desk.

Sylvie took aim and shot her gun three times toward where the figure had been standing.

The phone beeped again. The light now revealed no humanoid shadow.

The guy must have moved. She hadn't heard anyone fall.

She hastened to the cell, but when she reached the room, her hand hit an open door.

But who had opened it? Ian or the killer?

She looked to where she'd seen the shadowed figure. Had that been Ian? Had she shot him?

Loud breaths echoed through her head. She had to be alerting the killer to her location with every rush of air.

The front door burst wide and multiple flashlight beams infiltrated the dark. The back entrance also welcomed her backup. Preston had come through. Sylvie thanked God for getting her team to her so fast.

"I'm on the floor by the cell," she called out to them. "Ian Stone is in here somewhere."

And suddenly he wasn't somewhere, but beside her, pressing his head into her neck. "I'm right beside you." His arms engulfed her, and she returned the comfort with her own.

She couldn't stop herself. "Ian, I'm so sorry. Please forgive me. I shouldn't have put you in there. I shouldn't have let you leave my side."

"Shhh… I deserved it for sticking my nose where it didn't belong. I won't say another word about your son. You've done a great job raising him. You know what you're doing. Don't listen to me. What do I know? Nothing. I'm an idiot."

Sylvie shook her head and pressed closer to him, wanting to deny his remark, but also knowing she was unable to deny the fact that he had been spot-on about her lack of plans for her son if something were to happen to her.

The lights blared on overhead, revealing her team with guns drawn, but looking aimlessly around the office.

"There's no one here, Chief. The place is clean."

Sylvie released Ian and stood. But she stayed beside him. He offered his hand to her, and she held it tight. "Someone wants this man dead, and we cannot let that happen. It's going to be a long night, boys."

The cell phone on the desk beeped again.

"Which one of you left your phone here? I know we don't get the best signal up here, but you're still supposed to have them on you at all times."

"Sorry, Chief, that's mine." Preston stepped out from the rear of the room. His gaze jumped between Sylvie and Ian, a blatant question at their closeness in his eyes. But she had her own that took precedence.

"Yours? But I texted you for help. If your phone was here, how did you all know I needed you?"

Smitty raised his phone from his front pocket. "We all got the text, Chief. You must have sent a group text to all of us."

"I did?" Sylvie wasn't about to battle over silly matters. It was obvious she had, but in the darkness and in her adrenaline, she just hadn't realized she'd sent her message out to everyone. She sent a prayer of thanks to God for intervening. If she had sent the message to Preston only, he would have never received it, and she and Ian could be dead.

And Jaxon would be shipped off to Greg Santos.

Ian walked up to the hospital's front entrance with Sylvie guarding his back.

She spoke as the electric doors moved aside for them. "I've made arrangements for my neighbor, Margie Cole, to take Jaxon today. He won't like it, but I can't have him unprotected while this killer is walking around town and I can't have him with us."

Ian didn't like it, either.

"Your son needs you. If something happens to you because of me—"

"You need to accept my job as a cop, Ian. It's not going away, and I'm not, either."

They both wore bulletproof vests under their coats, but it still irked him to have her as his barrier to danger.

She peered over her shoulder to scan the horizon of the new day, but he knew she wasn't looking at the majestic beauty of the White Mountains.

She was looking for his shooter.

For what? To take the bullet for him? Ian shook his head in disgust.

"I hate you guarding me."

"I hate you doubting me."

Ian did an about-face "It's not about doubting you. It's about me being a man. I'm supposed to be able to handle myself, defend myself, but…" He stopped himself from sharing more than he needed to.

"That *but* is why I'm the one doing the guarding. I'm separated from this. It's got nothing to do with me and everything to do with you. Someone is after you. Someone doesn't want you making it home for the holidays. You're too close to this to be able to defend yourself. You're driving blind. Look at me as an extra pair of eyes."

"And if my shooter strikes, getting you in the process, how do I explain that to your son?"

They walked to the nurses station and got Jaxon's room number. "I'll tell him right now so you won't have to."

"Great. Now a kid is protecting me." They entered the elevator and Ian hit the button for the third floor.

"You really know how to make a guy feel less than adequate."

"But at least you're alive." She slapped a palm on his chest as the elevator doors opened to Jaxon's floor, stopping him from exiting first. Sylvie glanced down both sides of the hall before allowing him to move.

She kept her right hand over the gun on her waist as she walked. He knew her draw would be clean and quick if the need arose.

They reached Jaxon's room. She knocked and announced herself and Ian to her son.

The boy didn't reply. She pushed the door wide and revealed a man sitting in the bedside chair.

Sylvie fell back into Ian on a sharp exhale. Her fingers stayed over her gun. Ian knew this wasn't a pleasant surprise.

"Is everything all right?" he asked, reaching for her forearm for support, and suddenly he understood what she meant about the extra pair of eyes. Her ashen face told him she now was too close to this to make a good decision. She was too close, but he wasn't.

"Who are you?" Ian asked.

"Who are you?" the unknown man asked. It reminded Ian of his own encounter with a stranger in his hospital room in California a couple weeks ago.

But something told Ian this guy wasn't here to tell Sylvie she hailed from a rich family like *his* stranger had.

"I'm Luke Spencer," Ian said, knowing the Spencer name would hold a lot more weight than Stone.

The guy squinted, then flinched in confusion. The reaction was enough to give Ian the upper hand. "Luke Spencer's dead." The man slowly stood.

"So I'm told, but as you can see, I'm alive and well. I won't be able to say the same for you if you don't tell me who you are."

"He's Greg Santos," Sylvie answered for him, but the name meant nothing to Ian.

"What she means to say is I'm Jaxon's father."

Sylvie stepped in like a bulldozer. "You are not his father. Where is he? What have you done to him?"

The door behind them opened and Jaxon stepped in on quiet, unsure steps with his crutch. "He didn't do anything to me. I'm right here. I was in the bathroom getting ready to leave."

"With him?" She pointed to Greg.

"No, but I didn't know when you were coming. You didn't call to tell me."

"I couldn't, I was—"

"Yeah, I get it. You were working," Jaxon said and went to his bed to retrieve a department store bag. His outfit of blue jeans and red flannel was brand-new, the tags freshly torn and scattered on the bed. Ian figured dear old Dad had brought them as a bribe gift.

"Jaxon, your mom—" Ian started to explain why Sylvie couldn't make the call, but she cut him off with another palm to his chest.

Jaxon hefted his bag over his shoulder. He brought a winter cap down over his bandaged head and headed for the door, hardly in a rush with a boot on his broken leg.

Sylvie glared Greg's way. "You are not to go anywhere near my son. I will arrest you myself if you do. Pack your things and get out of this town."

"I plan to, but when I do, Jax will be with me, and there's nothing you can do to stop me. He's already told me everything I need to prove you are unfit to raise him, caring more about your job than our son."

"He's not your son," she repeated low and deadly.

"Saying it doesn't make it so. I've stood back long enough. But now the boy needs his father, and I plan to be there."

Greg pushed past her with little effort, but Ian stepped in to block him. He had to look down to meet Greg's eyes. "You have no idea what you're getting into. I can go for years in court. I can make you wish you never stepped foot in this town. Better get yourself a good lawyer, because you can be sure mine will be top-notch."

Ian let him go by, but not without brushing against his shoulders. The guy was short, but strong.

The door shut and Ian asked, "What does he do for a living?"

Sylvie breathed deep and slow. "He races cars. He's pretty successful. Stood in many winner's circles."

"Meaning he's rich."

Sylvie's lips trembled. This was the first time Ian had seen fear enter her eyes since the moment the first gunshot went off. "He's won many purses. What he's done with his money, I have no idea. I've never wanted any of it, but I'm sure he can last a lot longer in court than I can."

Ian placed his hands on the sides of her face. "But is he Spencer rich?"

She gave a slight shake to her head, her eyes questioning where he was going with this.

"Then don't worry. You will not lose your son to that man."

"How can you say that? I can't afford an attorney and neither can you."

"Ian Stone can't. But Luke Spencer can."

SEVEN

Sylvie pulled into the driveway of her tiny row house in downtown Norcastle. The houses were all the same with their single floors and one-car carports. Typically, Jaxon's Legends car earned the shelter, but with his smashed-up car sitting in a garage at the track, she pulled her cruiser up under the carport and put it into Park.

Jaxon sat in the backseat behind the glass partition. His choice. He'd gone for the back door at the hospital without a word. He'd yet to say anything. The crack that had been growing between them widened into a wedge, shifting Sylvie's world. Ian placed his hand on hers and squeezed. As much as she appreciated his comfort, she couldn't let Jaxon see the intimate touch. She quickly removed her hand and stepped out of the car.

She came around to the passenger side and opened the rear door. Jaxon was unable to get out without the back door handles and would also need her help with his broken leg. Sylvie extended a hand to him. "Go to your room and grab a few things. You'll be staying at Mrs. Cole's tonight."

Instead of taking her hand for help, Jaxon pushed her away.

On a gasp Sylvie recoiled at her son's unusual response. Sure, lately he'd been growing distant, but never rude. She glanced at Ian and wondered if her son had seen him take her hand. He couldn't have with the closed middle partition blocking his view.

A need for the comfort Ian offered came rushing back. *No, not comfort.* She was losing her son right before her eyes and didn't know how to stop this growing chasm.

Ian stepped out of the car and insinuated he wanted to try. Why he thought he, a complete stranger, would be successful where the boy's mother failed boggled her mind. But she let him pass.

"I once had my shoulder torn from its socket," he said to Jaxon. "My right one no less, the same one that took the bullet. So if you don't mind, I can offer some help, but it's got to be from my left arm. Go easy on me. I can't have two bum arms."

"What happened to your arm?" Jaxon asked as he let Ian lift him from the backseat of the car. "Was it a fight?"

They hobbled up to the back steps. "Why? Do I look like the fightin' kind?" Ian smiled down at her son, and something in Sylvie stirred at the sight…and then quickly turned to a nauseating roll. She slammed the door on the idea of a man in either of their lives. They'd come this far without one, and they would continue as so. It didn't matter if the man's smile did funny things to her, or his hand brought on a semblance of peace. Those things were all temporary. Soon after he would try to change her…like so many other people. She said in a gruff, perturbed voice, "I'll go tell Mrs. Cole we're here."

No response came from either of the boys. As they went inside the house, the two talked amongst themselves about how Ian had injured his shoulder. She doubted he was telling the truth when Jaxon laughed about an elephant playing a part in the fight.

Sylvie took a step toward her neighbor's house. It had matching yellow siding because Sylvie had gotten a good deal on the paint when she bought it off the Oops return shelf at the hardware store. She and Jaxon had spent the summer painting both structures, prettying up the neighborhood one house at a time, they'd said. Come spring they planned to plant pansies in the flower boxes. Or would it only be her...?

"Sylvie?" Ian had stepped back outside and now stood at the back door.

"Get inside the house where I know you're safe." The words came out clipped and angry, but didn't the guy realize the danger?

"Are you sure it's safe? Because someone's left you a message on your bathroom mirror."

"A message?" In confusion, Sylvie took two steps toward him. "What kind of message?"

"Jaxon found it. It says 'I found her.' Do you know what that's supposed to mean? Do you think it's a message from you know who about his estranged wife?"

Sylvie's stomach dropped like a heavy-handed fist. *He found her? But how?* Who had given up the location?

"Who wrote it? Sylvie, answer me! He was in your house."

Sylvie snapped her head up when she realized Ian had left the steps and stood in front of her. His hands gripped her shoulders, bringing her back to the present danger.

"You shouldn't be out in the wide open like this," she mumbled about Ian's situation while her mind worked on someone else's. Would she be too late?

"Forget about me and tell me what's going on."

Jaxon stepped out the door, fear on his face, and she realized her son could have been hurt. What if he had been home alone when Clemson came? She thought she could do this job and keep Jaxon out of it.

She rushed to the door and wrapped her arms around him. She held on for a few moments and noticed he did the same this time. They may be growing apart, but they weren't broken, yet.

"Jaxon, I need you to go to Mrs. Cole's and stay inside until you hear from me."

She helped her son down the steps, trying to take it slow while danger pressed in faster than she could respond. She pulled him along, wondering how long that message had been there. Yesterday? Last night? This morning? *Please God, let it be this morning.*

"Why do I have to stay inside? I'm not a baby. I don't need to be watched. Does this have anything to do with Bret Dolan?"

Sylvie tripped in the snow and stared at him. "What do you know about Bret Dolan?"

"I know you're butting into his family. He's been harassing me for weeks about what you're doing. He says you're trying to take away his mom."

"I would never do that. It may look that way, but… Forget it. I don't expect you to understand."

"I would if you actually took the time to tell me." Jaxon limped away on his crutch, crossing the yard to

Mrs. Cole's. The elderly woman opened her front door and waved to Sylvie, helping the boy inside as best she could. The woman wouldn't be able to do much to protect her son. A strong wind could take her down.

But Sylvie would have to take what she could and trust God to step in. She turned back to her cruiser and noticed Ian still standing under the carport.

Frustration whirled in her. "Didn't you hear me? It's not safe for you to be standing out in the open."

"And I said, forget about me."

"I can't forget about you. I need to keep you safe. It's my—"

"I know, your job. I get that. You're devoted to your job."

She reached her driver's side door. "Just get in," she told him, still not sure what she planned to do with him.

"Where are we going?"

"You can't come with me." She backed out of her driveway and knew where she could take him. "You're going to your brother's."

"Wade? But where are you going? To the woman you helped?"

"Yes. I pray I'm not too late. That message tells me her location has been found. She's in danger."

Sylvie hit her radio on her shoulder. "Carla, you read?"

"Go ahead, Chief."

"Has anyone reported a disturbance over at Evergreen Haven?"

"Nothing's come in." Sylvie let a little sigh of relief escape her lips as she drove. "Do you want me to send a car over?"

"No, I'm heading there now. But I do need Karl to

get over to my house and process it for a break-in. I had one this morning."

"10-4."

Next she called Wade, but no answer told her taking Ian there was out of the question.

"You don't have to worry about me telling anyone where this place is," Ian spoke over her thoughts of a plan B. "I wish I had such a place to go to when I was young."

Sylvie let the rest of her stress go in the heavy silence. She remembered him saying he came from an abusive home.

She looked to his shoulder, the one he'd told Jaxon had been injured by an elephant. "So the shoulder was no circus accident."

He laughed a sad laugh and shook his head. "Never been to the circus."

She swallowed hard as she made up her mind. "I suppose if he's found her, then the secret's out."

"Who is he?"

"Ben Clemson. He's a mean drunk. I'll need to find another place for his wife, but I'll also have to find another safe house. It won't be a safe place for anyone anymore. Just when I was so close to helping another woman leave her abusive situation."

"The other domestic violence situation you mentioned?"

She nodded as she raced on.

"Who? This Bret Dolan that Jaxon was talking about?"

Sylvie glanced his way. "Bret Dolan's mother. She called me late one night from a pay phone in town, saying she'd left and didn't know what to do. She feared for her life and begged me to help. I picked her up and brought her to the station. She didn't want to go to the hospital. Carla and I helped her with her injuries. But then I pushed her away. I rushed her."

"How?"

"She allowed me to photograph her injuries. All I wanted to do that night was go after Shawn Dolan and cuff him. I must have let it show too much. I tried to get her to press charges, and before I knew it, she was out the door. It was all too much for her."

"She went back to him."

Sylvie nodded. "Many times they go back. But I know she'll call me again someday, and this time, I'll have Evergreen Haven, a place to bring her to that would help her heal. Or would have, if Ben Clemson hadn't found the location. He'll tell everyone who will listen now, and I'm sure Mayor Dolan will be first in line."

"*Mayor* Dolan?"

"Affirmative. Bret's father is the mayor of Norcastle, and his wife's abuser. Told you, don't let the quaint little town fool you. Even Norcastle has ugly secrets."

"And you know them all. Are you sure you don't have people gunning for you, too?"

Sylvie took the turn into a campground that looked closed for the season. Cold little cabins dotted the hills that could be seen from the road, but as she drove farther into the property away from the traffic, he saw a large log cabin's chimney spurted smoke out the top. Beyond it, a red covered bridge gave access to the other side of the cold river that ran through town.

"It's peaceful here. You picked a good spot," Ian said.

"The bridge is a favorite spot. Jaxon and I have spent

years walking to it for spring fishing, or for just thinking. Spending long hours here got me thinking that
Evergreen Haven Campground would make a great location for a safe house."

"And only you and Carla know?"

"There are a few of my team who know. The ones I
know I can trust. Now you."

Sylvie parked the cruiser and opened her door. "Stay
here."

Ian opened his door and stepped out.

She sent him a frustrated look. "Fine, but if your
presence makes anyone uncomfortable, I'll need you
to back off."

"Got it."

They walked side by side up the front steps. Ian immediately saw the front door had been kicked in and
stood ajar. He shot an arm out to stop Sylvie.

"We're too late," she said and reached for her radio at
her shoulder. "Carla, I'm going to need that team over
here. There's been a breach."

Sylvie drew her gun. She took a step toward the
threshold, but Ian pulled her arm back.

"I'm a cop. This is what I do. I go in."

"You should wait for backup."

"You should wait in the car."

Neither of them was planning to follow the other's
orders.

He trailed her inside, watching her back. She held her
gun pointed up as she peered into the kitchen, her back
to the wall. She entered and Ian stayed in the doorway
to stand guard. He could hear something clicking. A
door opened and closed before Sylvie returned.

"The stove was on. This just happened."

"Which means the perpetrator could still be in the house. We need to exit until backup arrives."

Sirens off in the distance grew closer. A creaking sound from above blared louder in his ears. Someone moved upstairs.

"Go outside, Ian."

He shook his head, giving her a taste of his stubbornness. He wasn't leaving her side. "Consider me an extra pair of eyes."

Her own words thrown back at her seemed to do the trick. She waved her gun for him to move away from the stairs. He stood behind her as they approached the landing. She took the first step in silence, then another and another. At the top, she turned to put her back against the hallway wall, pointing the gun for Ian to do the same.

Together they slid down the hall and entered a bedroom.

From their standing point the room appeared empty. Ransacked but empty. Sylvie checked all corners then walked over to a rug and pulled it up off the floor. Except it wasn't only the rug that came up. A door in the floor did, too.

She placed a finger to her lips and closed the door. She brushed past him and whispered, "She's safe."

Ian looked at the trap door and realized Mrs. Clemson was inside, hiding from the intruder.

He heard the downstairs become a bustle of cops storming in from all entrances, but Sylvie moved on to a second bedroom.

"Freeze!" she yelled.

A gunshot went off and Ian watched her go down with a thud.

"Sylvie!" Ian fell to his knees and crawled over to her. His body iced over instantly with a fear he'd never experienced before. He pulled her out into the hall, but she pushed him away. He reached for her again, needing to know she wasn't hit.

She reached for her shoulder radio. "Perp went out the back bedroom window upstairs. He slid down the roof. He's wearing a black ski mask, and army green clothing. About five foot eight."

"We heard a shot. Are you down?" came the response.

"Missed. Now find him."

Ian dropped his forehead into his hand on a sigh of relief. A groan escaped from his panting chest. "Are you sure you're okay? You're really not hurt? Not shot? You scared me half to death!"

She jumped to her feet, carrying on as though he wasn't having a heart attack and she hadn't been in danger of losing her life. It was business as usual.

She scanned the overturned room. "This place is a mess." Ian realized Sylvie wasn't going to allow him or herself to lose focus. He didn't know how she cut herself off from feeling fear right now, but if he meant to help her, he would have to follow her lead. He pulled himself together for the task at hand.

"The guy was looking for something," he said through rapid breaths.

"Someone." She lifted her chin to the other room. "His wife."

"I don't think so. He spent more time foraging than looking for the woman."

"We'll start with her husband. If he has an alibi that checks out, then we'll look elsewhere. The only thing I do know now is the place is compromised." She stood and walked back to the other room.

"And don't forget the part about nearly being shot. You could have been killed," Ian said, on her heels. "If the shot had hit you in the head, you'd be dead."

"Telling me things I already know won't help us catch this guy." She hit her radio. "I need the 411, guys. Have you caught him?"

"He had a snowmobile tucked in the trees. He's long gone. We'll get the sleds, but he'll still have a pretty good lead on us. What do you want us to do?"

"Not another sled chase, that's for sure. Let him go. We'll get him with a warrant. I want an alibi for Ben Clemson."

"Ben Clemson? His wife recently left him. He's been down, but why would you think he would break in here?"

"Because she was living here."

No response came, and Sylvie let them chew on that.

She clicked off and stood. "Don't worry, Ian, I'm still looking for your shooter, too."

"My shooter, abusive spouses, your ex-boyfriend here to take your son. At what point do you reach your limit?"

"My last breath."

Ian sighed as she swept past him to help Mrs. Clemson from her hiding place. "How did I know you were going to say that?"

No reply came because Sylvie was giving a hand to two frightened women stepping out of the floor. Her soothing words caught him unaware. Her typical authoritative voice ceased in the presence of the ladies.

He followed them out to the cruiser. He overheard

the second lady say she was the home owner when she walked over to an officer to give him her statement. Mrs. Clemson climbed into the rear cruiser seat. Ian got in the front and Sylvie assured her he could be trusted.

Ian faced the frightened woman. "I'm sorry you've had to make this decision in your life, to leave everything behind in order to survive. If it's any consolation, I grew up in a home with an abusive father, and I wish my mother had known someone who could help her escape. You're blessed to have Sylvie."

The woman lifted sad eyes, but she nodded her agreement. "I am so thankful to her. Before she became chief, I never believed I could be safe. She saw me one day and just knew I needed help."

Ian glanced Sylvie's way, astounded at the amount of compassion this small woman offered to so many. Some people were all talk, but Sylvie wasn't afraid to get her hands dirty.

They drove in silence all the way to a shelter two towns over. Sylvie walked Mrs. Clemson inside to get her situated and returned deflated.

"I hope she'll be okay. This isn't my jurisdiction. I can't protect her here." She pulled out onto the street to head back to Norcastle.

"How did you recognize the signs?" Ian asked. "Did Greg hurt you? Because one word and his case is over." Ian mumbled under his breath, "His life just might be over, too."

"No. Even if he did I would have a hard time proving that. Yes, he left me pregnant, but he never hit me. But his abuse was more about his lack of respect for me. I think that's what I recognized in Mrs. Clemson and even Andrea Dolan. They're not valued by the men in their lives. When I see that, I take notice of what's not visible."

"How has it affected your relationships since Greg?"

"There haven't been many. I went out a few times when Jaxon was six. I thought I was doing him wrong by not having a male figure in his life, but the men didn't understand my goal of being a cop. At first, it's exciting for them, but then they start wanting to change me. To keep me safe at home. They don't understand that's not me. It's like they can't handle what I do. So Jaxon and I made our pact that it would be just the two of us, and we would be enough for each other."

"You never dated again?"

"No reason to."

Ian found her remark to be disappointing. He didn't know why, but perhaps it was because Sylvie had so much to offer. So much love and compassion and companionship. It wasn't just someone else missing out on receiving all she had, but she herself was on the losing end, not receiving that love in return.

Especially when she gave it so freely.

"Well, I'm sure Mrs. Clemson will always be thankful to you. You didn't just change her life—you believed her."

Sylvie searched his face in the darkness of the car's interior. With night falling, they were ensconced in uncertainty. Uncertain of what was around them outside. Uncertain of what was happening to them inside. All Ian knew was Sylvie hadn't just changed those women's lives—she'd changed his.

"How many people didn't believe you, Ian?"

He looked out the passenger-side window. "Too many to count. Honestly, I think my dad paid the police off. I don't know how he came up with the money, because we lived in a small cabin in the woods and he never worked, but he always had money."

"What about your mom? What happened to her?"

"She died of cancer when I was seventeen. As soon as she took her last breath, I was out of there. If I'd had someone like you to call, maybe things would have been different. What you're doing—"

"What I'm doing could get me fired. Carla covers me, but the town might not take too kindly to my clandestine efforts on their dime if they find out."

"But you're helping members of their town."

"Some might also say I'm breaking families up. There are some people who didn't like that I was a single mom, and it had nothing to do with the extensive duties of the job. That's why the council put me on a two-year probation. To give me ample time to prove I could handle the job. They weren't all for hiring me."

"I'll go out on a limb and say Mayor Dolan was one of them. Am I correct?"

Sylvie eyed him. "You're a smart man, Ian. You'll make a good Spencer."

Ian faced forward, unsure of how to respond. A smart man? That was a first. As for making a good Spencer, that was still up for debate. He didn't think he would even come close.

EIGHT

Sylvie pulled up to Clayton Spencer's prestigious Victorian home. Roni and Wade's uncle's sprawling house sat high upon the hill overlooking the town. The last time Sylvie had been here was last year for an intruder call when Wade and Lacey were in some danger of their own.

Lights glowed from all the windows, so Sylvie brought her cruiser to the gate and hit the button on the intercom.

"Is there a problem, Chief?" asked Clay when she stated her name.

"I need to see Wade if he's in."

"Yes, he's here. Roni's here, too. Lacey's in labor and everyone's hanging out. I'll open the gate. Come on up and join in the excitement."

Sylvie glanced Ian's way. "If you don't want to go up, we don't have to. We can head back to the station. There are officers there and you'll be safe. I won't let another breach happen."

"I say let's get this over with. With the whole family here, I'll be able to watch for the person who's out to kill me. Keep your enemies closer and all that."

"I wouldn't be bringing you here if I thought for a second one of them ordered the hit on you."

"Good friends, are they?"

"Only Roni."

"Then how can you be so sure?"

"I just know how much pain Wade and Roni have been through and how much they really want to put their family back together."

"And Clay Spencer, too?"

Sylvie paused to think about that. "Actually, I can't answer about him. The little bit I know isn't good."

"Like what?"

"Like he was friends with the man who had your parents killed. He says he had nothing to do with the murder, but there aren't too many people left to negate that."

"So what you're saying is Clay Spencer could have actually gotten away with murder. Did he gain anything from it?"

Sylvie drove up the curving driveway that encircled the property. Ornate lanterns lit the way, showcasing a stately home with huge wraparound porches and Victorian turrets signifying Norcastle's closest thing to royalty.

"Let's just say it was your mother who brought the money here. Your father and his brother, Clay, grew up downtown." She thumbed over her shoulder to point to the brightly colored Christmas lights down in the village storefronts. "And it didn't look like it does now. The factories closed up and most everyone was out of work."

"How'd my parents meet?"

"That would be a question for your family." She shut the car off. "But first you have to tell them who you are."

Ian opened his door and stepped out.

She rushed to his side. "You are supposed to wait until I come to your side. This place may seem secure with the gate, but I know for certain those barriers have been breached before, and could be again."

She had her gun out and they stepped up onto the porch. The door opened with Roni on the other side.

Her beaming smile died a fast death when she caught sight of Ian. "Don't tell me we're stuck with *him* again."

"Does it look like I'm coming willingly?" Ian thumbed over his shoulder at Sylvie. "She's got a gun."

"Will you two stop it?" Sylvie pushed Ian through the door Roni held wide. "I thought this would be the safest place right now. Even the station didn't sway the shooter. He broke in last night and nearly killed him."

"When she says *me* she means *her*," Ian corrected. "He nearly killed her."

Roni reached for Sylvie. "Are you serious? You were nearly killed because of this guy? Are you sure this is worth your life? What about Jaxon?"

"That's what I said," Ian said before Sylvie could state her pledge about serving and protecting. "It looks like we agree on something."

"That you're not worth her losing her life?" Roni said pointedly.

"Yeah, that too."

Roni's eyes squinted in speculation, but before she could retort, a man Sylvie had never seen before stepped into the doorway. Voices could be heard beyond him.

"It looks like we're barging in on a party," Sylvie said, ready to retreat to do this another time.

"Yeah, the whole family's home for Christmas. It's just perfect that Lacey will have the baby, too." Roni turned and smiled at the older gentleman in a black suit, his white hair neatly trimmed. "This is my grandfather."

The man offered a hand. "Chief Laurent, I've heard remarkable things about you. You go above and beyond your call of duty. I'm Michael Ackerman. Thank you for keeping my grandson safe."

"Your grandson? What are you talking about?" Roni asked, casting glances back and forth.

Michael smiled, his gaze on Ian. "Come in, Luke. We've been waiting for you."

Sylvie nudged Ian to move, but as he passed by Roni, her mouth hung wide in shock. Roni's sharp tongue had been officially silenced.

They all joined the group in the living room. Roni followed and took a seat. Her hands gripped around the chair's edges.

"Roni? What's wrong?" Wade asked his sister. She was growing as white as the snow starting to come down outside.

She stared at Ian, her eyes glued to him. She answered on a whisper, "Luke's come home."

"What are you talking about?"

Michael stepped up to Wade and put a hand on his grandson's shoulder. "What she's trying to say is your brother has been found. And he's decided to rejoin the family."

"Who said anything about rejoining the family?" Ian spoke up. "I'm here for one thing only. You told me I had to come back to claim my inheritance. So here I am."

Sylvie sighed and rolled her eyes. "Couldn't you have said that a little nicer? How about at least a 'Hello, I'm your brother. How've you been?'"

"And give these people another opportunity to take me out? I don't think so. And don't tell me they're innocent. You can't be totally sure someone in this room didn't hire the assassin out there. You can't be sure it wasn't one of them that nearly killed your team on the sleds and shot at you at the station."

Sylvie looked around the room. To Michael, Wade, Clay, even Lacey, who gripped her extended belly and breathed through a contraction as quietly as she could. Her dark brown hair was pulled back in a messy bun, but that was typically how she styled it on a regular day.

Sylvie looked at the clock and took note of the time. 11:20 p.m.

"All right," she said, removing a pad of paper from her belt. "If we're going to do this the hard way, I'm going to need to know where each of you were between eleven o'clock last night and five this morning."

The whole room broke into chaos. Shock turned to anger. But what surprised Sylvie was no one was angry about giving alibis for their whereabouts. They were angry that someone was trying to kill Luke Spencer.

Lacey whimpered from her spot on the sofa. Another contraction came swiftly. Sylvie glanced at the clock again. 11:22.

Sylvie slapped her notebook closed. "We'll have to pick this up later. Lacey, those contractions are two minutes apart. You're getting a ride in my cruiser." Wade and Ian jumped to. The two men stared at each other as they helped Wade's wife outside.

"Everyone else can follow," Sylvie said.

A dog barked and Sylvie realized Promise had been at Lacey's side. The golden retriever bounded for the door.

"Of course, you can come, too," Sylvie told her and rustled Promise's soft, clean coat of fur as they exited out into the falling snow.

Ian sat across the waiting room from his birth family. He fought to ignore their excitement, but found his lips twitching into a smile every so often.

"It's okay to be happy for them," Sylvie said beside him. "They're about to have an addition to their family."

Ian angled high eyebrows on her, waiting for her to grasp what she'd just said.

"Ian, there's room for more than one addition."

"They're trying to kill me to keep me out. Or at least one of them is." Ian studied Michael. The old man came from wealth. Ian was a penniless, illiterate construction worker. Why would Michael even contact him? The man was in the CIA. He had to know what Ian did for a living, the trailer he called home. The Spencers kept their cars in better places than where he lived.

Ian looked to Clay.

Sylvie said he didn't come from money, but earned it later in life. No, not earned, but inherited. He was no different than Ian. In fact, he would know exactly where Ian had come from because he'd been there. Just what would the man do to keep from returning to that destitute life?

The uncle's wife, Cora, held his hand. Ian wanted to know how the family's maid fit in with the family. Roni seemed to love her, judging by the way she hugged her repeatedly. But Ian figured if Clay raised Wade and Roni after their parents' deaths, then perhaps Cora filled a motherly role for them. But Ian wondered if she'd come into money because of Bobby's and Meredith's deaths, too. So far these two could have the most to lose.

"It's a boy!" Wade ran into the room at full speed, skidding to a stop to be inundated with hugs and shouts of joy. The family crowded together, linked to each other in one or multiple ways.

Sylvie stood from her chair and approached the group. She placed a hand on Roni's back and her friend turned to receive a hug. Sylvie released her to offer a hand to Wade.

"Congratulations, Dad," she said. Wade responded by pushing away her extended hand and pulling her up into a tight bear hug, lifting the tiny chief off the ground.

Ian pushed up in his chair at the sight, not liking it one bit. The words *get your hands off her* sprang to the tip of his tongue. The absurdity of thinking such a thing kept his lips sealed. Sylvie didn't belong to anyone and she wanted to keep it that way.

"Is he really my brother?" Wade asked. It was the first time the man had referenced Ian since the moment Michael had announced his identity. The car ride over he'd been focused on Lacey.

"That he is," Michael replied. "I wouldn't have told him otherwise."

"How did you find him?"

Ian wanted to know the answer to that question, too.

"When Luke was a baby he suffered two cracks in his inner clavicle. He fell off his changing table and displaced the bones. Plates were put in to realign the collarbone, but it was such a unique break I knew I just needed to search hospital records for someone with plates in their right shoulder. I've been looking for years. Then two weeks ago I was notified we found a match. An Ian Stone from Pasadena, California, entered a hospital for surgery on his shoulder. His X-rays showed evidence of the exact same break as Luke Spencer's. The plates were still intact. Although I'm not sure how, since there was evidence they underwent severe pressure. Some sort of altercation, I presume, but at any rate, I visited Luke in the hospital when he woke up. He was forthcoming in offering a blood test." Michael waved a hand at Ian. "There's no scientific doubt that this is Luke Spencer."

"He may be Luke Spencer, but that doesn't make him our brother," Roni spoke, her hard gaze locked on Ian's.

Ian caught Sylvie's frown at her friend's words, but he kept his expression blasé. Roni was right. He didn't fit in as a family member with these people, but he only needed his blood to claim his inheritance and start his life as a business owner. He could finally be a man to be respected.

"Just tell me what my take is and I'll be on my way."

"What is that supposed to mean?" Wade asked.

"Simple. You two have had your shares your whole life, while I've lived in poverty. Now it's my turn."

Wade scoffed. "Not so fast. I have questions that need to be answered first."

"Ask away. My life is an open book."

"Who are your parents?"

"Phil and Cecelia Stone."

Wade looked at Michael. His mouth dropped, and at his grandfather's nod, he closed it on a flare of obvious anger. "Stone. I knew I recognized the name. Phil Stone was our property caretaker when we were young. Before the car crash. Why would our old care-taker kidnap you?"

"I can't answer that one. They're both dead now, their secrets taken to the grave with them. Maybe our grandfather knows." Ian looked to Michael. "He seems to know more than anyone."

Michael shook his head, his hands opened palm up, empty.

"I know." Clay Spencer interrupted the exchange. His chin quivered before he blew out a breath.

The room fell to bated-breath silence.

"The Stones quit right away. Right after the accident, Phil came to me and said he and his wife couldn't take the aftermath of the accident and the injured kids. It was too much for them. I didn't fault them because it was too much for everyone. No one knew how to react."

"Uncle Clay, that doesn't tell us why the Stones took Luke," Wade pointed out.

Clay bobbed his head, his skin beaded with sweat. His breath grew erratic. "I overheard a telephone conversation between Meredith and Michael. After that I made a call to my friend and relayed it."

"Your friend. The one who killed our parents?" Wade asked.

Clay frowned, his shoulders slumped with a nod. He looked at Ian and said, "You have to understand why I trusted him. My friend told me my brother had married a Russian spy. I believed him. I was wrong to. I'm sorry, Luke."

Luke?

The name threw him. It didn't feel right. But before he could correct the uncle, Clay continued with what he knew of that horrifying day.

"Phil Stone had been in the house when I made the call to my friend. I didn't know Phil overheard me, but he must have. I told my friend they had taken a bag of gold and weren't coming back. I told him where it was hidden. Phil heard it all."

"I'm still not following. Why did he take Luke?" Wade's voice rose.

"Because Luke was the golden child," Michael answered for Clay. "Now I understand."

Ian scoffed. The title rubbed him in a degrading way, even more than being called Luke. It was a smack in the face when he wasn't worth two pennies. "Sorry, Gramps," he said. "I am not a golden child."

Clay looked him dead-on. "I'm surprised you're alive. Once Phil had what he wanted, he could have left you for dead."

"And just what did he want?"

"The gold," Michael responded. "I told Meredith to pack her family up and run. In my line of work, I have a lot of enemies, and one of them had found her. Clay's friend used him to get information on her and told my enemies where she was. They would kill her to get to me. Her mountain was no longer safe, so I told her they would never be returning to Norcastle. She had a bag of gold and jewels for such an occasion. It's the way of things when one works in the CIA. Or has family in it. I told her to hide the bag of gold on the baby. In Luke's diaper to be exact." Michael looked at Ian. "*Your* diaper."

"Ew," Roni said to no one.

Michael continued, "It was the one place my enemies wouldn't think to look. Honestly, through the years, I had always thought they figured it out and killed you somewhere else. I never understood why they wouldn't boast about it, though. Regardless of who took you from the scene of the crime, you were taken because you were the golden child. Literally."

"Well, it explains why my father always had money when he didn't work."

"Do you have any idea why Stone kept you?"

Ian knew it wasn't Phil Stone who'd kept him. "My mother couldn't have children. She was always very ill. She always told me I was the only one she could have. She went to her grave with her husband's secret. Maybe she knew it was dangerous to return, because someone has been trying to kill me since the moment I stepped foot into this town."

Ian eyed his family, each individually. Roni, who had given him flak from day one. Michael, who'd notified him, but could have come to regret his choice when he realized Ian only wanted his share of the money. Wade, who looked at Ian with anger. Clay, who knew the Spencers' killer and had relayed a message to him that got Ian stolen from the car in the first place. How much more was the man withholding?

"You shouldn't be surprised that I don't trust any of you," Ian said.

"I wouldn't kill you," Roni spouted. "I've spent every day since I learned you were alive out there looking for you."

Michael chuckled.

"What are you laughing at?" Ian asked. "You're in the CIA. You have ample ways to kill me."

"Son, if I wanted you dead, you'd already be dead."

Ian sighed in frustration, knowing truth when he heard it. He looked to Clay. The uncle raised his hands in surrender. "All I've ever wanted is to give you kids the best life I could. For my brother. He was my best friend. I owed him that and more. No, I am not trying to kill you. I rejoice that you're home, finally, where you belong."

Sylvie's cell phone rang. She turned around to take the call, saying, "Hello, Mrs. Cole. How's Jaxon doing?" as she moved away for privacy.

Ian said to Wade, "Well? That leaves you, big brother. You haven't said much, but that could be a cover-up, pretending to know nothing when you actually do. I bet you feel all protective of the family. Like you can't let anyone near them who might take advantage."

"That would be true."

"So, knowing I only want my share and couldn't care less about the rest of you must really irk you."

"Also true." Wade's jaw ticked.

"Ian." Sylvie had returned and now spoke behind him. He waved a hand as he attempted to get to the bottom of this with his brother.

"So you thought you could get rid of me before I made waves for everyone."

"Ian," she spoke again, a desperate tone in her voice.

He turned and was faced with stark-white fear. He reached for her and she let him take her in his arms. He grabbed her face to force her to look at him. "Tell me. What's wrong?"

"It's Jaxon. Mrs. Cole went to go check on him in the spare bedroom and he wasn't there. She can't find him anywhere. I have to go look for him."

"Let's go." Ian placed an arm on the back of her vest and nudged her forward.

"No." Sylvie dug in her heels. "I can't protect you while I search." To Michael, she said, "I don't believe for a second any of you are trying to kill Ian, but the truth is someone is. I've witnessed the attempts myself, so before I leave I need to know he'll be kept safe."

"Sylvie, I can take care of myself," Ian said. She placed a hand up to stop him. "I'm coming with you."

"Not to worry, Chief," Michael assured. "I've got my men all over this place now. No one will get near him."

"Your men are here now?" Sylvie asked.

"I don't go anywhere without them."

Sylvie looked around the room at the few people in chairs.

"If they could be seen, they wouldn't be working for me anymore."

"Right…" She cleared her throat. "Okay then, Ian, I think you're in good hands." She reached for his face and placed her left hand on his cheek. "Open your eyes. Don't be afraid to let them in." She whispered the last part as she leaned in to kiss his cheek.

The kiss felt final, like a goodbye.

No way.

Before Ian gave it a second thought, he maneuvered his face to meet her lips with his.

Her soft lips hardened beneath his purposeful ones. If Sylvie thought this was a farewell, she had another think coming.

Ian pressed in, pulling her forearms toward him. She didn't push away, but she also didn't kiss him back. He didn't care. Let her remember the feel of him. Let her second-guess her self-denial of a companion in life. So what if she'd had two tries blow up in her face?

As amazing as she felt in his arms, he knew she needed to find her son. Ian released her lips and arms and leaned away from her. She didn't move forward or back, stunned with a petrified look in her dilating eyes. Not the look he'd hoped for, but it would do. Sometimes fear got a person to make a move.

"Don't be afraid, Sylvie." He used her same words to make his point.

She snapped to attention. A look in the direction of his family flushed her cheeks. The tough and mighty chief of police was blushing.

And she was absolutely adorable.

Ian kept that to himself. He'd already sideswiped her once tonight. He'd save more of that for later.

And there would be a later.

She touched her fingertips to her lips. "I'll call you when I've found Jaxon. He couldn't have gone far. Thank you, Michael, for helping me. This doesn't mean I'm stopping my investigation into the shooter. My team is still on it, and I'll be back ASAP. Congratulations again, Wade. Give Lacey my love."

Sylvie turned tail and beelined it for the exit, a mother on a mission to find her son, even if she was a bit flustered doing it. Less than a minute later her cruiser's lights flashed red and blue as it sped out of the parking lot.

Now Ian found himself in the last place he wanted to be.

"Anyone up for a game of Go Fish?" he asked half-heartedly.

"Yeah," Roni answered. "Go fishing for your cut somewhere else."

"Enough," Wade said. "This is supposed to be one of the happiest moments of my life. I don't want any words said out of pain or anger to mess it up."

Roni let her hands fall to her side. "You're right. I'm sorry. Do you have a name yet for the little guy?"

Wade looked at Ian across the group.

"Oh, man, don't even tell me," Ian scoffed.

"Yeah, we had decided to name him after you. Luke Spencer."

Ian lifted his hands. "It's just as well. As much as you said you wanted me back home, you were really looking for a baby. The adult Luke will only prove a huge disappointment."

NINE

"Dispatch to Chief." Sylvie's radio chirped at her ear.

"Chief here. Go ahead, Carla."

"What's this story I hear?"

Sylvie rolled her eyes and touched her lips again. How fast news spread around here. The minty taste of Ian's lips hadn't even worn off yet. The press of his lips still tingled.

"It was just a kiss. It meant nothing. The man was showing off in front of his family. That's all."

"Whoa. Are you telling me someone kissed you, Chief? Now *that's* a story I do want to hear."

Sylvie groaned at her slip. That wasn't the tale Carla had been referencing. "Oh, you mean about Jaxon. He probably just went for a walk. I have an idea where he is. If I need help, I'll radio in."

"He's a teenager. They're flighty. I'm sure there's nothing to worry about. He's safe. No one would hurt the chief's son." Carla cackled.

"It's not hurting him that I'm worried about." Sylvie thought of Greg. Her son had to be with him. It was the only logical explanation for him leaving without permission. He wouldn't realize Greg wasn't here for

Jaxon's benefit, but for his alone. Greg would say all the right things to the boy and trick him into trusting him. Sylvie knew all his moves. She'd fallen for them once. A poor choice.

But then, there was always somebody who would find fault with any decision she'd ever made.

She's keeping the baby? How will she support it?

She's going to school? Who will raise the child?

She wants to be a cop? What if she dies and leaves the child an orphan?

She shook her head. *It's called life, people, and one makes the best decisions they can with what resources they have at the moment.* And up until this moment, what she'd done had worked.

So what changed? The answer wouldn't come until she found her son, but she knew it stemmed from more than Greg's return. The distance with her son had been growing for a couple months.

Her radio chirped in. "Chief, Preston here. You need help? And don't tell me to hold down the fort this time."

Sylvie smiled at her right-hand man's comment. She took the next left into downtown Norcastle. "I think I know where he is. I'm heading there now."

"Is Stone joining you?"

"No, I was able to arrange security detail for him. We need to catch the perp after him, though. I don't like having this lunatic out there on the loose. At least Stone is his only target. But have Smitty and Karl stick close to Stone in case the guy makes another move. He's at the hospital with the Spencers right now. Lacey Spencer had her baby."

"That's got to be uncomfortable for Stone, hanging with a strange family during a birth."

Preston didn't know the half of it. "That's why I need to retrieve my son and get back there."

A car up ahead was pulled off to the side of the road with its hood up. Sylvie slowed her car. "Preston, I've got a disabled vehicle on the south end of Chester Hill Road. I'll stop to let them know someone is on the way to assist them. I can't give them any more time than that. You got this?"

"You can count on me, Chief."

She signed off and slowed her cruiser as she approached the car. Her wheels crunched over hard snow as she brought her vehicle up behind it.

A pop followed by her steering wheel jerking to the right surprised her. Sylvie gripped her wheel through what could only be a blowout. The timing for a flat couldn't have been worse.

Before she could form a decision on her next move, a small Legends racing car came barreling down the embankment, aiming straight for her door.

Not a blowout, she realized.

A setup.

Ian's shooter must think he was still with her, and this was another attempt to get him.

Sylvie shot her body over to the passenger seat for the expectant impact. She shielded her head from any glass bound to come her way, but instead of crashing into her, the car spun out alongside the cruiser, door to door.

Sylvie lifted her head, but in the darkness couldn't make out the driver. He drove off down the road before she could get a better look.

She put her car into gear, but with a thumping driver's side tire she wouldn't get far. Soon, sparks flew up from her front end, and the car hobbled as it rode on its rim, the tire shredded.

The end of the road.

The Legends car had no taillights, race cars didn't need them, and that meant the driver had disappeared into the night. The perfect getaway car, even with the small motorcycle engine. With her wheel shot, she wasn't going anywhere. The one thing she'd learned from this incident was that their killer had access to the race track. Since most of the town worked at the track in some way, that left only 10 percent of the town in the clear.

She hit her radio. "Preston. The disabled vehicle was a trap. I was ambushed, my tire blown out. I've lost him at this point." She hit her steering wheel at being bested. "The guy pulled up alongside of me, probably looking for Ian. When he saw I was alone, he took off."

Preston chirped in, "Be there in three."

Sylvie veered her car over to the side of the desolate back road and parked it. A minute passed, then two. Three came with still no sign of Preston. She opened her door and got out to inspect her tire…or the burned rubber that was left.

She straightened and went to retrieve the jack and spare tire. She'd have to have a talk with Preston on his response time. It was going on five minutes.

She lifted the trunk on a creak and fumbled in the dark. The sound of the snowy wilderness around her hummed with a gusty wind whipping through the branches and swaying the leafless treetops. She had the car jacked up in record time. As she cranked the lug nuts off and looked down the road behind her, she hit her radio, getting more irritated by the second.

"Preston, where are you?" She reached for the tire and replaced the disintegrated one with the small doughnut. She wouldn't be chasing any bad guys on it, but she'd get to Jaxon all right.

No response came on her radio.

She gave a last twist of her wrench and stood. Dusting the snow from her pants, she keyed her radio again.

"Never mind, Preston, I got it. Thanks, but no thanks. I want you in my office come morning. I don't care if it's Christmas Eve."

She switched frequencies to the rest of her men. "Dispatcher."

"Here, Chief."

"I need a tow truck out on Chester Hill. There's a car I need an owner ID on. Not that I'm expecting it to be legit. The thing's probably stolen."

"You got it."

Sylvie threw the tools into the trunk of her cruiser, but before she shut the lid, a crunching sound came from behind her.

She had her gun drawn and was about to turn when a hard force hit the back of her head. Pain radiated through her whole body in shock waves as her knees gave out.

A groan escaped from her lips. Her body began to fall, but someone caught her up under her arms.

The world of trees and snow tilted and swirled around her. She fought to keep conscious, but darkness fought back with a vengeance.

She tried to focus on who had her, but her mind didn't function as it should. The blunt trauma to her head demanded its time to register throughout her nervous system.

She hit cold metal, and it took her a second to realize she was in her trunk, her face plastered against the tools she'd just used to change the tire.

Her body jolted when the trunk's lid slammed down in place. The car's engine roared to life. She was being moved to places unknown, and she couldn't lift a hand to stop it.

As the darkness of her mind won the battle over consciousness, her last image was of Ian smiling down at her son.

Roni ended a call on her cell phone. "Listen up, everyone. Spencer Speedway has trouble. Criminal trouble. I just took a call from our head mechanic. He called to tell me Brett Dolan's Legends car is missing. Someone's stolen it. He also said he's pretty sure someone cut the brake lines to the number eleven car. That accident on the track at the Jingle Bell Jam was no accident. It was sabotage."

"Aren't the Legends cars the ones Jaxon was driving?" Ian asked.

Roni looked at Ian like he'd sprouted a second head. "Didn't you hear me? The brake lines were cut on number eleven."

"So?"

"So, number eleven *is* Jaxon's car. Someone cut Jaxon's lines. He could have died in that wreck." He saw Roni shiver and reach for her neck. She pulled up her collar over the burn scars. Ian wondered how much she remembered from her crash, but something else raising the hairs on the back of his neck took a front seat.

"Someone tried to hurt the chief's son?" he said,

while his mind computed the details. "At the same moment someone took a shot at me."

"Are you sure it was at *you*?" Michael asked from his waiting-room chair. He stood and raised a handheld device. "Because my men have been looking for hours for someone trailing you or staking claim to finding you, and they don't have any leads. From what they can tell, no one's after you like you believe. Besides, Jaxon's brakes would have been tampered with before you arrived at the race. My gut's telling me the shots have been meant for Sylvie, not you."

"Sylvie? This whole time? The gunshots at the track as well as on the highway? The car explosion she…she nearly died in. The snowmobile tracks she would have followed off the mountain's edge to her…death. Even the shot at the department… It was all aimed at *her*?"

Ian looked to the hospital's exit, then remembered she'd sped off to find Jaxon.

"Why did that boy have to run off tonight?" he said in frustration.

Michael cleared his throat, but Ian was already on it.

"He didn't run off," Ian said.

"You're a smart man." Michael got on his device and started issuing orders to track down Sylvie. She was heading straight into another trap. And this time alone.

TEN

"Her cell still goes right to voice mail," Ian said as he handed Roni back her phone for the tenth time. "Sylvie might be in a place with no coverage." He hoped that was the case. "How familiar are you with Jaxon's birth father, Greg?"

Roni looked at Ian from the backseat. "He grew up here. Why? Did Sylvie tell you about him?"

"I met him."

"You met Greg? How? When?"

"The man's back in town. He wants custody of Jaxon. Says Sylvie's unfit. You and I both know that's not true."

"Greg's in Norcastle?"

"He was as of this morning. If he's got Jaxon, who knows where they are by now."

"Kidnapping wouldn't get him custody," Roni said.

"True, but feeding lies to the boy to get him to run away wouldn't be kidnapping. He would be able to use it as evidence of Sylvie's lack of parenting skills."

"Right." Roni pressed her lips. "Sylvie's going to need some money. She won't be able to fight him on her salary. I'll make sure she has it."

"Thank you." Ian felt a pang of disappointment,

wanting to be the one to help her, but what did it matter where the money came from as long as she had it?

Roni eyed him and he knew she was speculating.

"She's a friend, okay?" he said. "I know we just met this week, but she's the most genuine person I've ever known."

Roni nodded. "I guess we do agree on something… Ian."

She dropped her gaze to her lap. He knew she wanted to call him Luke, but something held her back. Something he saw, too.

He wasn't the Luke Spencer everyone wanted.

"I think we can also agree on the tasks ahead of us. Find Jaxon and Sylvie. Can we do that?" he asked.

She nodded and looked him in the eyes. Her ice blues matched his own, and for the first time he saw the resemblance. But eye color didn't make them family.

Michael pulled the SUV up to the police station. The four of them jumped out and barged in on Carla talking on the phone.

She took one look at their faces and said to the person on the line, "I gotta go. Something's come up." She dropped the phone on its cradle and turned to them. "Why do I get the feeling my shift's not over?"

"Have you heard from Sylvie?" Ian asked.

"Sure." Carla smiled up at Ian in a weird way. "Don't give up on her. She's bound to see you're worth breaking her life of singlehood."

Ian had no idea what the woman was going on about. "Just tell me when you talked to her."

"Humph." The woman moved her mouse to wake the screen up. "Perhaps you don't understand. I'm on your side, son. You could be really good for our chief."

"Your chief is good all on her own. Perhaps *you* shouldn't be giving up on her."

Carla paused her search on her screen, effectively chastened. "Of course, I just heard someone kissed her and thought—"

"Well, don't think. Just tell me when you spoke to her, and then I'll need you to radio her again."

Carla read from the screen. "Her call came in about an hour ago at 10:33 tonight. What's this about?" she asked as she reached for her microphone. "Dispatch to Chief."

Carla unclicked the microphone's lever and waited for Ian's answer while she waited for Sylvie to respond.

"Jaxon ran off and Sylvie went after him."

"I know that. That's what you're all upset about? They didn't give her the job for no reason. She knows what she's doing. She'll find her son, and if she needs help she'll call it in."

Carla clicked the microphone again. "Dispatch to Chief. Do you read?"

"We think it might have been a setup. We think the shooter has actually been after *her*. I've been in the way, indirectly foiling their attempts."

Carla's face washed white with red blotches. "Oh, no," she uttered. She looked at the screen. "I have access to all the channels assigned to the department, and I heard Sylvie radio Preston to tell him she was pulling over to help a disabled vehicle. It was most definitely a setup. She said someone in one of the Legends cars pulled up alongside her and drove off when they realized you weren't with her. She said they blew out her tire so she couldn't go after them. She had to change the flat. She radioed in to say she was all set and good to go. That was the last I heard from her." Carla pressed the lever. "Chief, I need a response, now."

Silence filled the station and one of the officers in the back of the bull pen came forward.

"What's going on?" he asked. Ian recognized him as Smitty.

"Sylvie's not responding. She ran into some trouble before, but checked back with me to say all was well. But now, something doesn't feel right."

"Where was her last location?" Officer Smitty asked.

"South end of Chester Hill. She was heading to find Jaxon. She thought he would be down there."

Officer Smitty made his way to the door. "I'll take care of this." He rushed out into the night.

Carla looked up. "Now what, Mr. Stone?"

"Spencer," Roni interrupted. "His name is Mr. Luke Spencer."

Carla's eyes grew wide with slow understanding. She sputtered, "Y-you're Luke Spencer?"

"I was," Ian confirmed.

"No wonder the chief wouldn't let you out of her sight. I thought maybe she, well, never mind. I was wrong. You were her responsibility, is all."

"Right, that's all," Ian said, ignoring the iron weight in his gut her words produced. Even if they were true. "Where does that road lead?" Ian asked, attempting to get back to finding Sylvie.

"To the boat landing for entry into the river. That's about it. That, and the back way into Evergreen."

"Evergreen. The campground?"

"That's right. You were there this morning, so you should know the place is pretty secluded. Not much out there but some trails, icy water and an old covered bridge."

"The covered bridge," Ian repeated, a memory clicking into place. "That's got to be it. She told me Jaxon liked to hike to it from their home. That must be where she was heading. I need a car."

"I'll take you," Michael said. "Roni and Clay, head back, but be ready for direction if we need you."

Carla opened her drawer and handed over a handheld radio. "In case she radios in, you'll hear her." Carla tossed the radio into Ian's waiting hand.

They moved for the door and out into the blustery evening, where snow whipped their faces with shards of ice.

Ian pulled up the collar of the police winter coat he still wore. He leaned into the wind and pressed toward Michael's SUV. "It's getting worse!" he shouted from over the hood of the truck, both jumping into the front seats, slamming the doors on the loud roar of wind.

"Do you remember the way?" Michael asked.

Ian gave out the directions while Michael sent a voice message to his men. "Fall in," he said.

Ian looked in his passenger-side mirror, wondering where the men were. He caught a glimpse of movement followed by car lights flickering on one by one.

"Eight cars? Do you always travel with this much heat?"

"I'm the former director of the CIA. Have I told you I have a lot of enemies?"

"You mentioned it, but how do I know you're not taking me to my demise? I'm still not totally convinced you invited me back here for a heartwarming family reunion."

Michael eyed him. He reached inside his coat pocket and removed a gun. The butt fit snuggly in his palm, his finger hovered over the trigger.

Ian's throat closed at the weapon, ready to fire. Would the guy off him right here in the front seat?

"Why so nervous?" Michael said with a laugh. "I checked you out and know you have a gun permit."

"So?"

"So I'm giving it to you." With that, the man passed the gun over to Ian. The metal felt warm from being close to the man.

"Why?"

"So you'll trust me. I mean you no harm. Finding you has been my life's mission. Bringing my Meredith's family back together for her has consumed me. She died because of this life I live. I couldn't die until I made it right. Keep the gun on me for however long you need to."

"What about your men? Won't they shoot me if they see I'm holding a gun on you?"

Michael spoke into his device to inform his men to ignore Ian's gun. Some laughs came back with a 10-4.

"Why did they laugh?"

Michael shrugged. "You have to understand, we're the closest thing to family each of us has. We keep a distance from our real families to protect them. Most of them are single for life. I'm a father to them, and they are my sons. But when they first come on board we have a time of earning each other's trust. I hand them my weapon until they know they can trust me. It always ends the same."

"How's that? Take the next right," Ian instructed.

"I give them my trust, and soon, they find themselves guarding me with their lives."

"And you think I'll do the same?"

"Just wait," Michael replied and pulled into the Evergreen Haven Campground.

They plowed through the new snow on the ground while more falling snow blinded the area to them.

"The covered bridge is up this road after you pass the big cabin."

Ian looked at the dark structure as they passed by. Yellow police tape blocked the door, leftover from the crime committed that morning.

Michael pulled the SUV up to the bridge and put the vehicle in Park. "End of the road, I'd say. This bridge was built for horse and buggies, not big military SUVs."

"Leave your headlights on. I'll go in and search inside."

Michael put a hand on Ian's arm to stop him. "I can have my men search it. I didn't bring you back here to die."

"You didn't bring me back here. I came for my own reasons."

"The money."

"To be worth something, and that means I go out there and find Sylvie."

Ian jumped out into the storm and pressed against its power. The wind mixed with the roaring water of the river below. He peered over the edge as he forged through the snowdrifts up to the covered bridge.

The headlights of the SUV and arriving cars cast light inside, but still there were shadows on the edges.

"Jaxon! Sylvie!" he yelled and tried to hear through the storm hitting the roof.

Nothing at first, but then a whimper off to his left pulled him around.

Ian followed the sound. "Jaxon? Is that you?"

His foot tripped on something. He dropped to the floor and touched a leg. A boot.

"Jaxon, it's just me, Ian." Ian's heart rate picked up. To the men outside, he hollered, "I found him!"

Jaxon shook with a viciousness of hypothermia setting in. Michael and his men bounded inside the old wooden structure, their boots thudding on the planks. They appeared around Ian to assist in moving the boy.

Jaxon let out a wail.

"Is it your leg?" Ian froze in lifting him.

He barreled his head into Ian's neck, but no response came. The boy was being as brave as possible. Ian wouldn't make him stay out here longer than necessary. He trudged through the snow to the SUV. Michael held the back door open wide. When Ian placed Jaxon on the seat beside him, the teen gripped stiff arms around him and cried aloud. Ian knew this wasn't about a pained leg. This was a cry of guilt.

"It's okay, Jaxon. No one is angry. Worried, yes, but not angry. Can you tell me what happened?" Jaxon shook, his teeth chattering while the heat roared around them.

Michael opened the front door and peered in. "She's nowhere around here."

Ian saw the influx of CIA agents perusing the bridge inside and below, down on the riverbanks, flashlight beams bouncing in every direction through the snow. Ian's heart sank.

"So she never made it." He sighed in frustration. "Michael, hand me the police radio." Once it was in his hand, Ian hit the button to speak. "In case you're listening, Sylvie, your son is safe. Hang on, sweetheart, we're coming for you next."

ELEVEN

Sylvie's eyes shot open on a sharp inhale. Pain struck her senses, and she reached for her head. She groaned as she touched dried blood in her loose ponytail.

How long had she been out? Hours? Days?

She licked parched lips and surveyed her surroundings.

Darkness ensconced her, but somewhere off in the distance a slip of light beckoned. Less than a crack, a sliver, but it had to open to so much more.

If she could reach it.

Sylvie pushed up on weakened hands. No binds of any kind hindered her. At her waist, she found her belt and gun gone. At her shoulder, her radio torn from its place.

She crawled a few feet toward the light and found dirt and old leaves beneath her. She lifted her chin to feel a breeze stir through the dank room. The outside was behind that crack.

She pushed to her feet, her hands on her knees until the dizzying pain subsided a bit. Her first steps slogged. At the crack, she pried her fingers inside and stood on tiptoes to see through to the other side.

Her eyes flinched at the sunlight's glare. Pristine, newly fallen snow blinded her. She squinted off to the right to allow her eyes to adjust. A black pipe came into view. No, too thick to be a pipe.

A smokestack.

Instantly, Sylvie knew her location.

She'd been dumped inside one of the vacant mills down by the river.

Knowing her location motivated her to use all her might to pull, push and break the wood to get to the other side.

Not a splinter budged from its place.

More elbow jabs and even a good high sidekick that sent her slamming back to the cement only jarred her teeth and nothing more.

She needed to find another way out.

She gave the board one more halfhearted kick before heading back into the darkness.

Careful steps led to a wall, a guide she used to feel her way from corner to corner. For all she knew she could be retracing her steps. At a point where the wall turned another corner, another crack of light gave her a destination. As she neared it a voice filtered to her ears.

Someone was nearby.

Her kidnapper?

She turned an ear to the sound and closed in. A conversation between two men drifted to her. One laughed and said, "We hit the jackpot with this one."

Sylvie paused. Were they talking about her? It couldn't be. She wasn't worth much. If they thought her family would pay out, they'd picked the wrong person.

She softly stepped up to the crack and found it to be

a door. Without her gun she couldn't burst in. A fool's move if there ever was one.

The other man spoke. "How much longer before you're in the Spencer accounts?"

Sylvie froze. Her breath crystallized in her lungs. Was she hearing right? Were these guys hackers?

She stepped back. Her foot chinked against a piece of wood, sending it over in an echoing topple.

"Shh…someone's here. Check it out. I got you covered." A chair scraped along the floor. A gun clicked.

Sylvie backed away against the dark wall. She picked up her steps and found another corner to hide behind just as the door opened wide, pouring light over the place she'd stood moments before.

A flashlight beam roamed across the floor by her feet. Just an inch more and the tips of her shoes would be seen.

Sylvie held her breath and her body in check. More than anything she wanted to know who the men were, but their weapon gave them the upper hand.

For now.

She knew their hideout. She would be back ASAP with her men.

But that was only if she made it out of here first.

With that being the only door she'd found so far, it might be a while.

"Cops are pulling up," the guy in the other room shouted on a rush.

Sylvie's pulse tripped. Help was here?

"Which cop?" the guy with the flashlight asked.

"Looks like Smitty."

The guy talking didn't seem worried that Smitty

was here. What did this mean? Was Smitty involved with these guys?

The thought sickened her. It couldn't be true. Smitty had been a devoted officer in this town for many years. He was like a father to her. He had helped her so much when she was young and pregnant, and then later getting situated at the department.

But he was also devoted to Reggie.

"What's he doing here?" the man at the door whispered back.

"Shh, just don't move and maybe he'll move on by."

Sylvie took their responses as confirmation Smitty was not a part of their ring. She sighed in gratefulness. But she wasn't about to stay silent.

Sylvie opened her mouth and shouted as loud as possible, "Help!"

Suddenly, the man at the door slammed it shut and a scuffle could be heard happening on the other side.

Sylvie rushed around the corner toward the door, but without the light, she tripped over a beam and fell to the floor with a grunt.

She seethed with scrapes and pushed up on her burning palms to gain her feet. By the time she got the door open, the men were gone.

She ran by the computers and out a second door. More darkness followed, but soon light reached her eyes and led the way.

An exit door finally came into view in the enormous mill. She stomped up the stairs out through the door, straight into Smitty's large, beefy arms.

"Chief!"

"Jaxon!"

"He's safe. Ian found him."

Sylvie sagged against him. "Quick, get the team here."

"What happened?" Smitty asked as he reached for his radio. "We've been looking for you all night. And Preston."

"Preston's missing?"

"Hasn't been responding since you radioed him last night."

Worry for her friend filled her. Quickly, she relayed what she'd overheard in the mill. "Smitty, they're running some sort of hacking ring here. Breaking into bank accounts. Can you handle it?"

He looked to the vacant building behind her with a nod.

"The setup needs to be confiscated right away for evidence before we lose any of it." She looked out into the snow-covered parking lot, the river roaring behind her. They were on the back side of the building, out of view from downtown. "There were two guys running the ring. They ran off as soon as I shouted. They couldn't have gotten far."

"Did they kidnap you?"

"That's what's weird. They had a gun, but they seemed surprised to have me in the building. I don't think they did. It's almost as if someone wanted me to find them."

"Or someone wanted them to find you snooping around their illegal activity so they would take you out."

Sylvie pondered Smitty's idea as she walked to the corner of the building. Snow tracks led from a side door straight to the river's edge. She followed the footprints and peered into the half-frozen rapids below. Empty. A bend in the river inhibited any further tracking. If this was the way they'd come, they wouldn't last long in the river.

She headed back to her officer.

"I think you need to get checked out, Chief," Smitty said. Sylvie reached for her head and felt the dried blood.

"It looks worse than it is. I can still handle the job."

"You can take time. Reggie's back to help."

Sylvie stopped short in the knee-deep snow. "Y-you called Reggie in?"

"I didn't just call him. I went and personally picked him up. He stepped right up, too." Smitty nodded matter-of-factly. "And has done a fine job running the show all night. It sure is good to have him back."

"Found her. And she's fine." The call came in from Smitty. The whole department, inside and still out searching for Sylvie, cheered through the radio lines.

Ian sat beside Jaxon on Sylvie's office couch, her window now boarded up behind them. He took his first full breath since the night before and squeezed wet-ness from his eyes. Pinching the bridge of his nose, he prayed. *Thank You, God. Thank You for keeping her safe.*

Then he reached for Jaxon. The boy threw himself into Ian's arms and buried his face into the crook of his neck. Wet tears poured out onto Ian's shirt and Ian pressed in and rubbed the boy's head.

He spoke soothing words as Jaxon released the fear he'd held at bay all night long. The boy, not yet a man, put on a good front for the officers. So stoic like his mother, but all along terrified inside.

Ian let Jaxon be that terrified boy now, even though

he wanted to jump from Sylvie's couch and grab the radio to demand where she'd been. What had she been through? Did she need comfort like her son? Would she accept it from him? He had so many questions he wanted to ask while he held her in his arms, but he could do none of that in front of her son. Maybe not even alone. Sylvie marked her boundaries clear.

There was no room for anyone but her son and her job.

Her very dangerous job.

Ian could see how the men she dated found it hard to let the reality of her job go. Sitting here with her son in the aftermath of only one night on duty of many nearly undid him. What would a lifetime be like, knowing she could walk out the door and never return because, like she said, her job was to always go in? Go into the danger. Go after the bad guys. Where would that leave him?

Ian pulled Jaxon tighter long after his tears and hiccups subdued. He needed the boy in this moment as much as Jaxon needed him.

Two men who shared their worry for Chief Sylvie Laurent.

But Ian would return to California soon. Jaxon would forever go through nights like this, always knowing they could end worse.

Sylvie's son grew quiet and his breathing steadied. His body listed in Ian's arms.

A glance down showed Jaxon had fallen asleep.

The poor kid had stayed up through the night, and now his body wanted sleep.

Reginald Porter paraded into Sylvie's office. He took note of her sleeping son, then moved forward without a word to her desk chair, looking mighty comfortable.

But then he had been an officer here for over thirty years. In fact he'd been present at the car crash that killed Ian's parents and got him kidnapped.

Could Reggie help him figure some things out about the crash?

"Do you remember the Spencer car crash?" Ian asked in a deep whisper.

His question stunned the man, but Reggie answered, "I do. I was a rookie at the time. Why do you ask?"

"I'm sure you're aware the baby might still be alive."

Reggie nodded. "I've heard something to that effect. Why do you ask?"

"I'm Luke Spencer. Been tested and everything. It's legit. I was kidnapped from the scene by the Spencers' caretaker, Phil Stone."

Reggie let out a long whistle. "Wow. That's…crazy."

"My thoughts exactly. I was wondering what you could tell me about that day."

"Well, Ian… Ah, Luke?"

"Ian's fine."

"Okay, Ian, I remember government officials busting in to take over, so I can't say I had any knowledge about your kidnapping. In fact, we all believed you to be inside the car."

"But you remember the scene."

"You can never forget something like that. Fire…" Reggie cleared his throat and dropped his gaze to his chest—the very chest that had recently gone under the knife. "I would have to think whenever fire is involved, things couldn't be worse, and not just for the victims, but for first responders, too. There's just nothing anyone can do."

"Meaning you have to let them burn."

Reggie swallowed. "I'm sorry. But I will say I sure am glad to see you weren't in that car after all. Wade got his sister out, but she was on fire and he couldn't get back inside to get you. I don't think he ever forgave himself for that. He was just a kid. Eight years old. He must be so relieved to have you back. But where have you been? You said Phil Stone got you out?"

"And kidnapped me for money."

"Kidnapped? There was more to that scene than the feds let on. I'm sorry to hear that. But at least you're alive." Reggie shrugged. "I saw the scene. You should be dead. I'm surprised you made it down the ravine in the first place. That car flipped repeatedly and…well, I'm sure your siblings can tell you what they endured. You don't need me for that."

"You say that, but I get the feeling you like being needed."

"Doesn't everybody?"

Jaxon stirred and mumbled. Ian lowered his voice. "How's your heart?"

Reggie covered his chest with a light rub. A slow smile spread over his face. "You must mean something to the chief for her to confide in you. I'll trust she had a reason, and just say medical technology is remarkable. My ticker is stronger than it has been in a long time. I gotta tell you, I thought I was done for, but now I'm in the best shape of my life. Lost a ton of weight, too."

"Any plans to return to work?"

Reggie rubbed the tips of his fingers along Sylvie's smooth wood-top desk. "I would be lying if I said I didn't miss the force. It's been my whole adult life. Retirement has its good days, but there's only so many repairs a guy can catch up on. I'm driving the wife mad."

Reggie gave a low laugh. "Coming back may save the marriage."

"But what would you come back as?"

"Well, that's something I wanted to talk with Sylvie about. If you don't mind—"

"Talk to me about what?" Sylvie stood in the doorway, catching them both by surprise. Her gaze traveled from Reggie sitting at her desk to Ian holding her sleeping son.

Her lips pursed. "Well, doesn't this look comfy. I see it didn't take you boys long to move right in."

TWELVE

"Those men at the factory did not kidnap me. I got the feeling they didn't even know I was there." Sylvie unlocked a cabinet and took out a spare belt. She buckled herself in and withdrew a gun next. Loaded and holstered, she was back in business again.

"I was dumped there. Now get out of my chair," she commanded Reggie.

Reggie relinquished the seat, but Ian had to wonder if the man's newfound health would pose a problem for Sylvie. Would he try to take over her seat permanently? How would she handle that along with everything else that was about to be thrown at her? She didn't even know about her son's brakes yet.

"Of course they kidnapped you," Reggie said, taking the opposite desk chair. "I really think you need to lie low for a while. Take your son up on the mountain for the holiday. Use my cabin. No one will bother you up there with no access roads. It's secluded and safe. Take the sleds and go. Let me stick around and help you here until we figure out who these guys are."

Ian kept his lips sealed as he observed the conversation between the two officers. Reggie's idea sounded reasonable. Sylvie and Jaxon would be safe.

"You want to help me?" She snatched a pencil from the cup on her desk. She marked off a point on the map with a heavy hand and traced the river to a spot farther down. "You can start looking for these guys here. They jumped in the river and could have made it to this bank. I'm sure they won't be running fast after their frigid swim."

"Crazy fools. But if you don't think they kidnapped you, you just might be a fool, too." Reggie stood to leave.

"Stop right there." Sylvie glared. "I won't be running off to the mountains for a vacation. But since you're so fired up to jump back into work, you can start with this. I want an update on the APB for Lieutenant Preston Wallace. Where you all have looked, every rock you have lifted in search of him and where you plan to look today. I want the laptops from the mill processed for an ID. These men were targeting the Spencers' bank accounts. I want to know how far they got."

Reggie nodded walked to the door.

"And one more thing. If you're planning to come out of retirement, you will not speak to me like that again. Now you may leave."

Reggie exited the room on a short huff.

Ian couldn't hold his tongue any longer. "They were hacking Roni's and Wade's accounts?"

She glared his way. "Yeah, it seems like you're not the only one looking for a cut of their money."

Ian cringed at her verbal strike. "Just my inheritance," he defended quietly. "Nothing more."

"Even if it kills you," she flung back.

"News flash. We figured out last night nobody's actually been out to kill me. I was wrong about that."

"Right, and the bullets flying your way have been blanks."

"No, they were very real, but they weren't flying my way—they were flying yours."

Sylvie shrunk back, confusion silencing her.

"That's right, Chief. This whole time the bad guy has been after you." Ian glanced down at Jaxon's lolling head of silky blond hair. More than anything he wanted to stand and reach for her. To hold her so he knew she was alive and well. Fill his arms with her even if she wouldn't stand for it—knowing she wouldn't stand for it. "Yes, Sylvie, you have been the target. You and Jaxon. His car crash at the track wasn't an accident. Someone cut his brake lines. That happened *before* I came to town. It's never been me."

Sylvie's eyes widened and her skin paled instantly. She grabbed at her stomach and dropped slowly into her chair. No more words or commands spilled from her mouth. Her gaze rested on her son's sleeping face as her green eyes misted up.

"He's fine. He's safe. There's no reason to cry. I'm sorry. I didn't mean to deliver that message so poorly. Aw, come on, Sylvie, please don't cry," Ian begged. Her growing tears pouring forth hurt more than splinters under his fingernails. "You can see he's sleeping peacefully."

"But…but he could have been killed. Who would hurt him like that? *Why?*" she wailed and covered her mouth to stifle the sob.

"Someone who wants to hurt you."

"Me. This whole time, it's been me the shots were for."

"I just kept getting in the way."

Sylvie locked her teary-eyed gaze on him and sobered. "You could have been killed. Oh, Ian, I am so sorry."

"Don't you dare apologize to me."

"How can I not? This should be a joyous Christmas for you. If you hadn't been shot you wouldn't have thought the Spencers were out to keep you from claiming your birthright. It could have been an amazing homecoming for you all. And still you sit here protecting my son for me. As soon as you learned you were safe, you should have gone home with your family. Instead, you went after my son."

"He was easy to find. He was right where you said he likes to go."

"The bridge?"

Ian nodded.

Jaxon stirred again.

Ian glanced down at Jaxon's childlike face. The child still present within the maturing boy showed through in his relaxed slumber.

Ian glanced up to find her watching him with a frown. She didn't come across as a jealous person, but perhaps where her son was concerned things were different.

"I'm not getting comfortable if that's what you're thinking," Ian said quietly.

She snapped to attention and looked back at the map. "Good."

"But I will say it's okay for the boy to have a male figure in his life."

"If you even think I am allowing his deadbeat father back in his life—"

"I didn't say anything about Greg. I just meant there will be things Jaxon will only want to talk with another guy about. It's natural. You must know that."

After a few slow seconds, she nodded. "I feel like I'm losing him. He's been so distant lately."

"You're not losing him. He loves you more than life."

She frowned again and reached into her top drawer. "I found this a couple weeks ago when I was doing his laundry. It's a poem." She unfolded the sheet of torn-out loose-leaf paper. "I didn't even know he wrote poetry." She sat quietly reading the words Ian couldn't see, then leaned across her desk and held it out for Ian to read.

He tilted his head and raised his eyebrows at her. "Even on a good day, Sylvie."

Understanding dawned on her face, and she whipped the paper back. "Oh, I'm sorry. I forgot you can't—"

"Read. It's okay, you can say it. It's nothing I don't already know."

Sylvie stood and came around her desk with the poem. She sat on the soft leather two-seater, fitting snuggly beside her son. She brought the piece of paper over for Ian to see.

"Jaxon has beautiful penmanship," she whispered and pointed a finger to the first word. Slowly, she read each word clearly.

Jaded eyes
Once so bright.
Seen too much
But miss so much
And yet, always watching.

She finished and they sat in silence. "Do you think he's talking about me? Have I failed him in some way?"

"Don't do this to yourself, sweetheart. He's a teenage boy. He's got a lot of confusion going through his head, and even fear. The world is changing for him. But what is constant in his life is you. He can always count on you, and he knows that."

Sylvie sighed and folded the piece of paper up. She slipped it into her son's pants pocket just as a loud snore broke from Jaxon's nose.

Sylvie covered her mouth to stifle a laugh. Her green eyes danced mischievously from above. Beautiful wasn't enough to describe her.

"I think your son is quite talented with his words and you should be so proud to have such a brilliant child."

Her hand dropped to her lap and gone was the laughter in her eyes. "You're smart, too, Ian. Getting letters mixed up doesn't make you an idiot. You've found ways to gain your knowledge a different way, and you shouldn't take that lightly. We're all different and our differences should be celebrated, not criticized."

"Tell that to my father."

"I can't. He died in a car crash thirty years ago." She looked at him pointedly over Jaxon's mussed hair, daring him to defy her.

Phil Stone was not his father. Never had been.

"So I guess it's no father for me, then."

"There's God."

Ian dropped his head back. "He's the most important Father to have, I know that now. I wish I had known it when I was growing up. Life was hard…and lonely."

"I'm sure Roni and Wade felt the same way."

"But they had each other."

"And would open their hearts and homes to you. Trust me. That's all they've wanted since they learned you might be alive somewhere."

"A family if I want it. Is that what you're saying?"

"Families also come with differences that should be celebrated. There will always be people who criticize, but in the end you can only do what is best for you. And only you know, Ian, what that is. Is it the Spencers?" She shrugged a silent answer. "Is it a business waiting for you in California?" She frowned at those words, but quickly pressed her lips to cover it up.

Did Sylvie want him to stay?

The thought of her desiring him in her life felt like what a gift under the tree might feel like.

Joyful.

Exciting.

Special.

Ian smiled at her over her son's head. Without thought, his head moved a few inches toward her beautiful petite lips. What a gift it would be to kiss her.

He'd kissed her at the hospital, but that had been a deliberate move to wake her up. This felt unprovoked.

Natural.

She looked at his lips, so close to hers. With her son sandwiched in between them, Ian would not be able to get any closer.

The next move would be hers.

Her chin quivered, and her eyes darkened. He watched how they misted up again.

"No?" he said, regret threading his one word.

Maybe he was wrong about being special.

"It's not possible. I also have a family to consider."

She broke the connection and looked at her son. "Please understand."

A tear slipped down her cheek and she swiped it away.

"I'm disappointed, but I understand." Ian wondered how the woman could crush him and put him in awe at the same time. He'd never met anyone like her. To have her on his arm would be a boost to his morale. A benefit to him—but what would she be getting out of the deal?

Money.

The idea of that being a reason for her to choose him felt all wrong. He was glad she didn't go there. Not that she ever would. Which just raised her even higher in his book.

He moved away and caused Jaxon to jolt awake.

"Mom?" her son said in a rush on finding her beside him. Jaxon launched his lanky arms at his mother and she seemed to melt into him as she welcomed him into her strong ones.

"I'm right here, Jax. I'm okay."

"Mom, what happened?" Jaxon burst into heart-wrenching tears. "Where were you?"

"At one of the vacant mills. Shh, honey, everything's fine now."

"Did you catch the bad guys?"

Sylvie pleaded with Ian over her son's head. She didn't want to tell her son of the danger she'd been in—and still was in. But that would mean keeping things from him. "I'm working on it, but I need you to promise me you won't run off again. It's still not safe."

"Someone's still trying to kill Ian?"

"No. Ian is safe now. Isn't that great?" She forced a smile on her lips.

"That *is* great." Jaxon looked at Ian and beamed. "Hey, you know what I just realized?"

Both Ian and Sylvie shook their heads, staring at each other.

"Today is Christmas Eve," Jaxon said, oblivious to the reality of the situation. Jaxon could be orphaned tomorrow, instead of celebrating the birth of Jesus. "Can Ian spend Christmas with us?"

She sent a startled look Ian's way. "I think Ian has his own family to spend Christmas with."

"In name only, and even that's up for debate," Ian cut in.

"Only by your choice. You should give them a chance before you burn that bridge. Besides, there's something healing about breaking bread with someone. Walls come down as the table grows."

"Then consider me at your table."

Sylvie locked her office door with her sleeping son inside.

When she took this job, she never thought she would have to keep him safe.

She poured herself a cup of coffee and took a second to regroup. With her back to her team, she sipped the lukewarm brew and noticed her hand tremble.

No time for that.

She faced the men and Carla at her desk. "All right, it's time to get to work."

"One step ahead of you," Reggie said from his seat in front of one of the hacker's laptops. "You were right about the Spencers being targeted. These guys were about to hit the big time. They already tapped into their bank accounts."

Sylvie moved to stand beside Ian, where he stood looking over Reggie's shoulder. His body emanated anger like an electrical charge.

"So they planned to take the money and run." Ian sneered and scanned the room. "I need to call them. To warn them. These thieves are still out there. Even if you have their equipment, they could still log in somewhere else and empty the accounts. Roni and Wade need to change their accounts and passwords."

The front entrance opened and Preston walked in holding an ice pack to his head.

"Where have you been?" Sylvie demanded, coming around to meet him.

"Climbing out of a ditch," the officer snarled back. He came around Carla and into the bull pen. He dropped the ice pack to his desk, exposing a purplish welt below his eye. "Someone pushed me off the road and I was knocked unconscious. I'll need a tow truck to get the car out."

"What's wrong with your radio?"

"Dead. Better the radio than me, I say. How much longer are we protecting this guy?" Preston curled a fat lip in Ian's direction. "Until we're all dead because of him?"

"You will do your duty, and that's an order," Sylvie commanded him into begrudging, but silent, submission.

"Except what she's not telling you," Ian inserted, "is she's the real target that someone wants dead."

Preston jerked a gaze in Smitty's direction.

"What are you looking at me for?" Smitty shouted back.

"Because we all know you've never been happy about Sylvie taking the chief position."

"Doesn't mean I would kill her. I uphold the law. I don't break it."

"Enough!" Sylvie shouted. "I know none of you are behind the threat to kill me, but someone *did* cut the brakes in my son's Legends car. That's attempted murder, and I want that person found. Right now I'll need a car to go out to the Spencers'. We're down two cruisers at this point. Smitty, can we take yours?"

"We? Why are you taking Stone there?" Preston asked. "If he's not in danger, send him home."

All eyes went to Sylvie. "About that, Pres. Long story short, the Spencers are his family. Ian is really Luke Spencer. Now if you'll excuse me, I need to inform Roni and Wade about the hackers. That needs to come from me. Police matters need to be handled by the book."

"Right," Smitty responded as he tossed her his keys. "We can't be picky and choosy about what we put on the books, right, Sylvie?"

The room fell to a deathly silence. An uneasy feeling ran up Sylvie's spine. Was he referencing her efforts to help the abused women escape? She didn't keep a file in the office to protect all parties, but she did document evidence on a USB drive that she kept hidden off-site. "Everything gets documented, Smitty. Always."

Ian placed a hand on her forearm, bringing her attention to him. "You ready?" he asked. He was anxious to go, but his touch also offered her support.

She stepped back for Ian to move past her for the exit. "Carla, don't let anyone into my office, and watch over my son. All doors are to stay locked. Preston, get yourself to the hospital."

Sylvie stopped at the front door. "Reggie, since

you're hanging around, keep looking for my cruiser, and my gun."

"Will do, Sylvie."

"It's Chief. And don't any of you forget it."

THIRTEEN

"It's astounding that any of you survived," Sylvie said quietly as she drove up the mountain road that led to the Spencer mansion. She slowed the cruiser and nodded to the passenger-side window. "That drop-off. That's the ravine you and your family went over."

Ian's stomach twisted at the sight before him. This was the place his life took a turn, or more like a dive, where a family was torn apart, never to be whole again. "Right here?" he asked. "They were… *We* were pushed over here? I can't imagine…"

Sylvie pulled the car over to the side of the road. The land dropped off mere feet from Ian's passenger window. "Something tells me Roni and Wade would both gladly erase their own bank accounts to go back and erase that horrifying day. There's not enough money in the world to make that ride worth it."

Ian's throat closed. He managed to push out, "The guy who did this. He's in jail?"

"For the rest of his life."

Ian stared out at a danger he unbelievably lived through.

Why?

"I don't know why I was spared. If I was just going to be kidnapped and treated like garbage, why wouldn't God just let me die? This one event led to a life of torment."

Her hand fell to his on his lap. Instant comfort flooded into him. "Believe me when I tell you, Ian, that Wade and Roni have thought the same thing. With Wade's post-traumatic stress disorder and Roni's burns, they have been tormented their whole lives, too. Perhaps you were spared to help them now. To help each other bring a family back together."

Their gazes stared straight out at the steep drop and the many trees that would have been unrelenting obstacles to the careening car that came their way. "Perhaps this is God's way of taking the evil thing done to you all and making it beautiful."

"He makes all things beautiful in its time." He quoted the Scripture from Ecclesiastes. "I know it in my head, but—"

His hand trembled and he fisted it. "Something Carla said has stuck with me."

He looked down at where they were linked, and then up into her expectant green eyes.

"She said the Spencers are always being attacked." Ian blew out a fast breath and continued. "Sylvie, I haven't been any different than any of the others. Worse, even. I'm their own brother and I'm out for myself like one of the greedy hackers."

"No, you're not like the hackers."

"I saw a way to rise above my circumstances, and I took it."

"First of all, you're not being honest with yourself if

you think you only came back here for the inheritance. You came back here for a family, and you know it."

Ian averted his gaze, staring back out at the drop-off.

"Second, you're not a thief. A third of Bobby and Meredith's estate belongs to you. Nobody can negate that. A judge would find in your favor. Your name is in their will as a beneficiary."

"Luke Spencer is in their will."

Sylvie inhaled sharply. "You don't think you can ever be Luke Spencer, do you?"

"I know I can't. I needed the money to say goodbye to Ian the Idiot. But to take the money would make me Luke Spencer, and those are shoes I can't fill. I can never be the golden child."

"They're not looking for a golden child. They're looking for their brother."

"Until they learn he's an illiterate drifter."

"Those are your circumstances. They are not who you are. I've been many things in my life that I could have let define me. Unwanted, irresponsible, pregnant out of wedlock, teen mother, sleep deprived, hungry, lost and lonely. But none of those details make me who I am. And neither do yours."

"How do you rise above them to be something better?"

"Well, first thing, money is not the answer. Wade told you that. Money did nothing for his wounds. He left it all behind, ran away to the army, only to gain more wounds. He took matters into his own hands, but that meant he tore down some bridges along the way."

"Yeah, well, I think I've incinerated mine."

"You're a builder. Rebuild them. Right now. It's not too late."

"I wouldn't even know where to start."

"Back when I was nineteen, pregnant and alone, I started with the bridge that was built for me. The one Jesus built from heaven to my heart. I know you said Alex brought you to church, but do you understand that Jesus brought you to God? Emmanuel means 'God with us.' And that's exactly what Jesus did when He stepped off His throne in heaven to come to earth on that first Christmas morning. He is the bridge that unites us to our Father in heaven. Jesus looked at us and thought we were worth leaving His throne for. He doesn't see our circumstances. He sees our true identities. Ask Him to help you see Wade and Roni the way He sees them, and I'm sure you won't have any problem reaching out to them."

"But I'm nothing like them. I don't even know who I am."

"That's because your identity was stolen from you. Literally." Sylvie leaned in, inches away. She searched his eyes and reached for his face. "Don't you want to take it back? Don't you want to know who you are? You were robbed of your identity, your whole life wiped away in one swipe."

"Just like what these hackers are doing to people's livelihoods. What they planned to do to my..."

"Siblings. Your brother and sister. You can say it. That's who they are. And whether you think you deserve the name, you are their brother, Luke."

Ian's eyelids dropped closed. His head bent forward to her forehead on a slight shake back and forth.

"Yes, you are Luke Spencer, and right now, I see you, not the details of Ian Stone, but who you are behind it all. Strong, noble, larger than life, helpful, resourceful and, most especially, brilliant."

Ian opened his eyes, but didn't lift his head away. Sylvie's eyes liquefied like sparkling pools on a spring morning. "Are you sure you're not seeing yourself in the reflection of my eyes? Because that's how I see you, among a few more characteristics you didn't mention."

"Like what?" She smiled out of one side of her lips.

"I could tell you, but then I would have to kiss you."

Sadness stole her sweet glimmer. Her hands fell away, but he grabbed hold of them. "We both know that can't happen."

Ian nodded but didn't lift away from her. His breathing picked up, and he was pretty sure hers did also. When she squeezed his hands, digging her fingers into his flesh, he knew she was struggling. All because he put her in this situation.

"I'm sorry," he whispered and turned his lips away. His eyes closed on a rushed sigh. "I want to respect your wishes. I do." Still, he held her hand, rubbing his thumb over her soft skin.

"My wishes. Oh, Luke, if you only knew," she whispered.

Abruptly, Ian lifted his face to see hers. He'd heard what she'd called him, but had it been a slip on her part? Or did she think he could really be a Spencer?

No. She may see Luke in him, but Ian knew otherwise. Wishful thinking didn't change anything.

"We better get to Roni's. Warning them is the least I can do before I head back to California."

Sitting across a glass-top table in the expansive Spencer dining room, Michael changed the accounts and passwords of the Spencer fortune on the laptop in front of him while Roni stared Ian down with her icy eyes so much like his. He expected her to kick him under the table at any minute. "So, you're worried our money will be taken and there will be nothing left for you, so you came to warn us. Is that it?" she asked point-blank.

Ian folded his hands on the glass. "I'm not surprised you would see it that way."

"You haven't given us any reason not to."

Ian mumbled under his breath to Sylvie, "I told you the bridge was gone." To Roni and Michael, he said, "You're right, Roni, I haven't, which is why I also came to tell you I won't be collecting my inheritance."

Michael looked up over the laptop. The reflection of the screen glared in his reading glasses but didn't block the surprise on his face. "I told you when I came to see you at the hospital, the money is yours. Meredith and Bobby left all money and insurance policies to their three children equally. That includes you."

"Honestly, I don't want it because I don't like the person I've become because of it. Just knowing it was mine to claim changed me in a few short weeks. 'O accursed hunger of gold.' Virgil's wisdom come true. Can even drive a person to kidnap a child they don't want. And here I thought money was what I needed if I was going to be something other than Ian the Idiot."

"Ian the Idiot?" Roni scrunched her nose. "Why would you call yourself that?"

Ian shrugged. "The name was commonplace in my house growing up." He dropped his gaze. "I have dyslexia."

Roni scoffed. "That's hardly a reason to call some-one an idiot."

Ian squared off to lay it all out on the table. "I can't read."

"So?"

"So, my father deemed that enough reason to call me names."

"Well, that's not your home anymore, so you can stop that."

"I'm homeless." Hey, why not bare all? he figured. "My present address is a trailer on a construction work-site. Or had been anyway. Without the money, I'll prob-ably be out of a job, too."

"Why?" Roni tilted her head, her scars peeking out from under her high-collared sweater. He'd seen them before, the shiny, stretched flesh left by the car fire, but after seeing the ravine that caused that fire and those scars, Ian saw how blind he'd been to Roni's pain. She may not have been taken from her home, but she'd suf-fered. Ian had been so in tune to her privilege, money, fashion, awards, that he'd missed seeing the person be-hind it all. He'd missed seeing all she had been through and triumphed over. He missed seeing the person Jesus saw when He looked at her.

Suddenly, Ian wanted to know that person, but why should she give him the time of day? "Well? Why will you be fired?" Roni asked.

"Alex won't fire me, but I'd been offered a part in the business, so that will go away."

"For how much?" she asked, crossing her arms and looking like she was about to do a little wheeling and dealing herself.

"Fifteen percent."

"Fifteen percent for how much?" she clarified.

"A million."

"A million! For fifteen percent?" She leaned forward and tapped the glass with her pointer finger. "You tell him you want fifty for that price. I don't care what fancy locations he's building his homes in, you're worth that. In fact, he'd be getting a deal."

Ian felt his eyebrows spike. The word *protected* filled his mind. How different of a person he would have been with family to watch out for him. "Well, it doesn't really matter now. I'll be going home empty-handed."

"I thought you said you were homeless."

"I just meant California."

"California is where your heart is, then?" Roni asked, her head tilted to let her long red hair drape over her shoulder.

Ian eyed Sylvie from the corners of his eyes before answering. "Actually, my heart is up for grabs."

"Good, then there's hope you'll find it here in Norcastle." Roni looked to the laptop screen. "Are we safe, Michael?"

Their grandfather turned the screen for all to see. "Your money is safe and secure with the highest protection. You'd have to know someone on the inside to hack these walls. Thank you, Luke, for coming here today to warn us. I'm sorry, Chief, that you had to find out the way you did. I'm glad you're safe now, and your son, as well. Great kid you have there. If you need my help figuring out who cut his brakes, let me know. I'd be happy to offer my men to your service. And to figure out who's after you, as well."

"You know, sir, that's not an option. The CIA is not allowed to work on American soil. I would have to call in the FBI before the CIA. It's critical that I keep things by the books. If the council gets word I have the CIA or FBI running the show in Norcastle's jurisdiction, they might use it as a reason to let me go. I'm still under probation for another two months. It's been a long two years. I can't wait for it to be over."

"Two years seems like a steep amount of time for a probationary period."

"It was the only way they would give me the job."

"And now it's coming to an end. Please don't think I'm trying to step on toes, but I might look into your council members. See if any of them might want you fired before your probation is up. Especially if one of them had been hesitant to hire you in the first place."

"Already on it."

"Any of them not a fan?"

Ian sneered. "The mayor himself."

"Mayor Dolan?" Roni jerked back and kicked.

"Ouch!" Ian hollered, bending over to rub his shin. "What was *that* for?"

"You can't go around defaming people without evidence. Tell him that, Sylvie. That's illegal."

Sylvie remained her stoic self.

"Sylvie?" Roni said slowly. "Is there evidence to support such an accusation against Mayor Dolan?"

Sylvie nodded once then swallowed hard. "Roni, I know this is a shock. Shawn Dolan is somewhat of a star around here. His success on the racetrack has made him a success at the polls, but things aren't always as they seem."

Roni pulled down her collar to reveal her scars more fully. "You don't have to explain appearances to me. You forget I've spent most of my life covering up the truth for the sake of appearances." To Ian she explained, "I used to wear silk scarves to cover my scars up. I told myself it was for everyone else's benefit, but the truth went deeper than that."

Sylvie replied, "I haven't forgotten. That's why I know you'll understand if I have to go against popular opinion someday and arrest Shawn Dolan."

"Arrest him? For what?"

"I'm not at liberty to say. I pray someday the truth is out and all parties are safe." Sylvie pressed her lips together and looked to Ian. He reached out and held her hand on the table.

"I second that," he said. Such a small hand for such a dangerous job. Impending doom hovered over Sylvie, but she wouldn't allow it to deter her from doing her job of taking down the bad guys.

"Do you have evidence to make a case against him?" Michael asked.

Sylvie nodded. "I'm ready with everything I need when the time comes."

"Does he know you have it?"

"I don't think so. Only a couple people do."

Michael asked, "Who?"

"My most trusted team members. Carla and Preston, of course, and… Reggie. But I think Smitty also knows. Reggie must have told him, because Smitty said something today back at the station that leads me to believe so. He made it sound like I'm keeping things off the books. I document every call, but this file is hidden for protective reasons."

Roni shook her head in denial. "I can't believe Shawn would break the law. He's such a sweet guy who everyone adores. He's funny, and whips those Legends cars around the track faster than anyone I've ever seen."

"He races the same type of car Jaxon does?" Ian asked. "They're so small. I can't believe an adult can fit in them."

"Shawn's not a tall man. It's like the cars were made for him, and he was definitely made for racing them. He draws a big crowd and delivers great wins."

"Well, as long as I am chief, he won't win this one," Sylvie stated. "As soon as my probation period is over I'll have more capabilities to make a case without the threat of Dolan firing me."

Michael cleared his throat. "Chief Laurent, like I said, I don't want to overstep, but it appears this Shawn Dolan knows your plans, and will hold nothing back to stop you. Not even the trigger of his gun. I have to ask you, are you prepared to die over this?"

Ian felt her hand stiffen in his. "Not gonna happen," he said to assure her, as well as himself. "Not with me watching her back."

Sylvie tilted her green eyes his way. Appreciation filled them, but he also recognized a stern rejection of his offer.

"Just try to stop me," he dared.

"I have a gun."

"That you've lost once already."

"I will use it if I have to, Ian."

"What's another hole in my body if you're safe?"

"I don't need you."

"Yes, you've made that perfectly clear many times, yet I'm still here. Anything else you want to throw at me? I can go all day."

Sylvie pursed her lips in anger, then quickly gave in

with a short laugh, but not before she stuck out her cute little tongue in his direction.

Ian stilled at her bright-eyed smile. Her face lit up the room and for this moment took away the darkness surrounding them.

If only they could stay in this moment.

FOURTEEN

Ian surveyed the station's parking lot for any potential threat. "Wait." He grabbed Sylvie's forearm before she stepped out of the cruiser.

"I've already secured my surroundings. I was scanning the lot before I pulled in. There are three cars. One is Carla's, and the other two were impounded. The tree line is clear. Thanks to bare branches, I can see far into the woods. It's safe." She pushed the door wide and Ian kept up with her brisk gait to the front entrance.

He reached for her hand. "It's not safe, though. How can you go on with work as usual when you know someone wants you dead?"

She looked down at where they were linked, but his hand stayed firm. Let her get used to the feel of him. Maybe she would grow to welcome his touch, want him to reach out more, and not just for help, but for comfort and affection.

She ripped her hand away.

Maybe not.

"I'm a cop, Ian. I make people mad at me every day. Doing my job means stopping criminals and bad people from succeeding in breaking the law. The key words there are *bad people*. I wouldn't expect anything else but retaliation. That's part of being bad. But part of being an officer of the law is serving and protecting my jurisdiction. I go in. Remember? That means I don't run home and hide whenever someone might decide to get back at me for ruining their plans. It also means I put on the uniform and come back here every day."

"With no one to protect you."

"Well, usually that would be Preston, but with him being injured…"

"With him being injured, that leaves me."

"I shouldn't allow it. It's too dangerous, but…but I am grateful you were there for Jaxon when he went to the bridge." She exhaled, proof that she understood the gravity of the situation, the danger still lurking. "I thank God he's safe, but it's time to get back to work." With that she unlocked the door and made her way inside.

She didn't make it five feet before she squeaked to a stop on the linoleum.

"What's wrong?" Ian asked.

"Carla's desk is empty." Sylvie grabbed the butt of the gun at her waist. Her footsteps barely made a sound as she walked around Carla's work space, glancing at the contents on top.

A cola can, tipped over and lying in its own sugary spilled contents. Her cell phone in the mess.

"Carla," Sylvie called, searching through the empty bull pen. "Her car's out front. She should be here."

Ian went to pick up the can.

"Stop." Sylvie's harsh voice halted him. "Until I say otherwise, don't touch anything. Any tampering with the scene contaminates trace evidence."

She walked to her office, the door still closed as

she'd left it. With the boarded-up window, visual access inside wasn't possible. On a flash, she pushed the door wide and pointed the weapon as she burst inside.

He ran in to follow. She stood by her sofa where her son had slept just hours ago.

Jaxon was gone.

Sylvie's head lifted and turned slowly to look at Ian. "There's a note." Her lips trembled, her face paled. "He's been taken." She read the typed note to him on a growing cry.

How does it feel to be separated from your family? Come to the bridge or get used to a life without your son.

Sylvie stumbled back. Her knees bent and Ian reached out just in time before she crumpled to the floor.

"I've got you. You hear me, Sylvie? I've got you."

A wail escaped from deep down inside her and she let Ian fold her into his arms. He could feel her gun against his shoulder, and he reached up to take it from her. Her fingers dug deep into his back, as though she struggled to hold on for dear life. "Sylvie, a crime has been committed here. I need you to tell me what to do. What would you do if this was anyone else's child?"

She stilled. Slowly pulling away, he saw the horror in her wide, darkening eyes.

"Stay with me and tell me what I need to do. What we need to do. You said yourself, you can't go home and hide. Stay with me, and tell me what comes first."

At her shaky nod and sniffle, he knew the stoic Sylvie was back to work. She reached to her belt. "All units, this is your chief. Carla and Jaxon are missing. A note left behind points to a kidnapping. I'm issuing an APB for them both. I want checkpoints set up on the edges of town. Stop every car. Do you copy?"

"Smitty and Reggie here. Copy that."

"Buzz and Karl copy."

The rest of her team returned the radio call except for Preston.

"Preston, do you copy?" Sylvie asked. "Preston," she called again.

"The hospital kept Preston overnight," Reggie responded.

"Good to know. I'm also going to need two of you to go to Mayor Dolan's house to notify him."

Silence returned over the radio.

"Do you copy?"

"I'll go," Smitty responded.

"If he's not there, find him. If you can't, I need to know. I'm going to the covered bridge. I'm supposed to go alone, so be discreet when you arrive."

"10-4," her team signed off with their orders.

The map Sylvie had been studying earlier still sprawled across her desk. The tiny letters jumped around the page, making it impossible for Ian to understand. Jaxon's crutch lay on top of it. Ian was sure it hadn't been there before. Had there been a fight between the boy and his kidnapper? Had the crutch been thrown onto the desk?

"He left his crutch. He would need it to walk. Why wouldn't he take it?" Ian asked.

"Another reason I need to get to the bridge. He can't get away on his own."

"I'm going with you."

"You can't. I won't risk Jaxon's life. Or yours. The note says come alone or he dies. This one I have to do by myself."

"But why the bridge?"

Sylvie frowned. "It's where I hid the Dolan evidence. That's why I want Dolan found. If Shawn Dolan is MIA, then perhaps he's Jaxon's kidnapper." With that, she took the gun from Ian's hand and walked out.

He raced to the door. "If not me, take one of your team."

Sylvie pointed to Carla's desk. "They have one of them already. And the rest will meet me there. I hope."

The exit door slammed behind her, leaving Ian alone and feeling useless. A feeling he'd had for far too long. Ian the Idiot came shining through at a moment when he needed to be something else. He needed to be daring and brave, smart and quick. He needed to be like… like his family. He needed to be a Spencer.

But I am a Spencer.

"I am a Spencer," he said in frustration to the empty room. "I am a Spencer," he repeated. The message wasn't meant for anyone but himself—the only person stopping him from taking back what had been stolen from him.

His name.

His home.

His family.

His inheritance.

But he had been wrong about the kind of inheritance. It wasn't money that made him Luke Spencer.

His inheritance was his identity.

It was how God saw him.

The man Jesus was willing to leave His throne for.

The real Luke Spencer behind all the circumstances.

That's who he wanted to be…again.

"I am Luke Spencer. And today I'm taking it all back."

Sylvie said she saw brilliance in him. It was time to dig deep and find that brilliance.

Luke turned to Jaxon's crutch. He nearly reached for it but stopped when he saw the leg pointed to a small outline of a house.

A cabin was drawn on the map.

It had to be a message from Jaxon, one that didn't need to be read with letters.

"What are you trying to tell me, Jaxon? Did you know where you were being taken? God, you've brought me this far. Is this where you're leading me next?"

Luke grabbed the map in one crinkling swoop and headed for the door. He knew the answer was a yes, but first, he had a stop to make.

Every brilliant person has a team, and he was going to claim his.

Sylvie pulled her car up to the desolate campground and parked in front of the covered bridge. The darkened interior displayed only a shadow of a single person too wide to be Jaxon.

Where was her son?

She exited cautiously, her gun at her side, ready to take aim. Her boots crunched in the snow as she made tracks to the mouth of the bridge. The person at the other end came into view.

Sylvie's boots hit the old wood boards with thuds. At the halfway point, she could see enough to make an ID.

Carla.

"Carla, where's my son? What's going on?"

"Where's the file? Just give me the file and this all goes away."

"Goes away? My son's been kidnapped. Someone tried to kill him. Please tell me you're not a part of this. You were supposed to protect him. How could you do this to me? To Jaxon? You love him. Please rethink what you're doing and stop this before it goes any further. Tell me where Jaxon is. Please."

"I have a gun," her dispatcher said. Her voice shook on the last word.

Sylvie looked to Carla's hands as she stepped up to her, just a few feet away.

"Your hands are empty."

Carla didn't say a word. She only stared at Sylvie, except she wasn't looking at her eyes. Carla latched on something above Sylvie.

"There's a target on me, isn't there?"

Carla swallowed hard. "Where's the file?"

"Someone is forcing your hand. Is it Shawn Dolan?"

"Just give me the file and nobody gets hurt."

"Is that what they told you? I think it's safe to say they lied to you."

"Please, Sylvie. There's a gun on me, too," Carla rushed out with a tremble.

Sylvie holstered her gun and stepped back. She reached the loose floorboard. Jaxon had found the board when he was younger and it became his secret place to hide his trinkets.

She lifted it now.

Nothing lay beneath.

Sylvie bent low to see if the drive had shifted, but even in the growing darkness, she could tell it was gone.

On bended knee, she dropped her head, trying to think of her next move. Things could go really bad from here. She lifted her head to see Carla fidgeting. The woman glanced over her left shoulder. Whoever had taken her and Jaxon was behind her on the mountain somewhere. But how far? At the top, or nearby behind a tree?

"Come on, Sylvie. Hurry!"

"It's not here."

Carla's face drained. "Don't play this game right now."

"I'm not playing a game. I'm serious. The file is gone. I put it under this board—"

A blast from the mountain echoed through the air. Sylvie waited to fall from the gunshot, but found herself flinching involuntarily and not hitting the floor.

She didn't fall, but Carla did.

Sylvie rushed forward and turned her dispatcher and friend over in her arms. She dragged her into the shadows of the bridge. Carla's eyes opened wide, but after a few gasps, her eyes fluttered closed.

"Carla!" Sylvie looked to the mountains as she grabbed her radio. "This is your chief! I—I'm at the covered bridge. Carla's been shot." Blood covered Sylvie's shaking hand.

"On our way, Chief," Reggie responded.

Sylvie watched the mountain. "Did you get Dolan?"

"Wasn't home. His wife says she hasn't heard from him in two days."

So he could be on the mountain taking shots now.

"Tell the paramedics the GSW went through Carla's right lung. She's bleeding out fast."

"Two minutes," Reggie responded. "But your man should be there before that."

My man?

A whiny motor reached her ears from somewhere far off.

A snowmobile.

Sylvie searched the mountains. A single sled and driver came barreling down the mountain. The red-and-black suit told her it was emergency-personnel attire. It was one of her men.

Is that what Reggie meant?

The sled came screaming up to her and skidded to a stop at the back entrance of the bridge. A face lay hidden behind a black helmet. Sylvie held her breath waiting for the driver to remove the shield and reveal himself.

But instead of lifting the helmet, the driver lifted a gun.

Sylvie drew her weapon.

"Drop the gun and get on!" a male voice bellowed, but with the motor she couldn't ID it.

His gun aimed at her cued her to do as he demanded. He'd already proven he would shoot. With one last look at Carla, Sylvie released her gun to the floor and raised her empty hands.

Plans B and C whirred in her mind as she stepped forward.

As though the man could read her mind, he pushed back and yelled, "Drive!"

Sylvie climbed on and immediately felt the gun push into her back. She still wore her bulletproof vest, but at this close range, a bullet could cause serious damage, even death. She could only hope that man Reggie mentioned would get here soon.

Or was this the man Reggie meant? Perhaps Reggie wasn't sending help, but a killer.

Stalling came to mind, but the gun moved to her head and changed it.

Sylvie zipped the sled back up the mountain, but without the proper gear, the cold temperatures instantly cut through her like a knife. Frigid wind smacked her in the face. Her hands stiffened with instant pain. But none of the dangers she faced from the elements came close to the danger behind her. She may be in the driver's seat, but a killer was now in charge.

FIFTEEN

Luke raced past Sylvie's empty cruiser on his snowmobile and drove through the covered bridge. A body lying on the other side stopped him on a sliding skid. Carla lay unconscious, blood pooled out behind her. He jumped off and knelt beside the woman, feeling for a pulse.

She was still alive, but barely. He lifted his visor and spoke. The radio inside the helmet he'd taken connected him to backup. "This is Luke Spencer. I'm at the bridge. Carla is still alive, but Sylvie is nowhere to be found. Snowmobile tracks tell me she's been taken up the mountain."

Sirens neared. "We'll be there in a matter of seconds," Buzz replied.

"I hear you, and I'm going up after her."

"Watch your back."

"He won't get me a second time." Luke leaned over the dispatcher. "Carla, help is on the way. Hang in there."

The woman's eyes remained closed as two ambulances screamed up to the bridge's entrance. The paramedics jumped from the vehicles and thudded across with a stretcher and bags.

She would be taken care of from here.

Luke ran back out from the bridge, but before he jumped on the snowmobile, bullets sprayed the snow at his feet. He retreated back.

"Hey, Michael!" he shouted into the radio. "I've got a shooter separating me from the sled. Do you see where they're coming from?"

Luke looked up just as his grandfather's CIA helicopter crested the mountain peak. Gunshots sounded from one of his men standing at the side opening.

"We've got you covered, Luke," Michael spoke through the radio from above. "Go get her."

Luke took a deep breath and raced forward. He didn't let the air out from his lungs until he had the sled zipping away from the bridge and up the trail following the tracks left behind.

The path narrowed and grew steeper. Snowy pine trees smacked him as he raced past them. He wondered how Sylvie had fared coming through here without the right gear. The higher he went, and the lower the sun dropped out of the sky, the more the cold seeped through his gloves and stiffened his fingers. She had to be in agony. Snowflakes began to fall, at first in a light flurry, but quickly changing to a heavy dousing the higher he went.

"Michael, I'm going to need a little direction. I've lost her tracks. Can you lead me to where that cabin is supposed to be?"

"According to the map, you're not that far off, son. Stay to the right. You'll soon come to a stream you'll need to get across."

"Got it. And thanks for being my eyes."

"Anytime."

"Apparently so. You even make holiday hours. Probably not how you planned to spend Christmas."

"Are you kidding? I live for this stuff. What's not to love about a high-speed holiday?"

Luke grinned beneath his helmet. He kept his gaze straight ahead, but felt protected knowing his grandfather hovered overhead reading the map for him. Sylvie would say his resourcefulness was shining through. He never let his dyslexia stop him from gaining the knowledge he needed to learn. So what if his letters danced in wavy lines? He'd found a way to make his path lead straight to Sylvie. And it started with his family.

Sylvie killed the sled's engine and stared at Reggie Porter's mountain log cabin. It stood hidden beneath a canopy of snow-covered pines. Her masked captor pushed his gun into her back. "Move it!" he yelled.

She listened for a familiar voice…like Reggie's.

"Is Jaxon here?" she said, hoping for a reply. With the weight Reggie had lost, the gunman could be him.

No answer came. Just the gun pointed her way.

The whomping sound of a helicopter closed in from somewhere beyond the trees.

Without hesitation Sylvie ran out from under the trees to get the pilot's attention. A bullet from the masked man's gun sent her flailing through the air. She crumpled against the cabin's steps, her lungs emptied in a whoosh. "Who…are…you?" she asked, gripping her chest. Pain radiated in her rib cage. She unclipped the vest to check for the bullet, but a kick to her leg stopped her.

"All you had to do was give Carla the file," the guy yelled. He grabbed her arm and dragged her up the steps, tossing her inside on the wooden floor.

Nausea rolled and her whole body shook. Grabbing at her ribs, she didn't think the bullet had gone through the vest and touched skin, not like in Carla's case. "So you shot Carla?"

"You think I shot her with this?" The guy slammed the door behind him and held up his 9 mm. "I didn't, and believe it or not, I saved your life."

"So you could kill me up here? If you're going to claim to be a hero, then at least show your face."

With that the guy walked past her. He opened a door and a minute later, he reappeared with Jaxon bound and gagged.

"Jaxon!" Sylvie pushed past the pain to kneel. Her son fumbled his way on his boot to meet her before she gained her feet. Sylvie wrapped her arms around him, ignoring the throbbing in her ribs the contact caused. She would rather face the pain than ever let go of her son again. "Are you hurt?"

Jaxon's soft hair pressed against her face as he shook it back and forth. His mumbling voice reminded her of the gag. She pulled the tied cloth down. Immediately, he rushed out a rapid cessation of frantic words. "I heard a gunshot! I thought you were dead. Oh, Mom, I was so scared!"

"Shh, I'm okay. I'll be bruised, but the vest did its job. It's all good, Jaxon. Nothing to worry about."

"So he did shoot you." Jaxon twisted from her grasp. "You promised! You said you wouldn't hurt her. You wouldn't hurt anyone. You lied!"

The man in the helmet stood by the window, looking out to the wilderness beyond the smudged glass.

"She'll live. For now."

"Who are you?" Sylvie asked. "What do you want?"

"I want the file. Give it to me, and I'll disappear from your life forever."

"I don't know where the file is. It wasn't where I hid it on the bridge."

The guy pointed his gun at her again. "I don't believe you. Hand it over, and I'll ride out of here with you both alive and well."

Sylvie couldn't distinguish the muffled voice through the thick helmet. "Are you Shawn Dolan? You're about his height."

"I said give me the file!"

"And I said I don't have it."

"I know where it is," Jaxon said quietly.

"What?" She startled at his confession. "How?" She searched his guilty face. He avoided eye contact and stared at his bent knees.

"That's what I went to the bridge for yesterday. I didn't just go for a walk. I went to get the file. I'm so sorry, but I knew that's what Bret was looking for. He told me you had a file on his dad. He tried to get me to give it to him. He punched me after school one day. He said you were trying to break his family up. He said if you did, then he would do the same to us." Jaxon swallowed. His lips trembled.

"So you went to the bridge to get it? How did you know it was there? You haven't hidden anything in there in years."

He shrugged. "I wanted to use the hiding place again."

"For what?" Sylvie felt the wedge between her and her son double in an instant. It was more than growing distant. He'd also been hiding things from her. "Jaxon, are you doing drugs?"

"No!"

"Then what could you possibly need to hide from me so badly that you would start using your old hiding place?"

"You won't understand."

"Try me," Sylvie said, then thought of a better way. "No, trust me. Come on, Jaxon, it's always been just us. We made a pact, remember? You can trust me."

He nodded. "I know. It's just personal."

"Does this have anything to do with your poems?" She tried to keep her voice calm.

His face jolted. "Yeah. I didn't want you to find them so I went to the bridge a few weeks ago to hide them, but when I lifted the board I found the envelope with the drive in it," he said in one long fast rush. "I put it back, but I thought it might be what Bret was attacking me for."

"What did you do with it?" the masked man demanded, still watching from the window.

"Do not address my son." Sylvie released Jaxon and pushed to her feet, blocking the guy's view of him.

A sick laugh erupted from behind the helmet. Her reflection in the visor shrunk back at the sound.

The next moment the guy lifted the helmet off his head.

Greg stood before them, an angry glare on his face. "Except he's my son, too. And he better start talking or he'll be getting more than a broken-up family. He'll be getting a dead mother."

Sylvie lurched her body at the man who had treated her so cruelly fifteen years ago. How dare he kidnap them and threaten their lives now. Her hands reached out to knock him to the ground. They hit the floor with astounding force and rolled.

Greg threw her off his back, but something inside Sylvie, smothered for so long, must have contributed to a strength she'd never believed possible. She was a mama bear pushed past her limits. Perhaps all these years training to be the best cop she could be had really been preparation for the day Greg would return to hurt her again. Had she always known it would come?

Sylvie elbowed his hold on her arm away, kicking back into his knees at the same time. He bent his head down in pain, and she twisted around to slam his nose back toward the ceiling.

Blood splattered the wood above as well as spraying lightly across her face.

"Ah!" Greg hollered in pain, holding one hand to his face, leaving the other to hold off her assault. "Stop! Just stop!"

He might as well have been speaking a different language.

Sylvie went in for his throat, landing on his chest with her forearm across his neck.

Greg gurgled and twisted with all his strength.

"I will kill you if I have to," she said, inches from his face.

Greg stilled. "Can't…breathe."

"I know."

"Please."

"I'm going to release you, but then you are going to tell me exactly why you are back in town. And spare me the melodrama about it being a desire to have custody of a child you never wanted to begin with. Got it?"

No response.

Sylvie pushed into Greg's trachea a bit more. The pressure sent his legs kicking and body twisting again. His voice strained with incomputable words.

She released the pressure. "I said, got it?"

"Y-yes," he struggled to say, but it was enough for Sylvie to let off her hold enough for him to converse.

Releasing him entirely was out of the question, even if he'd been disarmed in the takedown. She reached for her cuffs at her back and flipped Greg over with her knee to his back. *Click, click,* and he was apprehended.

She left him facedown to stand guard above him. She reached for his tossed 9 mm on the floor and checked the chamber for the ready bullet. She circled him slow and steady, each footfall creaking on the floor until she came around to his face. The tips of her boots brushed his hair.

Greg lifted his head and dropped it again, unable to hold it up. "You broke my nose."

"'And though she be but little, she is fierce.' That's what Ian says about her," Jaxon informed Greg with a smug smile.

"Who?"

"Jaxon means Luke Spencer," Sylvie said. "You remember him?"

"Oh, your rich boyfriend." Greg spat blood from his snarled lips.

"Boyfriend?" Jaxon asked. "What's he talking about?"

Greg laughed. "Keeping secrets from your son, are you, Sylvie?"

"Nothing, Jaxon. Luke is only a friend. Why don't you go back into that room while Greg explains why he's back in town," Sylvie said. "I'd hate to have you see the ugly tactics of my job. Even though this man isn't a part of your life, I'm sure the things you'd see would pain you almost as much as him." Sylvie stepped on his fingers just enough to show she meant what she said.

"Okay!" Greg shouted.

Good, he heeded her warning.

"I came back to break your little family up. Believe it or not, it would have saved your life."

"Saved my life? You shot me!"

"I shot your vest."

"FYI, you still could have killed me. I could be bleeding internally right now and die before nightfall. You'd go down for killing an officer of the law."

Greg sagged and whimpered. "I just wanted to make him go away. To end his blackmailing once and for all."

Sylvie pursed her lips. "You're back in town because someone's blackmailing you? What did you do wrong that you would commit murder to cover it up?"

"I didn't plan on committing murder. I thought if I separated you from Jaxon that would be enough. I figured it would hurt you more than any life-ending bullet."

Sylvie glanced to her son, who'd yet to move. The thought of losing him did bring on a painful effect that surpassed the bruised ribs ailing her. "Go on."

"But going to court for custody would cripple me, especially with your boyfriend's money. You don't think I remember the Spencers? How someone like you ever captured a Spencer's attention is mind-boggling. Especially with that manly attire."

"You mean my uniform? It's not about fashion. It's about being practical. You never know when you'll have to take someone down. Shall I demonstrate again?"

"No."

"Then keep talking. What did you do that has someone blackmailing you?"

"I've cheated on a few races."

"That's all?"

"They were important races. They boosted my career."

"Ah, and someone found out. Was it Shawn Dolan? I think I remember the two of you being chummy when we were younger. Is he your blackmailer?"

Greg's mouth remained zipped.

"I'll take that as a yes. So he blackmailed you to return to Norcastle to hurt me, either by taking Jaxon from me or by death. Either would work for him. And if you didn't comply, he would report you and have your prize cups stripped. Correct?"

Nothing.

So far she had nothing to arrest Shawn Dolan on. She needed a confession.

"You'll find out soon enough. When I don't deliver that file, he'll be at this door to collect it himself."

"Who will? Tell me who wants that file enough to kill for it! Is it Shawn Dolan?"

"I want a lawyer."

As much as she wanted to scream, Sylvie kept her cool. "You're going to need one, but fine, we'll do this your way." To her son, she said, "Jaxon, where is the file?"

"I'm sorry, Mom."

"You are forgiven. Whatever you did with it, I forgive you. Just tell me where it is."

"I gave it to Bret."

Sylvie pressed her lips tight. "Okay, when?"

"The night I went to the bridge. That's the real reason I went. Bret took his Legends car and drove over to the bridge. I gave it to him."

"Bret was driving the Legends car that night?"

"Yeah, why?"

"I had a little run-in with it on my way to find you. It came out of nowhere and nearly hit me. I followed it for a little while, but without lights, I lost it. Plus, my tire had been blown out. When I pulled over to change it, I was ambushed, knocked out and kidnapped. Preston was also pushed off the road."

"By Bret? I hate him!"

"Stop. We need to keep our heads clear and figure this out. Know who our enemy is and be prepared for when they arrive. Or even better, go get them first."

The sound of a loud motor had her running to the window. The helicopter was back. It was hard to see it with the tree growth all around. She also didn't think the cabin could be seen from above. She wasn't even sure if this was help or more danger coming her way.

"Let's go, Jaxon." Sylvie helped her son to his feet. "Can you walk on your boot to get to the sled?"

"A little. Where are we going?"

"To get the file."

"From Bret?"

"He's apparently kept it from his father, or Greg wouldn't have to bully it out of us. That tells me Bret has had an eye-opening experience with what he found on it."

"But what about… Greg?" Jaxon nodded to the man on the floor. Sylvie took note that he didn't call the pathetic man his father. "Are we just going to leave him here?"

Sylvie grabbed Greg's helmet and handed it to Jaxon. There would be no more hiding for Greg. And by the end of the day, she would be able to say the same for Shawn Dolan. "He won't get far with no gear." Sylvie took his boots off just to be sure. "Don't worry, Greg. You'll be in a nice warm cell by Christmas."

The man grunted but kept his face down on the floor. His life as he knew it was over.

Sylvie helped her son to the door, but when she opened it to the darkening night, a shot echoed through the air, splintering the doorjamb an inch from her head.

Jaxon screamed and fell to the porch. She went down after him.

"Are you hit?" she demanded.

"No," he cried in fear. "I don't think so."

Sylvie squeezed her eyes shut. *Dear God, I'm calling out to You again. You've always been with me, a Father for my son. I'm begging You now to please get him off this mountain safely.*

The helicopter's blades grew louder by the second. Would there be gunfire from above as well as the trees?

Another shot blasted through the night. Sylvie fell over her son to block him from flying bullets. She needed to get the vest on him. With quick work, she ripped it from her shoulders.

"I'm putting the vest on you," she said as she pulled his arms through the openings.

"What about you? What will protect you?"

"Don't worry about me. I'm going to get you out

of here. But if something does happen to me, promise me you will keep driving down this mountain. Understand?"

"Mom—"

"Understand?"

Jaxon sniffled. "Yes, I understand."

"God is with you, Jaxon. You won't be alone." At his nod, she said, "Okay, on my count, jump on the front and start the engine. I'll ride on the back. Do you follow?"

"10-4."

She smiled at his use of police code. "When I say go, this will be the fastest race of your life. I know you can do it." She waited for him to take a deep breath and let it out. "Go!"

Sylvie lifted her son with all her strength. Putting her body in front of his, she twisted around to run backward toward the sled. She tossed him to the front, and was already getting in place behind him when he had the motor up and running. The snowmobile jerked her so hard she nearly fell off the back when Jaxon put it into motion.

Bullets whizzed by her exposed head. She heard them over the motor of the sled and the engine of the helicopter above. A glance up and she saw someone rappelling down the chopper ahead of them.

Jaxon whipped the sled into a spraying side stop.

Sylvie saw the guy land and come running at them at the same time she noticed what had stopped Jaxon from going any farther.

The headlight of a lone sled faced them ten feet away. In the dark, all she could see was a driver in black, a helmet blocking his identity.

"Sylvie!" the guy from the helicopter coming at her from her right called out. She pointed her gun at him and then at the sled rider, and then back at the man coming at her again. In the dark she couldn't be sure who the good guys were. "Sylvie! It's me, Wade. Let me have your son."

"Wade!" she shouted. "Yes, take him. Take him to safety!"

Wade lifted Jaxon off the sled and suddenly rose up off the ground and into the air with her son securely in his hold. She moved her aim to the rider before her. He also took aim with his gun.

"Drop it!" she shouted over the motors. He may not be able to hear her order, but he could read her lips with his light on her. If he said anything to her, she couldn't tell. All she could make out was his shadowed figure and the unmistakable outline of a gun aimed at her. "I said drop it! I will shoot to kill!"

She felt the whiz of the bullet flying past her left ear before she heard the shot. The man had shot at her.

Before she pulled her own trigger, she was jolted from behind. Someone had rear-ended her, sending her forward.

Or had that been the person the shooter had fired at? Perhaps he hadn't been shooting at her, but protecting her from the one sneaking up on her from behind.

But who was the shooter, then?

She brought her sled under control and whipped it back around to see both riders coming at her. Her headlight glowed on an emergency uniform, and she realized it was one of her men.

Reggie's words came back. *Your man is on his way. Your man.*

Was it Ian?

No, not Ian. Sylvie knew beyond a doubt this was none other than Luke Spencer.

The helicopter hovered above, and she knew the Spencers had come to help her. A whole family affair, including the long-lost golden child.

But her man?

Why would Reggie call him that? Luke Spencer wasn't her man.

The rider who had rear-ended her took aim at her. Luke raced his sled at the gunman, slamming into the side of his snowmobile and flying off his own to push the gun away.

The weapon exploded in the night.

Sylvie's heart squeezed so tight, she would have thought the bullet entered her own chest.

In horror, she watched Luke's body jerk back with the force of a blizzard wind, once again taking a bullet meant for her.

He landed on his back in the deep snow, a billow of the flakes scattered around him. Sylvie had no time to assess the damage done to him and could only hope his bulletproof vest blocked the slug. The shooter took aim at her and pulled the trigger before she could even raise her gun.

When no bullet came her way, she realized his gun had jammed. He banged his palm on the handle and took aim again. The extra second allowed her to get her own shot off.

Her bullet clipped his shoulder and sent him back down in his seat. It also sent his gun flying into the darkness. Sylvie pulled the trigger again, but the driver hit the sled's gas and raced away in time to send her second bullet askew.

Sylvie turned to sit back in her seat and go after him, but a quick glance back showed Luke lying motionless in the same position he'd landed.

A blotch of red grew large in the snow on his right side.

Sylvie jumped off her sled and fumbled her way to him in a cumbersome run. The snow went past her knees. Her body fell and landed a foot from him. Sylvie crawled and fell again, unable to reach him fast enough.

"Luke!" she yelled, her throat clogged with tears. Her bare hands touched his gloved one, and she pushed her body up to land closer to him. With the depth of the snow, she couldn't kneel beside him without sinking. "Luke, can you hear me?"

He made no movement in response. She reached to his helmet and pushed the visor back to reveal an unconscious Luke Spencer.

Snowflakes falling from the sky hit his face and collected peacefully on his lashes.

Sylvie leaned over him to judge where the bullet had gone in. She felt for the edge of his vest and followed it down to his right side. Wetness came away on her fingers when she reached a spot the vest had left uncovered. The bullet had entered under his armpit and blood poured out at a deadly rate. It must have hit the axillary artery. She remembered when Reggie went in for his cardiac surgery, he'd said the doctors were going in through his axillary artery. She didn't need a medical license to know this needed to be clamped or he would bleed out.

But what could she clamp it with up here on a snowy mountain?

She grabbed at her head in frustration, tearing her hair from her ponytail. Her silver hair clip loosened from her head. Sylvie yanked it out and tested its strength. If she could locate the vein she might be able to stanch the blood pouring out of him with it.

Warm blood had her small fingers slipping in their search. When she thought she found the artery she squeezed it and noticed how the blood slowed. "I found it, Luke. I found the vein. Stay with me." And what? Die from exposure up here instead of bleeding out? She wondered what was crueler. All she knew was that neither worked for her. Luke couldn't die. He had a family to claim. She couldn't believe God would keep Luke alive as a baby and bring him back here only to die when he was so close to becoming a Spencer again.

Sylvie's fingers slipped. Another onslaught of blood poured around her hand. She quickly relocated the vein and clamped it again. She grabbed her hair clip and opened it wide enough to cover the sides of the vein and let it close tight. She kept her other hand on the vein and slowly released to test the strength. Blood seeped, but it didn't gush.

And then it broke.

"No! No!" She rushed to find the vein again. But now what? Would letting go be kinder? Could she even let go?

She gazed upon his face, so peaceful. More snow had found its way inside the helmet. She brushed the flakes away gently. She should close the visor from the elements, but doing so felt like giving up. It felt like saying goodbye.

This wasn't how she thought their goodbye would be. She knew it would come, but she was okay with that because he would finally be with his family. She would be able to walk away knowing he was loved.

Now he would die on a mountain because of her.

Sylvie sniffed and felt the tears flow down her cheeks. Slowly, she leaned over him and laid her head on his chest.

"I'm here, Luke. I'm right beside you. You're not alone. I'll be by your side the whole time. I promise."

She reached for the visor to pull it down.

"Luke, are you there?"

The sound of Michael's voice came from inside Luke's helmet.

He had a radio.

Sylvie's heart rate sped up with hope. She rushed forward to speak, but her words tripped over each other. "It's Sylvie. Luke… Help." She took a deep breath and tried again. "Luke needs help. He's been shot and is bleeding out."

"We're on our way back." Michael's words had her shaking with anxiety.

"You're going to make it. Do you hear me, Luke? You're going to make it, even if I have to hold your artery with my hand the whole way." Her fingers pressed tighter. "You're going to make it," she said again to confirm her belief. "You're going to spend Christmas with your family."

The helicopter's motor grew close. Soon it hovered above them and the rope fell off to their side. It jerked with movement as Wade descended a second time. He was by her side reaching for Luke as he landed in the snow.

"I have to hold his artery!" she shouted to be heard.

"I've got him, Sylvie."

Wade's hand covered where she held on and took over.

"Promise me you won't let go!"

"I had to let go once before. That's never happening again!"

She knelt back and relinquished Luke to his family.

"I'll send the rope down for you!"

A team of snowmobiles flew out from over the crest, coming her way.

Her team had arrived.

"No! Get him to the hospital!" she shouted. She would ride down. Besides, she had a couple arrests to make.

She watched as they zipped back up to the helicopter in record time. The chopper flew away as she knelt in the snow, covered in Luke's blood. Fresh snowflakes quickly worked to cover the presence he left behind. The approaching engines reminded her of her sworn duties.

Sylvie stood, climbed on the sled and waved for her men to follow her to the cabin for the first arrest. Greg would get that jail cell tonight. Shawn Dolan would be next.

She knew she'd clipped him. He'd sped off to lick his wounds, but he couldn't hide forever. He had to know the jig was up. But that only made him more dangerous. Sylvie would be keeping a sharp vigil until she had him in custody. She didn't expect him to make it easy. He would go for the kill.

But so would she.

As Sylvie pulled up to the cabin and hauled a defeated Greg out to her men, Reggie stood by her sled, his helmet off. "What happened to Luke?"

"He took a shot meant for me. Again."

"Bad?"

She gave a single solemn nod. "He's with his family now. They'll take good care of him."

Sylvie climbed on her sled, but before she took off, Reggie handed her his helmet. He removed his vest and handed it over to her.

She stared at it hanging there between them.

"Someone wants the chief of police dead. You're our family, and we protect our own."

At her acceptance of his duty, his gloves came next. He stuffed one of her bloody hands inside his glove. When the inside warmth touched her hands, she realized how frozen her appendages were. It was almost like her whole body had somehow distanced itself from her situation.

Reggie lifted her second hand to stuff it into his glove. "I'm going to pray for your man. I'll pray he comes home to you."

Sylvie shook her head. "He'll go home to his family. He's waited long enough."

"Family isn't always about blood. They're the people your heart claims."

"My heart can make no claims on Luke."

"I wasn't talking about yours. I was talking about his." Reggie walked to his sled. Once in his seat, he waited for the chief to give the signal.

But Reggie's words struck her still. She wanted to take solace in the fact that Luke would finally be able to claim a family of his own, but if Reggie was right, then maybe it wasn't Roni and Wade but her and Jaxon.

Even after she'd made it clear there was no room for him in her life.

Or was there?

Sylvie pushed the idea away and dropped her visor. She had a pact with her son. She'd made a promise. It would always be just the two of them. There was no room in her life for Luke.

In her heart, well, that would be different.

Sylvie revved her engine and waved her left hand, speaking into the helmet's microphone to the team. "Time to catch us a bad guy. We ride!"

SIXTEEN

I'm here, Luke. I'm right beside you. You're not alone. I'll be by your side the whole time. I promise.

"Sylvie!" Luke jerked awake. A beeping sound somewhere close by sped up to a rapid cadence. A white tiled ceiling came into focus, then a strange woman's face filled his view. Her dark skin and hair didn't trigger a memory.

Not Sylvie.

"Who are you?" he rasped. "Where's Sylvie? She promised she would stay beside me."

"Now, now, your family's here. Everything's going to be fine. I'm your nurse. We've been waiting for you to wake up all night."

"We?"

She moved her round face away and stepped back to reveal the packed room. A few faces registered, a few didn't.

Still, no Sylvie.

"Welcome back, brother."

Luke turned to his left in time to see Roni step up to his bedside. He shrunk back. "Are you going to punch me?"

"Not today."

He squeezed his eyes tight to pull on a memory. Or had it been a dream?

"I was shot. Again."

Luke opened his eyes to find Wade Spencer.

"You," Luke said. "You were there. I saw you."

Roni said, "Wade carried you the whole way to the hospital."

Wade fisted his hands and his dog, Promise, bounded up by his side. She licked his hands and he began to pet her. After a minute, he said, "Your axillary artery under your arm was hit. I arrived on the scene in our grandfather's helicopter. I rappelled down to get you. Chief Laurent had already located the artery and was working to stabilize it." He swallowed hard. "I've, ah, seen my share of main-artery wounds in war. They're not pretty, but don't give me the credit for saving you. Chief deserves it all."

"Where is she? Why isn't she here?" Luke scanned the room, squinting at the unfamiliar faces, wondering if he should know them.

"I'm Ethan Rhodes, Roni's husband," said a blond, wavy-haired man. A set of baby blue eyes contrasted with his serious face.

"The FBI agent," Luke said when it clicked. "I thought you were undercover."

"Made it home for Christmas."

"Christmas. Did I miss it?"

A few laughs went up in the room. "No, you're just in time." Ethan smiled. "Roni's told me all about you. Filled my ear all night long, actually."

Luke looked at his sister and knew it couldn't have been anything good. "About that, um, you should know I have no intention of taking what belongs to them."

Now Ethan looked perplexed. "I'm not following." He glanced his wife's way.

"Oh, I left that part out," Roni explained. "It's nothing. Just a little misunderstanding. You know how we had so many people coming out of the woodwork claiming to be our brother. We had to be sure he was really him before we could give him his inheritance. We hope you can forgive us, Luke."

"Forgive *you*? What have you done with my sister?"

Ethan chuckled, elbowing his wife. "He's got you pegged. It's not too often you hear an apology from Ron—"

Roni sent a warning glare her husband's way.

Ethan cleared his throat. "Never mind. I'm glad I was able to meet you. I'll have to thank our amazing chief of police for coming to your rescue. I've come to rely on her a few times. She's top-notch."

Luke figured there was a story there, but all he cared about was laying eyes on Sylvie. He looked farther into the room and stopped on the sight of a baby.

"I'm Lacey, Wade's wife," the beautiful mother holding the tiny baby said.

"I remember," Luke said. "We met at Clay's." Luke looked to the baby. "He's beautiful. Luke, is it?"

"Kaden Luke, actually." Lacey smiled a brilliant teary smile. "We were going to make his first name Luke, but seeing as the name was so new for you, we didn't want you to have to share it right out of the gate. I hope you don't mind that his middle name is Luke. It would mean so much to us."

He looked to Wade. "But you don't even know me."

"I know all I need to know. You're my brother, and you have come home. That's all that matters."

Luke dropped his gaze to the baby. His brother and sister could have both moved on to their own families and left him behind, but instead they were here by his side.

Luke moved to reach his forefinger to the child, but pain skyrocketed right down the arm. He inhaled and pulled back until it subsided.

"Now, Mr. Spencer." His nurse was back readjusting his position. "You need to be still for a while. Don't make me get the doctor in here before the gifts are handed out."

Luke looked straight down the bed to where Clay and his wife, Cora, stood arm in arm. "Gifts? What gifts?"

The two separated to show the window ledge had been turned into a mock fireplace hearth, decked out with all the Christmas trimmings. Tinsel and garland and even a wreath hung in the window. But it was the stockings he'd seen at Roni's house that were all hung and waiting to be distributed that clenched his heart.

"You have a stocking, too," Roni announced and ran to the ledge to remove the one in the middle. She carried it back almost reverently. As she neared, Luke noticed the dulled fabric of reds and greens. This wasn't a new stocking.

"It's yours from when you were a baby. Our mother made them. She wasn't a seamstress, but they were made with love. I think they're beautiful."

Luke reached his good arm for the stuffed stocking and brought it close, squinting to read the embroidered letters.

"It says 'Luke.' She embroidered each of our names on them."

"I can't believe you kept it all these years."

"Kept it and displayed it every year," Roni said proudly.

Luke glanced up quickly. "But you thought I was dead."

Roni looked back at Cora and at the woman's nod, she said, "Every Christmas I would help Cora bring up the decorations, and I would always insist on hanging your stocking. Maybe because deep down I knew you were alive. I was too young to have a clear picture of the crash. When I was finally able to speak, Cora tells me I cried for you constantly. I knew someone had taken you. I knew you were out there and needed us." Roni's lips trembled, but she pressed them tight. Her husband wrapped an arm around her shoulders and pulled her in close to him. But Roni kept her eyes on Luke. "Can you forgive us for not coming for you?"

At Luke's silence, she continued, "I know life was so hard for you. I know you suffered tremendously at the hands of your kidnapper. We should have—"

"No. Stop," Luke demanded. "Stop right now. Whatever happened thirty years ago was not our fault, and we cannot blame each other and we can't blame ourselves for it. To do so would mean they won. Maybe you're willing to lose, but I'm not."

Roni's eyes widened. She pulled away from her husband, nearly pushing him over. "Lose? I *never* lose. And don't you forget it."

"I wouldn't dare. You might hurt me."

"That's what big sisters are for. Gotta keep the little brother in line."

The two smiled at each other for the first time since they met.

Family. So this was what it was like. And probably why Sylvie wasn't here. Hospital policy of family only. But the room didn't feel complete without her and Jaxon.

"Thank you for my gift. I thought all I would get for Christmas was two gunshot wounds." He laughed with everyone, but inside felt the pain of another hole, this one burrowing into his heart with each second that went by without knowing why Sylvie wasn't present.

Suddenly, Luke realized someone else besides Sylvie was missing, too.

The man was nowhere to be found. "Where's Michael?" he asked.

Uncomfortable glazes dropped to the floor.

"Wade?" His brother would be honest with him. He didn't know him too well yet, but Luke already knew he was a man who could be trusted.

His brother sighed. "He's, ah, going to bat for Chief Laurent."

"Going to bat for Sylvie?" Luke pushed up. Pain shot through his body, but it meant nothing next to the torture of knowing Sylvie was in trouble. "Was she—she *hurt*? What happened to the shooter?"

"She was fine, but we don't know about the other rider. He took off."

"He's still out there?" Luke pushed up to a full sitting position. The room tilted sideways and nausea rolled up in a wave.

"Whoa!" Ten different hands reached for him before he fell off the bed. It could have been less, but his vision was seeing double, or maybe it was triple.

"Get back in this bed, Mr. Spencer," his nurse said. He wished he could read her name tag, but that was out of the question and it had nothing to do with his dyslexia.

"How am I going to help her? She's in danger." Luke laid his head back on the pillow in torment.

"Michael will do everything he can."

"What happened after I was shot? Tell me everything."

Wade began his briefing again. "The chief got a shot off on the guy's right arm before he took off. Then her and her team came back to town last night, planning the arrest of Shawn Dolan. Apparently, the chief has something on him that has him out for blood."

"He beats his wife," Luke announced to the room. The ladies all inhaled at the same time. "I take it you didn't know. Go on."

"When Sylvie arrived back in town, there was a message from the council, releasing her from her position."

"Why?"

"Well, technically she was still on probation. They don't have to give any reason at all. But with Carla being taken and shot, and the loss of the cruisers and other expensive inventory, they felt she couldn't handle the job."

"Those had nothing to do with her, and everything to do with your town's mayor. Once everyone knows he's behind it all, they'll see she can handle it."

"Except Michael and his CIA team assisted. They're using that as a means to prove she broke the law by working with the CIA on American soil."

"But I would have died, and there was a child. They can't be serious.

"I have to get out of here. I have to help her."

"You're not going anywhere, Mr. Spencer. Over my dead body," his nurse announced.

Luke sized her up. "What's your name?"

"Mary, but some patients have called me Bulldog. I don't take any offense to it. Better make yourself comfortable." Mary leaned back over him as she had when he woke up. "Because like I said, you're not going anywhere."

A knock came on the door.

Luke had to think of a way out of here. Maybe his grandfather could chopper him out by saying he was being transported to another hospital. But using the CIA's helicopter might paint Sylvie in even more of a bad light. It might be best to have Michael go dark with his men.

"Hi, Preston. Any news about your chief?" Wade asked of the person in the doorway. Luke's ears perked up at the mention of Preston's name.

"I'm being released, but I heard Ian was here and I wanted to stop in. It looks like a party in here. I don't want to intrude."

"Forget it, come on in." Wade stepped back to let the officer in. "Glad to see you're on the mend. Any idea who slammed into you?"

Preston stepped into the room, sporting an ugly purple bruise below his eye. He fidgeted with the cuff of his officer's uniform. "Not yet."

"Have you heard about Sylvie?" Luke asked him.

Preston glanced his way with a nod. "I just checked in with the department and heard the news. I'm heading there next. I just can't believe it. Look, Ian—"

"Luke. Call me Luke."

"Luke, I'm really sorry I wasn't there last night for Sylvie."

"You were injured. You wouldn't have been much help."

"But she and I have been together for years, partners long before she become chief. We watch each other's back. I should have been there. I promise, I'm going to stand by her through this. I won't let her down again."

Preston turned to leave.

"Preston, real quick. Can you give her a message for me?" Luke asked.

"Sure."

"Tell her…" He glanced at his family, then at the stockings on the window ledge. There were two more stockings needed before his family would be complete. But knowing her feelings, he would have to get used to it. "Tell her I don't regret anything and I would do it again. All of it."

"I will."

"And thank you for being such a good partner. You mean the world to her." Luke lifted his good arm and offered it to Preston for an olive branch shake. Preston hesitated, then quickly took it. Luke gave the man's hand a firm shake, but when Preston winced, he let go. "Sorry, man, we're both not our typical selves these days. Take care of yourself."

Preston nodded. "I'd say your life is heading into the black. Wish you the best."

The door clicked closed, leaving the room in silence.

"Interesting guy," Cora said with an awkward laugh. "What do you suppose he meant by that?"

"I'll cut him some slack," Clay said. "He's been slammed into and knocked out. You saw his head."

"And apparently his arm. Was he your patient, Mary?"

"When?" The nurse lifted her face from studying a chart.

"He came in yesterday to get checked out after being driven off the road. The hospital kept him for the night."

"Not *this* hospital," she said matter-of-factly. "I've been doing rounds all night. I would have checked in on him."

Luke shot a pointed glance at Wade, who sent one to Ethan. He didn't have to say a word. His FBI brother-in-law skirted the bed and met Wade by the door in less than a second.

"Wait!" Luke called. "I'm going with you!"

"Oh, no, you're not." Mary shoved him back on the pillow. "Don't make me sedate you."

Luke looked to Roni in near hysteria. He had to get out of here!

A slow smile grew on his sister's face. But it was the wink she sent his way that told him his sister was about to break him out of here.

Luke had to think growing up with her wouldn't have been dull. They might have fought like cats and dogs, but when it counted, she would have been on the front lines to protect her little brother. And if the wheelchair race out of the hospital that preceded a car ride at a speed he'd never thought possible was any clue, life with his big sister would have been a hurricane in motion. Luke was so glad she was on his side…for today anyway. He knew that would change like the weather, but he looked forward to every sibling squabble to come. Being a Spencer never felt so right. Sitting by Roni as they raced into town in her Porsche, he didn't even have to read the Welcome to Norcastle sign to know he was home.

But would he feel the same if Sylvie Laurent wasn't beside him? Or worse, if she could never be because she was killed before he could track her down?

"Can't you go any faster, Roni?"

His sister burst out with a sinister laugh and hit the gas. "You asked for it, little brother. You asked for it."

The weight of her badge always gave Sylvie assurance that what she was doing had value. She placed the metal symbol of authority gently on her desk beside her spare gun, barely making a sound as she did.

Reggie slid them across the desk toward himself and put them in the top desk drawer. "It's only for a little while."

She eyed him dead-on. "You really believe that?"

"No, but what else am I supposed to say? We both know the council is making a big mistake, but neither of us have means to prove it."

"I know it was Shawn Dolan behind everything. If only I still had the file on him to prove to the council he's not the man they believe him to be."

"You know very well you wouldn't be able to release that file without charges being brought by his wife."

"I don't get it. He's hurting her. Why doesn't she want it to stop?"

"Would you want her to just to save your job? Or is it her safety that you care about?"

"Her safety, of course."

"Well, perhaps you could convince her to as a friend now. No longer as chief of police. No one is stopping you from being her friend."

Sylvie smiled for the first time since receiving the

notice of termination from the police department that morning. Merry Christmas to her.

"You're right, Reggie. There are many ways I can still help people being hurt at the hands of others." Sylvie reached a hand across the desk. "You're going to make a great chief."

Reggie shook it firmly in both hands. "Not as good as you, and every man in this place knows it. We're losing as much as you are today. More."

"Thank you for saying that. Now, if you'll excuse me, I'm going to go home and spend Christmas with my son."

"I'd like you to take an escort."

"I'll walk, if you don't mind. There's just something degrading about being dropped off in a cruiser like I did something wrong."

Reggie smiled and came around the desk to walk her out. They made it to Carla's desk. Sylvie touched the empty chair of the dispatcher who had sat in it longer than Sylvie had been alive.

"She deserves a medal. Make sure she gets it."

"Will do, Chief," Smitty said from his desk.

"Just Sylvie," she corrected.

"Always Chief," Smitty responded with nods from her men.

Tears pricked her eyes. A quick blink and an inhale held them in check. "Merry Christmas, team."

She turned away one last time from the men and station and stepped out into the crisp, sunny morning. She passed by her cruiser, which the men had found down by the river. It had been pulled up from the bank and would need an overhaul for Reggie.

She started the short mile-long trek home. Her boots

fluffed through loose snow and crunched on the older, harder stuff below. An engine off in the distance had her looking ahead. The red and blue lights sitting on top of the car told her it was a police vehicle.

The car slowed as it approached and the driver's window dropped down as the car came to a stop across the street from her.

"Preston," Sylvie said with a smile. "I guess you heard."

"I'm not happy about this, Sylvie. They had no right."

"They had every right. I was still on probation. You and I both knew this might happen. You thought it would be from within the department, though."

"That I did, which made me miss the outside enemy approaching. I failed you."

"No." Sylvie crossed the street and approached the car. "Don't ever think that, Preston. You were my right hand, and I'll always be grateful for the years as partners and then your work as my assistant."

He placed a hand over the one she had resting on the car door. He gave it a squeeze and when she thought he would pull the platonic gesture away, he kept it there with a little rub from his warm fingers.

A bit of unease chilled her and she withdrew her hands and stuffed them into her coat pockets. "Well, I better be getting home to Jax. Merry Christmas, Preston. I hope you feel better soon. Sorry you got hurt in all this."

He touched his face but waved his other hand as if to say *no big deal*. "It's all part of the job. And speaking of the job, when I was at the hospital yesterday, I did a little investigating and found out the two hackers who jumped in the river checked in for hypothermia."

The cop in Sylvie stepped to. "Did you get IDs?"

"Of course. You taught me well. They're brothers. James and Brian Miller. A little pressure and they squawked on who hired them."

"Let me guess. Greg Santos."

Preston's face dropped. "Yeah, how'd you know?"

"That was one of the things I got out of Greg before he lawyered up. They're friends of his. He brought them in to wipe out the Spencers' accounts, so Luke wouldn't be able to help me in a custody battle."

"And now? Will the infamous Luke Spencer be helping you?" The edge in Preston's voice brought on another sickly wave of unease. Was Preston angry at Luke?

"What is that supposed to mean?"

"Never mind. Forget I said it. I'm still sore and it's making me cranky. Forgive me?"

She offered a halfhearted smile. "Of course. So, have you arrested the Millers?"

"Not yet. I overheard them talking about meeting someone at the salt tent today. I wanted to come get you to do the honors."

"Me? You know that's impossible now."

"What's the council going to do, fire you? I'll be the one on the books making the arrest. You're just along for the ride. Just like how you took Spencer along for all the rides this past week."

"That's different. I was protecting him from someone who wanted to kill him."

"But no one was trying to kill him. It was you they were after. You shouldn't be out here walking alone on the streets. It's not safe. You better hop in and let me guard you while I go make the arrests." Preston's eyes twinkled with a bit of the mischief she'd seen in them on so many nights working with him.

She smiled back, knowing he was a crucial part of her success in gaining the chief position. He was a true friend.

"I know what you're up to."

"You do?" His eyes darkened.

"Yeah, you always did take a little too much delight in sticking it to the powers that be who feel they can do our jobs better than we can."

"Oh, right. So what do you say? One last ride, Chief?"

Sylvie looked down the road. "Actually, I was going to stop off at the Dolans' and see Andrea. I may not be chief anymore, but that won't stop me from being an advocate against domestic violence in this town. Dolan hasn't seen the last of me, and now he has nothing to hold over me."

"I figured you would do that. Can't let that go, can you?"

"Never."

Preston whistled. "Talk about sticking it. But you know you can't make Andrea Dolan turn her husband in."

"I can at least try to help her see reason."

"But in the end she's going to make the best choice for her life, regardless of what you think she should do."

She stilled at Preston's words. They were her same reasons for her choices through the years. When so many people criticized her every decision along the way, in the end, she made the ones that worked for her.

"You can't fix the world, Sylvie. But you can get a few bad guys off the streets here and there. So what do say? Let's go take these guys and save some innocent people they're targeting with their thefts some heartache. Go out with a bang."

"A bang, you say," she said pensively. "Well, when you put it that way, how can I say no? But we'll have to use your gun. I just turned mine in."

Preston smiled. "I was planning on it."

SEVENTEEN

"She's not at her home and she's not at the department. They also checked Preston's apartment," Luke told Roni as he clicked off her cell. "Wade and Ethan just left her house and made sure Jaxon was safe next door with the neighbor where they brought him last night. But Smitty guarding the place has alerted Jax that something is up with his mom. I was hoping to avoid that. He's been through so much. The kid just wanted to spend Christmas with us."

Roni's sculpted eyebrows raised. "Us? As in Sylvie *and* you?"

"Funny, Sylvie looked the same way when he brought it up. She wasn't thrilled about it, either."

"Don't get me wrong, I'm totally pleased about it. I've been trying to get her to date for years, and now to think she might consider dating my cute little brother, believe me, I'm excited."

"Spending Christmas together isn't a date. She's made it clear that will never happen."

"But you mean to ask her for one as a present, right?" Roni smiled coyly at him.

"First, we need to find her."

She sobered. "Right. Where do you think Preston would take her?"

"I'm trying to think if she mentioned a place that meant something to them, but I don't recall. That worked once for finding Jaxon, but it won't this time."

"Okay, let's think. If all this time it was her partner taking shots at her, where was he taking them from?"

"The first day was at the racetrack. The next time was from the road. I don't see a pattern there. But if he was the one to kidnap her, he would have been the one to bring her to the old mill building." Luke huffed. "He probably left her there unarmed to be killed by those guys when they found her. He wanted them to do his dirty work for him. Sylvie always said that as a cop she goes into the danger, no matter what. Preston probably figured she would barge in on their setup even without a gun, and they would take her out. Preston could mourn the loss of the chief along with the whole town with no worries of ever being arrested."

"Obviously, he forgot the chief is brave but not stupid. So, okay, let's check the mill." Roni floored the gas pedal and they headed downtown to the industrialized section of Norcastle.

It had been days since Luke had been to the apartment he'd rented. Passing by it now he thought of his belongings still strewn about. His Sarno Construction shirt left on the floor, his past as Ian Stone scattered with it. He could honestly never go back to collect his meager belongings, and saw no reason to. Luke instead faced forward and concentrated on putting together his future. Sylvie beside him like she'd promised him on that mountain came into his mind. He couldn't envision his future any other way. He wouldn't settle for a good friend. He wanted more. He wanted her to be his family.

"I think I got it," Roni announced. "Maybe Preston has been in love with Sylvie for years. She's always made it clear she would never date again. But then you came to town. Rich, handsome Luke Spencer turned her head."

"I wish. Anyway, that doesn't jibe. He tried to hurt her and Jaxon before I came to town. He's been planning this all along. I just got in the way." A salt truck rambled by spraying the street. Roni waited for it to pass and pulled up to the old mill building. "There's no sign of them. No car tracks, no foot traffic in the snow. No one's been here since the place was swept." She chewed on her nail as they scanned the area around them. Then she looked back at the departing truck. "I wonder if Preston was the one to rile the townspeople up over the salt tent. There have been picketers for months. If he wanted to hurt Sylvie, he might have created fire where there was only smoke. All the times she kept sending him to calm the crowd, he was probably setting up shop over there and gaining a following."

"So, then he might want her to see his handiwork and take her there."

"I like the way you think. We must be related."

"It doesn't look like anyone's around," Sylvie said as Preston drove up to the tent and pulled around to the back to hide their vehicle. The lot was empty, except for a few plow trucks left in the rear of the parking lot. "The plow drivers are out clearing the streets after last night's storm."

"The Millers are supposed to be here. Let's see if they're hiding out inside."

Sylvie and Preston exited the car and kept in step as they approached the tent on stealthy feet. Preston held his gun at chest level and opened the door first, while Sylvie backed up off to the side. "This is like old times, partner," she whispered. She couldn't think of a better finish to a career than to end it as it began.

"It's not over yet," Preston whispered back. "On my count, you run in. I've got your back…as always." At her nod, he counted, "One, two, three."

"Hands up! Police!" she yelled and ran into the cavernous tent. The stench of salt pricked her nose and watered her eyes, but from what she could see, the place stood empty of any other people. She walked the makeshift aisle between piles of rock salt. There was nothing to hide behind straight back to the rear of the tent, where the salt reached near the ceiling. Some sunlight breached the ceiling fabric and she could see corrosion on the beams.

"I thought you said you had been keeping an eye on this place and the picketers didn't have any cause to make a ruckus." She pointed to the damage. "What do you call that?" She turned just as Preston stuck a rectangular plastic box with a red light blinking in the corner onto the tent interior wall.

Sylvie studied the object, then his emotionless face. "Is that what I think it is?"

"A bomb? Yes. It's a plastic explosive. And there's more than one."

Sylvie's thoughts tripped in confusion. "M-more?"

"They're all over town. The opera house, the town-square clock tower, the covered bridge, even the racetrack's grandstand will be coming down momentarily. They're set to go off one after another, and no one will be able to stop them."

A shiver raced up her spine as her body temperature dropped instantly. Chills shook her appendages as an image of the pure chaos that was about to ensue flashed in her mind. She couldn't believe it was Preston who was about to cause such terror and destruction.

"Why are you doing this, Preston?" Her voice sounded desperate to her ears. "Why?"

"To stick it to the town, of course. Just like I said. One last bang. Maybe I should have said 'bangs' as in multiple, because there are so many."

Bile rose up from her stomach. "Just how many? Like more than the places you just mentioned?"

"One more."

A groan escaped her throat. "No, Preston, I don't want this. Please tell me you don't have these positioned where there are people."

"Don't worry."

She sighed in relief.

But then he said, "The hackers will go down for it."

"Meaning people *could* get hurt? Oh, Preston! What are you thinking? The bombs go off, and I'll be the one to take the Millers in? Is that your plan? To get my job back? I'm supposed to be some hero? This is crazy, Preston. Where is the other bomb located? Tell me!" She swallowed hard. Could she hope people wouldn't be out of their homes because of the holiday?

"The Spencer mansion garage, where they house their fancy-schmancy cars." His eyes flashed bright… and deranged. He'd have to be to come up with a plan like this. "It will look like the Millers were going after the Spencers personally again."

All Sylvie could think was the whole family would be there.

Luke.

No, Luke was in the hospital. His family would be with him, but there were still people at the house.

But it was also so far from town. Could she get all the bombs confiscated in town *and* the one on the Spencers' home? Or would she have to go up the mountain and let the ones in town detonate and hope no one was nearby?

She reached for her phone. She needed Reggie. "Ugh! No connection."

Click, click.

Sylvie raised her gaze to the familiar sound and met the black abyss of the inside barrel of Preston's gun.

No, not Preston's gun…*her* gun. Her missing gun. "Preston, why do you have my gun? The one taken off me when I was dumped at the mill?"

"Drop the phone."

She did as he said and the missing piece to her puzzle slid in. "It was you? I don't believe it. It's been you all along?"

"Yes. Now kick the phone over to me."

Sylvie kicked it across the concrete, her hands raised up behind her head. "You don't plan on me bringing anyone in. You never did."

"Unfortunately, you're not going to make it in the scuffle with the Miller brothers. You'll get a shot off on each of them, but they'll turn the gun on you and kill you."

"And when does this all go down?"

"It already has." He looked at his watch. "Ready? Wait for it. Five, four, three, two, one."

An explosion off somewhere downtown blasted through the serene holiday morning.

Sylvie jerked and covered her mouth at the sound.

"There goes the bridge."

The bridge?

She ran to Preston's left to get to the door, but a quick leg out sent her sailing through the air, colliding with a pile of rock salt. She landed in a slump against it. Granules slid down the pile like a mountain avalanche of displaced snow. As the salt spill slowed, a man's hand protruded from the side of the heap right by her head.

Sylvie fumbled backward at the shock of seeing a human hand pointing at her in its rigor mortis state.

One of the Millers, she could only assume.

"Please, Preston, tell me you didn't do this. Please tell me you didn't kill them."

"Actually, ballistics will show you did."

"Me?"

He waved the gun around. "With your gun. After this place blows, the weapon will be found, along with your body, or what's left of it, and prove you were here to do the deed."

"But why me?"

"Because you couldn't leave well enough alone with Shawn Dolan. The man wanted to put my name out there to lead a special task force with the governor, but if you ruined him, his word would mean nothing. I've tried to bring this up to you. I've proven that I'm worth more than the menial tasks you give me. But every time I brought it up, you shrugged it off. This was going to be my big break, to do something other than cruise around the streets of Norcastle for you for the rest of my life. But you, you just couldn't let Andrea's whimpering go. You had to keep building a case against Shawn, trying to convince his wife to tarnish his good name. If only I could find the file you created on him. I searched your house and Evergreen. Anywhere I could think you hid it."

"Wait. That was *you* who broke into Evergreen? *And* my house to leave the message? You broke procedure about the safe house and put Mrs. Clemson at risk just so you could look for the file?"

"That's not all I broke. I even broke my nose to give me some time away from the station to look for it."

"And to get rid of me. Don't forget that."

"I couldn't. Shawn made it very clear that I couldn't. Get the file and make this case go away, or there would be no governor's job for me. But I knew even if I found the file, you were never going to stop. You said so yourself this morning. Dolan thought if you lost Jaxon, it would break you and take your searchlight off him while you fought a custody battle. He dragged your useless ex back here to take Jaxon from you, but I knew that wouldn't be enough. I knew the only way to stop you was to silence you forever. If Spencer hadn't shown up and ruined everything, I would be celebrating with Mayor Dolan right now and all would be well."

"*Well?* What about Andrea? It's physical abuse."

"Andrea didn't want your help. Nobody wants your help."

"Well, they're going to get it anyway. Tell me how much time until the other bombs go off."

"Why? So you can save the town? You don't have what it takes."

"How much time?" she shouted.

As she'd hoped, Preston checked his watch. "The clock tower blows in five min—"

Sylvie took the brief moment given to her and threw herself into the air at him. Her focus was his right arm, which held the gun. With her right shoulder she landed and jammed it into his chest, shoving him back while her right hand grabbed the gun and pushed out to his side. It would be harder for him to take aim again if she moved the weapon away from his body. At the same time her left hand banged into his wrist so hard it cracked.

Preston screamed out in pain. "My arm! You broke my arm!" His lips snarled as grunts and growls were directed at her.

Sylvie responded with the gun now turned on him. One press of her finger and it went off.

Preston went flying back to the cement floor. His head slammed hard, knocking him out cold. Blood pooled out behind him as she approached him. The shot went through his left shoulder.

"I don't have what it takes? Take that." Her rapid breaths pushed against her ribs. "Now you have a hole to match the other one I gave you last night." She leaned over Preston and felt for a pulse. "You'll live to stand trial, though. Then you can tell everyone about your... aspirations."

The door swung open. Luke stood on the threshold. "Sylvie!" He rushed in. "I thought..." He looked at Preston on the ground. "I thought that was you. Are you all right?"

"Get out!" she yelled, halting him. "Now! There's a bomb!"

Sylvie reached for Preston's dead weight and attempted to drag him out of the building.

Luke moved in beside her.

"Didn't you hear me? I said get out!"

"I'm beside you, Sylvie. I won't ever tell you not to do your job, but I will stand beside you while you do it."

She searched his face, breathless at the words she thought she misheard, but prayed she hadn't. "Do you mean that?"

"Only if you promise to never let go again."

"I thought…"

"I know what you thought. That what I needed was my family. But that includes you and Jaxon, too."

She slowly smiled, then nodded on a cry. "Help me get this maniac out of here, so I can kiss you."

"Gladly."

It dawned on Sylvie that Luke was injured and should be in the hospital, but as they dragged Preston's body far away from the shed, it felt so right to have him beside her.

Her man.

They dropped Preston in a snow pile, and none too gently.

Luke reached for her, but she held a hand up, remembering the other bombs. "No, wait. You need to get your family out of their house." She grabbed Preston's radio off his shoulder. She pushed the button. "This is Ch— This is Sylvie Laurent calling for Reggie."

"What's your location, Sylvie?" Reggie called back. "I'm sending the chopper to pick you up."

"Salt shed. You need to get a couple of bomb squads together. Five is more like it. There are plastic bombs set to go off all over town."

"Bombs?" Luke said. "Where are they located? And why does my family have to leave their house?"

Sylvie looked at Luke while she told Reggie the locations. "The salt shed, the opera house, the bridge, the clock tower, and…"

Luke raised his eyebrows waiting for her to tell him.

Sylvie felt her lips tremble. "I'm sorry, Luke." To Reggie she spoke loud and clear. "The Spencer mansion. It's in their garage."

Luke's face paled as Roni walked over to them from her Porsche. "My family's there by now." He spoke as though he hadn't fully comprehended the weight of it all yet.

Luke said, "We'll never make it in time." He grabbed the radio from Sylvie. "Reggie, this is Luke. I need you to contact Michael Ackerman. He needs to get to my family's home and get everyone out."

The radio answered with static, then Michael's voice came over. "Already on it, son. I have Reggie in the helicopter with me. I just told Wade. He and Ethan are taking care of it as we speak. The question is, does the chief want my men's help in diffusing the rest of the bombs in town?"

Luke glanced her way, his eyebrows raised. Sylvie shook her head and said, "That call's up to Reggie now."

Michael chuckled. "Actually, you're chief again. Reggie is awaiting your command."

"What? How?"

"The council changed their minds when they read your file. They realized their illustrious mayor had a reason for wanting you gone. He's been arrested."

"Arrested? But that means…"

"It sure does. Andrea Dolan and her son are pressing charges. Bret gave them the USB with all the evidence you'd collected. But we'll get to that later. Right now I need direction from the chief of police. Do you want my men's help?"

"Yes!"

Michael laughed again. "Good, because they're already on the ground. And I'm on my way to pick you up."

"Preston's been shot and he's unconscious. I'll need to go with the ambulance."

"My helicopter will be faster. I don't want that guy dying."

Before Michael clicked off, she said, "Michael, I need to know—were there any casualties in the explosion?"

"We're looking into it, but we're thinking everyone was home for Christmas, where they belonged. You did lose your bridge. You'll be needing a good builder. Have I told you how handy my grandson is? Brilliant, really. I've seen his work."

"Your grandson?" Sylvie looked at Luke and said, "He says you're brilliant. You want the job?"

"What I want is you in my arms, now."

Sylvie looked to Luke's arms outstretched to her, open and...*bleeding*?

"Luke! You popped your stitches." She rushed for him.

"I know. It's just a couple, though. I felt them pop, but I'm okay."

"Are you sure? You could start bleeding out again."

"Well, to be on the safe side, I'll have Mary the Bulldog take a look at them when we get to the hospital."

"Who?"

"Oh, wait until you meet her. I think you'll like her. She's got the same commanding voice you do."

Luke flashed a grin her way, and she made her way into his arms.

Luke pulled her in closer with his good arm and threaded his fingers through her hair. With a gentle tug, he pulled her head back to lift her face to his. His ice-blue eyes danced with a happiness that had to match her own.

Luke let out a huge sigh. "Hey, Roni," he called to his sister. "I think I'm finally home."

Roni let out loud whoop that made them both laugh before growing serious.

"Home," Sylvie whispered a breath away from him and closed her eyes. "Now about that kiss."

Luke took her lips in his typical no-holds fashion. Fast, sure and with abandon. Everything that she saw in Luke Spencer, and she loved it. She loved his kisses. She loved his presence that didn't suppress her, but made her stronger. She loved him, and as she let herself love him, her arms reached around his neck and gave his exuberance right back to him. She was never letting go again.

And neither was he. She knew it without a doubt.

The helicopter blasted over the trees and came down in a snow-stirring landing, but the two of them were oblivious to anyone and anything but them. When someone tapped her on the shoulder, they still held on to each other, but slowly, with a smile on each of their giddy faces they unlocked their lips and looked to the person who had so rudely interrupted.

Jaxon stood less than a foot from them, his eyes wide with…what?

Confusion?

Disappointment?

Anger?

Sylvie's smile slipped from her face. With the sound of the helicopter, she couldn't give her son a very detailed excuse. She opened her mouth and closed it with useless attempts to explain.

But still her arms stayed fastened around Luke. She was never letting go again. But how could she make her son understand?

"Jaxon!" She reached a hand out to him. "I love him, Jaxon. I love Luke! Please understand!"

Jaxon's eyes widened and he looked to Luke.

Luke touched Sylvie's face and turned her cheek to face him, his eyes misting up at her words. She could see he was astounded.

She nodded and mouthed, "I love you."

His lips trembled as a huge smile broke his tanned face. He shouted over the helicopter, "I love you, Chief Sylvie!" Then he looked to Jaxon and shouted, "I love your mom, and I love you!"

Jaxon reached out with both hands, but before she knew what he planned, he launched his arms around them both. Wet tears hit her cheek, and she knew he was crying with them.

Sylvie felt Luke's sigh of relief. She beamed a smile up at him, knowing exactly how he felt. Without a word, they wrapped their arms around her son and brought him into the fold.

A family they would be. Forever linked and never letting go.

EPILOGUE

The rushing spring water gushed below Norcastle's covered bridge and lifted a cool breeze to the people inside.

Sylvie stood with Jaxon on one side and Luke on her other. Six months had passed and Luke had worked diligently on rebuilding the bridge into a perfect replica of its former rustic feel.

In the crowds around them, too numerous to count, there were many who'd joined in to repair the structure, getting to know the missing Spencer child and coming to love the man he'd become. Almost as much as she loved him.

His old boss, Alex Sarno, had flown in and was here somewhere. He'd come to help, but was pleasantly surprised Luke had it covered. Well, not really surprised. He said he'd always known Luke had a natural talent for building, but something else Alex said really hit home. He said his greatest accomplishment will always be the bridge he'd built, but not this one, as magnificent as it was. It was the bridge he'd built to his family. Alex said he would miss Luke, but wished him well on his own construction business, which he would be full owner of here in the Northeast. Especially because they wouldn't be competing for jobs. He said that with a wink.

Sylvie looked up at her soon-to-be husband and smiled. She dropped her head on his shoulder and he wrapped an arm around her to pull her in close.

"You ready to be sworn in as chief of police, love?"

"Let's make it official…but first, we need to become a family."

A few happy cheers rose up behind Luke. Sylvie peered over his shoulder to see his whole family there with huge smiles on their faces. She returned their grins and couldn't wait to be a part of their clan. Their numbers astounded her, and from the news Roni shared last week, they would be growing again. Sylvie glanced at her friend with her husband's arms draped around her from behind. Ethan's hands rested on Roni's abdomen so casually, but Sylvie knew of his awe for the child growing inside her.

Sylvie moved her attention to Lacey. She made a beautiful mother to her little boy, but right now little Kaden was being loved by his grandparents up from South Carolina. Sylvie wondered if Luke knew his family extended far beyond Norcastle.

Promise barked, bringing everyone's attention to her sweet smiling face. She barked again and ran up to Sylvie to be pet.

"She must sense your jitters," Luke leaned over and whispered to her.

"Nonsense. I've never been surer of anything in my life."

Luke flashed his striking grin, his teeth still so white against his tanned skin. She had to wonder when his tan would fade to match the pale skin of the Northerners, not that she would complain if it didn't. His golden-brown skin just reminded her of how special he was.

"You ready, golden boy?" She smiled.

"I was ready months ago."

"I know. I just wanted to be married on the bridge, and I wanted to be sworn in as chief under my married name, which means I had to wait until the probation period and trials were over."

"The council would have lifted the probation period, you know."

"And take a special privilege? Not my style."

"And speaking of style, have I told you how beautiful you are?"

"Only about twenty times since I arrived, but go ahead, you can say it again. I'm made of sturdy stuff. I can take it."

"No worries about all the flattery weakening you?"

"Funny about that. I think it actually makes me stronger."

Luke leaned in. "In that case, let me compare you to—"

"Stop right there, mister. No reciting someone else's work. Not on my wedding day."

Luke looked past her to Jaxon and winked. "Well, now that you mention it, Jax and I have been working on a little special something. What do you say, Jax? Shall we share it?"

Jaxon gave an emphatic nod.

"You're on, Pastor," Luke said.

The elderly man cleared his throat and began. "Dearly beloved, we are gathered here today to join two people who adore each other and wish to join their hearts as one, along with their families. Luke Spencer and Sylvie Laurent, it is a joy to officiate your marriage to one another. I do believe you have your own vows?"

"Luke's going to wow us with his words," Sylvie said loud enough for all to hear.

She giggled just for him. Then he reached into his tux pocket and pulled out a piece of folded-up paper. Ever so slowly, he unfolded it and any mirth left his eyes. When he focused so thoroughly on the paper, Sylvie's smile evaporated even faster. "Oh, Luke," she whispered. "You're going to read it?"

He gave her a timid smile. "Jaxon and Roni have been helping me. It's amazing how much you can learn when you take name-calling out of the mix. And these have helped, too." He reached into his pocket and pulled out a pair of rose-colored glasses.

"Glasses to help with dyslexia?" She laughed with anticipation. "I always knew you were resourceful. You know what you want, and you go after it."

He locked his eyes on her. "I know a prize when I see one. Not even bullets will deter me from claiming it." He held the glasses up with one hand and lifted the paper. "Now will you let me read? And just so you know, this is only the first of many readings. I have a whole new world to explore with these things."

She beamed at his excitement at finally being able to read. He had a lifetime to make up for. "Well, then, what are you waiting for, Mr. Spencer? Put those lenses on, and let's get this show on the road."

* * * * *

An eternal optimist, **Hope White** was born and raised in the Midwest. She and her college sweetheart have been married for thirty years and are blessed with two wonderful sons, two feisty cats and a bossy border collie. When not dreaming up inspirational tales, Hope enjoys hiking, sipping tea with friends and going to the movies. She loves to hear from readers, who can contact her at hopewhiteauthor@gmail.com.

Books by Hope White

Love Inspired Suspense

Hidden in Shadows
Witness on the Run
Christmas Haven
Small Town Protector
Safe Harbor
Baby on the Run
Nanny Witness
Mountain Hostage

Echo Mountain

Mountain Rescue
Covert Christmas
Payback
Christmas Undercover
Witness Pursuit
Mountain Ambush

Visit the Author Profile page
at Harlequin.com for more titles.

CHRISTMAS UNDERCOVER

Hope White

May the God of hope fill you with all joy and peace as you trust in Him, so that you may overflow with hope by the power of the Holy Spirit.
—*Romans* 15:13

ONE

FBI agent Sara Vaughn awoke with a start, her heart pounding against her chest. Darkness surrounded her and it took a second for her eyes to adjust.

Panic took hold. No, she was beyond that. She'd outgrown it.

She counted to three, taking a deep breath, then exhaled. She clicked on her headlamp. Tall, majestic evergreen trees stretched up toward the starlit sky.

The mountains. She was in the Cascade Mountains following a lead that her supervisor, Greg Bonner, said was a waste of time.

Sara knew better.

The sound of deep male voices echoed from beyond a cluster of trees to her left.

"Be reasonable, David!" a man shouted.

David Price was one of the three business partners who were on this mountain getaway. The other men were Victor LaRouche and Ted Harrington, and together they owned the drug company LHP, Inc.

Sara made her way toward the sound of raised voices.

She was proud of herself for managing to get on the trail guide team hired to lead them up Echo Mountain. This isolated spot in the Cascade Mountains of Washington would surely give the men the privacy they needed to solidify their plan.

Getting a dangerous drug into the hands of unsuspecting consumers.

"Why do you have to make this so hard?"

She recognized Vic LaRouche's voice because of its Southern twang.

She stayed off the main trail, not wanting to alert them to her presence, and made her way through the brush. Edging around a large boulder, she stepped over a fallen branch in silence. She needed to stay invisible, hidden. Something she was good at.

The men were no doubt having this discussion a safe distance away from the lead guide, Ned, so as not to wake him. It didn't take much to wake Sara. Even in sleep, she was always on alert.

"It's not right and you both know it," David said.

"It was an anomaly, a mistake," Ted Harrington said.

"A mistake that could kill people."

"Don't be dramatic," LaRouche said.

This was it—the evidence she'd been looking for.

She pulled out her phone, hoping to record some of their conversation. If she could catch them admitting to their plan, it would go a long way to proving she was right, that she wasn't just an "overzealous" agent trying to prove something.

She crept closer, shielding herself behind a towering western hemlock. Digging her fingers into the bark, she peeked around the tree. The three men hovered beside a small campfire, the flames illuminating their faces. LaRouche and Harrington were tall, middle-aged men, older than David Price by at least ten years.

"I'm not in business to hurt people," David said.

"We're helping people, sport," Harrington said, slapping David's shoulder. "Letting them sleep like they never have before."

"And they don't wake up."

"That hasn't been irrefutably proved," Harrington said.

"Even one death is too many."

LaRouche, a tall, regal-looking man, jumped into the conversation. It grew into a shouting match, giving Sara the chance to sneak even closer. She darted to another tree, only ten feet from the men.

She clicked off her headlamp.

Hit the video record button on her phone.

And held her breath.

"I didn't sign on for this!" David said.

"Majority rules," Harrington countered.

"Then, I'm out. I'll sell you my share of the company."

Harrington threw up his hands and paced a few steps away.

"If you leave, stock prices go down," LaRouche said calmly.

"I don't care. Some things are more important than money."

"Like your family?" LaRouche taunted.

"Is that a threat?" David said.

"Sure, why not?"

David lunged at LaRouche. Harrington dived in between them. "Enough!"

The two men split apart, David glaring at his partners.

"Calm down. Let's talk this through," Harrington said.

"Talk? You mean threaten me?" David said.

"I like to think of it as persuading you, David," LaRouche countered.

"No, I'm done." David started to walk away.

It seemed as if the conversation was over.

Then LaRouche darted around the fire, grabbed David's arm and flung him...

Over the edge of the trail.

The chilling sound of a man crying out echoed across the mountains.

Sara gasped and took a step backward.

A twig snapped beneath her boot.

LaRouche and Harrington whipped their heads around and spotted her. They looked as stunned as she felt. The three of them stared at each other.

No one moved. She didn't breathe.

Heart racing, she watched the expression on LaRouche's face change from stunned to something far worse: the look of a murderer who was hungry for more.

"It was an accident," Harrington said.

LaRouche reached into his jacket, no doubt for a weapon.

In that millisecond, her only conscious thought was survival.

Sara clicked on her headlamp and took off, retracing her steps over the rugged terrain. She was outnumbered and couldn't retrieve her off-duty piece quick enough. She had to get safe and preserve the video evidence against them.

Shoving the phone in her pocket, she hopped a fallen branch and dodged the boulder on the other side. As she picked up speed, she heard a man grunt as he tripped and hit the ground behind her.

"Where are you going? We need your help!" Harrington called.

Beating back the tentacles of fear, she searched for

a trail, or at least a more even surface. She'd left everything at the campsite but the clothes on her back, so her odds for survival weren't great, especially considering the cold temperatures in the mountains this time of year.

Stop going to that dark place, she scolded herself. She had to figure out how to contact her boss and report the murder before the men reported it as an accident.

Call her boss, right, the man who'd ordered her to take time off. He didn't even know she was chasing a lead he'd proclaimed was a dead end.

"David fell and we need your help!" Harrington yelled.

David fell? Is that what you call it when you fling a man off a cliff?

She sucked in the cool mountain air, pumping her arms, trying to get a safe distance away where she could get a cell signal and call for help.

"Let's talk about this!" Harrington pressed.

Like they'd "talked" to David Price? The memory of his desperate cry sent shivers across her shoulders.

She found the trail, but if she found it, so would they. They were taller than her five foot three, their strides longer. It wouldn't take them long to catch her.

And kill her.

They'd probably fabricate a story about how she was responsible for David's death. That would wrap everything up in a neat bow—just in time for Christmas.

No. She wouldn't let them win.

A gunshot echoed across the mountain range.

She bit back a gasp. How would they explain her body riddled with bullet holes? Unless they hoped wild animals would rip it apart, making cause of death that much harder to determine.

Suddenly she ran out of trail. She peered over the mountain's edge into the black abyss below.

"Think," she whispered.

She realized her rope was still hooked to her belt. She hadn't planned to drift off to sleep earlier, so she hadn't taken off her gear. She wrapped the rope around a tree root jutting out from the side of the mountain below the trail and pulled it tight.

For the first time in her life, she appreciated Uncle Matt's insistence that she take wilderness survival courses, along with self-defense. She used to think he'd forced her to take the classes because her small frame made her a target for bullies. She eventually realized it was because of the nightmares. He thought the classes would empower her, make her feel safe.

Sara had never felt safe.

She dropped to her stomach and shimmied over the edge. Clinging to the rope, she let herself down slowly, hoping to hit a ledge or plateau where she could wait it out. She clicked off her headlamp. At least if she could disappear for a few hours until sunrise, she might be able to make her way out of Echo Mountain State Park.

She calmed her breathing, questioning her decision to follow this lead on her own. Was her boss right? Was she too determined for her own good?

Sara gripped the rope with gloved hands and steadied herself against the mountainside with her boots.

"What do you want to do?" Harrington said.

His voice was close, right above her close. She held her breath.

"We'll send Bill to find her," LaRouche said. "He's got climbing experience."

"Wouldn't it be better if we—"

"No, we need answers, like who sent her and what she heard. Then she needs to disappear."

Disappear. They were determined to kill her. Sara's pulse raced against her throat.

As she hung there, suspended in midair, she searched her surroundings, trying to see something, trying to stay grounded.

All she could see was a wall of black, which reminded her of…

Stay in here and don't make a sound.

But, Daddy—

I mean it. Take care of your brother.

Suddenly someone tugged on the rope, yanking her out of the memory.

"Sara Long, is that you?" LaRouche said.

She was relieved they only knew her undercover name, Sara Long. That should keep them from discovering her true identity.

Then, suddenly, they started pulling her up. No, she wouldn't let them get away with it, killing people, innocent people.

Killing her.

She released the rope and grabbed the tree root, then edged her way down the side of the mountain, grabbing onto whatever felt solid.

She grabbed onto a branch…

It pulled loose from the earth and she started to slide. Flailing her arms, she reached for something, anything, to slow her descent.

But it was too dark, and the fall too steep.

It wouldn't surprise the guys in her field office if she died out here like this: alone, on some rogue assignment gone south.

She didn't care. At least this time she'd taken on the enemy instead of hiding from him.

I'm sorry, Daddy. I should have done something to save you.

She came to a sudden stop. Her head whipped back, slammed against something hard, and she was swallowed by darkness.

Will Rankin approached the end of the trail and made the final turn. His breath caught in his throat at the stunning view, sunlight sparkling off the calm, turquoise water at the base of Echo Mountain, with the Cascade Mountain range spanning the horizon behind the lake. This was it, the perfect place to open his heart to God, hoping for peace to ease the resentment lingering in his heart.

Intellectually Will knew it was time to let it go for so many reasons, not the least of which being his daughters. They needed a loving, gentle father, not a bitter, angry one.

Will thought he had coped with Megan's death pretty well over the past two years, but the dark emotions continued to have a stronghold over his heart. He was still angry with his wife for shutting him out as she battled cancer, and he struggled with resentment about his mother-in-law, who challenged nearly every decision Will made about Claire and Marissa.

I love my girls so much, Lord. Isn't that enough?

Apparently not to his mother-in-law.

No, he wouldn't think about that today. Today he'd commune with nature and pray: for his daughters, for emotional peace and for the strength to get him through the upcoming Christmas season, the girls' second Christmas without their mom.

It was unseasonably warm at the base of the mountain. Although a recent light snowfall dusted the area around the lake with a layer of white, it would probably melt off by noon. He smiled, thinking about how much the girls were looking forward to playing in the snow.

Then something else caught his eye across the lake.

A splash of red.

Curious, he pulled out his binoculars and peered through the lenses. It looked like a woman in a red jacket, jeans and hiking boots. Her long brown hair was strewn across her face.

She looked unconscious, or worse.

Will shoved the binoculars into his pack and took off. He had to get to her, had to save her. He glanced at his cell phone. No signal.

Please, Lord, let me save her.

As he sped toward the unconscious woman, he wondered how she'd ended up here. Was she a day hiker who hadn't brought enough hydration? He didn't see a backpack near her body, yet even day hikers knew better than to head into the mountains without supplies since the weather could change in a flash.

By the time he reached the unconscious woman, his heart was pounding against his chest. He shucked his pack and kneeled to administer first aid. "Ma'am?"

She was unresponsive.

"Ma'am, can you hear me?"

What had happened to this fragile-looking creature? He wondered if she got separated from her party or had fallen off a trail above.

He gently brushed jet-black hair away from her face.

She had color in her cheeks, a good sign. He took off his glove and pressed his fingers against her wrist to check her pulse.

"No!" She swung her arm, nailing Will in the face with something hard.

He jerked backward, stars arcing across his vision. He pinched his eyes shut against the pain. Gripping his nose, he felt blood ooze through his fingers. He struggled to breathe.

"Don't touch me!" she cried.

"I'm trying to help."

"Liar."

He cracked open his eyes. She towered above him, aiming a gun at his chest.

"Please," he said, putting out one hand in a gesture of surrender. "I'm sorry if I upset you, but I really do want to help."

"Yeah, help them kill me."

He noticed a bruise forming above her right eye and lacerations crisscrossing her cheek.

"You're hurt," he said.

"I'm fine."

Will guessed she was frightened and confused. Maybe even dehydrated.

"I'm Will Rankin, a volunteer with Echo Mountain Search and Rescue."

"Sure, and I'm Amelia Earhart."

"Check my pack. My driver's license is in the side pocket."

It was worth a try, although he knew all the sensible conversation in the world may not get through to someone in her condition.

Narrowing her eyes, she grabbed his backpack and

stepped a few feet away. Never lowering the gun, she unzipped the side pocket.

"May I sit up to stop my nosebleed?" he asked.

She nodded that he could.

He would continue to act submissive so she wouldn't see him as a threat. It was the best way to keep her from firing the gun by accident. He sensed she wasn't a killer, but rather she was disoriented and frightened.

Sitting up, he leaned forward and pinched his nose, just below the bridge. He'd have dual black eyes for sure and didn't know how he'd explain that to his girls, or their grandparents.

You've got bigger problems than a bloody nose. He had to talk this woman down from her precarious ledge.

She rifled through his wallet and hesitated, fingering a photograph of Claire and Marissa.

"My girls," he said. "They're in first and third grades."

She shot him a look of disbelief and shoved his wallet and the photos haphazardly into his pack.

"Did you fall from a trail above?" he asked.

"I'm asking the questions!" She straightened and pointed the gun at his chest again. "And you'd better give me the right answers."

"Please," he said. "My girls… I'm all they've got. Their mother…died."

He thought he'd gotten through to her.

She flicked the gun. "Get up."

He slowly stood, realizing how petite she was, barely coming up to his chest.

"Where are they?" she demanded.

"Who?"

"LaRouche and Harrington."

"I'm sorry, but I don't know what you're talking about."

"Right, you randomly happened to find me."

"I did."

"Uh-huh. And you're out here, in the middle of no-where, why?"

"I'm spending a few days in the mountains for—" he hesitated "—solitude."

"You're lying. There's more to it."

"I'm not lying, but you're right, there is more to it."

She waited and narrowed her eyes, expectant.

"I come to this spot by the lake to find emotional peace—" he hesitated "—with God's help."

"Yeah, right. Great story, *Will*."

He didn't miss the sarcastic pronunciation of his name, nor the paranoid look in her eye.

She dug in her jacket pocket and pulled out her phone. She frowned.

"You have a phone?" she asked.

"I do."

She shoved hers back into her pocket. "Give it to me."

He pulled it out, dropped it between them and raised his hands. "You won't get a signal here, but there's a spot by my cabin where I can usually find service."

"Your cabin?"

"I'm renting a cabin about a quarter of a mile north."

She eyed his phone, must have seen there weren't any bars, and shoved it into her other pocket.

"Let's go." When she picked up his pack, a groan escaped her lips.

"Do you want me to—"

"Walk," she demanded, her eyes watering.

They were obviously tears of pain. He guessed from

the rip in her jacket and strained look on her face, she might have cracked a rib or two.

With a nod, he turned and headed toward the cabin. She was hurt and confused, and the worst part was, she wouldn't accept his help.

He'd have to rely on patience, kindness and compassion to make her feel safe. That would go a long way to ease her worry and earn her trust.

Hopefully that would be enough.

Sara wasn't sure how far she'd get before passing out from the excruciating pain of her headache, but she'd fight until she dropped. She had somehow survived the fall, and wouldn't allow herself to die at the hand of a hired thug.

It figures LaRouche and Harrington would send a handsome, clean-cut guy to find her—a real charmer, this one. Will or Bill or whatever his name was, had to be over six feet tall, with chestnut brown hair and green eyes, and he spoke with such a gentle, calming tone. What a story he'd crafted for himself: he'd come out here to pray?

He'd laid it on thick, all right. Those were probably his little girls in the photograph, girls who had no idea what their daddy did for a living.

In her ten years with the FBI, Sara had learned plenty about sociopaths and how they used their cunning intelligence and polished charisma to convince an interrogating agent of their innocence.

Clutching the gun, she took her finger off the trigger in case she stumbled and pulled it by accident. He wouldn't know the difference. As long as Will thought she aimed a gun at his back, he'd do as she ordered.

The trees around her started drifting in and out of focus. She blinked to clear her vision, and stumbled on a rock jutting out of the ground.

Strong, firm hands gripped her arms, keeping her upright. Will's green eyes studied her face, as if assessing her head injury. He must have realized his mistake, that he was still holding on to her, because his hands sprung free and he raised them, as if to say, *please don't shoot me.*

She stepped back and dropped the backpack on the ground. "It's throwing me off balance."

He picked up the pack and adjusted it across his shoulders with ease. "That bruise above your eye—" He hesitated. "Are you experiencing blurred vision?"

"I'm fine." She flicked the gun barrel toward the trail.

He continued walking.

"I have ice packs at the cabin," he said. "And pain reliever."

She hated that he was being so polite. It was an act, his strategy to discover how much she knew. Those were LaRouche and Harrington's orders, right?

Much like her official orders had been to leave it alone, put aside the LHP, Inc., investigation due to lack of evidence. But she'd pushed and pushed until Bonner had had enough, and told her to take a couple of weeks off.

So she did, and spent her vacation going undercover and buying her way on to the trail guide team that LaRouche, Harrington and Price had hired to take them up the mountain. Her goal: watch and listen, glean whatever information she could from the men who were on vacation with their guards down.

"Would you like some water?" Will offered.

She ignored him. Sara might be hurting, but she wasn't stupid. It would be too easy for Will to slip something into her water, rendering her unconscious.

"Guess not," he said softly.

She took a deep breath and bit back a gasp at the stab of bruised ribs. She decided it was a good thing because the pain would keep her conscious and alert.

He slowed down, closing the distance between them.

"Keep walking," she said through clenched teeth.

"I thought you might need to rest."

"I don't."

With what seemed like a frustrated sigh, he continued. Sure, he was frustrated. He wanted to finish this job quickly and move on to his next high-paying assignment.

She focused on his backpack as she struggled to place one foot in front of the other without losing her balance. It wasn't easy when she felt as though she'd stepped off the Tilt-A-Whirl at the county fair.

They continued in silence, her pulse ricocheting off the inside of her skull with each step. She had to make it, had to put these arrogant criminals behind bars.

She hoped they could pull the video recording off her phone, even though she'd noticed it had been damaged in the fall.

Will's phone was working just fine. Maybe they were close to getting reception. She pulled his phone out of her pocket, but her trembling fingers dropped it. She snapped her gaze to Will, fearing he'd seen her weakness. He continued up the trail.

She waited until he was a good distance away and knelt down to retrieve the phone. When she stood, her vision blurred and she could barely make out Will's form. She squinted through the haze to see him.

He was no longer within sight.

She shoved the phone into her pocket and clutched the gun grip with both hands. Where did he go? Had he taken off up ahead, waiting to ambush her? She approached a sharp turn, blocked by a boulder.

Took a slow, shallow breath…

Darted around the corner.

And spotted Will, on his knees, with his hands interlaced behind his head.

"What are you doing?" she said.

"Waiting for you."

"Get up."

He stood, his back to her. "Are you all right?"

"Go on, keep moving."

He continued along the trail and she followed. He was waiting for her? More like he was messing with her head, and doing a good job of it.

"The cabin's not far," he said.

She ignored him, knowing how these guys worked. They insinuated themselves into your psyche and destroyed you from the inside out. This guy was luring her with his father-of-the-year, single-parent story. She'd seen the wallpaper on his phone of two adorable girls with strawberry blonde hair and big smiles. This guy was a master.

They trekked the rest of the way in silence, Sara focusing on breathing through the pain and shutting out the panic taunting her from the fringes of her mind. She was in the middle of nowhere with an assassin, and her next step could be her last.

No, she was tough. Even if others didn't believe it, she knew it in her heart.

If only she'd been tough when she was twelve.

They turned a corner to an open field with a cabin in the distance. Surely she'd be able to get a signal out there, in the middle of the field.

He marched in the direction of the cabin.

"Stop," she said. She'd be a fool to let him go inside with her. No doubt that was where he kept his tools of the trade—coercion tools.

"Sit down, over there." She jerked the gun barrel.

He sat down beside a fallen tree.

"You have rope in your pack?" she said.

"I do."

"Get it."

He unzipped his pack and pulled out what looked like parachute cord.

"Toss it over here. And put your hands behind your back," she said.

He did, not making eye contact. With a fortifying breath, she grabbed the rope off the ground and climbed over the downed tree.

"Lean forward."

He did as ordered. "I'm not going to hurt you."

"You're right, you won't."

She quickly bound his wrists behind his back, and secured him to a limb of the fallen tree. She stood and started walking.

"Drink some water," he said. "It will help with the headache."

"You can stop now."

"The best cell reception is over there, by that cluster of boulders." He nodded, ignoring her comment.

With determination and focus, she marched toward the field, on the other side of a narrow creek. That had to be the spot where she'd find a signal. It would also put her out in the open, making her vulnerable, an easy target. No, these guys usually worked alone. She checked his phone, hopeful and more than a little desperate, but she still had no bars.

She glanced up. A ray of sunlight bounced off the creek and pierced her vision. Pain seared through her brain. She snapped her eyes shut, but it was too late. A sudden migraine blinded her.

She stumbled forward. Had to get to…had to get service. Call her boss…

"What's wrong?" Will shouted.

She broke into a slow jog. Had to get away from him. Get help.

Breathing through the pain, she stepped onto the rocks to cross the creek. One foot in front of the other. She could do it.

But she slipped, jerking forward. She put out her hands to break her fall.

And landed in the water with a splash.

The man's shouts echoed in the distance.

She feared he would somehow free himself and finish her off.

She crawled through the creek, her soggy clothes weighing her down. Pain bounced through her head like a pinball.

With a gasp, she surrendered—to the pain, to her own failure—and collapsed into the cold, bubbling water.

TWO

"Ma'am!" Will shouted, pulling on the rope binding his wrists. She was down, unconscious in the creek. Was her head even above water?

"Hey!" He realized he didn't even know her name. "Ma'am, get up!"

She didn't move.

"Argh!" he groaned, pulling violently on his wrists. This was not going to happen. He was not going to sit here and watch a woman die in front of him.

"Get up!" he shouted.

She didn't move.

He yanked on his wrists and dug the heels of his boots into the ground, trying to get leverage. This craziness wasn't going to do him any good. He took a deep breath and forced himself to be calm.

"Think," he said. He remembered that his pocket-knife was clipped to the side of his backpack.

He stretched out, making himself as long as possible, practically dislocating a shoulder in the process. With the toe of his boot, he caught the strap of his pack and dragged it across the soft earth. In a low crouch, he kicked it behind him until his fingers could reach the knife.

He flicked it open and sawed away at his bindings, unable to see what he was doing. A sharp pain made him hesitate when the blade cut his skin. He clenched his jaw and continued.

"Ma'am!" he called out. "Ma'am, answer me!"

She didn't move.

He continued to dig at the rope with the blade, and accidentally cut his skin again. Didn't matter, he had to get free and—

Snap! He jerked his wrists free, reached around and started working on the rope that bound him to the tree.

"Come on, come on," he muttered. The parachute cord he kept in his pack was meant to be strong, which was why it felt as if it was taking forever to cut himself loose.

Please, God, help me get to her in time.

He finally sliced through it, pocketed the knife and grabbed his pack. Racing across the property, he focused on the woman, who was only partially submerged in the creek. What if she'd swallowed water and it blocked her airway?

He rushed to her side, looped his forearms under her armpits and dragged her out of the creek.

He leaned close. She wasn't breathing.

"No," he whispered.

With one hand on her forehead, and the other on the tip of her chin, he tilted her head backward. He hoped it was only her tongue blocking the airway. He pinched her nose and administered two deep breaths.

She coughed and a rush of relief whipped through his chest. Will rolled her onto her side. "It's okay. You're okay now," he said, although his heart was still racing at breakneck speed.

He had to call for help, get Echo Mountain Search and Rescue up here and quick. He spotted his smartphone, partially submerged in the creek. He snatched it out of the cold water. It would dry out and be usable at some point, but until then Will was on his own.

The shiny glint of metal caught his eye. The woman's gun lay mere inches away from him. He wasn't a fan of guns, but couldn't leave it here for a random stranger to pick up. He shoved it into his pocket.

The woman coughed. "P-p-please don't hurt me."

He snapped his attention to her shivering body. She was clutching her jacket above her heart, terrified.

"You don't have to be afraid of me," he said. "I'm going to help you."

She closed her eyes, as if she didn't believe him. He wondered if she saw him pocket the gun and assumed the worst.

"Do you think you can get up?" he said.

"Yeah."

He extended his hand. She ignored it and shifted onto her hands and knees. A round of coughs burst from her chest. That didn't sound good. He feared the water in her lungs might lead to something worse.

She stood, but wavered. Her eyes rolled back and he caught her as she went down. Hoisting her over his shoulder, he marched to the cabin. He had to get her dry, tend to her head wound and then determine what other injuries she'd sustained. It was obvious she had a severe headache, and most likely suffered from dehydration. He could treat those easily enough, but didn't have the ability to treat internal bleeding from her fall, or other, more serious injuries.

He'd do his best. The rest was in God's hands.

Taking quick, steady steps, he made it to the cabin and laid her on the single bed. He grabbed logs and started a fire to warm the room. Once he got it lit, he refocused on the woman.

The woman. He wished he knew her name.

He pulled her into a sitting position, leaning her head against his shoulder to remove her jacket. He noticed it was water-resistant.

"Smart girl," he whispered.

Most of her clothes, except for her jeans, were dry thanks to the jacket. She could remove her jeans to dry out when she regained consciousness. He wouldn't do anything that would make her feel uncomfortable.

He adjusted her on the bed, covered her with a wool blanket and pulled the bed closer to the fire.

Rushing into the kitchen area, he grabbed more first-aid supplies from the cabinet. Her groan echoed across the small cabin. Cracking an ice pack a few times to release the chemicals, he grabbed a kitchen chair and slid it close to her.

"Let's get a better look." He analyzed the lacerations on her face, retrieved an antiseptic wipe from the first-aid kit, and pressed it against the scrapes scarring her adorable face.

Adorable, Will? Really?

Shaking off the thought, he cleansed the debris from her head wound, and then placed a bandage over the cut. He pressed the ice pack against a lump on her head that was sure to swell and probably leave her with at least one black eye, if not two.

"Uh," she groaned.

"I'm sorry, but this will reduce the inflammation."

She pinched her eyes shut as if in extreme pain, which indicated a concussion.

"Where else are you hurt?" he said.

She didn't answer. He noticed she gripped her left wrist against her stomach.

"Your wrist?" he said. "May I see it?"

She buried it deeper into her stomach. Yeah, it was injured, all right. Her reaction was similar to Marissa's when she'd broken her wrist after falling off her bike last spring.

The mystery woman wasn't making this easy, but he wouldn't force the issue. He suspected that dehydration intensified her confusion and fear, and he wouldn't risk making it worse.

He grabbed a water bottle out of his pack. "You need to hydrate."

Supporting her with his arm, he sat her up and offered the water. Slowly, her eyes blinked open.

"You really need to drink something," he encouraged.

She pursed her lips, and her blue eyes clouded with fear. Ah, she thought he'd put something in the water.

"It's filtered water, see?" He took a swig, and made sure to swallow so she could see him. "Delicious."

He sounded as though he was trying to convince five-year-old Marissa to eat her broccoli.

The woman nodded and he held the bottle to her lips. He tipped it and she sipped, but coughed. He pulled her against his chest and gently patted her back. How long had it been since he'd comforted a woman like this?

Lord knew Megan wouldn't accept his comfort during the last months of her life.

The mystery woman leaned into Will and he held his breath. Maybe she'd decided to trust him?

"What's your name?" he said.

She pushed away from him.

He put up his hands. "I'm sorry."

Clutching her wrist to her stomach, her blue-gray eyes widened, her lower lip quivering.

"At least let me wrap your wrist?" he said.

She glared.

"The longer we wait, the more it will swell. I'll wrap it, then ice it to reduce the inflammation. It might hurt less once it's iced."

She didn't shake her head, so he thought she might be open to the idea. He pulled an elastic bandage out of his first-aid kit and extended his hand. "May I?"

She tentatively placed her wrist in his palm. It didn't look broken, but they wouldn't know for sure until she had it X-rayed.

"Did this happen when you fell in the creek?" he asked.

She nodded affirmative.

"It's probably a sprain." He slid his palm out from under her wrist. "I need you to hold this steady between your thumb and forefinger," he said, placing the bandage just right.

He wrapped the bandage down to her wrist and back up between her thumb and forefinger, noting how petite her fingers were.

"They'll obviously do this better at the hospital," he said, guiding the bandage to circle her wrist a few times. He secured it with a plastic clip. "I've got some pain reliever."

He dug in his backpack and found ibuprofen. When he turned to her, she'd scooted away from him again, her eyes flaring at the sight of the bottle.

"What do I need to do to convince you I'm a friend, not an enemy?"

"Give me my gun."

"I'd rather not."

She clenched her jaw.

"You're dehydrated and not thinking clearly," he explained. "The gun could go off by accident."

She pulled her knees to her chest, her hands trembling.

He grabbed an extra blanket off the foot of the bed and shook it open. He started to drape it across her shoulders, but noticed she'd gone white. He hesitated. Yet he had to get her warm somehow.

Gently draping the blanket around her, he pulled it closed in front.

"Hold it together," he said, as softly as possible.

She reached up with her right hand and their fingers touched.

She burst into a more violent round of shivers.

It tore Will apart that she was having this kind of reaction to him. Maybe it was a physical reaction to near hypothermia.

"We need to warm you up. Let me try something." He rubbed her arms through the thick blanket.

He thought he was being gentle, but after a minute she pinched her eyes shut as if suffering severe pain. He snapped his hands from her body and stood abruptly.

"You can't get warm with those wet jeans soaking

your skin. You can take them off, and wrap this around your waist." He pulled his spare blanket out of his pack and laid it on the bed. "And ice the wrist. I'll go try to get the phone working."

He shifted his backpack onto his shoulders and turned to leave.

"Wait," she said.

He hesitated, hopeful.

"My gun?"

His heart sank. He pulled the weapon out of his jacket pocket and slid it onto the kitchen table.

"I'll be outside if you need me." Will shut the door and strode away from the cabin, kicking himself for his last remark. Of course she wouldn't need him. She thought Will the enemy, a man out to kill her.

"She's dehydrated," he muttered. "And confused."

Which made him a complete idiot for leaving her alone with the gun. Although he'd removed the clip, there was still one bullet in the chamber.

Talk about not thinking straight—he'd been thrown off-kilter since he'd found her. What else would explain his behavior? She'd practically broken his nose, yet he still wanted to help her. She'd tied him to a tree, and he'd cut his own skin to free himself so he could save her life.

He glanced at his wrist. He should have bandaged it while he was in the cabin, but had completely forgotten about his own wounds, and he'd left the first-aid kit behind. The cuts weren't that bad. A good thing since the woman would probably lock him out of the cabin.

The woman. He still didn't know her name.

He took the phone out of his pocket and removed the battery. Trying to power it up while wet could cause more problems, so he'd try to dry it out. He sat on a rock and dug into his pack for the small can of compressed air. His friends often teased him about the random things he carried in his pack, but after Marissa had dropped his phone into the town's water fountain, he knew anything could happen where his girls were concerned, and he had to be ready.

Glancing at the cabin, he realized he hadn't been ready for today's events. He hadn't been prepared to stumble upon a wounded, vulnerable woman in the mountains, nor had he been prepared to have to fight so hard to help her.

He aimed the compressed air nozzle at his phone and squeezed. As it blew away the moisture, he considered that maybe he should accept the fact he would never win this woman over. Perhaps he should cut his losses and head back to town, leaving her to her own devices until SAR could make the save.

He stilled, removing his finger from the compressed air button. No, he was not his father. He did not abandon those who needed him. Wasn't that exactly why he'd gotten involved in Echo Mountain SAR?

A crack of thunder drew his attention to the sky. Clouds rolled in quickly from the south. Not good.

Although the compressed air might have helped, he knew he'd have to wait a few hours before reinserting the battery and trying it out. He pocketed the phone and battery, and headed back to the cabin.

He hoped she wouldn't shoot him on sight.

As soon as he left, Sara grabbed the gun and sneaked out of the cabin. Maybe not the smartest move, but then staying with this man, this very manipulative man, could prove much worse.

She was actually starting to believe him.

As she trudged up a trail, clutching a wool blanket around her shoulders, she realized how close she'd come to dying back there at the hands of her captor.

Dying because he was so good at his job.

He'd nearly convinced her of his sincerity as he'd gently tended her wounds and warmed her body with his strong hands. And to think, when their fingers touched, she'd felt a sense of calm she'd never felt with another man.

Dehydration. A concussion. General insanity. Check on all of the above. LaRouche and Harrington must have paid big bucks to send such a master manipulator out here to find her.

At least she still had her gun. She pulled it out of her pocket, only then realizing the clip was missing. "Great."

Her head ached, her ribs ached and now her wrist was throbbing thanks to breaking her fall when she went facedown in the creek.

The creek. Will the assassin had saved her life after pulling her from the water. He hadn't had to do that, had he?

She focused on the rugged trail ahead to avoid any missteps. There'd be no one to catch her this time.

A flash of Will's green eyes assessing her injury as he'd held her upright taunted her. A part of her wished he'd truly been the man he'd claimed to be: a single dad on a hiking trip to commune with God.

But then, Sara wasn't a fool. She knew how *that* relationship worked—people prayed and God ignored them.

She stuck her gun back into the waistband of her wet jeans. At least she had one bullet left in the chamber.

A deep roar echoed through the woods. She froze.

Another roar rattled the trees.

She snapped her gaze to the right…

And spotted a black bear headed her way.

Everything in her body shut down—her mind, her legs, even her lungs. She couldn't breathe. Frozen in place, she stared at the beast as it lumbered toward her.

Closer.

Don't stand here, idiot. Run!

Could she outrun a bear? Were you even supposed to try? She struggled to remember what she'd learned about bears, but her brain had completely shut down. One thing she did know was that she couldn't defend herself if he decided she'd make a good appetizer.

"Don't run or he'll attack," a deep male voice said from behind her.

Will.

"Wh-wh-what are you…doing here?" she whispered, unable to take her eyes off the bear.

"Listen to me carefully. Do not look into the bear's eyes. Okay?"

She nodded and redirected her attention to the ground.

"Now back away slowly. Toward the sound of my voice."

She hesitated.

"It's okay. Slow movements shouldn't spook her," he said.

Sara followed his directions and backed up, but the bear kept coming. Will stepped in front of her.

The bear roared, aggravating her headache.

"What does she want?" she said.

"Probably the same thing you want. To be left alone. Maybe she's got cubs nearby."

"I have the gun."

"That'll only make her angry. Back up slowly."

She took a step back, then another.

"That's it," he said.

As she and Will tried to distance themselves, the bear slowly followed.

"This isn't working," Sara said, panic gripping her chest.

"Easy now. Don't make eye contact. You're doing great."

Sara continued to step back. "What if she charges us?"

"We make ourselves big and threatening. I have a feeling you'll do great."

Was he teasing her? As they were both about to be torn apart by a bear?

They kept backing away and Sara was stunned when the bear hesitated.

"That's right, we're boring hikers, mama bear," he said in a hushed voice.

That smooth, sweet voice he'd used on Sara.

They backed away until they were out of sight. Will turned and gripped her arm. "Let's move."

"You think she'll follow us?"

"Doubtful, but we're safer in the cabin. What were you thinking, taking off with nothing but a blanket?"

"I was… That you were—"

"Enough. I don't want to hear any more about how I'm going to kill you. The dehydration is messing with your head." He stopped and looked deeply into her eyes.

"If I wanted you dead, I would have let Smokey eat you for dinner, right?"

True. An assassin wouldn't have risked his own life to save a mark from a bear, only to kill her later. In La-Rouche's and Harrington's minds, a dead witness was the best witness, yet Will have saved her twice.

Which meant she'd been abusing this innocent man, Good Samaritan.

Single father.

She sighed as they kept walking.

"Thanks," she said. "For the bear thing."

"You're welcome. I don't suppose that warrants me knowing your name?"

"Sara."

"Nice to meet you, Sara. I'd rather you not run off again and get eaten by wild animals on my watch."

"No promises," she half joked.

"Ah, you like pushing back for the fun of it," he teased.

But he'd nailed it. Sara was always pushing, although, not necessarily for fun.

"Why do you think someone wants to harm you?" he asked.

"I witnessed a crime."

They turned a corner and he stopped short.

"What?" She looked around him.

A man was coming out of the cabin.

"Do you recognize him?" she said.

"No." He motioned to a nearby tree. "Hide back there. I'll check it out."

"It could be dangerous."

"Or simply a hiker lost in the mountains. Kinda like you." Will smiled and nodded toward the tree. "Go on."

"Maybe you should take this." She offered him the gun.

An odd smile creased his lips. "Thanks, but you keep it."

She nodded and watched him walk away, shielding herself behind the tree. From this vantage point she could watch the scene unfold, not that she had a great escape plan. Hiking back up the trail meant crossing paths with the bear, but sticking around meant being interrogated by the real assassin, if that's who the stranger was.

If it was the man hired by LaRouche and Harrington, that meant Will, a single father of two girls, was walking into trouble.

For Sara.

"No," she whispered, and peered around the tree, wanting to go to him, to tell him not to take the chance.

A gunshot echoed across the property.

And Will dropped to the ground.

THREE

Will hit the dirt, thinking Sara had come after him and took her best shot. But that didn't make sense. She was smart enough to know it was safer where he'd left her, camouflaged by the trees.

Sara might be confused, but she wasn't foolish.

He struggled to slow the adrenaline rush flooding his body.

"Hey, sorry about that," a man's voice said.

Will eyed a man's hiking boots as he approached.

"I saw a mountain lion and wanted to scare him off."

Will stood and brushed himself off, irritated both by the hiker's decision to discharge a firearm and by his own reaction to the gunshot. It was a defense response developed from growing up in a house with a volatile, and sometimes mean, drunk.

"I'm B. J. Masters." B.J. extended his gloved hand and Will shook it.

"Will Rankin."

B.J. was in his late thirties, wearing a top-quality jacket and expensive hiking boots. He didn't seem like an amateur hiker, nor did he seem like the type to be hunting a helpless woman.

"Whoa, what happened?" B.J. motioned to Will's face.

Bruising must have formed from Sara nailing him with the gun.

"Embarrassing hiking moment," Will said. "Would rather not go into the details. I noticed you were in my cabin."

"Yeah, sorry about that," B.J. said, glancing at the ground. "I thought maybe it was abandoned, but once I went inside I saw your things and the fire going. Didn't mean to trespass."

"No problem. You on a day hike or...?"

"Yeah, I'm scouting places to hold a retreat for guys at work. I'm with Zippster Technologies out of Seattle." He handed Will a business card. "I was surprised to see a cabin in this part of the park."

"A well-kept secret. Where are you headed today?"

"Squawk Point."

"That's a nice area," Will said.

He eyed Will's cabin. "You rent the cabin through the park website?"

"I do."

"I wonder how many guys could fit in there?"

"Probably eight to ten," Will said. "After that it might get a little crowded."

"Yeah, well, probably not big enough for our team." B.J. gazed across the field, then back at the cabin. "But a nice area, for sure. Well, thanks for not calling the cops on me for breaking and entering."

"Actually, I dropped my phone in the creek. Don't suppose I could borrow yours to call my girls and let them know I'm okay?"

Will figured he'd call SAR.

"Wish I could help you out, but the battery's dead. This new-model smartphone is worthless."

"What if you run into trouble?"

"I've got a personal locator beacon. Besides, what trouble could I possibly get into out here?" He gazed longingly at the mountain range.

"You'd be surprised," Will muttered.

"Well, nice meeting you." B.J. extended his hand again.

"You, too. Have a good day."

With a nod, B.J. headed for the trail.

Will went to the side of the cabin and pretended to get wood for the fireplace. Once B.J. was out of sight, he'd retrieve Sara and bring her to the cabin. Made no sense letting B.J. know of her presence, especially if the men who were after her questioned random hikers about seeing her.

When he'd found Sara just now, he noted her pale skin and bloodshot eyes. At least she was walking around, and maybe even thinking a little more clearly than before.

That woman was tough, no doubt about it, tough and distrusting.

Will wandered to the side of the property to search for a cell signal. The sooner he could get Sara medical attention the better.

He pressed the power button, but the phone was still dead.

He gazed off into the distance. B.J. was turning the corner, about to disappear from view. Will waited until he could no longer see the hiker, then started for the trail where he'd left Sara. She was already on her way down, clutching the gun in her right hand.

"Who was that?" she said.

"A techie from Seattle scouting out retreat spots."

"And you believed him?" She scanned the area.

"Sara, it's okay." He reached out.

His mistake.

She jerked back as if his touch would sear her skin. "Get inside."

He put up his hands and prayed for patience. What more could he do to make her feel safe?

"Are you hungry?" he said, going into the cabin. "I thought I'd heat up some red beans and rice for supper."

She followed him inside and shut the door. "I'm fine."

"I didn't ask if you were fine. I asked if you were hungry."

"Stop being nice to me."

"Would you rather I be mean to you?" He pulled out supplies for dinner.

"He could have been working for Harrington and LaRouche," she said.

"Doubtful. He gave me his business card." Will offered it to her. She took it and sat on the bed, still clutching the gun.

He pulled out a pot and found a can opener in a drawer. "As soon as the phone dries off, I'll get a signal and call SAR, but it might not be until tomorrow morning."

"Go ahead. Ask me," she said.

"Ask you what?"

"What I'm doing out here, and why men from a tour group I was assisting with are after me."

"My goal is to get you back to town for medical attention. If you want to tell me what's going on, that's completely up to you."

He heard the bed creak and her soft groan drift across the cabin. She was hurting. The adrenaline rush from her encounter with the bear had probably masked her pain, and now that she considered herself relatively safe, she was feeling every ache, every pinch of pain.

"How about some pain reliever?" he asked.

"Yeah, probably a good idea."

"Check my backpack, side pocket," he said, pleased that she was accepting his help. "You'll find a small container with ibuprofen and vitamins. Probably wouldn't hurt for you to chew on a few vitamin Cs to boost your immune system."

Filling the pot with water, he went to the fireplace to warm it. He didn't look at her for fear he'd scare her again, that she'd retreat behind a wall of paranoia and fear.

"Wouldn't hurt to drink more water," he suggested. "To help the dehydration, and probably the headache."

She grabbed the water bottle off the bed and sipped.

"Why are you here?" she said.

"It's my cabin, at least for a few more days."

"Why don't you leave me alone?"

"That wouldn't be very gentlemanly of me."

"Gentlemanly, huh?" she said.

"You sound as if you've never heard the word before." He stirred their dinner.

"Or I haven't met many—" she paused "—gentlemen."

"That's unfortunate."

"It's life."

He dropped the subject, not wanting to antagonize her with a philosophical discussion on how men were supposed to be gentlemen, especially to women, that men weren't supposed to think solely of themselves.

And abandon their children to a volatile mother.

Whoa, shelve it, Will. This getaway was supposed to be about easing the resentment from his heart, not battling the scars from childhood.

Out of the corner of his eye, Will noticed Sara shivering as she popped off the top of the ibuprofen bottle.

"If you remove your wet jeans we can dry them by the fire," he offered.

"No, thanks."

"Okay."

"No offense, but I won't get very far without my pants."

"Nor will you get very far if you come down with pneumonia."

"Okay, Dad."

He sighed. "Sorry, guess I clicked into parent mode."

He refocused on the water heating in the pot. For whatever reason, she still couldn't completely trust him.

Understanding comes from walking in the other person's shoes. Reverend Charles's advice when Will struggled to understand Megan. No matter how hard he'd tried, he couldn't make sense of why she'd pushed him away.

Since he and Sara would be stuck in this one-room cabin for a while, he tried seeing the world from her point of view to better understand her reactions. She seemed clearheaded, not as delusional as before, and she feared someone was out to harm her. That was her reality. He had to respect that fact. She was also wounded and stuck in a remote cabin with a stranger who, in her eyes, was somewhat of an enigma because he considered himself a gentleman.

The fact that the thought of a good man was so foreign to Sara probably intensified her distrust.

Will realized that in order to take care of her, he needed to respect her space, and not act aggressive or domineering. He hoped she would open her mind to the possibility that he truly wanted to help.

Gripping the gun firmly in her hand, Sara found herself struggling to stay awake. Not good. Things happened when she slept.

Bad things.

"Do you have any coffee?" she asked.

"Sure."

Will went into the kitchen. She eyed the bottle of ibuprofen in her lap, then the chewable vitamin C tablets. She'd taken both, thanks to Will's suggestion.

Will. A stranger with really bad timing who'd happened upon a woman with a target on her back. A stranger who wouldn't leave her, even after she'd told him her life was in danger, that she could be putting his life in danger.

"It's instant," he said, returning to the fire to warm water.

"That's fine." She handed him the chewable vitamin bottle. "You could probably use some extra C, as well."

He popped one into his mouth. "Thanks."

She watched his jaw work and his Adam's apple slide up and down as he swallowed. He fascinated her, this gentle, strong and honorable man.

He scooped coffee into a mug and added water. "You can take up to five of those vitamin Cs if you want."

"What I want is to be home," she let slip.

"Which is where?" He handed her the mug.

She noticed blood smudging his skin. "What happened to your wrist?"

"Ah, nothing," he muttered. He dug into his pack and pulled out an antiseptic wipe. "I'll bet you're a city girl."

"That obvious, huh?"

"A good guess."

"What about you?" she said.

"I live in Echo Mountain," he said as he cleaned blood from his wrist.

"What's that like, living in a small town?"

"It's nice, actually." He opened a dehydrated packet of food, poured hot water into it, sealed the bag and set it aside. "Never thought I'd end up living in a small town, but I've been here for ten years and can't imagine living anywhere else."

"You moved here from…?"

"Denver," he said. "My wife was from here originally, but she wanted to live near the Rockies so she got a job in Denver after college. We met on a group hike and…" He glanced at the fire.

"What?" Sara asked.

Will stood and went to the kitchen. "I should find us something to eat on."

She sensed he regretted talking about his wife. Sara wondered what had happened to her but wouldn't ask.

"Tell me more about your girls," she said.

Walking back to the fire, he handed her a spoon. She used it to stir the instant coffee.

"Claire's my eldest daughter. Eight going on eighteen." He shook his head and sat in a chair beside the fire. "I'm not sure how I'm going to make it through her teenage years without getting an ulcer."

"That's a ways away. Perhaps you'll remarry."

The flames danced in his green eyes as he stared at the fire. "Perhaps."

"How long were you married?" she pushed, sipping her coffee.

"Ten years. Claire was six when her mother died, and little Marissa was only three."

"It's hard for kids to lose a parent."

"So I've been told," he said.

There wasn't a day that went by that Sara didn't ache for her mom and dad.

She pulled the blanket tighter around her shoulders. They spent the next few minutes in silence. Will seemed temporarily lost in a memory about his wife, and Sara beat herself up for not getting enough evidence to put LaRouche and Harrington away sooner.

Sure she'd recorded their conversation and the murder, but when she'd checked her phone earlier, she'd noticed it had been damaged in the fall. Hopefully a tech could retrieve the file.

Will opened the packet of rice and beans, dumped it onto a metal plate and handed it to her.

"What about you?" she said.

"I'll eat whatever's left over."

She hesitated before taking it.

"Go on, it's not bad," he said.

"But it's your food."

"I've got more."

She took the plate, avoiding eye contact. The more time she spent with Will, the more frustrated she became about her situation, and relying on his good nature.

Relying on anyone but herself was dangerous.

Since she hadn't eaten in nearly eighteen hours, she took the plate. "Thanks."

"Tell me more about the man who is after you," he said.

"Hired by two businessmen who killed their partner." She took a few bites of food and sighed. "I saw them toss the guy over a cliff."

"They killed their partner?" he said. "Why?"

"Who knows, money?" She didn't want to share too much with Will because it could put him in danger.

"I can see why you've been so frightened," he said. "I'm sorry if I haven't been patient enough."

Her jaw practically dropped to the floor. What was he talking about? He was apologizing after everything she'd done? Given him two black eyes and verbally abused him?

After a few minutes, she handed him the half-empty plate.

"You sure?" he said. "I can always heat up something else for myself."

"No, go ahead."

With a nod, he accepted the plate and started eating. She took a deep breath, then another, staring into the fire.

Maybe it was the flames dancing in the fireplace, or the sound of his spoon scraping against the plate. Whatever the case, she found herself relaxing, fighting to keep her eyes open.

Stay awake!

"Relax and I'll keep watch," he said, as if sensing her thoughts.

Will might think they were safe in the cabin, but

Sara knew better. Danger was almost always on the other side of a closed door.

The warmth of the fire filled the cabin and she blinked, fighting to stay alert. Exhaustion took hold and she felt herself drift. She snapped her eyes open again, and spotted Will lying on the floor on top of his sleeping bag. He wore a headlamp and was reading a book.

He was definitely a trusting man, but was he really so naive to think they weren't in danger? He was a civilian determined to protect her. Yet she'd brought the danger to his doorstep.

For half a second, she wanted to believe there were quality men like Will Rankin who rescued failed FBI agents, and protected them from bears and assassins.

Comforted her with a gentle hand on her shoulder. She drifted again…

Don't make a sound…

She gasped and opened her eyes. Will was no longer on the floor beside the fire. She scanned the room. She was alone.

The door opened and she aimed the gun. Will paused in the threshold. "Needed more wood." He crossed the small cabin and stacked the wood beside the fireplace.

"What time is it?" she said.

"Nineish," he said.

"I've been out for…"

"A couple of hours. Your body needed it."

Her mind ran wild, panicked about what could have happened in the past two hours. How close the assassin was to finding her.

"Give me your phone."

He handed it to her. She stood and headed for the door.

"I don't think it will work yet," he said.

"I've got to try."

"Want me to come with?"

"No." She spun around and instinctively pointed the gun at him. The look on his face was a mixture of disbelief and hurt.

"Sorry." She lowered the gun. "Just...stay here."

"Try a few hundred feet that way." He pointed, and then turned back to the fire, his shoulders hunched.

The minute she stepped out of the cabin a chill rushed down her arms. She should have brought the blanket with her, but wasn't thinking clearly. Why else would she have pointed the gun at Will?

His hurt expression shouldn't bother her. She hardly knew the man. Yet shame settled low in her gut.

Focus! It was late, but she had to call her boss if she could get a signal.

The full moon illuminated the area around the cabin. She pressed the power button and practically jogged toward a cluster of trees up ahead.

"Come on, come on." She held the button for a few seconds. The screen flashed onto the picture of the two redheaded girls.

"Yes," she said.

But still, no signal.

She waved the phone above her head, eyeing the screen, looking for bars.

The click of a gun made her freeze.

"There you are."

FOUR

A firm hand gripped a fistful of Sara's hair. "Did you think you could outrun us?" a man's deep voice said.

Us? They'd sent more than one of them after her?

"Nice to meet you, Sara. I'm Bill." He snatched the gun from the waistband of her jeans and pushed her toward the cabin.

"What do you want?"

"Why'd you run off from the group?"

"I had a family emergency."

"Sure," he said, sarcastic. "Who sent you in the first place?"

"No one. I work for Whitman Mountain Adventures."

"Convenient how you showed up out of nowhere and worked your way onto LaRouche and Harrington's camping trip."

"I needed the job."

"Yeah, yeah. We're meeting up with them tomorrow so you can explain yourself. We'll sleep here tonight."

Sleep here? In the cabin? Where Will was innocently stoking a fire?

"No," she ground out.

"Yes." He shoved her forward.

She opened the door to the cabin, but Will was gone.

"Where's your friend?" the man asked.

"What friend?"

He pushed her down in a chair. "The guy I met earlier today. Before our pleasant chat, I noticed your torn jacket on the bed. I guessed you were close. Where'd he go?"

"I have no idea."

A thumping sound echoed from the front porch.

"You sit there and be quiet while I go hunting." Her attacker bound her wrists in front.

When she winced at the pressure against her sprained wrist he smiled as if taking pleasure in hurting her. He leaned close. So close she was tempted to head-butt him. Instead, she stared straight ahead, acting like the innocent victim she claimed to be. He tied another rope around her midsection, securing her to the chair.

"Behave," he threatened.

He turned and went outside in search of Will. Why had Will gotten himself involved in this? Why had he had to help her when he'd found her unconscious body next to the lake?

Silence rang in her ears as fear took hold. The assassin would kill Will, leaving two little girls without a father. No, she couldn't let that happen. Couldn't let those girls suffer through the kind of mind-numbing grief Sara had experienced, especially since Will's girls had already lost their mom.

"Never give up," she ground out. And she wouldn't, ever, unlike the cops who'd given up on finding Dad's killer.

She dragged the chair into the kitchen, awkwardly opening drawers in search of a weapon.

She found a multipurpose fork in a drawer. It would have to do.

The door swung open with a crash.

She spun around, aiming her weapon...

At Will.

"You're here," she gasped.

He rushed across the small cabin. "Are you okay? Did he hurt you?" Will untied her and searched her face, as if fearing she'd been beaten up.

Sara shook her head. "I'm sorry, I'm so sorry."

"It's not your fault." He led her back to the fireplace, removed his backpack and dug inside. "Let me find—"

The assailant charged into the cabin, wrapping his arm around Will's throat.

"Let him go!" she cried.

Will tried to elbow the guy in the ribs but the assassin was too strong. Digging his fingers into the guy's arm, Will gasped for air. Sara darted behind the guy and wrapped her arm around his neck. The guy slammed her back against the cabin wall, sending a shudder of pain through her body. She collapsed on the floor.

He dragged Will outside and Sara stumbled after them. "Stop! Let him go!"

He threw Will to the ground and stomped on his chest, over and over again. "You like that?"

"Leave him alone!" Sara charged the assassin. He flung her aside, but not before she ripped the gun from the waistband of his jeans.

He continued beating on Will, unaware she had his weapon.

Sara scrambled to her feet. Aimed the weapon. "Stop or I'll shoot!"

The assassin was drowning in his own adrenaline rush, the rush of beating a man to death. She squeezed the trigger twice and the guy went down. She rushed to Will, who'd rolled onto his side clutching his stomach.

"Will? Will, open your eyes."

He coughed and cracked them open. "That was… the guy who was after you?"

"He was hired to find me, yes."

"So someone else will come—" he coughed a few times "—looking for you?"

"Not tonight. He was supposed to take me to meet up with them tomorrow."

"Is he dead?"

"I don't know."

Will groaned as he sat up, gripping his ribs. "We need to check. If he's not dead, we need to administer first aid."

She leaned back and stared at him, stunned by his comment. "He tried to kill you."

He pressed his fingers to the assassin's throat. A moment later he nodded at Sara. "He's gone."

Will coughed a few times as he scanned the area. "We can't leave him out here. Animals."

She didn't have a response for that, either, speechless that Will could show compassion for a man who most certainly would have beaten him to death if she hadn't shot him first.

She eyed the body.

The dead body.

She'd just killed a man.

Her fingers tightened around the grip of the gun and

her hand trembled uncontrollably, sending a wave of shivers across her body.

"Whoa, whoa, whoa," Will said, rushing to her. "Let's get you inside."

She thought she nodded, but couldn't be sure.

"Relax your fingers," he said, trying to take the gun away.

Staring at her hand, she struggled to follow his order but couldn't seem to let go.

"Sara, look at me."

She took a quick breath, then another. With a gentle hand, he tipped her chin to focus on his green eyes. Green like the forest after a heavy rain.

"That's it," he said. "Everything's okay. You can let go now."

But she didn't feel okay. Her hands grew ice cold and thoughts raced across her mind in a random flurry: her boss's disappointed frown, her cousin Pepper's acceptance into med school, the look on her father's face when he savored a piece of coconut cream pie.

A long time ago. Before…before…

Her legs felt as if they were melting into the soft earth.

She gasped for air…

And was floating, her eyes fixed on the moon above before she drifted into the cabin.

It was warm inside. It smelled like burning wood, not death. She was placed on the bed in front of the fire, but she didn't lie down because she didn't want to sleep, to dream, to be held captive by the nightmares.

"Keep the blanket around your shoulders," Will said.

It was then that she realized he'd carried her inside.

He pulled the blanket snugly around her, and poked at the fire. It flared back to life.

He kneeled in front of her. "You're probably going into shock, but you'll be fine."

Those green eyes, brimming with promise and sincerity, made her believe that things would actually be okay.

It only lasted for a second.

Because in Sara's life, things were never okay.

"I'll be right back." Will squeezed her shoulder and left.

That was when the terror of her life came crashing down on her.

If she were a religious person, she'd go as far as to say she'd sinned in the worst possible way.

She'd killed a man.

She'd become like the monsters she'd sworn to destroy.

Like the monster that killed her father.

Will clicked into overdrive. He tossed logs out of the wood container, rolled the body onto a tarp and dragged him across the property.

A part of him was shocked, both by the murder of a stranger, and by his own reaction. He found himself more worried about Sara than the ramifications of this man's death.

It should be justified in the eyes of the law, since she'd shot him to save Will's life. The guy would have surely beaten Will to death, leaving his children parentless. Will wasn't sure Sara had had another option. The man was about brutality and death, and that was how his life had ended.

But taking another man's life was a sin, so after Will placed the body and weapon into the wood container, he kneeled beside it and prayed. "Father, please forgive us. In our efforts to live, we took another man's life."

Guilt clenched his heart. He still couldn't believe what had happened. But he couldn't dwell on it, not while Sara was going into shock. He needed to tend to her.

As he went back to the cabin, he noticed the man's blood on his gloves. He took them off and dropped them outside the door. The sight of blood might upset her further. He stepped inside the cabin.

Sara was not on the bed where he'd left her. He snapped his head around. "Sara?" His heart slammed against his chest. Had she left again? Was she wandering aimlessly in the mountains in a state of shock?

"Sara!"

The echo of his own voice rang in his ears. He turned, about to race out into the dark night.

Then he heard a squeak. Hesitating, he waited to see if he'd imagined it. Another squeak drifted across the room. He slowly turned back. The sound was coming from under the bed.

Will went to the bed and checked beneath it. Sara's terrified blue eyes stared back at him.

"He won't see me in here," she said in a childlike whisper.

"No, he won't. That's a good hiding place." He stretched out on his back and extended his hand. She looked at it. "Your hands must be very cold," he said.

She nodded. "Like ice-cycles."

"My hand is warm. May I warm the chill from your fingers?"

Her eyes darted nervously beyond him. "What if he comes back?"

"He won't. He's…" Will hesitated. Reminding her she'd killed a man would not help her snap out of shock. "He's gone."

"Are you sure?"

"One hundred and ten percent." The number he used with his girls.

She eyed Will's hand. He motioned with his fingers to encourage her to come out.

"I'm only safe if I stay hidden," she whispered. "He won't see me in here."

That was the second time she used the phrase *in here*. Where did she think she was? Will suspected she might be drifting in and out of reality, the present reality mixed with a past trauma, perhaps? At any rate, he needed to keep an eye on her condition by making sure she was warm and comfortable. If she felt most comfortable under the bed, then that was where she'd stay.

"Are you warm enough?" he asked.

She shrugged.

"How about another blanket?" He snatched one off a chair and placed it on the floor.

Her trembling fingers reached out and pulled the blanket beneath the bed. "Thanks."

"Is there anything else I can do for you?" he said.

"No, thank you."

He positioned himself in front of the fire. A few minutes of silence passed as he stared into the flames. The adrenaline rush had certainly worn off, because he was feeling the aches and pains from the beating he'd survived.

Survived because of Sara. She'd saved him from an ugly, painful death.

As energy drained from his body, he struggled to stay alert. Will needed to protect Sara, take care of her.

He glanced left. Her hand was sticking out from beneath the bed. Was she trying to make a connection with him? He positioned himself on the floor and peered under the bed. She'd changed positions and was lying on her side, bundled up in the blankets.

Bending his elbow, he brushed his hand against her petite fingers. She curled her chilled fingers around his.

"Wow, you are warm," she said.

"Yeah," he said, barely able to speak. This connection, the fact that touching Will comforted her, filled his chest with pride.

"Do you have a fever?" she said.

"Nah. The warm body temperature is a family thing. My girls run hot, too."

"Your girls." She closed her eyes and started to pull away.

Will clung to her hand. "No, don't. I… I need the connection."

She opened her eyes. "You do?"

"Yes."

"But I've been horrible to you. Accusing you of being an assassin, tying you up." Her eyes widened. "Oh, my God, that's why your wrists were bleeding. You had to cut yourself free."

She snatched her hand from his and rolled away.

Well, good news was she'd returned to reality and was no longer caught up in some trauma from her past. The bad news was she blamed herself for whatever pain Will had suffered.

He went to the other side of the bed. The fire didn't light this part of the room so he couldn't see her face, but he still tried to connect with her, there, in the dark.

"It's not your fault," he said. "You were terrified and confused, and most likely suffering from dehydration."

"I gave you a bloody nose."

"I startled you."

"You were trying to help me." She sighed. "I'm so ashamed."

"Why, because you were protecting yourself from men who wanted to harm you? You should be proud. You escaped. You survived."

"No, they were right. I don't belong out here."

"Where, in the mountains?"

She didn't answer him.

"Sara?"

She rolled over again and he went to the other side of the bed. He bit back a groan against the pain of bruised ribs as he stretched out on the floor next to her.

"Could you do me a favor and stay in one position so I don't have to get up and down again?" he teased.

"I'm sorry."

"It's not that bad. But the ribs are a little sore."

"I meant, I'm sorry for everything that's happened."

"Sara, it's not your fault."

"Yes, it really is."

Silence stretched between them, punctuated by the sound of the crackling fire. Will sensed there was more behind her words, but he wasn't going to challenge her. He tried another strategy.

"Thank you," he said.

"For what?"

"For saving my life out there."

"You saved mine first." She extended her hand again and he grasped it. Unfortunately it was still ice cold.

"Do you want to sit by the fire to warm up?" he offered.

"Maybe later."

He sensed she was still frightened and probably felt vulnerable. But the more he knew about her situation, the better he could help her.

"Are you up to talking about what's going on?" he asked.

"Sure."

"Men are after you because you witnessed a murder?"

"Yes. They want to know what I saw, and what I heard."

"Did you hear anything?"

"Yes."

He waited.

"I shouldn't involve you further," she said.

"How can I help you if I don't know what's going on?"

"I would never forgive myself if you, or your girls, were threatened because of your association with me," she said.

She was a strong, determined woman, and an honorable one, as well. He couldn't fault her for that.

She yawned and pulled the blanket tight around her shoulder. She hadn't coughed in the past few hours, so he felt hopeful she wouldn't come down with pneumonia.

"Perhaps we should sleep," he suggested. "To be fresh for tomorrow. We'll need to hike a bit to find a cell signal."

"Okay, sleep sounds…good." She yawned again.

Although he knew sleep would help him function tomorrow, he doubted he could relax enough to drift off. He decided to brainstorm the necessary steps to get them safely back to town.

As options whirled in his brain, exhaustion took hold, making his mind wander to other things like his girls, his latest work assignment, Megan's death and the gray cloud of grief that hung over his house for so many months afterward. Could he have done something differently to help his girls adjust? No, ruminating about the past wouldn't help him raise his girls with love and compassion.

Sara squeaked and squeezed his hand. She must have fallen asleep. Will focused on the feel of her cool skin clinging to him, and decided he'd been given another chance to help someone.

And he wasn't going to blow it this time.

When Sara awoke, it took her a minute to figure out where she was, and whose hand she clung to.

Will.

Embarrassed, she considered pulling abruptly away, but didn't. She wanted another moment of peace, and it felt so comforting to be holding on to him.

He slept on his back, breathing slow and steady. She envied him for such a peaceful sleep. Since childhood she'd struggled with nightmares that often left her feeling exhausted in the morning.

With a sigh, he blinked open his eyes as if he knew she was watching him. He turned his head toward her.

"Good morning," he said, his voice hoarse.

"Good morning."

"Did you sleep okay?"

It was then that she realized she hadn't been plagued by nightmares. "Yeah, actually, I did."

"Good." He eyed his watch. "It's eight. We must have needed the sleep." He stood and offered his hand.

"I'm good," she said.

"Want me to make coffee?"

"That would be great." Sara climbed out from beneath the bed and stretched. "Uhh," she moaned. Her body ached from her fingertips to her toes.

"Hey, easy there." He went to her, touching her arm to help her sit in the chair.

"I'm okay, just sore." She looked up into his eyes. "Coffee will make it better."

"You got it."

A sudden pounding on the door made her gasp.

FIVE

"Where's the gun?" Sara said, anxiety rolling through her stomach.

"Outside in the wood container."

The pounding continued.

Will grabbed a log from the woodpile by the fireplace and motioned for Sara to get behind him. But she was no weakling, and no matter what injuries she'd sustained, she wasn't going to let Will fight this battle for her. He'd done enough.

Ignoring the pain of her injured wrist, she also grabbed a log and got on the other side of the door. If someone broke it down, he was going to get an unpleasant welcome.

The muffled sound of men talking on the other side of the door echoed through the thick wood. There were more than one of them? Not good. How had they found the isolated cabin? Then again, Bill had found it easily enough.

Another knock made her squeeze the wood so tight a sliver edged its way into her forefinger.

"Will? Will, you in there?" a male voice called.

"Nate?" Will dropped the log and reached out for the door.

Sara darted in front of him.

"Nate's a friend of mine, a cop," Will said. "It's okay."

She didn't step out of his way. She trusted Will but didn't trust the situation. It was too much of a coincidence that Will's friend happened to be hiking nearby.

"Sara, it's okay," Will said, touching her shoulder. "Trust me."

Maybe it was his gentle tone, or the sincerity of his rich green eyes that eased her worry. With a nod, she stepped aside, but didn't drop the log.

Will opened the door and shook his friend's hand. "Man, am I glad to see you."

Nate was tall, like Will, with broad shoulders and black hair. He wore a heavy jacket and gloves. An older gentleman with gray hair stood beside Nate.

"Hey, Harvey," Will greeted. "What are you guys doing up here?"

"Got a SAR call," Nate said. "We knew you were up here and figured you might be bored so we decided to swing by and pick you up." Nate studied Sara with a raised eyebrow. "Obviously, not bored."

The older man snickered.

"Right, sorry," Will said. "Nate, Harvey, this is Sara. Sara, Nate's a detective with Echo Mountain PD."

Sara placed the log on the floor and shook hands with the men. "Nice to meet you."

Nate redirected his attention to Will. "I didn't know you were dating anyone."

"Dating? Wait, no, not dating," Will said.

She thought he blushed, but couldn't be sure.

"We met when…" Will glanced at her.

"Will saved my life," she explained to Nate. "I witnessed a murder, and I'm on the run from men who are out to kill me because of what I saw."

Nate narrowed his eyes at her. "Direct, aren't you?"

"We've had a long night," Will said. "A guy tried to kill me and Sara shot him. The body's in the wood container."

"Wait, you killed a man?" Nate said.

"I had no choice," Sara answered.

"We've gotta get her to the hospital," Will redirected. "She's got an injured wrist, possible head trauma and who knows what else. We need to move fast before they send someone else after her."

"Can you hike?" Nate asked her.

"Hiking's not good for her concussion," Will said.

"Let her speak." Nate studied Sara.

"Not far, and not very fast, unfortunately," she admitted.

"I'll stay with you two for protection and call dispatch to send another team with a litter. Shouldn't take more than an hour since they're already on their way. Harvey, go ahead and help with this morning's rescue."

"You got it. It was nice to meet you, ma'am," Harvey said.

"You, too."

Sara instantly liked Harvey. He reminded her of what her father might have been like had he lived.

She went back into the cabin and sat at the kitchen table. Why did she have to think about Dad today? She didn't need that guilt and sadness dragging her down while trying to puzzle her way out of this dangerous situation.

"Sara?" Will said.

She absently looked at him.

He studied her with a concerned expression. "You okay?"

How could he possibly know that she'd gone to that dark place again?

"Yes, I just want to get out of the mountains and go home."

Will sat beside her, and Nate leaned against the kitchen counter. "And where is home?"

She sensed him clicking into cop mode and she could understand why. If someone was out to get Sara, innocent civilians could be at risk.

"Seattle, but I'd taken a temporary job with Whitman Mountain Adventures out of Spokane Valley," she said. "They needed extra help with groups they were taking up into the mountains."

"So you're a tour guide?"

"A cook, mostly." It had been a good cover considering she'd cooked for her dad and brother after her mom had died. She felt it wise to maintain her cover for now.

"How long have you been with Whitman Mountain Adventures?"

"Nate," Will interrupted. "Can't you do this later? She's been through a lot."

"So you said," Nate studied her. "You shot a man."

"Because he was beating me to death," Will interjected. He yanked his shirt up to expose his bruised torso.

Sara had to look away, but noticed Nate's expression harden.

"Give it a rest," Will said. "I'll go get water to make coffee." He grabbed a metal bucket and headed for the door. Will hesitated and turned to Sara. "You'll be okay?"

"Sure."

Will shot one more cautionary nod at Nate, then left.

"You cold?" Nate said, wandering to the fireplace.

"A bit."

Nate stacked some wood in the fireplace and shoved kindling beneath it. It was awfully quiet all of a sudden, and Sara realized she missed Will's grounding presence.

Whoa, not good. She'd have to separate from him completely once they made it back to town because somehow she'd grown dependent on him.

"Ya know, Will's had a tough couple of years," Nate said, his back to her as he started the fire.

"He told me."

Nate snapped around. "What did he tell you?"

"That his wife died, that he has two little girls."

Nate refocused on the fire. "Then, you can understand why residents of Echo Mountain are protective of him."

"Yes, that would make sense."

"Very protective."

"I understand. You have nothing to worry about from me. I plan to distance myself from Will as soon as we get off this mountain."

An hour later, Will finally took a deep breath as they were headed down the trail toward town. Sara was secured to the litter carried by two SAR volunteers, while a second team handled the recovery mission of the dead body in the wood container.

It turned out they'd had an abundance of SAR volunteers for this morning's call, so they'd sent half of them to the cabin for Sara. Will, Sara and Nate hadn't waited long for a team, which was good because the tension in the cabin had been palpable.

Will wasn't sure what had transpired between Sara and Nate while he was getting water, but she didn't say much after Will's return. She stretched out on the bed and rested until the team arrived. Will asked Nate what had happened, but instead of answering, Nate fired off questions, asking Will what he really knew about this stranger. He went as far as to caution Will to keep his distance.

When they arrived at the hospital, SAR friends hovered around Will, worried about his condition. Surrounded by the group, he felt the love of family, even though they weren't blood relations. Then he spotted Sara, all alone, being wheeled into the ER. Will started to follow her but Breanna McBride, a member of the SAR K9 unit, blocked him.

"What happened to your face?" She eyed his bruises. "I thought you were on vacation."

"I was, but I went hiking and found an unconscious, wounded woman."

"Then, you should have called for help, not played hero," Grace Longfellow, another K9 SAR member scolded as she approached.

"I appreciate the concern," Will said. "I'd better find a doctor and have my ribs looked at."

"Your ribs, what happened to your ribs?" Breanna asked.

"And who gave you the black eyes?" Grace pushed.

"Ladies, I need to speak with Will," Nate interrupted, walking up to them.

"You can't. He has to see the doctor," Grace said.

"I'll make sure he does." Nate led Will away from Breanna and Grace.

"Thanks for the save," Will said.

"You're welcome, but I really do need to talk to you."

Will strained to see the ER examining room door. "I'd like to know how Sara's doing."

"Take care of yourself first."

"But—"

"Get looked at by a doctor. Then if Sara's story checks out, you can see her." Nate stopped and looked at Will. "Although, if someone's after her, wouldn't it be better to keep your distance?"

"But you're going to protect her, right?"

"We need to get all the facts."

"You don't believe that she's in trouble? Who do you think that guy was that she shot and killed? He would have killed her after he finished me off."

Nate planted his hands on his hips and sighed.

"What's wrong with you?" Will said, realizing his accusatory tone bordered on rudeness.

"I guess I'm a little more cautious than most," Nate said. "I don't necessarily believe people until I have proof. A man is dead—this is serious."

"You don't have to tell me that. Wait, are you thinking about arresting Sara? You can't. It was self-defense."

"I understand that, Will, but I still have to question her as soon as possible."

"I get it, but make no mistake that she's in danger. And she's all alone."

Nate put his hand on Will's shoulder. "Once they fix her up, I'll question her, confirm her story and we'll go from there, okay?"

Will nodded, but he wasn't totally satisfied. He didn't

like the way Nate was talking about Sara, as if she was the suspect, not the victim.

"You'll see a doctor?" Nate said.

"Sure."

Nate nodded that he was going to stand there and watch to make sure. With a sigh, Will went to the registration desk, described his injuries and was told to sit in the waiting area. He found a corner spot, away from people.

He closed his eyes and pressed his fingers to the bridge of his nose, needing to think, to pray. For Sara.

Please, God, keep her safe in your loving embrace.

"Am I intruding?" Breanna said.

Will opened his eyes. "No, but I'm not very good company right now."

She sat down next to him. "You look worried."

"I am."

"About that woman? The woman you met yesterday?"

"Stupid, huh?"

She glanced sideways at him. "Hey, are you calling me stupid?"

"What? No, I—"

"I'm the one who rescued a semiconscious man from the mountains, remember?"

Will cracked a half smile. "Oh, yeah, forgot about that."

"Then, you're the only one. My family still hasn't let me live that down."

"But they like Scott. We all like Scott."

"Not at the beginning they didn't. I rescued a wounded man with amnesia, who couldn't remember why men were shooting at him, and he had an unregistered gun in his hotel room. They thought I'd lost my mind."

"I have a feeling Nate shares that same opinion about me."

"Well, he didn't find her, did he? He didn't look into her eyes."

"Or comfort her," Will let slip.

"Or comfort her." Breanna leaned toward him. "Don't let anyone make you feel ashamed about that, okay?"

He nodded.

"William Rankin?" a nurse called.

"That's me." Will stood and nodded at his friend. "Thanks, Bree."

"Anytime."

The headache was the worst part of her physical injuries. Sara could tolerate pain from the sprained wrist and various aches whenever she moved, but the headache was nearly paralyzing.

Detective Nate Walsh's questions didn't help matters. His voice was starting to wear on her. She'd learned he'd been promoted to detective just last year, so he was probably trying to make a good impression on his superiors.

He was only doing his job by conducting his interview as soon as possible, but right now she was desperate to turn off the lights and sleep.

"So, Miss Long, you witnessed two men from your tour group, Mr. LaRouche and Mr. Harrington, throw a third man, Mr. Price, off the mountain. Why would they do that?"

"I don't know." It was the best she could come up

with considering she wasn't ready to expose herself as an FBI agent, make that a rogue FBI agent on leave, which complicated things even more.

"You must have overheard something…"

Oh, she had. She'd heard LaRouche and Harrington try to convince David Price to get on board with their plan.

A criminal plan to distribute the dangerous drug Abreivtas into the United States.

"Sara?" the detective pushed.

"I'm sorry, what was the question?"

"What did you hear before they supposedly pushed Mr. Price over the edge?"

Supposedly. Right. The detective didn't believe her.

"They were arguing about a business decision, I think. David said he was done and started to walk away. Mr. LaRouche grabbed him and…" She hesitated. "Hurled him over the edge."

"And Mr. Harrington did nothing?"

"No, sir. I think he might have been in shock."

"Then what?"

"They heard me and turned around…"

The memory shot adrenaline through her body as she recalled the predatory look on LaRouche's face.

"Did Mr. LaRouche say anything?" the detective asked.

"No, sir. But he looked—" she hesitated "—furious. So I ran."

"Is it possible they got into an argument and the fall was an accident?"

She eyed the detective. Was he on LaRouche and Harrington's payroll? No, that couldn't be possible. Nate seemed like a solid guy and he was Will's friend, which went a long way in her book.

Will. A man you barely know. Maybe she didn't know him all that well, but she trusted him. Will was what her father used to call "good people."

"Ma'am?" Nate said. "Could the fall have been an accident?"

"No, I don't think so." She studied her fingers interlaced in her lap.

"Okay, so you took off and left your gear behind?"

"Yes, sir."

"Did they chase you?"

"Yes. I tried to escape down the side of the mountain and fell. Will found me the next day."

"And the man who attacked you and Will? Did you know him?"

"No, sir."

"Then, how did you know he was an enemy?"

"The way he yanked on my hair and threatened me."

"What did he say specifically?"

"He said, did I really think I could outrun them, and that he was ordered to bring me to a meeting the next day so I could explain myself."

"And then?"

"He tied me up and went to find Will. They fought— the man was kicking Will to death, so I shot him." She eyed the detective. "Wouldn't you have done the same?"

Someone tapped at the hospital room door.

"Hey, Sara," Will said, joining them.

He went to the opposite side of the bed and gently placed his hand over hers. Although she sensed the gesture might be inappropriate in Nate's eyes, the contact instantly calmed her.

"How are you feeling?" Will asked, ignoring Nate, and searching her eyes.

"I'm okay. My head hurts, though."

"Want to buzz the nurse for a pain reliever?"

"No, I've already taken something. It should kick in soon."

Nate cleared his throat and raised an eyebrow at Will's hand, gently covering Sara's. She started to pull away, but Will wouldn't let her go. It wasn't a forceful grip; it was a comforting one.

Will looked at Nate. "I think she needs to rest."

"Is that right, Dr. Rankin?"

"She's not going anywhere. Can't you wait until she's feeling better to finish your interview?"

Nate directed his attention to Sara. "We're pretty much done, although I'd prefer you stay in town until we wrap this up."

"Of course," she said.

Nate directed his attention to Will. "I'll need to take your official statement, as well."

"I can swing by the station this afternoon."

"No, now. You can start with how you got the black eyes," Nate said.

"That was my fault," Sara said.

"A misunderstanding," Will offered.

"*She* gave you the black eyes?" Nate said.

"It was an accident," Will defended.

Nate raised an eyebrow.

"When I found Sara, she was unconscious," Will explained. "She regained consciousness and she thought I was one of the guys trying to hurt her. In an effort to defend herself, she nailed me with her weapon."

Sara didn't miss Nate's speculative frown.

"Continue," Nate said.

"I took her back to the cabin to tend to her injuries."

She appreciated that he didn't describe how horrible she'd been to him, verbally abusive and threatening, making snide remarks when all he wanted to do was help her.

"Last night she went outside to find a cell signal and I went to get more wood. I saw a man approach Sara from behind and force her into the cabin at gunpoint. I recognized him as a man I'd met earlier in the day. He seemed so innocuous. I've got bad instincts, I guess."

"Sociopaths can be charmers," Sara muttered, realizing the drugs might be loosening her lips a little too much.

"You saw him take Sara into the cabin. Then what?" Nate prompted.

"I tried luring him outside."

"Even though he had a gun and you didn't," Nate said disapprovingly.

Will seemed to ignore the tone of Nate's voice and continued, "He came outside, I knocked him out with a piece of wood and went to check on Sara," Will said. "I guess I didn't hit him hard enough because he came after me in the cabin, dragged me outside and kicked me until I nearly passed out. I heard two shots and he stopped kicking."

"As I said before in my statement, I shot him because I feared for Will's life, and my own," Sara added.

"You shot him with *your* gun?"

"No, the attacker's gun. I grabbed it when he was beating up Will and I was trying to pull him off."

"You shot him in self-defense?" Nate asked Sara.

"Yes."

"Then I put the body in the wood bin to keep it away from animals," Will said, directing the detective's attention away from Sara.

"Why didn't you call for help?" Nate asked Will.

"I couldn't get a signal at the cabin, and I didn't want to leave Sara alone in search of one. She was exhibiting symptoms of shock. I'd hoped she'd be better by morning, at which time we'd hike a short distance to find a signal. Then you showed up."

"We'll have the deceased fingerprinted, which might give us some answers. That is, if he's even in the system."

"Oh, he will be," Sara said, her cop instinct stating the obvious.

"You sound pretty sure," Nate said. "Had you ever met him before?"

"No, sir, but I know his type."

"What type is that?"

Nate and Will looked at her, expectant. Oh, boy. She'd better come up with a good answer.

"Bullies," she said. "They're usually not one-time offenders, are they, detective?"

He hesitated, as if puzzling over her answer. "No, they're not."

Sara closed her eyes, hoping the detective would take the hint and leave. She needed time alone, without doctors and medical staff poking at her, and without the local police's pointed questions.

"Sara, have you ever shot a man before?" Nate asked.

She snapped her eyes open. "Of course not."

It was the truth. In her tenure with the FBI, she'd never found herself in a situation where she had to shoot and kill someone.

Until last night.

In order to save Will's life.

He was only in danger because of you.

"If you don't mind, I could really use some sleep." She rolled onto her side away from Nate and slipped her fingers out from under Will's hand. The guilt of putting him in harm's way weighed heavy on her heart.

"Will, you and I can finish your interview in the lounge."

"Okay," Will said. "Sara, I'll be close if you need me."

She had to distance herself from this man before he was even more seriously hurt because of Sara and her quest to nail LaRouche and Harrington. More seriously hurt? He was almost killed last night. The bruising below his eyes and swollen nose made her stomach burn with regret.

"No, you can leave," she said.

"Excuse me?"

"Just go, Will. You've done your bit."

"My bit?"

She mustered as much false bitterness as possible in order to drive him away. "Yeah, saving the damsel in distress. You're relieved of your duties."

She closed her eyes, hypersensitive to the sounds in the room: the clicking of the blood pressure machine, a car horn echoing through the window...

Will's deep sigh as he hovered beside her bed.

She'd hurt him with her acerbic comment, but it was for his own good. So why did she feel like such a jerk about the silence that stretched between them?

"Come on," Nate said.

She felt Will brush his hand across her arm—a good-bye touch.

A ball of emotion rose in her throat. This shouldn't hurt; she shouldn't feel anything for a man she'd only met yesterday.

Her emotional pain was a side effect of her injuries, that was all, the trauma of the past twenty-four hours. It had nothing to do with Will and his gentle nature, or his caring green eyes. She sighed, and drifted to sleep.

Sara awakened with a start.

Where was she? She sat up in bed and searched her surroundings. Right, she was in the hospital. It was dark outside; dark in her room. Someone had turned off the lights, probably to help her sleep.

"You're okay," she whispered.

But then why was her heart pounding against her chest?

She flopped back on the bed, remembering the nightmare that had awakened her—running down the middle of a deserted street, LaRouche and Harrington chasing her in a black limousine. Even as she slept, the corrupt businessmen were terrorizing her.

The intensity of her nightmare drove home how much danger she was in—even here, in a hospital. She was a target and she would continue to be a target until she put them behind bars.

Holding onto her IV pole, she went to the closet and found her now dry jeans. Although she favored her sprained wrist, she dressed herself, remembering how Will had offered to dry her jeans by the fire.

How he'd taken care of her.

Talk about a weak moment. After the shooting, she'd

completely fallen apart, sucked into the black emotional hole of her past, remembering the sound of her father fighting for his life downstairs.

The sound of the gunshot that had taken his life.

If Will hadn't been there last night to talk her down from her traumatic shock, to offer her a blanket and a warm hand to hold on to, she would have spun herself into a blinding panic attack.

"You can't keep relying on him," she reminded herself. "You've got to do this on your own."

On her own. By herself. That had been Sara's mantra since childhood, even after her aunt and uncle had taken her into their home.

Today was no different. She had to protect herself, call in and update SSA Bonner about what had happened. He was going to be furious that she'd pursued this case against his orders, and she might even lose her job.

She hesitated and gripped the IV pole. Maybe she should wait to contact him until after she retrieved the recorded argument between the men—proof that there was truth to her claims about LHP, Inc.

Unless she had firm evidence in the death of David Price, it would be her word against LaRouche's and Harrington's. The word of two slick businessmen against Sara's, a rogue FBI agent with a chip on her shoulder who couldn't follow orders and took extreme measures to prove her point.

Maybe she should have dropped this case months ago and kept her mouth shut instead of hounding Bonner. But she couldn't watch the corporate hacks at LHP, Inc., get away with introducing a dangerous drug into the United States and promoting it as a safe and effective sleep aid. She'd uncovered solid evidence, buried reports from the pharmaceutical testing, even if Bonner thought them innocuous. She knew what Abreivtas could really do.

It could kill. She had to stop them.

She went into the bathroom and splashed water on her face. It wouldn't look good to local authorities if she left the hospital, but staying here made her a target. Detective Walsh didn't seem to be taking her story seriously, and even if he did, the local cops couldn't protect her from the likes of LaRouche's and Harrington's hired goons.

Drying her face with a paper towel, the image of Will being kicked, over and over again, flashed across her thoughts. She hated that she'd been responsible for such a violent act on a gentle man.

A widower and single parent. Hadn't he suffered enough?

Slipping into her jacket, she felt for her wallet and phone. They were both tucked into her inside zippered pocket. Good. She took a deep breath and pulled the IV out of her hand.

She peeked around the corner. All clear. She was far enough away from the nurse's station that they wouldn't see her leave, and even if they did, they couldn't stop her, right?

She hurried to the elevator, but decided it was too risky. She didn't want to take the chance Nate Walsh had come back with more questions or, more likely, Will had returned to check on her.

She ducked into the stairwell and headed down. Gripping the handrail, she took her time. No need to rush and pass out before she got safely away.

Her head ached from the emotional tension and physical movement. She focused on taking slow and steady breaths.

A door opened and clicked shut from a floor above.

She hesitated.

"Sa-ra?" a man called in a singsong voice.

Her blood ran cold.

"I need to talk to you," he said.

She stumbled down the last few steps, tripping and slamming into the door to the first level. Whipping it open, she shuffled away from the stairwell. Eyes downcast, she wandered through the ER waiting area toward the exit.

And spotted a tall, broad-shouldered man coming into the hospital and heading toward her.

Don't be paranoid.

In his midthirties, he wore jeans, a fatigue jacket and military-grade boots.

Their eyes locked.

"Sara?" he said, reaching into his jacket.

She spun around and took off.

SIX

Will wasn't sure why he'd returned to the hospital. Sara had been pretty clear that she didn't want him around.

But something felt off. Her voice said one thing, but he read something else in her eyes. It was almost as if she thought sending him away was the right thing to do, yet she desperately wanted him to stay.

"Or you're losing it," he muttered as he parked the car.

At any rate, he'd decided to check on her. Maybe she'd be asleep, which would be the best scenario. He needed to see her and know she was safe, then he could leave.

Yeah, who was he kidding?

"What are you doing here?" Nate said from a few cars away. Apparently he'd had a similar thought, only a different motivation.

"Don't bust my chops," Will said. "I want to make sure she's okay."

"She's fine."

"I'd like to see for myself." Will continued toward the hospital entrance.

"Do I have to get a restraining order against you?"

Will snapped his attention to Nate. The cop's wry smile indicated he was teasing.

"Sara and I have been through a lot," Will said. "And last night…" He shook his head.

"Last night, what?" Nate challenged.

"I know it's your job to be suspicious, especially because she shot a man, but trust me, it was not something she enjoyed doing. She was traumatized afterward."

"She's not your responsibility."

"I didn't say she was."

"But you're coming here at—" Nate checked his watch "—nine fifteen to check on her?"

They entered the hospital and went to the elevators. "I've got nothing better to do. The girls are spending another night with their grandparents."

"Uh-huh."

"Hey, don't give me a hard time for being a good guy."

"Good guys finish last, remember?"

"I didn't know it was a race," Will countered.

"Just…be careful."

Will nodded his appreciation for his friend's concern. A lot of folks in town seemed concerned about Will since Megan had died. Did they all think him that fragile? Or incapable of making good choices?

As Nate and Will stepped out of the elevator onto Sara's floor, a frantic-looking officer named Spike Duggins rushed up to them.

"I went to grab a coffee," Spike said. "She was sound asleep. The nurse was going to keep an eye out."

A chill arced across Will's shoulders. "Sara's gone?"

"I notified security," Spike said, directing his answer to Nate.

"How long?" Nate said.

"I don't know, five, ten minutes?"

"You had her under surveillance?" Will asked Nate.

"Spike, you start at the north end," Nate said, ignoring Will's question.

"Spike, this is security, over," a voice on Spike's radio interrupted. "I think I spotted her in the lobby."

Nate grabbed Spike's radio. "Keep her there."

"She's already gone. I must have scared her off."

"Which direction?" Nate asked.

"Toward the cafeteria," the security officer said.

"Head to the south exit," Nate ordered him. "Spike will go north and I'll check out the cafeteria."

"Roger that," the security officer responded.

"What about—"

"You stay here in case she returns," Nate ordered Will.

The two men jogged off and disappeared into the stairwell.

Will couldn't stand here and do nothing. The security guard said he'd scared her off, so what made Nate think he and Spike would have better luck?

Was she having another flashback, like the one she'd had last night? If so, she wouldn't trust a stranger, or even a cop.

But she'd trust Will.

He went into her room and checked the closet. Everything was gone. She definitely hadn't planned to come back.

He took the stairs closest to the cafeteria and headed down.

Will had to find her, had to make her feel safe so she wouldn't run away. Perhaps if Nate had told her he'd left a police officer to guard her, she wouldn't have felt so vulnerable.

But Will sensed Nate's motivation had been to keep her under surveillance, not protect her from a violent offender. Will never should have left the hospital, even after she'd asked him to.

What was the matter with him? Why did he feel such a deep need to protect this woman?

Because of the look in her eyes and the sound of her voice when she'd hidden under the bed. He'd seen that look before on his sister's face when they'd hid from their raging mother. Will had perfected the role of protector at an early age.

He got to the ground floor and headed to the cafeteria, readying himself for the lecture he'd surely get from Nate. Will entered the empty dining area as Nate stormed out of the kitchen.

"I told you to stay upstairs," he snapped.

"She's frightened and she trusts me."

"Whatever. I'm going to check the security feed." Nate continued down the hall. "Go home, Will," he called over his shoulder. "You don't belong here."

Nate disappeared around the corner. His words stung, but only for a moment. Will knew Nate's comment was born of concern for Will.

As Will scanned the cafeteria, he considered the extent of Sara's injuries. She had winced if she moved too quickly, or put pressure on her wrist by accident. A woman in that kind of pain couldn't run for long. More likely she would hide until she saw an opportunity to quietly slip away.

He wandered through the cafeteria. The tables were empty, but a few visitors were standing at the coffee station filling up, probably in anticipation of a long wait ahead of them tonight.

His gaze drifted to a cluster of office plants in the opposite corner of the cafeteria, and he remembered what she'd said last night.

He won't see me in here.

Hiding meant safety to Sara. He approached the plants, fearing he was wrong and she wouldn't be there, in which case, she might be wandering the property somewhere, completely vulnerable. He clenched his jaw, fighting back his worry.

As he got closer, he saw the reflection of a woman hugging her knees to her chest against the glass window. With a relieved sigh, he devised a plan to ease her out of hiding. He wanted this to be her idea; he wanted Sara to feel in control.

He went to the hot drink station and plopped teabags into two cups, poured hot water and gave the cashier a few singles. He carried the hot beverages across the cafeteria and sat down near the plants.

"Sara, it's Will," he said. "I thought you might still be cold." He slid a cup toward her.

She didn't take it.

"Sorry it couldn't be something better, like a scone or a muffin, but food service pretty much shuts down at this time of night. That's herbal tea. It's orange blossom," he said. "The girls like that one, and I like it because it's caffeine-free and won't keep them awake."

"You shouldn't be here."

"I came back to check on you."

"No, you really shouldn't be here. It's dangerous."

"What do you mean?"

"I heard a man behind me in the stairwell. He said my name—they sent him to get me. I ran, and another man was blocking the exit."

"I think that was actually a hospital security officer."

"No, he was wearing military-grade boots. He also knew my name and was...was..."

"It's okay. You're safe now, and I'm not leaving until you believe that."

She reached out and took the cup. At least her fingers weren't trembling like they had been last night.

"How did you know I'd be here, behind the plants?" she asked.

"It seemed like a logical spot to hide out." He finally glanced at her. She looked tired, worn down and still frightened. "Did the man threaten you?"

"He said he needed to talk to me."

"But nothing else?"

"No, why? You think I'm crazy, too?" she snapped.

"Sara." He hesitated. "I'm on your side, remember?"

She tipped her head back against the glass and sighed.

"Here's a thought—why don't you work *with* the police instead of shutting them out?" Will said. "Detective Walsh can protect you."

"Detective Walsh doesn't even believe me."

"Don't be put off by his tone. He's a big-city detective turned small-town cop. He's got an edge to his voice, sure, but you want a tough guy like that on your side, don't you?"

"What I want is to get out of here, without putting anyone else in danger."

"Let me call Nate and have him escort you back to your room."

"Where I'm a sitting duck."

"Not if he offers twenty-four-hour police protection." He wasn't about to say that he would also stay close, because he knew she'd fight him on that decision.

"Okay, I guess that's the best choice, if you can get him to believe me."

"I'll talk to Nate. If he doesn't believe you, I'll talk to the chief. I've got some pull in this town."

"Yeah, I noticed how everyone surrounded you when we first arrived at the hospital. You have a great support system."

"I am blessed. For sure." He remembered how friends from church and SAR had rallied around him after Megan's death. How they wouldn't let him wallow, brought him meals and offered to entertain the girls.

But that was two years ago. He'd mostly healed and was a strong man, and a good father, even if his in-laws didn't always think so. Sure he'd stumbled a few times along the way, but today Will felt confident in his abilities to raise his girls with love and compassion.

"Okay, let's head back to my room," Sara said.

Will stood and offered his hand.

"Can you hold my tea?" she said.

"Of course." He'd wanted to take her hand, but would not force the issue. Taking her cup, he restrained himself as he watched her stand. It was frustrating to see her struggle against the pain. He tossed his cup into the garbage can behind him, and reached for her again.

"No, I can do it," she said.

He should respect her determination, not be hurt by

it. The rejection wasn't a criticism of his abilities, but he sensed her need to rely on herself.

She straightened. "Thanks." She stepped out from behind the plants and started across the cafeteria.

Will noticed a slight waver in her step and he reached out to steady her. His hand gripped her upper arm, and she snapped her gaze to meet his.

"It's okay to accept help," he said. "I won't expect anything in return, promise." He smiled, hoping to lighten the moment.

"No, you wouldn't, would you?" she said in a soft, almost hushed voice.

For a moment, he couldn't breathe. It was as if she saw right through him, into his wounded heart.

"We found her, sir," a man's voice said.

Sara ripped her attention from Will and paled at the sight of a man heading toward them. He was in his thirties, wearing jeans and a fatigue jacket. Will assumed it was the security guard, since he held a radio in his hand. Then Will noticed his boots—military grade.

"Are you the security officer?" Will clarified, to ease Sara's worry.

"Yes, sir, Jim Banks, hospital security. Are you taking her back to her room?"

"I am," Will said.

"Why aren't you wearing a security uniform?" Sara pointedly asked.

"I'd already changed into street clothes when I heard the call go out that you were missing, so I thought I'd help find you before I left," Jim said. "I'm sorry if I frightened you."

She nodded, but didn't look convinced.

"I'll accompany you both to her room," Jim said.

"Thanks," Will said.

Sara didn't look happy. For whatever reason, the security officer intimidated her. Will wasn't sure why. The guy seemed okay to Will, but then Will hadn't been the best judge of character or he would have figured out the friendly hiker from yesterday was really a hired thug.

They walked in silence to the elevator. As the doors opened, Nate came rushing around the corner.

"Someone was after her, here in the hospital," Will blurted out.

Nate nodded at Jim. "Thanks, I've got this."

Jim hesitated for a second, then with a nod, he said, "Have a good night."

"You, too," Will offered.

Will, Nate and Sara got into the elevator. Nate pressed the third-floor button. Sara leaned against the elevator wall, and Will shifted himself between her and Nate. It was an instinctive, protective gesture.

"When you disappear like that it makes you look as if you're hiding something," Nate said, eyeing the elevator floor numbers.

Sara didn't answer at first. Will knew if he answered for her, Nate would only criticize him and come down harder on Sara. She needed to explain her actions.

Will squeezed her hand and nodded, encouraging her to respond.

"I'm sorry. I was scared," she said. "I had a nightmare that reminded me how much danger I was in. I freaked out and took off, and some guy was stalking me."

"What did he say?" Nate said.

"That he needed to talk."

"Did you recognize him?"

"I didn't see him. I heard him."

"Where did this happen?"

"The stairs at the end of my hallway."

Nate sighed. "I'll post a uniform outside your room."

Will squeezed her hand.

"Thanks," she said.

They reached her floor. Will and Nate escorted Sara to her room, where Spike waited.

"I'm so sorry, ma'am," Spike said. "I stepped away for a minute and—"

"Officer Duggins will be relieved by Officer Pete Franklin in about half an hour," Nate said, narrowing his eyes at the young cop. "I'll also hang around for a while."

"No one's going to hurt you here," Will said, looking at Nate for confirmation. "Right?"

Nate nodded.

"Thanks." She glanced at Will as if she was going to say something. Instead, she offered a grateful smile, turned and went into her room.

Nate narrowed his eyes at Will. "I'll be here and Pete will show up soon."

"I'm still here," Spike offered.

"Don't push it," Nate warned, and then looked at Will. "You can really go now."

"I know." Will didn't move.

"But you're not going anywhere, are you?"

Will shrugged.

The next day Sara convinced doctors that her minor concussion and sprained wrist didn't warrant her staying in the hospital any longer, although once they released her she wasn't sure where she'd go. Nate had requested she stay in town until they finished their investigation of David Price's death.

There was still no word from LaRouche and Harrington. She wondered how they'd talk their way out of this one.

It didn't matter. At this moment what mattered was finding a safe place to stay, a place where her mystery stalker wouldn't torment her further.

She put on her torn jacket and left her hospital room where she found Will, camped on the floor, working on a laptop.

"Will?"

"Hey, Sara," he said, shoving his laptop into a briefcase and standing to greet her.

"What are you doing here?"

"I thought you might need a ride."

His wavy chestnut hair fell across his face, and he was wearing the same clothes he wore last night.

"You never left the hospital?" she said.

"Didn't have any place to be."

"What about your girls?"

"They're with their grandparents. I wasn't supposed to be home until the day after tomorrow anyway. I thought I'd let Nanny and Papa spoil them one more day."

"Where is—"

"Your protective detail? Officer Franklin's shift just ended and Nate left earlier this morning. He figured you'd be released today and apologized about not having the manpower to offer you protection 24/7. He was going to send an officer to drop you off wherever you needed to go, but I said I was already here. I could do it."

"Oh, he must have loved that," she said sarcastically.

"Yeah, well, I think he gave in because he knew it was a losing battle. So where can I drop you?"

"Really, that's not necessary. I can get a cab."

"What, do I smell that bad?" He sniffed his armpit teasingly.

"Stop," she said, almost smiling. "I appreciate the offer, but I think you've done enough."

"Miss Long?"

She turned and saw a police officer headed toward her.

"Yes?"

"I'm Officer Petrellis. I was sent to give you a ride."

"Officer, I'm Will Rankin." They shook hands. "Did Nate Walsh send you?"

"Yes, sir."

"Guess I lost that argument after all," Will said, frowning.

"Where can I drop you, ma'am?" Petrellis asked.

She looked reticent to tell him, so Will stepped in. "No, really, Officer, I insist."

"Detective Walsh said it's fine if you want to drive her, but I need to follow to make sure she gets safely settled." He turned to Sara. "Ma'am, are you okay if Mr. Rankin gives you a ride?"

"Of course she is." Will turned to Sara. "Aren't you?"

She could tell from the expression on Will's kind face that it was important for him to do this, to help her. After everything she'd put him through, she didn't have it in her heart to disappoint him.

"Sure, that would be fine," she said.

Will motioned Sara toward the elevator.

She put on her emotional mask, needing to embody her undercover identity—Sara Long, tour guide assistant.

"We'll start by finding you a comfortable place to stay," Will said. "Nate suggested we book you a room at Echo Mountain Resort."

"Right, so he'll know where I am."

"No, because it's a very secure facility." They stepped into the elevator. Officer Petrellis joined them, but didn't participate in the conversation.

"They've had some experience protecting people at the resort," Will continued.

"Oh, really?" she said with a raised eyebrow.

"Long story. You hungry? We could stop for something to eat first."

"Actually, I desperately need a cell phone."

He pulled his smartphone out of his pocket and offered it to her. "It's working again."

"Thanks, but I need my own."

"Ah, calling your boyfriend, huh?"

She shrugged and decided not to answer, letting him draw his own conclusions. Having a boyfriend would certainly discourage Will from continuing to help her.

They stepped out of the elevator onto the main floor.

"What type of vehicle are you driving, sir?" Officer Petrellis asked Will. "In case we get separated."

"A gray Jeep."

"Plate number? Again, in case we get separated."

Will gave the plate number and the officer wrote it down. He was being awfully accommodating, Sara mused, especially since she was under the impression Nate didn't have the manpower to spare. But then this was small-town law enforcement. They were about building relationships and protecting their community.

"We can swing by the Super Shopper and get you a

phone, some clothes and whatever else you need since you left your backpack up in the mountains," Will said.

She fingered the rip in her jacket. "That's probably a good idea. Tell me more about Echo Mountain Resort."

"It's on the outskirts of town," Will said. "I know a few people who work there, and the manager, as well. I'll give them a call to see what's available."

They went outside and headed for his Jeep.

"I feel bad that you're still involved in this, in my drama," she said.

"No worries. I want to see this through to the end."

Sara knew Will Rankin had no clue what he was signing on for.

Will called the resort. "Hi, Nia, it's Will. I have a friend who needs a room….Wait, that's *this* weekend? I completely forgot…" He shot Sara a defeated look. "Okay, I'll try something in town….I hope you're wrong about that….Sure, I'll bring the girls by." He ended the call as they approached his truck.

"Bad news?" Sara asked.

"I forgot about the resort's big festival this weekend. It's booked solid. We'll try a B and B in town. How about we get you set up with a phone, and we'll make calls while we eat lunch? Sound good?"

"Sure."

He opened the door for her and she got into his Jeep. She noticed how he was careful to make sure she was settled before closing the door. He was the true definition of a gentleman, she thought, as she watched him walk around the front of the vehicle. What other kind of man would invest himself in a stranger's dangerous situation like Sara's?

One who, no doubt, had white knight syndrome tendencies. Well, she'd accept a ride from him, and buy him lunch to thank him for everything he'd done. Then, after he dropped her off at a B and B or wherever she ended up staying, she'd offer a firm goodbye.

They picked up supplies at the Super Shopper, and Sara made her call, but didn't look happy about the outcome. Will decided not to ask too many questions. He didn't want to push her away by being nosy.

Something still felt off, as if she acted a good game, but felt utterly alone, maybe even abandoned. Will decided he would not abandon Sara, then he cautioned himself not to feel so responsible for her.

He couldn't help it.

As they stood by his Jeep, she slipped on her new blue winter jacket and smiled at her reflection in the window. The smile lit her face, and he forced himself to look away. His gaze landed on the police officer's car a few parking spots away, reminding Will that Sara was still in danger.

"Well, I kinda like it," she said.

He snapped his attention to her. "I do, too."

"Then, why'd you look away?"

"Sorry, got distracted. Is it warm?"

"Yeah." She half chuckled.

"What's so funny?"

"You're such a dad."

"Is that a bad thing?" He opened the car door and she slid onto the front seat.

"No, but be warned, at some point with your girls it's going to be about looking good, not being warm."

"Don't remind me." He shut the door and went to the driver's side of the Jeep. He got behind the wheel and said, "You ready for lunch? There's this great new spot a few minutes away. My girls love it."

"What, is the menu all candy?" Sara teased.

Will pulled out of the lot. "Actually, it's called Healthy Eats." He smiled. "Don't let the name scare you."

"You're assuming I'm a junk-food person." She shifted in her seat and winced.

"Bad, huh?" he said.

"No, I'm fine. Looking forward to a nice room with a soft bed, and no police officers questioning me."

He understood her frustration, but she had killed a man in the mountains—to save Will's life. The primary reason he would not abandon her.

"There are three B and B's in town," Will started. "Annabelle's, Cedar Inn and The White Dove. Maybe you should give one of them a call?"

"Okay."

With each call, he could tell she grew more frustrated. A few minutes later they pulled into the lot at Healthy Eats.

"Don't worry," he said. "I know Lucy, the owner at The White Dove. They keep a spare room open in case her daughter shows up in town unexpectedly. I'll talk to her."

"Thanks."

Will sensed she was starting to fade. Food would definitely help renew her energy.

A few minutes later, they were seated in a booth ordering tea, scones and sandwiches from the owner of the restaurant, Catherine, who was Nate's sister.

"Shouldn't take long," Catherine said. "You two look

as if you could use some of my healing broth. I'll bring some out, on the house."

"We really appreciate it, Catherine," Will said.

"Anything for you, Will." She winked and walked into the back.

"Someone's got a crush on you," Sara said.

"Who, Catherine? Nah, she's on the 'help Will' team."

"Help you what?"

"At first, it was to help me recover from my wife's death."

Sara reached across the table and touched the hand gripping his tea mug. "I'm so sorry, I did not mean to bring that up."

"It's okay. I've been grieving long enough. A lot of the folks in town, and especially from church, can't stop looking out for me. I'm blessed with good friends, yet sometimes…" His voice trailed off.

"Sometimes what?"

"All the attention can be suffocating. It makes me feel as if they think I'm incompetent." He didn't know why he said it, and wanted to take it back.

"You're the opposite of incompetent, Will," she offered. "Look at everything you've done for me."

"Thanks. I wasn't fishing for a compliment, honest."

She cracked a smile.

Again, he had to look away. That adorable smile of hers was enchanting. "I'll call Lucy about her daughter's room at The White Dove Inn."

"That would be great, thanks."

He pulled out his phone.

"Will? What are you doing here?"

Will looked up and spotted his in-laws crossing the restaurant toward him.

"And what happened to your eyes?" his mother-in-law, Mary, asked.

He got out of the booth to greet them. "Hiking accident," he said. Will shook hands with his father-in-law, Ed, who then went to the register to pick up their order.

"Where are the girls?" Will asked.

"Susanna Baker called and invited Claire and Marissa to join her and the twins for a movie." Mary studied Sara with judgment in her eyes.

"What movie?" Will asked. "Is it PG? Because the last PG-13 movie Marissa watched gave her nightmares."

"It's fine." Mary waved him off. "They were going to an animated film. Why are you back early? And who's this?"

He wouldn't sugarcoat it, nor would he go into great detail, either.

"Mary, this is Sara. I assisted Sara when she was injured in the mountains."

Sara offered Mary a smile. "Nice to meet you."

"Search and rescue...so that's what cut your vacation short," Mary said disapprovingly. "Are you expecting to pick up the girls tonight? Because we'd planned a trip to the children's museum tomorrow, and they were looking forward to tea at Queen Margaret tea shop."

"That's fine," Will said. "What time will you be dropping them home?"

"Between seven and seven-thirty."

"Sounds good. I'll be ready."

Mary cast one last look at Sara. "I most certainly hope so."

Ed joined them, gripping a to-go bag in his hand. "What'd I miss?"

"Will cut his trip short to save this young lady."

"Sara," she introduced herself.

"Ed, nice to meet you." He nodded at the bag. "I've worked up an appetite. Those girls never stop, do they?" He smiled at Will.

"No, they surely don't. Thanks again for watching them."

"Don't be silly," Mary said. "They're our grand-daughters. We love them. You'll be home by seven to-morrow to greet the girls?"

"Of course," Will said.

"Goodbye, then." She turned and left.

Ed shrugged at Will and nodded at Sara. "Good to meet you."

"You, too."

Will watched them leave. Only after they'd pulled out of the lot did the tightening in his chest ease.

"Are you going to sit down?" Sara asked, with a question in her eyes.

"Yeah." He slid into the booth.

"What was that about?" Sara said.

"What?"

"She seemed awfully—"

"Judgmental? Critical? Close-minded?"

"Something like that." Sara smiled again.

The tension in his shoulders uncoiled. He shrugged. "It's complicated."

Catherine approached their table with soup. Good timing. He didn't want to get into the ugly story about how his in-laws had grown resentful of Will after

Megan lost her battle with cancer, and how they questioned his abilities as a father.

"This is amazing," Sara said, spooning a second taste of soup.

They spent the next hour enjoying delicious food and natural conversation. He wasn't sure how that was possible, since he'd only known her for a day, yet he felt comfortable chatting about whatever topic drifted into their discussion.

He wondered if she also enjoyed their companionship. Then she offered to pay for his lunch and he wondered if this was her way of thanking him for saving her in the mountains, nothing more.

He called Lucy at The White Dove Inn and was able to secure Sara the room reserved for Lucy's daughter.

They finished their meal and he drove her across town to the inn, pointing out highlights of Echo Mountain, including the Christmas tree in the town square.

"We'll light it next weekend at the Town Lights Festival, not to be confused with the Echo Mountain Resort Festival," he said.

"Wow, there's a lot of celebrating going on for such a small town."

"There's a lot to celebrate this time of year," he offered.

She turned to look out the side window, as if she wasn't so sure. In that moment, he pictured himself showing her how beautiful Christmas could be: drinking hot cider in the town square amongst friends and neighbors, attending Christmas church services and singing songs praising the Lord.

But Sara seemed lost in a dark memory, one he wished he could replace with new ones.

A few minutes later he pulled up in front of The White Dove Inn and Sara's eyes rounded with appreciation. "It's lovely."

He reached for his door.

"Don't."

He turned to her.

"Your journey ends here," she said.

"I'm confused. Did I somehow offend you?"

"No, nothing like that." She hesitated. "Let's face it, Will, it's in your best interest to steer clear of me."

"How do you figure?"

"I saw the way your mother-in-law looked at me, at this—" She motioned at the space between them. "I mean, I really appreciate everything you've done."

"But?"

"I need to ask you not to seek me out anymore."

"Seek you out? You make me sound like a stalker. I thought I was helping a friend."

"We don't know each other well enough to be friends. Maybe we could have been, if the situation were different."

"This has something to do with the call you made earlier, doesn't it?"

She didn't answer, glancing at him with sadness in her eyes. "You're a good man, Will. I wish you all the best." She leaned across the seat and kissed him on the cheek.

He couldn't breathe for a second, stunned by the kiss. She quickly grabbed her bag of supplies and hopped out of the Jeep, slamming the door and hurrying up the steps to the B and B.

She hesitated as she reached the door.

Turn around. Come on, change your mind, turn around and let me help you.

She didn't. She knocked on the door and a moment later it swung open. Lucy waved at Will over Sara's shoulder. He offered a halfhearted wave and Lucy shut the door.

Will glanced through his front windshield at the neighboring houses decorated in green, red and gold lights. Sara was right, of course, yet it still stung.

At first he thought he was drawn to her because she needed him, needed someone to take care of her, which was dysfunctional on so many levels. As he sat in his Jeep after being told to keep his distance, he realized it was something else that made him want to stay close.

He had connected with this stranger on a level he hadn't experienced with another woman since Megan. How was that possible?

"You're sleep deprived," he muttered, and pulled away from the curb.

He'd better catch up on his sleep if he wanted to be fresh and energized for the girls tomorrow. As he drove away from the B and B, he spotted the unmarked police car across the street. Officer Petrellis was on the phone, and nodded at Will as he passed.

Will was grateful that Nate had changed his mind about offering Sara protection, and decided to call him using his hands-free device.

"Will," Nate answered. "Was about to call you. Turns out the man Sara shot and killed had a rap sheet for assault and battery, and attempted murder, which he skated on thanks to high-priced attorneys he couldn't afford."

"You think LaRouche and Harrington paid the bill?"

"That'd be my guess. The DA doesn't see any reason to press charges against Sara for killing him in self-defense."

"That's great news. Listen, I wanted to thank you."

"For what?"

"For putting protective surveillance on Sara."

"Yeah, Spike's been sending me text updates all day."

"Spike? You mean Officer Petrellis."

"What are you talking about? Officer Petrellis took early retirement last spring."

SEVEN

A chill shot across Will's shoulders. "Petrellis said you sent him to protect Sara."

"No, Spike offered to give her a ride from the hospital to make up for messing up last night."

"I've gotta get back to Sara." Will spun the Jeep around. "I just dropped her off at The White Dove Inn."

"I'm on my way."

"How long will it take you to get there?"

"Five, maybe ten minutes."

"Hurry."

"Will, wait for me."

"I'll see you when you get there." Will ended the call, unable to agree to wait for Nate. It wasn't in Will's DNA to sit by and do nothing while someone stalked her.

He pulled up to the inn, a safe distance behind the unmarked cruiser. Drumming his fingers against the steering wheel, he peered into Officer Petrellis's car.

His empty car.

Will gripped the steering wheel with unusual force. Five minutes—he tried talking himself into waiting five minutes for Nate to arrive. He scanned the inn, studying every window for signs of trouble, then realized he wouldn't be able to see Sara from here since her room was by the dining room.

In the back where it was dark, where an intruder could easily sneak in unnoticed.

He was driving himself crazy sitting here, waiting for something to happen.

Worrying about what could happen.

Worrying about being too late.

He whipped open his door and took off toward the house. Would Petrellis harm Sara in front of an inn full of guests? No, he wouldn't be that bold. Besides, Will doubted the cop had been hired to hurt Sara. More likely he'd been ordered to get information and report back to the men who were after her.

Will decided to bypass the front entrance and enter through the back. As he walked along the dark side of the house, he saw a shadow up ahead, lit by a floodlight.

"Hey!" he called out.

The person turned around...

It was Lucy, owner of the inn.

"Hi, Will. What are you doing back here?"

"I wanted to check on Sara."

Lucy, in her late thirties, with short dark hair, planted her hands on her hips. "And you decided not to use the front door?"

"Sorry, I heard someone back here and thought I'd check it out."

"Just me, composting dinner scraps."

"Did a police officer stop by?"

"No, why? Am I in trouble?" she teased.

"Did you see anyone else out here tonight?"

"No, but then I wasn't looking." Her smile faded. "What's going on?"

"Let's go inside." He motioned her toward the house, hoping that Sara was okay.

As Will and Lucy climbed the back stairs, he scanned the property one last time before they went inside.

What if Petrellis had sneaked inside while Lucy was disposing of the dinner scraps?

"Maybe I should go in first," he offered.

Without argument, Lucy stepped aside and let him enter the kitchen. Pots and pans were stacked in the sink, and plates were lined up on the countertop.

No sign of Officer Petrellis.

"Sara's room is where?" he asked.

"Over here." Lucy led him through the dining room to a door off a small hallway.

He took a deep breath and tapped on her door. "Sara?"

No response.

"She said she was exhausted," Lucy offered.

He looked down at the soft glow reflecting from beneath the door.

Tapping harder, he called out, "Sara, it's Will. Are you all right?"

Again, silence.

"Please open the door," he said to Lucy.

"I don't feel right going into a guest's room while she's inside."

If she was still inside.

"It's an emergency," Will said. "I think she's in danger. While you were out back, someone could have made his way into her room."

The front doorbell rang repeatedly.

"That's probably Detective Walsh," Will said. "Go ahead and let him in. He'll explain the urgency."

With a worried nod, she went to greet Nate. Will continued to tap on the door. Maybe there was a simple explanation. Yeah, like she didn't want to talk to him. She'd said as much when she'd left his Jeep, right?

"Sara, please open the door," Will said.

Nate marched up to Will. "I told you to wait for me."

"Officer Petrellis wasn't in his car," Will said. "I couldn't wait, and now Sara's not answering her door."

Nate nodded at Lucy. "Please open it."

She pulled a master key out of her pocket. "Sara? We're sorry to intrude." She opened the door.

The room was empty.

Will noticed open French doors leading outside. "He took her."

Nate went to the doors, and turned to Lucy. "Where does this lead?"

"The driveway."

Nate checked the door. "Someone messed with the lock." Nate went outside to investigate.

Will couldn't move. The walls seemed to close in around him. His fault; this was his fault.

"Lucy, are you down here?" a guest called from the living room.

Lucy placed her hand on Will's shoulder. "I have to take care of my guest."

Maybe Will nodded, maybe he didn't. He couldn't be sure of anything right now, except for the fact he'd failed Sara.

As he struggled to calm his panicked thoughts, he noticed the backpack she'd bought at the Super Shopper beside the bed, plus the sneakers she'd worn out of the store. She'd been so happy to get out of the stiff, dirt-covered boots and into a pair of comfortable shoes.

She'd taken them off, and wore what out of here? The uncomfortable boots again? No, he didn't see that happening. Will snapped his attention to the armoire. He approached it and tapped gently with his knuckles.

"Sara, you in there?"

There was no response. He held his breath and cracked one of the doors open.

It was empty except for wood hangers and an ironing board.

"No one's outside." Nate came back into the room and shut the doors behind him. "And the sedan you described is gone. Spike's not answering my texts. I have to assume he wasn't sending the messages. Petrellis must have somehow gotten his phone. Hope Spike's okay." Nate patted Will's shoulder. "Hang in there, buddy. We'll find her."

"Okay." Will's mind raced with worst-case scenarios.

Nate hesitated before stepping out of the room. "This was not your fault, Will."

"Yeah, okay."

"I mean it." Nate left the room, his voice echoing across the first floor of the inn. "Base, this is Detective Walsh. I need you to ping Officer Spike Duggins's cruiser and get me that location. Also, send an officer to Stuart Petrellis's house, over."

As Will shut the doors to the armoire, he considered what could have happened. If Petrellis had broken into her room she wouldn't have gone willingly with him, and Will hadn't been gone that long, maybe five minutes, tops. He surely would have heard her protests.

Her cries for help.

His gaze drifted to her newly bought sneakers. Convinced she was still in the house, he went into the living area. Voices drifted from the kitchen, Lucy's voice, and another woman's—not Sara's.

Sara was hiding. He could feel it.

As he wandered through the living room, he noticed a door built into the wall beneath the stairs. His girls would definitely consider that the perfect hiding spot. Could Sara be in there? Or was he kidding himself, denying the reality of the situation?

The possibility that she'd been taken, and might be dead by morning.

Will went to the door and tapped gently.

"What are you doing?" Nate said, gripping his radio.

Will knocked again. "Sara, it's Will. You okay in there?"

A few tense moments of silence passed.

Please, Lord, give her the courage to open the door.

"I'm brewing tea," Lucy said from the kitchen doorway. "And warming scones."

"I needed a snack," her female guest said from the kitchen.

"Tea and scones, how about it, Sara?" Will tried again.

Either she was scared and hiding, or Will was making a complete fool of himself.

"Nate's here. You're safe," Will encouraged.

With a soft click, the closet door opened. Will offered his hand and Sara took it. As she stepped out, she glanced at Nate then at Lucy.

"Sorry," Sara said. She slipped her hand out of Will's and went to her room. Will and Nate followed.

"I'm so embarrassed," she said.

"What happened, and why were you in the closet?" Nate asked.

"I thought I saw a man outside my window. I was being paranoid."

"No, you're being careful," Will said. "And that's a good thing, right, Nate?"

"Yes. Especially given the circumstances."

"What circumstances?" Sara said, worry coloring her blue eyes.

"We'll explain on the way," Nate said.

"Where are we going?" she asked.

"We need to find you another safe house. Better yet, we've got an open cell at the station."

"No, you're not locking her up," Will said.

"For her own good," Nate argued.

"I've got a better idea."

It felt wrong on so many levels, Sara thought as she looked out the loft window to the parking area below. Will and Nate were outside having a heated discussion, probably about Sara, and why Will needed to stop helping her. Nate had been clear—Sara could remain free as long as she promised to stay in Echo Mountain until they finished investigating the stranger's death, and the supposed death of David Price.

Supposed, right.

To think that without Will's help Sara would be locked in a cell right now. Her gaze roamed the loft that his deceased wife had used as her art studio. It had a peaked ceiling with wood support beams, and lace curtains covering the rectangular windows. It was a peaceful place, a place where one could dream, imagine and create.

The loft wasn't meant to be used as a fortress.

It felt wrong to be here, not only because of the danger Sara brought with her, but also because of the lie she had to hide behind. Would Will see her differently if he knew the truth, that she was an FBI agent who'd failed miserably as she'd watched a man being murdered?

She didn't like lying to Will or the local authorities, but she wasn't ready to go public, not until she spoke with her supervisor. Unfortunately Bonner wasn't answering her calls. She wondered if it was a tough love thing, that he thought if he ignored her she'd get back to relaxing on a beach somewhere. Then she realized he wouldn't recognize the new phone number. She'd been hesitant to leave a message regarding the situation, she wasn't sure why. So she decided to keep trying until he picked up.

The last thing she wanted was to blow her cover and expose herself as FBI to LaRouche and Harrington. They'd surely destroy evidence that could be used to build a case against them.

Evidence. She felt in her pocket for her broken phone. She had to get it to a tech person and retrieve the recorded murder of David Price.

"How do I find one of those?" she whispered to herself.

Maybe she'd ask Will, since he seemed to know most everyone in town. Yes, she'd tell him she wanted to retrieve photos from her ruined phone.

She sighed, eyeing Will's commanding presence through the window as he spoke with Nate. She wanted to stop lying to Will, to the man who had continually offered support and encouragement. No man, besides her uncle, had ever done that for her. Most of the men she'd dated had seemed too self-absorbed, and the male agents at work were focused solely on their careers.

There was no room in the FBI for weakness. She thought she'd covered hers pretty well with sheer grit and determination to nail criminals. Instead, Bonner criticized her for her tenacity, saying it had gotten her into trouble, that she saw crimes where there were none. He even insinuated she was overcompensating for something, like her small stature or even...

A past failure.

That seemed like a low blow, considering Bonner knew about her father's death.

She stepped away from the window and unzipped her backpack, still frustrated with herself for hiding when she felt the threat looming outside her room at the inn. She should have stood up for herself and taken the guy down. Any other FBI agent would have detained him for questioning.

"Yeah, with bruised ribs and a sprained wrist?"

The sound of footsteps echoed against the stairs. Putting distance between her and Will was getting more and more difficult, especially since she was staying in his wife's art studio.

That's not the only reason, Sara.

She felt herself opening up to him, allowing herself to be vulnerable for the first time since...

Had she ever really been vulnerable to a man before?

"It's not a five-star hotel, but it's pretty nice, huh?" Will said, stepping up to the top floor.

"It's charming." She glanced at him. "But I don't like putting you or your family in danger."

"You aren't. This place is a few blocks from my house, and isn't in my name, so no one will be able to make the connection between us."

"Who owns it?"

"A couple that travels ten months out of the year. I'd agreed to maintain things around here in exchange for Megan's use of the loft. I kept doing it, you know, as a favor."

Sara suspected it was more than that. She suspected he liked being around his wife's former space.

"The daybed isn't bad," he said. "Megan spent her share of nights here." He looked away, as if he hadn't meant to admit that.

"I'm sorry," she said.

He frowned. "Why?"

"You two were having trouble?"

"No, it wasn't that…well, not initially. It was the cancer. She wanted to spend the last few months here with the caregiver so I could get used to raising the girls alone. At least that's what she said."

"That must have been rough."

"Yeah, well, we had the loft cleaned out, so no cancer germs," he joked. He closed his eyes and sighed. "I don't know where that came from. I'm sorry."

"You don't need to apologize. You've been through a lot, and you have a right to react any way you want."

"Yeah, but that made me sound like a heartless jerk."

"Not even on your worst day could anyone think of you as a heartless jerk."

Will snapped his gaze to hers. Sara felt her heartbeat tapping against her chest.

Don't do this, Sara. He's a man still grieving for his wife, and you happen to be standing in her space.

"Hopefully a room will open up at the resort in the next day or two and I can move over there." She refocused on emptying her backpack of clothes and setting them on a wooden bench. "Oh, I meant to ask if you knew of a place in town where I could get my phone looked at?"

"The new one?"

"No, my original phone. It was damaged in the fall and I'd like to retrieve things from it, like pictures."

"I know a techie who could help."

"Great, thanks."

"Nate has assigned a police officer to keep watch."

"What about Spike, the one who Nate thought was looking after me?"

"They found him wandering by the highway, disoriented, and took him to the hospital."

"Officer Petrellis did that to him?"

"Nate suspects so, yes, and that Petrellis took Spike's phone and was texting updates to Nate."

"Is Spike okay?"

"He'll be fine. He's a tough kid who came on the force a few months ago. He's probably wondering if that was such a good idea right about now."

"Did they track down Petrellis?"

"No one was home when they checked his house. No car in the driveway, and the blinds were all closed. They've got a bulletin out on him. Anyway, a police officer should be arriving shortly to keep an eye on things here."

"I thought Nate didn't have the resources, or are they worried I'll flee the county?"

"Nate is concerned about your safety."

She nodded, hoping the detective truly believed her.

"Sara?"

"I'm fine. You don't have to stay."

"Okay, well…" He ran an anxious hand through thick chestnut hair. "There are fresh towels in the bathroom, and you bought toiletries at the store so you should be all set."

"Yep, looking forward to a good night's sleep."

"Okay, well, until tomorrow."

"Will, you don't have to—"

"Don't tell me not to check on you, Sara."

"You're awfully determined."

"Sometimes not determined enough. I won't make that mistake again."

She frowned, trying to figure out what he meant.

"Have a good night," he said in a firm voice. "The door automatically locks when I shut it. You can flip the deadbolt if you want, as well."

"Okay, thanks."

With a nod, he went downstairs and shut the door with a click.

She felt so alone in this strange place, a place where Will's wife had withdrawn from the world, which was kind of what Sara felt as though she was doing.

She could neither withdraw from the world, nor her current situation. There was a case to solve, two men to put away for murder, at the very least.

She pulled out her newly purchased cell phone and called her boss, this time deciding to leave a message.

"This is Agent Bonner. Leave a message."

"It's Agent Vaughn. There's been a development in the LHP case and I need to speak with you immediately. Here is my new number." She rattled it off. "The suspected drug case is now first-degree murder. I witnessed LaRouche kill David Price."

She ended the call and stared at the phone. That should get him to call her back.

Exhaustion took hold, and she flopped down on the

daybed. The echo of car doors slammed outside, and she figured the new surveillance officer had arrived.

Sara took a deep breath and relaxed, knowing she'd think more clearly after a decent night's sleep. She felt safe for now. No one knew where she was. LaRouche and Harrington couldn't find her here.

She sighed and drifted off to sleep.

Sara awoke with a start. She wasn't sure how long she'd been asleep, perhaps not long because it was still dark outside. She grabbed her phone. It was nearly ten.

Then she heard what had awakened her: the creak of wooden floorboards. Someone was coming up the steps.

Sara sat up, her heart racing. She'd left the desk lamp on, which she often did, so she wouldn't be disoriented if she awakened. She searched the room for a closet, a place to hide.

No, she wouldn't keep hiding like a coward, a weak and fragile woman who didn't belong in the field. But she needed a better position from which to defend herself.

She noticed a rock candleholder on the desk across the room. She grabbed it and crouched beside a set of file cabinets.

Her attacker was pretty smart to have eluded the police officer outside. Was Petrellis coming up the stairs? She bit her lower lip with worry, remembering he was at least six feet tall. Sure, she could call 911, only they wouldn't get here in time to prevent the assault. They'd arrive after the fact, after she'd been taken, or beaten up, or worse.

She focused on the sound. Silence rang in her ears. Was she was imagining things?

No, she wouldn't be swayed by her boss's comment that, at times, her overzealousness bordered on irrational.

Another creak of floorboards echoed across the loft.

Focus, Sara. Breathe.

Creak, creak.

Now it sounded as though the creak was coming from the other side of the loft.

The intruder was up here, with Sara. Coming closer.

Closer.

Weapon in hand, Sara waited...

EIGHT

Will had drifted off to sleep on the sofa when the phone awakened him.

"Yeah?" he said.

"Is Claire with you?" his mother-in-law said.

"What?" He sat up.

"Susanna can't find her. She thinks she might have gone home."

The phone pressed to his ear, Will searched the house. The beds were neatly made. No Claire. "She's not here. What happened?"

"Claire got upset and Susanna thought she went into the bedroom, but now she can't find her. One of the girls thought she heard her go out the back."

"I'll go look for her. She shouldn't be walking around at night."

"You're preaching to the choir. That girl should be grounded for life."

"I'll call when I find her." He pocketed his phone, grabbed his house keys and headed outside, figuring he'd walk to Susanna's house and hopefully run into his daughter making her way home.

He tamped down the panic, knowing it was a senseless emotion, yet a natural one. What happened that upset Claire? She'd been moody lately, and he wondered if something was happening with her friends or at school, and she couldn't bring herself to talk to Will about it. Listening and giving advice had always been Megan's role.

He walked a few blocks and automatically glanced to his right, across the park at the house with the upstairs loft that his wife, and now Sara, used as a refuge.

A shriek echoed across the park.

More lights popped on in the loft.

And a little person sprinted out of the house, past the patrol car parked out front.

Claire?

He took off toward her. What was she doing at the loft? Unless…

She missed her mom.

And found a stranger in her mother's space.

That must have been confusing, not to mention frightening for his daughter.

Will caught up to her on the lake path.

"Daddy! Daddy!" she sobbed.

Will whisked her into his arms. "Hey, baby girl. It's okay. I'm here."

"There was a…ghost in the loft!"

"No, honey, there's no such thing as a ghost."

"I saw her!"

She continued to sob against his shoulder and he debated taking her home, or going back to the loft to clear this up. A uniformed police officer headed toward them. The one thing Will did not want was for Sara's protective detail to leave his post.

Carrying Claire in his arms, Will headed toward the loft.

"Where are we going?" Claire said.

"To show you it wasn't a ghost, then I'll take you home. What were you doing at the loft anyway?"

"Nothing."

"Claire Renee Rankin."

A few seconds passed, then she said, "I go there sometimes, that's all."

"You go inside?"

"Yeah. I found a secret way inside."

He approached the police officer and recognized Officer Ryan McBride, Bree's cousin. "Hi, Ryan," Will said.

"I didn't even see her until she came racing out of the house. Is she okay?"

"Yeah, just scared. What about Sara?"

They both turned to look at the house. Sara stood in the doorway on the first floor, gripping a blanket around her shoulders.

"See, that's the ghost!" Claire cried into Will's shoulder.

"No, honey. That's Sara, a friend of mine," Will said. "I'm sure she feels badly about scaring you. Let's go talk to her."

Claire shook her head no.

"Look, you weren't supposed to be at the loft in the first place, were you?"

She shook her head again.

"Okay, then, let's face the consequences of your actions and sort this out." He nodded at Officer McBride and continued to the house.

"Will, I'm so sorry. I thought it was an intruder,"

Sara said, pulling the blanket tight around her shoulders with one hand.

"Let's go inside."

The three of them went upstairs. Will sat on a gray wingback chair and adjusted Claire on his lap. His little girl buried her face against his shoulder.

Sara sat on the daybed across the room. "I'm so sorry," she repeated.

"So is Claire, aren't you, baby girl?" Will said.

"I'm not a baby anymore, Daddy."

"No? So you're a big girl, and big girls can run off without telling anyone where they're going?"

She didn't answer.

"What happened, sweetheart?" he said, softening his voice.

"Nothing."

"Claire?" he pushed.

"We were making cookies."

"And…?"

"Olivia wanted to make snicker doodles, and Marissa said, you mean snicker poodles."

"That upset you because…?"

She leaned back and looked at him. "Those are Mommy's special cookies."

"Right. And it made you miss your mom?"

She buried her face against his neck. "It made me sad, so I went for a walk. Don't be mad, Daddy."

"I'm not angry. I was worried. So was your grandmother, Mrs. Baker, and what about your little sister? Remember the buddy system? You're never supposed to leave her alone."

"She was eating cookie dough. She didn't care."

"Of course she did. As a matter of fact, I'd better

call over there. First, let me introduce you to my friend, Miss Sara. She was hurt in a hiking accident and SAR rescued her. I offered to let her stay here."

"This is Mommy's place," Claire's muffled voice said.

"I know, but Mommy's not using it right now, and Miss Sara needs a place to sleep." He shot a half smile across the room at Sara.

Sara's gaze was intent on the back of Claire's head.

"How about it?" Will said. "Can we show Miss Sara our gracious hospitality by letting her stay here for a few days?"

"I guess." Claire leaned back and looked at Will. "What happened to your face, Daddy?"

"I had a hiking accident, too."

"Did they have to rescue you?"

"No, I walked down on my own."

"You look like you were in a fight."

"Do I look like I won?" he teased.

"Yeah." Claire giggled.

"Good answer," he said. "Now, I'd better call your grandmother before she sends out the National Guard." Will shifted Claire off his lap and made the call.

By holding the blanket loosely around her body, Sara managed to hide the fact that she was still trembling. The adrenaline rush hadn't worn off from the past few minutes.

Will's daughter studied her with fascination and fear coloring her eyes. To think Sara had nearly conked the girl on the head with the rock candle.

Yet she hadn't because as Sara had been about to

jump out of her hiding spot, the little girl had whispered, "Mommy, where are you?"

Sara had put down her weapon and stepped out from behind the file cabinet. Unfortunately revealing herself had terrified little Claire.

Mommy, where are you?

Hadn't Sara asked the same question a hundred times as a child? Wondering why her mom had had to go live at the hospital, and then why she'd never come home.

Sara's heart ached for Claire.

"It's fine. She's fine," Will said into the phone.

Sara noticed how he inadvertently stroked Claire's hair while speaking to his mother-in-law.

Claire hadn't taken her eyes off Sara.

"I'm sorry if I frightened you," Sara said.

"Why were you hiding?"

"I was scared."

"Of me?" Claire said, incredulously.

"I didn't know it was you," Sara explained. "All I heard was someone coming up the steps."

"Oh," Claire said, thinking for a minute on that one. "Can you draw?"

Sara bit back a smile at the random nature of her question. "No, not really."

"Mommy says everyone can draw."

"She created wonderful things." Sara eyed the sketches pinned to the walls.

"No, I'll take her home and pick up Marissa on the way," Will said into the phone. "I think she should be grounded, don't you?" He glanced at Claire.

His daughter shook her head no, that she didn't want to be grounded.

"Nonrefundable, huh?" Will continued. "Okay, I

guess you can swing by in the morning and pick them up… See you then." Will pocketed his phone and looked at Claire. "Nanny and Papa spent a lot of money on tickets to the museum, so I'm going to let you go with them tomorrow, and then tomorrow night we'll talk about the consequences of your actions."

"Don't ground me next week, please, Daddy. It's after-school art camp."

"We'll talk about it later."

The little girl looked as if she was going to burst into another round of tears. Sara did not envy Will's job of being a single parent.

"Let's go," he said, reaching out for Claire. "Sara needs to get some sleep."

Claire ignored her father's hand and studied her shoes.

"Claire?" Will prompted.

"Whenever I come here—" she hesitated "—I usually say a prayer for Mommy."

Will's expression softened. "Good idea."

Claire pressed her fingers together in prayer, as did Will.

Sara hadn't prayed since…well, she couldn't remember the last time she'd prayed. She figured, why bother? It hadn't helped when Mom was sick, and what kind of God would take Sara's father away from her?

"Don't you know how to pray?" Claire asked Sara with a frown. "It's easy. You put your hands together, see?" She nodded at her own fingers.

Sara had to stop thinking about her own pain and consider little Claire's emotional recovery. Sara pressed her hands together, the feeling so awkward and uncomfortable. "Like this?"

"Yes, then close your eyes."

Sara did as requested. How could anyone deny such a sweet little girl who was still grieving for her mom?

"Dear Lord," Claire began. "Take good care of my Mommy because she always took good care of us. I hope she's helping you in Heaven, and I hope she'll never forget us. I love you, Mommy. Amen."

"Amen," Sara and Will said in unison.

She didn't know about Will, but Sara could hardly speak past the ball of emotion in her throat.

"Good," Will said in a rough voice. "Good prayer."

"You did good, too, Miss Sara," Claire offered.

"Thank you."

Claire went to take her father's hand.

"Hopefully there won't be any more excitement," Will said to Sara. "I'll see you tomorrow."

"You don't—"

"I'll bring breakfast by after my in-laws pick up the girls."

"We want to come for breakfast," Claire said. "Please, Daddy, please?"

"Enough, sweetheart. Let's get your sister and go home. We'll figure out the rest tomorrow."

Claire grinned. Sara wondered if the little girl had Will wrapped around her finger.

"Until tomorrow, then." Will escorted Claire to the top of the stairs.

"Good night, Will," Sara said. "Sweet dreams, Claire."

Claire smiled at Sara. "I'll say a prayer for you tonight so you won't be scared anymore."

Claire started down the stairs and Will glanced at Sara.

"She's adorable," Sara said.

"Yeah."

With an odd, almost sad smile, Will disappeared down the stairs with his daughter.

After everything that had happened today and this evening, Sara realized spending time with Will and his girls for breakfast tomorrow was a horrible idea. She'd be hiding behind a shield of lies, and that was starting to feel terribly wrong.

As she stretched out on the bed, she heard Claire's prayer: *Take good care of my Mommy because she always took good care of us.*

That was what Will and his girls needed most: someone to take care of them. Sara was a dangerous diversion from that goal, although Will didn't know how dangerous.

She felt something brewing between she and Will: a closeness, a connection. She couldn't let that happen.

"Stop thinking about them."

No matter how much a part of her enjoyed watching Will interact with Claire, listening to Claire pray for her mother and taking refuge in the loft, the reality was, Sara had a job to do. If only her boss would call her back.

Until then, she had to stop involving innocents like Will and his girls, for their own good.

Sara got up early the next morning and tried to leave, but Officer McBride asked her to wait until Nate arrived. Asked? More like ordered her to stay put, up in her tower.

Sara could have argued, but she wasn't an idiot. Making enemies with the local cops wasn't a great idea, especially since she'd need their support, not their suspicions.

As she gazed out the window, she imagined what it would be like to live in a small town like Echo Mountain. Sara had hopped from one place to another after high school, first switching colleges to get the best criminal justice degree, then taking jobs to support her goal of becoming an FBI agent.

Yet life seemed so peaceful in Echo Mountain.

She sighed. Things always looked different from the outside. Like the bureau, and how it was nothing like she'd imagined. They didn't rush out and nail the bad guys. They had to follow protocol and procedure, and sometimes that meant a criminal wouldn't be prosecuted.

As she gazed at the mountain range in the distance, she wondered if LaRouche and Harrington had come down from the mountain, and what story they'd tell.

She spotted Will's Jeep cross the property. He parked and got out, with both little girls in tow.

"Will, no," she said. Bringing the girls here would only make things harder.

He carried what looked like a pastry box. Sara couldn't believe he'd awakened his daughters this early to bring her breakfast.

"Sara?" Will called from the bottom of the stairs.

"Come on up!" It's not as if she could turn them away. She wouldn't be that cruel, especially not to two little ones.

Will, Claire and her little sister came up to the loft. "Marissa, this is Miss Sara," Will introduced.

"You look like Mommy," Marissa said matter-of-factly.

"She does not," Claire argued.

"Girls," Will said. "Show Miss Sara what we brought her."

Claire shook her head disapprovingly at her little sister, then placed a box on the desk. She opened it slowly, reverently, as if she was showing off the crown jewels instead of creatively designed pastries. "These are Maple Bars, these are Chocolate Chipmunk Bars and these are Penelope's Pink Pansies."

Marissa leaned over the box, her green eyes widening. She looked a lot like her father. "Pansies are my favorite."

"I'm guessing these didn't come from Healthy Eats," Sara said.

"You'd guess right." Will smiled.

"We only get these on special occasions," Claire explained.

"Yeah, special occasions," Marissa echoed.

Was that what this was, a special occasion? Sara was in deeper trouble than she thought.

"Wow, how do I rate?" she asked Will.

"Thought it might help your aches and pains. Here." He pulled napkins out of his pocket and put them on the desk. "We're calling this first breakfast."

"Yeah, because Papa likes to eat breakfast out so we'll have second breakfast with him," Marissa said, licking the frosting off her Pink Pansy pastry.

For a brief second, Sara enjoyed the warmth of family, of children. In that moment, she shoved aside all thoughts of LaRouche and Harrington.

She reminded herself that this, the smiles of little girls licking frosting off their lips, was only an illusion, one that would evaporate soon enough.

Claire lifted a doughnut out of the box and raised it to her lips, eyes rounding with delight.

"It's terrifying, isn't it?" Will said.

Sara looked at him. "What?"

"The expression on her face when she's about to eat copious amounts of sugar and fat."

"If you think that's terrifying, how about this?" Sara grabbed a Maple Bar, took a bite and rolled her eyes from side to side, and up and down.

The girls giggled.

"You look crazy," little Marissa said.

"She looks happy," Claire countered.

"Happy doesn't look like this." Marissa imitated Sara. "It looks like this." Marissa cracked a broad grin, exposing frosting on her teeth.

"Gross. You are so immature," Claire said.

"I'm not manure."

"I didn't say…" Claire sighed. "Oh, never mind."

Will and Sara shared a smile.

"Tell Miss Sara where you're going today," Will said, plucking a chocolate doughnut for himself.

"A doll museum," Claire said with awe in her voice. "They have dolls from all over the world. Even Russia."

"Is that far away?" Marissa said.

"Of course it is," Claire countered.

"How do you know? Have you been there?"

"You know I haven't been there."

"Then, how do you know it's far away?"

"I learned it in school, silly."

"Oh." Marissa thought for a second, then looked at Sara. "Do you draw?"

"No, not really."

Marissa looked at her sister. "Mommy said—"

"Miss Sara hasn't learned yet," Claire explained.

"Let's teach her." Marissa scrambled off her chair and rushed to the other side of the room. She grabbed a sketch pad and dashed back to her sister.

"Pencils?" Claire said.

Again, Marissa raced across the room, went to a shelf and snatched a few pencils.

"Good." Claire cracked her knuckles.

This was quite the operation, Sara mused.

Claire nodded at the doughnut in Sara's hand. "You'll have to put down the doughnut."

"Right." Sara laid it on a napkin and brushed off her hands.

"Hold the pencil between your fingers like this." Claire demonstrated. "Watch me."

Marissa studied her sister and mimicked her every move.

Sara caught Will's expression, a mixture of pride and sadness, punctuated with a thoughtful smile. Drawing obviously reminded him of his wife.

"Then you draw a *t* in the middle of the page."

"Why are you drawing a *t*?" Sara said.

"It's how you draw a face. You connect the corners." Claire nibbled her lower lip. Marissa imitated the motion of drawing a circle. "And there you have the outline of the lady's head." Claire held up the sketchpad.

"Why are you drawing a lady?" Marissa asked.

"Men are boring. Ladies have hair and makeup and fun stuff like that," she answered her sister. She pointed to her drawing. "Then you'll draw the eyes here." Claire pointed. "See, the eyes are above the cross line, like on a real face. You try." Claire handed Sara a pencil.

Sara made a *t* and drew an oval shape by connecting the tips of the letter.

"That's good, now make the eyes," Claire said.

Will's phone buzzed.

"Whoops, that's Nanny and Papa. They're wondering where you are. Let's go, girls."

The girls grabbed their doughnuts and headed for the stairs. Claire turned to Sara. "Don't eat all the Pink Pansies or you'll get a tummy ache."

"Okay, I won't." Sara smiled.

"I'll be back in twenty," Will said.

"I'll be here, practicing my drawing."

Marissa ran up and hugged Sara's legs. "Don't worry. You'll be able to draw someday."

So stunned by the display of affection, Sara didn't immediately return the hug. Her heart sank. She never realized what she'd been missing. Just as she wrapped her arms around the little girl, Marissa sprung free and skipped up to her dad and sister.

"Dolls, dolls, dolls!" Marissa chanted.

Will cast one last smile at Sara and led the girls downstairs. Sara went to the window. She watched them get into Will's Jeep and pull away.

An ache permeated her chest. They were such a lovely family: a protective, gentle father and two sweet, albeit precocious little girls. Will's family seemed so perfect, so...

She turned back to the room. How could they be so grounded and at peace after having lost a mother, a wife?

Sara wandered to the table where they had practiced drawing. A day hadn't gone by since her father's murder that Sara hadn't felt the burn of anger.

The Rankin family had suffered a great loss, but didn't seem to let the grief shadow their conversations.

Their every thought.

All of Sara's decisions since Dad's death had been motivated by anger and the need for justice. Get a criminal justice degree, work her way into a job with the FBI and hunt down bad guys and put them behind bars.

Make them pay.

Because her dad's killer was never caught, never served his time.

Now, in her thirties, Sara was all about her career. She had no personal life, no boyfriend or even close friends for that matter. She never had time to nurture those kinds of relationships.

Being with Will and his girls, seeing how the community rallied around him and protected him, triggered an ache in Sara's chest for that which she would never have.

"One more reason you need to get out of here." She grabbed her backpack and considered her options. If Officer McBride wouldn't allow her to leave until she spoke with Nate, perhaps she could talk him into taking her to the police station to wait this out. One thing was for sure—staying here, in Will's deceased wife's studio, was messing with Sara's head. Big-time.

She glanced around the loft to make sure she hadn't forgotten anything. Her gaze landed on a photo of Will's wife with an arm around each of her little girls. Sara had a photo a lot like that one, of Sara, her dad and little brother, Kenny. It was taken at the beach. They were happy, laughing.

A perfect moment lost in the chaos of murder.

You and your brother hide in the closet. Do not come out until I say it's okay.

The slamming of a car door outside ripped her out of the memory. Time to distance herself from Will and his girls. It was stirring up too many memories and buried grief.

Grief she'd been able to neutralize with determination to get justice.

She headed downstairs, deciding she'd sleep in a cell if she had to. She'd be safe at the police station, and a lot safer emotionally than if she continued to stay here.

As she headed for the patrol car, she saw Detective Walsh talking on his phone. He didn't look happy. Then he shot her a look, and she slowed her step. Something was very wrong.

"I understand. Text me the coordinates and I'll pass them along to SAR. We'll send a team. Once they're down I'll want to interview each of them individually.... Yes, I have her in custody."

In custody? Sara dug her fingers into the strap of her backpack.

Nate ended the call and turned to Sara. "Mr. La-Rouche and Mr. Harrington finally called in. They said David Price disappeared after he got into an argument with you."

NINE

"What?" Sara said in disbelief.

"They claim the last time they saw Mr. Price, you two were arguing over money."

"Unbelievable," she muttered.

"Is it true? You were arguing about money and, what, he fell?"

"Absolutely not."

"Just the same, I need you to come with me to the station."

Her heartbeat sped up. "Are you arresting me?"

"I'm bringing you in for questioning."

"They're lying. I don't care about money," she ground out. "I only care about…"

Don't say it. Not yet.

"Ma'am?" Detective Walsh prompted.

"Forget it." Of course they'd pin the murder on her. It was an easy solution to fix their problems. And they'd get away with it. They'd discredit Sara and make her a viable suspect.

"Is there anything you want to tell me?" Nate asked.

She clenched her jaw, wanting to tell the detective who she really was. Sara feared losing traction with this case if word got out and LaRouche and Harrington discovered she was FBI.

She noticed Will's Jeep heading toward them. Perfect. This would drive him away, Will and his adorable girls, girls who didn't need to be exposed to the ugliness of Sara's life.

"Do what you have to do," she said to Nate.

Nate studied her with creased eyebrows. "Let's go." He motioned for her to get into his unmarked squad car.

Will pulled up beside them and hopped out. "Hey, what's going on?"

"I've been accused of murder," Sara said. "Okay? I'm dangerous. Stay away from me."

She climbed into the car and Nate shut the door. She couldn't hear what they were saying because they'd stepped away from the car, but she could tell Will argued fiercely with the detective.

Finally, Nate shook his head in frustration and got into the car.

She stared at the headrest of the seat in front of her, trying to block out Will's presence. He tapped on her window and she glanced out at his confused face. He looked as if he wanted answers.

As if he deserved answers.

She ripped her gaze from his emerald eyes. "Are we going or what?"

As Nate pulled away, Sara's eyes watered. *Goodbye, Will.*

She felt utterly alone. She wasn't working in an official capacity for the FBI, her supervisor hadn't returned her calls and now she'd pushed away the one person who truly wanted to help her.

"He deserves the truth."

She snapped her eyes to the back of Nate's head. "Meaning what?"

"Will saved your life and put himself at risk by protecting you. Don't you think that deserves complete honesty?"

"It doesn't matter."

"Oh, yes, ma'am, it does. Will Rankin is one of the most honorable men I know. For some strange reason he's decided you're worthy of his protection. He's usually got good instincts about people."

She gazed out the window as they passed a park filled with children.

"So? Were his instincts right about you?" Nate pushed.

She sighed. If LaRouche and Harrington were going to frame her, she'd better get ahead of this thing and confide in the local police.

"Yes, his instincts are good."

"And?"

"I'm FBI."

"Really," he said, disbelief in his voice.

"Yes."

"And you didn't bother to tell me or Will that before now because…?"

"I'm undercover."

"Then, you should have brought me into your investigation." Nate got a call and answered his radio. "Detective Walsh, go ahead, over."

"Someone saw Petrellis at the Super Shopper, about half an hour ago, over."

"He's still in town?" Nate muttered to himself, then responded into the radio, "Send a unit to check it out.

If the officer sees Petrellis, he needs to call for backup. Do not approach him alone, over."

"Ten-four."

He clicked off the radio and eyed her in the rearview. "We'll finish our discussion at the station."

Nate focused on driving, visibly frustrated by the call.

"You think he should have left town?" she said.

"Wouldn't you? I mean, we suspect that he drugged Spike, and was following you around all day for some nefarious reason."

"What happened with Spike, exactly?"

"Petrellis saw him outside the hospital and approached him, acting as though they're buddies. He congratulated Spike on the new job with Echo Mountain PD and slapped him on the shoulder. Hard. Spike says he thought he felt a pinch, like a bee sting. That's pretty much all he remembers." Nate shook his head. "What is happening to my town?"

Sara gazed out the window, feeling even guiltier that she brought trouble to the community of Echo Mountain.

Within minutes Will was on the phone calling Royce Burnside, the best lawyer in Echo County. Will had done search engine optimization marketing work for Royce's law firm and knew of their stellar reputation.

As a favor to Will, Royce said he'd meet him at the police station right after lunch. Will stopped himself from marching into the station alone, all fired up. He worked on marketing projects for the next few hours in his home office. Unfortunately, the image of a bruised and fragile Sara being aggressively interrogated kept seeping into his thoughts, distracting him.

Will leaned back in his chair and pulled his fingers off the keyboard. What was Nate thinking? Sara wasn't a criminal or a violent woman. She'd gone into shock after shooting a man, and had experienced traumatic flashbacks.

Although he sensed that Sara wanted to go this alone, the more she pushed Will away, the more determined he was to help. Sure, he knew once this case was resolved and she was given her freedom, she'd probably leave town and he'd never see her again. It didn't matter. She needed help and he wanted to be the one to give it to her.

He warmed up butternut-squash soup from Healthy Eats for lunch, hoping Nate at least had the decency to feed Sara. Maybe Will would bring some soup just in case. He had plenty.

Minutes stretched like hours as he waited for one o'clock.

"This is ridiculous." Although it was only twelve fifteen, he packed up a container of soup, grabbed a small bag of crackers and headed for the station. He brought his laptop as well, figuring he'd get some work done while waiting for Royce.

Will wasn't even sure Sara needed an attorney, but it wouldn't hurt to have one in her corner.

He parked in the lot, pulled out his laptop and moved his seat back so he could open it up and work. The whole work thing lasted about five minutes. Glancing at the building and knowing she was inside being questioned about a murder she didn't commit drove Will nuts.

Some folks would call him nuts for believing in a complete stranger.

But they weren't strangers. She'd exposed herself to him in a way he suspected she hadn't with many, if anyone. When she'd hidden under the bed, clutching the blanket to her chest, she'd seemed like a child, fearing for her life.

Something terrible had happened to Sara in her past, and it had all come rushing back after the shooting.

Will tucked the laptop into his backpack and grabbed the soup bag. He didn't care if he was early. He'd text Royce to meet him inside.

As he headed for the building, he spotted a familiar car parked across the street from the police station.

Officer Petrellis's unmarked sedan.

Surprised and concerned, Will glanced away, so as not to be obvious. He pulled out his phone and texted Nate about the car. They were looking for the retired officer to question him about yesterday, about drugging Spike and stalking Sara.

"Hello, Mr. Rankin."

Will glanced up. Petrellis was heading toward him.

"Officer," Will greeted, then hit Send on the text to Nate.

"What brings you to the station?" Petrellis said.

"Visiting my friend Nate."

"And what about your other friend Sara? How is she doing?"

"I wouldn't know. I've been busy with work."

"How well do you know her, if you don't mind my asking?"

"I don't know her at all, actually. I helped rescue her after a nasty fall. That's it." He glanced at his watch. "Whoa, I'm late. Excuse me."

Will turned to walk away, to put distance between

him and the retired officer with questionable motivations.

Something stabbed Will in the arm and he instinctively jerked back. "Hey!"

"You need to come with me."

"Excuse me?"

"I need to ask you some questions."

"I don't have time. I've got to get inside and…and…" Ringing started in his ears, and his surroundings went in and out of focus.

"Here, let me help you." A firm hand gripped Will's arm and led him away from the police station, away from Sara.

"No." Will yanked his arm away. "I have to talk to her."

"Her? You mean Sara?"

A part of Will knew he'd said too much. His brain was floating on some kind of wave, pulling him away from the shoreline of reality.

They found Spike wandering the highway, Nate had told Will.

That must be what was happening to Will.

"Relax," Petrellis said as they approached his car. "It will be over soon."

Over? As in…

Was Petrellis going to kill him? Leaving the girls with no parents, and judgmental grandparents to raise them?

"No!" Will shouldered Petrellis against the car and fired off punches.

"Will!" Nate called from across the street.

Petrellis yanked Will forward, kneed him in the gut

and cast him aside. Will collapsed on the pavement and watched Petrellis's car speed off.

"No," Will croaked, wanting Petrellis to come back, to tell them why he was after Sara.

Sara. The beautiful woman with the big blue eyes.

"Will." It was Sara's voice.

He looked up, into her worried eyes.

"No, I want all patrols to be on the lookout," Nate's voice said from behind her. "He's headed south on Main Street toward the interstate, over."

"Will?" Nate said.

All Will could see were Sara's blue eyes.

"Nate didn't arrest you, did he?" Will asked her.

"No." She placed a comforting hand on his chest. "What happened?"

"Dispatch, I need an ambulance," Nate's voice said.

"No," Will said. "No ambulance."

"Will, you're hurt," Nate argued.

"Drugged like Spike. Felt him stick my arm."

"Then, an ambulance can take you to the hospital."

"Everyone will know. My in-laws—"

"This wasn't your fault," Sara said.

"Stop worrying about them, Will," Nate said. "The ambulance will be here shortly."

"Have to get home… The girls."

"They're not coming home until seven, remember?" Sara offered. "It's only twelve-thirty."

"Oh, yeah." He closed his eyes, then opened them again. "Are you okay?"

"I'm fine." She frowned. "I'm worried about you."

"What's going on?" Royce said, joining them.

"Who are you?" Sara said.

"Your attorney," Royce said. "Will hired me."

"Ambulance is here," Nate said.

Will stood, Sara holding onto one arm for support, while Nate gripped the other. He flopped down onto a stretcher, but wouldn't let go of Sara's hand.

"I need to—"

"Go find Petrellis," Sara interrupted Nate. "I'll ride with Will."

As Will was being examined by medical staff, he worried what his in-laws would think, what they would say. This would be the second time he'd been examined by doctors at the hospital in the past few days. In Mary's and Ed's minds, he probably threw himself onto the path of danger yet again by interacting with a suspected...what? What was Officer Petrellis, exactly? Will still didn't know.

Once they reached the hospital, Will was given a medication to counteract the drug. His brain fog began to clear and he was able to focus again. Sara said she'd be in the waiting room speaking with Royce, who had followed them from the police station.

Will puzzled over Nate's sudden turnaround from almost arresting her to letting her accompany Will to the hospital.

"How's your vision?" the nurse asked.

"Good, excellent," Will answered.

"Are you nauseous or dizzy?"

"No, ma'am. I'm much better now, thanks. Can I go?"

"Where's the fire?" Dr. Kyle Spencer, a member of SAR asked, coming into the ER. "Hey, buddy, I heard you were brought in."

"Hey, Spence," Will said.

"How's the head?"

"Fine."

"No headache?"

"No."

"Blurred vision?"

"Not now."

"So…when?" Spence studied him with concern.

"After I got stuck with the drug."

Spence pulled out a penlight and checked Will's eyes. "Did you fall and hit your head again?"

"Not that I know of."

Spence was referring to an altercation in the mountains last year. That injury had left Will with temporary, selective amnesia. At the time Will didn't remember that Megan had passed away. Once his memory returned, reliving that grief had left him gutted, as if she'd just died.

"The medical team identified elements of the drug we found in Spike's system and were able to give him, and now you, something to counteract the effects," Spence said.

"Yeah, so they told me."

"It wouldn't hurt to rest this afternoon."

"Okay, doc." Will shifted off the gurney and planted his feet on the floor.

Spence studied him. "A-OK?"

"Solid as a rock, thanks."

"Excellent." They shook hands. "Until our next mission, then."

"Yep." Will left the examining room and found Sara in the waiting area with Royce.

"Hey, how are you?" Sara went in for a hug.

It was a brief embrace that shocked Will. He didn't want to let go.

"I'm okay," Will said. "Was Royce able to help you?"

"Turns out it wasn't necessary," Royce said. "In case

you do need me, you've got my card." Royce smiled at Will. "Glad you're okay. Take care."

"You, too."

Royce left the ER waiting area and that was when Will noticed a uniformed officer by the door.

"Okay, someone's going to have to draw me a map here," Will started. "This morning Nate was arresting you, then he did a one-eighty and let you accompany me in the ambulance and now he's posted a police officer, I'm assuming for your protection?"

"Yeah, you and I need to talk. It's rather crowded here. Officer Carrington will take us to the station, unless you need to go home and rest?"

"No, I'm okay."

Will and Sara left the hospital with Officer Carrington, Sara's eyes constantly scanning their surroundings. She seemed different today, stronger, more sure of herself.

He almost wondered if she was the same person he'd found in the mountains. Of course she was, yet something had definitely changed.

And he liked it, especially the hugging part.

The ride back to the station was somewhat quiet. Will was desperate to know what was going on, but didn't dare ask in front of a third party.

Officer Carrington escorted them into a conference room at the station. Sara wandered to the window and looked outside.

"First, I need to apologize for bringing this danger to Echo Mountain—" she turned "—and into your life."

"I don't see a need to apologize. Go on." He pulled out a chair at the table and sat, hoping she'd join him.

She leaned against the wall and crossed her arms over her chest.

"The truth is, I'm FBI. I was on an undercover mission to find evidence against a company called LHP, Inc.—LaRouche, Harrington and Price's company. I suspect they plan to distribute a sleep medication that will make them millions, and potentially put lives at risk."

"You followed them on a hiking trip?"

"I bought my way onto the guide team, hoping they'd let their guard down and I'd find evidence of their plan. Then I saw Vic LaRouche throw David Price to his death. Wasn't expecting that."

"Have you told Nate this?"

"This morning, when he picked me up. He kind of—" she hesitated "—guilted it out of me."

"Yeah, I could see him doing that."

"Now I feel even more guilty because of what happened to you this afternoon."

"You didn't stick me with the drug."

"Don't be so literal here, Will. This is my fault. Maybe if I would have made a different choice."

"What choice? You've been in survival mode ever since you witnessed the murder."

She cocked her head slightly. "How do you do that?"

"What?"

"Offer so much compassion for someone who has been making your life a mess."

"What? I don't see a mess."

"Will, Petrellis knows you and I are connected, so now you're a target. The smartest thing for me to do is leave town and somehow draw them away from Echo Mountain."

"Why did Nate take you in this morning?"

She pulled out a chair and sat at the table. Good, she was getting closer.

"LaRouche and Harrington reported David Price missing this morning," she said. "They claim he disappeared after he and I got into an argument."

"So they're turning this around on you?"

"Looks that way."

"But you're FBI."

"They don't know that, and they can't." She reached across the table and placed her hand on Will's. "Only you and Nate know who I really am," she said. "It has to stay that way. If these guys find out the FBI is on their trail, they'll bury evidence so deep we'll never find it."

His gaze drifted to her hand, and she slid it off.

"You seem different," he said, glancing into her eyes. "More grounded and confident."

"It feels better to have people know the truth, people I trust." She cracked a slight smile.

The door opened and Nate joined them wearing a frown. He planted his hand on Will's shoulder. "Doing okay?"

"Yeah, I'm good. How's Spike?"

"Embarrassed, but otherwise good."

"And Petrellis?" Sara said.

"In the wind. For now."

"What's his motivation?" she asked Nate.

"Have no clue. Yet."

"Why did he take early retirement?" she said.

"He had issues at home and it interfered with his work."

"What kind of issues?"

"Not sure. He was a private guy." Nate slapped a folder onto the table. "We've got a bigger problem."

Will and Sara shared a worried look.

"One, your investigation has made Will a target," Nate said.

"Hey, Nate—"

Nate put up his hand to silence Will. "And, two, according to your supervisor, there is no case. Officially, you're on vacation, so that makes you a rogue agent with a vendetta."

TEN

"That's not true," Sara said, her face heating with anger. Why couldn't Bonner support her and admit she had been working on a case?

"Sara, what's going on?" Will said with a puzzled frown.

"It's easy, Will," Nate said. "Your friend here has been lying to us and manipulating us this whole time."

Will studied her with such pain in his eyes. "You've been lying to me?"

Regret coursed through her. No, she had good intentions, even if her execution was off.

"Will." She leaned forward. "I'm sorry, truly. But I'm doing the right thing here. My boss probably threw me under the bus because he's tired of me hounding him about tough cases, the criminals that get away." She glanced over her shoulder at Nate. "You worked in a big city—you know what I'm talking about."

Nate didn't answer, so she continued, redirecting her attention to Will, wanting him to know everything.

"LaRouche and Harrington were trying to convince David Price to go along with their plan to distribute a dangerous drug that could kill people. Because of who they are and their influence and who knows what else, they're going to get away with it. That's why LaRouche shoved David Price off the cliff—because he was going to walk away from the company, which would have raised suspicion and tanked their stock. So yes, I came out here because I didn't have enough evidence, and I decided to find more. Call me nuts, call me rogue, I don't care, as long as I put these guys away before they kill anybody." She glanced at Nate once more. "Didn't you ever watch a suspect walk away with a cocky smirk on his face when he should have been in cuffs?"

Nate tapped a pen against his open palm and studied her. "How do you know the drug is dangerous?"

At least he was listening to her. Now if she could get Will to forgive her for lying.

"They were arguing about an anomaly in the test results," she explained to Nate. "David Price said it wasn't right, that it could kill people. I recorded it on my phone, which was damaged in my fall. I was hoping a tech could still retrieve the video. That's my nail in their coffin."

"What motivated you to follow them into the mountains?" Nate asked.

"An email exchange between LaRouche and the drug testing company. I printed them out. My supervisor said it wasn't enough."

"Why not?" Nate said.

"It was too—" she made quote marks with her fingers "—vague."

She glanced at Will, who still looked like a man who'd just met her for the first time. As if he didn't recognize her. Shame burned her insides, both for having lied to him, and for putting him in danger.

She shifted in her chair and waited for more questions from Nate.

"He said once you got your teeth into something, you weren't giving it up," Nate said. "Even if there was no basis for an investigation."

"Nice," she muttered.

"He told you to let this one go," Nate continued.

"Well, I couldn't."

"You ignored a direct order."

"He ordered me to take vacation time—"

"Because you hadn't taken time off in five years."

"I didn't have any reason to."

"But you had reason to go against a direct order and pursue this case?"

"If it could save lives, yes," she countered. "I can't believe you've never done the same."

"We're not talking about me. We're talking about you, and why you're so tenacious. Your boss said—"

"What, that I'm an aggressive head case because I hid in a closet while a random home invader broke in, killed my father and made me and my little brother orphans? As if we hadn't been through enough after Mom died."

Sara shook her head in frustration and stared at the gray laminate table. Silence filled the room. There, she'd said it, what everyone who knew her, and knew about her past, thought whenever she did anything off book.

Someone knocked on the door and a secretary poked her head inside. "The chief wants to see you, Nate. It's important."

"I'll be right back." Nate followed the secretary out

of the room and shut the door, leaving Sara and Will alone.

With her shame spread out on the table, exposed for him to see.

She clenched her jaw, wishing she could be anywhere else, be anyone else at this moment. Will's opinion of her mattered more than it should.

"Sara?" he said.

She couldn't look at him. He pushed back his chair and came to her side of the table. He knelt beside her, reached for one of her hands and gently clasped it between his.

"I am so sorry about your father," he said.

She nodded.

"How old were you?"

"Twelve."

"Oh, honey." He pulled her against his chest and stroked her back.

She almost started crying and stopped herself. It would only prove that they were right about her: that she was weak and fragile, and had no business in law enforcement.

"Don't." She pushed away and stood, pacing to the opposite side of the room. "I appreciate your compassion, but it only makes me feel worse."

"Why?"

She hesitated. Never in her life had she confided in anyone about Dad's death, not even her uncle. Right now, in this conference room, she ached to talk about it with Will. He wouldn't think her weak or damaged, would he? Knowing Will, he'd offer to hug her again.

She'd gone a lot of years without hugs. Maybe she should appreciate them while she could. Besides, once this case was done she'd leave town and never see Will again, never see the look of pity on his face because he knew the truth about Sara failing her dad.

"I guess," she started, "I don't deserve your compassion."

"Don't say that."

"Why not? I lied to you."

"You thought you were doing the right thing."

"Oh, Will. I'm not worthy of your compassion. I failed Dad and I keep failing victims who depend on me to protect them."

He took a few steps closer. "What victims?"

"People like the Williamsons, whose daughter was killed by members of a drug gang. She went missing and we were called in to find her. I was this close." She pinched her fingers. "Bonner, my supervisor, took me off the case. He said we'd invested too many man-hours in the investigation. Local police in Detroit found the girl's dead body a week later. I could have found her, Will. I know I could have."

"I'm sorry," he said.

"Yeah, well, sorry is for losers." She snapped her attention to him, afraid she'd hurt his feelings again. Surprisingly, he shared a look of understanding.

"No," he said. "Being sorry is a way to share a friend's burden. I'd like to share yours."

"Why?"

"I feel as if we've become friends. I wish you'd stop trying to push me away."

"But I lied to you about who I was."

"Because you were working a case. I get it, even if I'm disappointed that you felt you couldn't completely trust me."

"Stop being nice to me."

Will leaned against the wall and crossed his arms over his chest. The corner of his mouth turned up in a slight smile. "That's the second time you've said that. Now it's my turn to counter—toss that chip off your shoulder and get on with your life."

"What life?" she muttered.

"So it's really all about work for you?" Will said.

"You wouldn't understand. You have a family."

"And friends, and a church community," he added.

"Rub it in, why don't ya," she said teasingly.

He didn't smile. "My point is, there are many dimensions to life, not just work or family. Maybe, while you're in Echo Mountain, you could experience some of those other things."

"My goal is to not only nail LaRouche and Harrington, but also to keep my distance from people so I don't put them in jeopardy."

People, meaning Will. From the disappointed look on his face, he obviously got the message.

The door popped open and Nate came into the room. "I spoke with our chief. We think it best if you stay undercover for the time being to continue the investigation of LaRouche and Harrington."

"You believe me?"

"Yes, I do," Nate said. "Although I don't appreciate you lying to me. The chief and I also realize we have a bigger problem." He looked at Will. "You've become a target, my friend."

"Because Petrellis came after me?" Will said. "No, I happened to be at the wrong place at the wrong time. That's all."

"Let's assume Petrellis is working for LaRouche and

Harrington, that they hired him to find Sara, find out what she told authorities. He knows the two of you are connected, which means he can get to her through you. And possibly get to you through your girls."

Sara's heart ached. She'd done this. She'd dragged two adorable little girls into the ugliness of her work.

"Will, I'm so—"

"What do you recommend, Nate?" He cut Sara off.

"We'll put police protection on the house tonight while we look for a place to relocate you and the girls," Nate said.

"Where to?" Will asked.

"How about the resort?"

"They were booked last time I checked," Will said.

"Maybe the resort's had some no-shows," Sara offered, trying to be both helpful and hopeful.

An emotion so foreign to her, yet she'd embrace hope if it might help the girls. Help Will.

"How about Bree's cottage at Echo Mountain Resort?" Nate suggested. "She's got an extra room upstairs, and a state-of-the-art security system. Plus, with everyone around for the festival, Petrellis wouldn't be foolish enough to try anything."

"I'd hate to impose on her like that," Will said.

"Come on, buddy, you know Bree. She'd be offended if we didn't ask for her help."

Will nodded. "True."

"Why don't you call her, Will?" Sara said.

"It's settled," Nate said. "You call Bree and I'll send Sara's phone to the lab in Seattle to see if they can pull the recording off it."

"How long will that take?" she said.

"Depends how backed up they are."

"Or we could take it to Zack Carter at the resort," Will said. "He's an amazing tech specialist."

"Can't. It's a chain of evidence thing," Nate explained. "I take it from Sara and it goes directly to the lab. Otherwise, once this goes to court they could challenge the third-party intervention."

"Oh, right," Will said.

Nate extended his hand for Sara's phone. She hesitated. "No offense, but this is not just a recording. It's my life."

"I understand," Nate said. "I'll make sure it gets into the right hands. I'll put a rush on it."

Will shot her an encouraging nod.

Sara handed Nate the phone, trying to process this new feeling—this feeling of genuine trust.

"I'll set up police protection for tonight," Nate said. "Tomorrow we'll covertly relocate you and the girls."

"We have church in the morning," Will said.

"I'll assign myself to that detail and keep watch outside. Sara, I'd advise you to stay in the loft until further notice."

"I can't do that."

"Excuse me?" Nate said.

"I'm responsible for Will and his girls being in danger. I want to be close enough that I can be part of your protective detail."

"Absolutely not," Nate said. "You're a trouble magnet."

"Nate," Will admonished.

Sara didn't let the comment affect her. "No one will know I'm there. I'll change my appearance, whatever is necessary, but I won't abandon Will and his girls."

"Even if that could prove dangerous for them?" Nate said.

"Then, we find Petrellis first. We'll use me as bait to catch him."

"Sara, no," Will said.

"I will not keep looking over my shoulder," Sara said. "And I certainly don't want him terrorizing your family, Will." She redirected her attention to Nate. "How about it?"

"Okay, let's get Will and the girls settled, then we'll cast a line for Petrellis."

"I wish you wouldn't do this," Will said to Sara.

"This is my job. On a normal day I'm pretty good at it."

"But you're hurt—"

"I'll be fine."

She'd do whatever was necessary to make sure Will and his girls were out of danger.

Sara sipped her hot tea as she sat at the counter in the town's most popular diner. It was a long shot, but the best plan they could come up with on short notice.

Nate waited outside with another officer in an unmarked car. The agreement was Sara would text them when Petrellis showed up. Surely someone in this crowded restaurant knew Petrellis, and many of them had heard of her—the strange woman who'd been rescued from the mountains. She could tell from their expressions, from their curious frowns as they passed by.

But somehow she was going to disguise herself when she joined the protective detail for Will and the girls? Who was she kidding? She was probably the town's biggest celebrity.

Which she hoped worked in her favor right now. Hopefully her diner visit would start a buzz about the mysterious lady who fell off the mountain and had been rescued by the local bachelor. Sara was under the impression locals were not only protective of Will, but also wanted to find him a suitable mate.

Sara was not at the top of that list, even on her best day. Will was about compassion and raising his girls in a healthy environment. Sara was about…well, you wouldn't call her lifestyle necessarily healthy.

For the first time in years, she caught a glimpse of her obsessive nature, a nature that turned people off, especially her superiors at work. And now she was so obsessed with keeping Will and his girls safe that she was putting herself in danger. Yeah, *obsessive* was a good word to describe her current decision. It was part of the job, a job Will would never truly understand.

The restaurant wall clock read nine fifteen. She wondered what Will was serving his girls for dinner. Probably something healthier than the cheeseburger and fries sitting on the counter in front of her. Would Will read Claire and Marissa a bedtime story? Work on their Christmas lists?

The waitress, a middle-aged woman with black hair pulled back, came by with a water pitcher. "How was the burger?"

"Good, thanks."

"Need more water?"

"No, I'm good."

"Can I ask you something? I mean, if I'm being rude just tell me."

"Go for it."

"Are you her? The woman who fell off the mountain and was rescued by Will Rankin?"

Success! Word had spread. They knew who she was.

"Yes, that's me."

"Where are you from?"

"Seattle."

"Ah, so hiking was a new experience for you."

Sara shrugged. She'd hiked plenty as a kid.

"Good thing Will happened to be out there," the waitress offered.

"Yep."

But not so good in Sara's book. Finding Sara had sent Will's life into a tailspin of trouble.

"Will's a nice man," the waitress said.

"Exceptionally nice."

"He's been through a lot."

"Yes, he has."

"So you know about his wife?"

"Yes, Will and I have become friends."

"Oh," she said, disappointed. A customer caught her eye and she walked away.

Sara's phone buzzed with a text. It was from Will.

You okay?

She responded.

All is well. How are the girls?

She glanced over her shoulder toward the door. The waitress stood beside a table of customers, three elderly couples who seemed to be glaring at Sara.

Oh, boy. Her friendship with Will was causing her

to be the most disliked person in town. She redirected her attention to her phone. Will hadn't responded. She didn't want to look back at the locals in the corner. Their message was clear. "You should be ashamed of yourself for involving Will."

Oh, she was very ashamed of herself for putting him in danger. Yet, she kept hearing Will's voice: *I wish you'd stop trying to push me away.*

He appreciated their friendship, or whatever you could call what was developing between them. Every time she tried drawing a boundary line, he'd reach right across and hold on tighter. What kind of man did that?

A compassionate, generous man.

One who deserved better than a damaged friend like Sara Vaughn in his life.

The waitress returned and placed the check on the counter. A hint that Sara had overstayed her welcome?

"Thanks," Sara said.

With a nod, the waitress walked away. Sara flipped over the check, and noticed a message written in ink: "Meet me out back."

She scanned the restaurant. A few people still stared at her, but chances were none of them had written the message. She placed cash in the bill sleeve and shifted off the barstool. Cradling her sprained wrist against her stomach, she went down the hall leading to the bathroom. At the end of the hall was a bright red exit sign over a back door.

This could be it. Either Petrellis waited outside for her, or it was a local wanting to give her a lecture about staying away from Will. She pulled out her phone to text Nate, and hesitated.

Once Petrellis was brought in for questioning, he'd

clam up like his kind usually did, hiding behind his lawyer.

She couldn't let that happen.

Pocketing her phone, she pushed the door open. A gust of wind sent a chill across her shoulders.

"Hello?" she called down the dark alley.

Her voice echoed back at her. Anxiety skittered across her nerve endings.

She knew what she was doing, she told herself. She was a smart agent who was going to get information out of Petrellis.

Suddenly someone gripped her shoulders hard, and shoved her forward.

"You don't have to restrain me," she said. "It's not as if I'm in any shape to fight back."

He led her to his car and pushed her into the driver's seat, then across into the passenger seat. She hit the record button on her new phone, hoping maybe this time the evidence wouldn't be destroyed.

Aiming the gun at her chest with one hand, Petrellis started the car and pulled out of the alley.

"Where are we going?" she said.

"Someplace we can talk."

"About?"

"Who you really are."

She stilled. Did he know? Had her cover been blown?

He shot her a side-eye glare as he headed out of town. "Because you're not some random trail assistant or you'd be terrified of this." He waved his gun. "But you're not. Which means you have experience with guns."

"I was taught to shoot as a kid."

"Let's cut to the truth. Who sent you and what did you hear out there in the mountains?"

"So they did hire you to find me."

"What are you after?" he demanded.

"It was a job, that's all."

"You killed David Price, why?"

Whoa, so LaRouche and Harrington were telling their own people that Sara had killed him?

"I didn't kill him. LaRouche did."

"Stop lying. I need the truth!"

"I told you the truth."

"No, you didn't, but you will."

He turned onto a farm road and hit the accelerator. The car sped up, the speedometer needle reaching sixty miles per hour.

"Why are you doing this?" she cried.

"I have nothing to lose. My life is over."

The car sped toward an abandoned barn in the distance. Faster. Faster.

"Slow down!"

"Either I get answers from you or we both die. Makes no difference to me."

ELEVEN

Great, Sara had been kidnapped by a man with a death wish? No, there was more to this.

"What have they got on you?" she said.

"Tell me who hired you!" he countered.

"Are they blackmailing you? What? I know you're a cop—"

"Not anymore I'm not."

"I heard you had to retire early because of family issues. Have they offered you money?"

He sped up. Seventy miles per hour.

"Okay! I'm FBI!" she cried.

He shot her a look of disbelief.

"LaRouche and Harrington are the enemy here, not me," she protested.

The flash of police lights lit the car from behind.

He eyed the rearview, then refocused on the barn in the distance.

"You might want to die, but don't be a coward and take me with you. And what about the people who will die because of a faulty drug?"

He looked at her again.

"They didn't tell you about that, did they?" she said.

His foot eased up on the gas.

"You were a cop, a good cop," she said. "Getting the bad guys is in your blood. Help me stop them."

"I can't."

"Then, don't stop me from putting them away!"

She was grasping at the wind, but she had to try to get through to him. As the sirens wailed louder behind them, her heartbeat pounded against her chest. She didn't want to die this way.

Use your training. Talk him down.

"Innocent people will die. Do you want to be remembered as a murderer by your family? Your wife and kids?"

An ironic chuckle escaped his lips. "My kids don't care about me."

Okay, she'd hit a nerve. She was getting through to him.

"I don't believe that. They're going to be devastated when their father dies and is branded a criminal. There's still a chance to save yourself, Petrellis. Help us nail these guys."

A tear trailed down his cheek.

"Remember why you put on your uniform in the first place," she continued. "I could really use your help here, Stuart," she said, remembering his first name from the file she'd read at the police station.

He eased his foot off the accelerator. The barn loomed in the distance. He pressed down on the brake. The car came to a stop.

"I'm sorry," he said, and started to raise his gun.

To his own head.

She lunged, wrestling the gun away.

It went off, shattering the front windshield. Officer

McBride whipped open the driver's door and pulled Petrellis from the car. Nate opened Sara's door. She shoved the gun at him and stumbled away from the car, trying to catch her breath, trying not to throw up.

She'd almost been killed. Twice. First by the suicide crash into the barn, then when she'd disarmed him.

What was she thinking?

That she couldn't watch a man die because of criminal jerks LaRouche and Harrington.

"Take a deep breath," Nate said.

"I'm fine, I'm fine." Her face felt hot and cold at the same time.

"Why didn't you text me when you saw him?" Nate said.

"Didn't want him lawyering up."

"You could have—"

"Don't leave him alone. He's suicidal. He tried shooting himself in the head. They've got something on him, Nate. Find out what it is. I think he'll help us if you can destroy whatever they've got on him."

"Okay, okay, breathe. You're going to hyperventilate."

"How's Will? Is he okay?"

"He's fine. Let's get you out of here."

As Will fed the girls dinner, he tried to stay present and engaged in their stories about the museum, and their grandpa ordering monster hash for lunch.

Thoughts about what was happening with Sara's plan to draw out Officer Petrellis kept taunting him.

A few hours later, as he tucked them into bed, little Marissa asked, "Are you mad at us?"

Both girls looked at him with round green eyes.

"No, why would I be upset with you?" he said, glancing across the room at Claire.

"Because you've got that grandma look on your face," Claire said.

"What look?"

"You know, like this." Claire scrunched up her nose and pursed her lips in the patented grandma, disapproving frown.

Will smiled. "I look like that?"

Marissa nodded that he did.

"I'm sorry, girls. The fact is, I'm distracted because I'm worried about a friend."

"Miss Sara?" Claire asked.

"Yes. She's having a tough time and I think she could use a friend or two right about now."

"Doesn't she have any friends?" Marissa asked.

"I don't think so. She works so much and has no time for friends."

"That's sad," Claire said.

"But God's her friend," Marissa offered.

"Let's say a prayer for her." Claire climbed out of bed and kneeled, interlacing her fingers. Marissa followed suit, and Will's heart warmed. They were such good, loving girls.

He interlaced his fingers. "Who wants to lead?"

"I do, I do!" Marissa said.

The room quieted.

"Give us this day our daily bread—"

"Wrong one," Claire corrected.

"Oh, yeah." Marissa cleared her throat. "Dear God in Heaven, we are praying for our friend Miss Sara, who can't draw, and has no friends, but she's really nice and we like her anyway. We pray that she…" Marissa hesitated and looked at Will.

"Is safe," Will said.

"Is safe," the girls echoed.

"Is at peace," Will said.

"Is at peace."

"And will open her heart to the wonder of grace. Amen."

"Amen," the girls said.

"Okay, back into bed. I've got a surprise for you tomorrow after church."

"What kind of surprise?" Claire said.

"It wouldn't be a surprise if I told you." He tucked her in and kissed her forehead. "I think you're going to like it."

He went to Marissa's bed and tucked her in, as well.

"Love you, Daddy."

"Love you, pumpkin."

Will went to the door and switched off the light; the ceiling lit up with the twinkling of glow-in-the-dark stars.

He shut the door, appreciating the moment, realizing in a few years Claire wouldn't want to share a room with her little sister.

Will had plenty of work to catch up on, which he hoped would keep his mind off Sara. He fixed himself a cup of tea and went into the living room to enjoy the colorful lights on the Christmas tree while he worked.

He opened his laptop and forced himself to focus. One of his best clients, Master Printing, had had their website hacked and taken down by search engines. He'd rewritten the code and corrected the problem, so he signed on to check if their website was back online.

There wasn't much an SEO specialist like Will could do to force the search engines to reupload the pages. Still, he let them know the situation had been rectified.

A soft knock sounded from the door. He wondered if he'd imagined it. He stood and peeked through the window. Sara stood there with Nate behind her.

Will opened the door. "Thank God you're okay."

Sara wrapped her arms around Will and squeezed. Tight.

"Let's go inside," Nate said, looking over his shoulder.

"Sorry," Sara said, releasing Will.

"Why? I was thinking of doing the same thing." He put his arm around her and led her to the sofa.

"Actually, could I use the bathroom?" Sara asked.

"Sure, at the end of the hall on the right," Will said, and offered a smile.

It looked as if Sara tried to smile, but couldn't get her lips to work. She disappeared around the corner.

"You got Petrellis?" Will asked Nate.

"We got him."

"You don't sound happy about it."

"She went rogue on me, Will," Nate said, frustration coloring his voice. "I told her to text me when she saw Petrellis. Instead, she got into his car, and he…" Nate shook his head.

"He what?" Will fisted his hand.

"He almost killed them both, then tried to shoot himself in front of her."

"Oh, Sara," he whispered.

"She disarmed him, but she shouldn't have been there in the first place," Nate said, frustrated. "I apologize for bringing her here. She was insistent."

"No, it's okay," Will said. "I would have been up all night worrying about her anyway. At least I can see she's okay, sort of."

"The chief is trying to get Petrellis to work with us. The guy's pretty messed up. I guess his wife's in bad shape."

"How so?"

"She's got multiple sclerosis. Living in a nursing home in Bellingham, very expensive. LHP's security chief tracked Petrellis down and offered him a boatload of money to find Sara and figure out what she was up to. Petrellis needed the money to keep his wife in the Bellingham facility." Nate hesitated. "I had no idea she was so sick."

"How did LaRouche and Harrington track him down so quickly?"

"Companies like LHP employ top-notch IT specialists who probably went through bank records and personal histories to identify someone they could manipulate. I wonder who else they targeted in town."

"And no one knew about Petrellis's wife?"

"Nope. I feel bad about that. Why didn't he talk to the chief?"

"Sometimes if you don't talk about it, you can pretend it's not happening," Will offered, speaking from personal experience. "What I still don't understand is how LaRouche and Harrington discovered Sara was in Echo Mountain."

"The whole town knew she'd been rescued by SAR. Wouldn't be hard for them to figure it out."

"What happens next?"

"Waiting to hear from the chief," Nate said. "I still

want to move you and the girls to the resort. Did you speak with Bree?"

"She graciously invited us to move into her cottage."

"And Aiden's holding a private room for Sara at the resort."

"So you'll set her up there, as well?"

"That's the plan, not that she'll take orders." Nate's phone buzzed.

"You get that. I'm going to check on Sara," Will said.

"Detective Walsh." Nate wandered to the front window.

As Will headed for the hall, he heard the echo of little girl voices.

"I like those the best," Marissa said.

"That's because they're little, like you," Claire said.

"You make that sound like a bad thing."

It was Sara's voice. Will hesitated, not wanting to interrupt the moment.

"She always teases me about being little," Marissa said.

"I was little when I was a kid," Sara offered.

"You were?" Marissa said.

"Yep. Sometimes kids made fun of me, but my dad used to call me his little darling, which made it all okay."

"Does he still call you that?" Claire asked.

Will took a step toward the bedroom, wanting to intervene.

"My dad's in Heaven," Sara said.

"With Mommy." Marissa hushed.

The room fell silent. Will stepped into the room and froze. Sara was lying on the floor between the girls' beds, her hands folded across her chest.

"Hey girls," Will said.

Marissa jackknifed in bed. "Sara was little, too, Daddy."

"No kidding?"

Sara sat up and hugged her knees to her chest. "Sorry, they spotted me when I was walking by and asked me to come say good-night."

"I'm glad they did."

"Will you be here tomorrow, Miss Sara?" Claire asked.

"Maybe. We'll see. I'd better go so you can get some sleep."

"Daddy has a surprise for us tomorrow." Marissa clapped her hands in excitement.

Sara reached for Will, and he extended his hand to help her up. When she stood, they were only inches apart.

"Be careful of the mistletoe in the hallway," Claire said in a singsong voice.

Marissa giggled.

"Okay, girls, bedtime. For real," Will said. He motioned Sara out of the room and shut the door so adult voices wouldn't disturb them.

"They're so…" Sara started. "Precious."

"You sure you don't mean precocious?"

She stopped in the hallway, inches from the dreaded mistletoe, and placed an open palm against his chest.

"You're right, you are so—" she hesitated as if she struggled to form the word "—blessed."

In that moment, everything seemed to disappear: the danger, his anxiety about his in-laws and the fact that his best friend stood in the next room.

Will leaned forward and kissed Sara on the lips—a brief, loving kiss.

When he pulled back, her blue eyes widened and she pressed her fingertips to her lips.

Giggling echoed behind him. He turned and spotted his girls watching from a crack in their door.

"Bed," he ordered.

They slammed the door. When he turned around, Sara was walking into the living room.

Will sighed. Had he upset her?

He followed her into the living room where Nate continued his phone call.

Will sat next to Sara on the couch. She studied her fingers in her lap.

"So…am I in trouble?" Will asked.

She snapped her gaze to meet his. "No, but I am."

He studied her blue eyes, trying to discern the meaning of her words. Had something happened with the case, or was she referring to the kiss? Did she share the strong feelings he was developing for her, and decided that was unprofessional?

"Okay, I'll figure it out. Thanks, Chief." Nate ended his call and turned to Will and Sara. "Petrellis has been medicated for now. He went nuts on the way to lockup and they rushed him to the hospital. The chief likes our plan about relocating you at the resort, but suggested Sara head back to the station with me and spend the night in a cell."

"Nate, come on, why can't she stay at the loft?" Will said. "No one knows about it."

"The station is harder to breach, plus someone is always there. I can't put twenty-four-hour guard on both your house and the loft."

"Then, let Sara stay here, at the house."

"Will—"

"My home office doubles as a guest room." He interrupted Sara's protest, and looked at Nate. "You've got us under police protection anyway. This makes the most sense."

"Not to me, it doesn't," Sara said.

Nate sighed. "He's got a point. Keeping you all in one spot will make our job easier. I'll call the chief and let him know. I'll take the first shift. Better get my overnight bag from the truck." Nate went outside.

"I shouldn't be staying here, Will," Sara said.

"You don't belong in a jail cell." He stood and extended his hand. "Come on, I'll show you to your room."

She took his hand and he gently held on, anticipating her wanting to pull away.

She didn't.

He led her down the hallway and flipped on the light. Papers were scattered across the daybed.

"Sorry." He rushed over and collected them and then placed them on his desk. "The bed's only been slept in a few times, when Megan's sister came to visit. Clean towels are in the guest bathroom, which we rarely use. What else?" He looked around the room.

She reached out and touched his cheek. "Thank you."

"Of course."

"For so many things."

The walls felt as if they were closing in, and he could hardly breathe. Her gorgeous blue eyes studied him, as if she was trying to tell him something, something important, and intimate.

"Whatever happens, please know how much I appreciate you…" She hesitated. "Your generosity and your strength. You amaze me."

"My ego thanks you."

His gaze drifted to her lips. He wanted to kiss her again.

"I… I could use a glass of water," she said, her voice soft.

"We've got that here," he teased. "In the kitchen."

She didn't move. Neither did he.

Will's heart pounded against his chest. He sensed she needed to put distance between them, and he understood why. It was important they stayed focused on remaining safe, and not get distracted by their attraction to one another, or the promise of…did he dare say love?

Two loud cracks echoed from outside the window.

Followed by a crash.

And the house went dark.

TWELVE

Sara protectively yanked Will away from the window and pulled him into a crouch.

"Daddy! Daddy!" the girls cried.

"Go to the girls," Sara said calmly. "And stay down."

They both felt their way into the dark hallway.

"Where do you keep flashlights?" she asked.

"Everywhere. Kids are afraid of the dark. Got one in here." He opened a hall closet and fumbled for a second, then handed her a flashlight.

"What about you?"

A light winked from inside the girls' bedroom. "Claire's on it."

"Daddy!" Claire called.

"Go." Sara pointed the flashlight so he could make his way down the hall.

"You aren't going outside, are you?"

"No. Go on, they need you." She gave him a gentle shove. Once he was in the room with his girls, Sara went into the living room and peered through the curtain. The entire block was dark.

Neighbors opened their doors. She spotted a neighbor across the street starting down his front steps to investigate.

"What is going on?" she whispered.

She watched a few more neighbors wander outside, then head toward the end of the block. She went to another window to search the dark street. Someone flipped on their car headlights, illuminating a vehicle that had collided into an electrical pole. It must have damaged the transformer.

"Yikes." She wondered if the driver had been under the influence, or if he'd hit the gas instead of the brake by accident.

Another set of headlights clicked on, illuminating the street in front of Will's house. She snapped her attention to Nate's car and spotted someone kneeling beside Nate, who was on the ground.

"Oh, no," she said in a hushed tone.

She wanted to check on him, but figured he'd be furious if she left the house. She called 911, but they'd already been alerted about the accident and downed police officer.

"What happened?" Will said coming into the room.

Little Marissa dashed to Sara and wrapped her arms around her from behind. Tense from the past hour, Sara fought the urge to untangle the girl's arms from her waist. *Stop thinking about yourself and consider how much this little girl needs female comfort.*

"Looks as if a car hit the transformer," Sara said, stroking Marissa's hair. "Your neighbors are taking care of things."

"Can I see?" Claire said.

"No," Sara said.

Claire stopped dead in her tracks. Will looked at Sara in question.

"The car is pretty smashed up, and the driver is probably…" She hesitated. "Well, images like that can give you nightmares for weeks. Trust me, I've had my share of those."

"You have?" Marissa said, looking up at her.

"Yup. Better idea, let's light some candles and have a party."

"A party, cool." Claire started for the kitchen, where Sara assumed they kept the candles.

"Me, too," Marissa said, chasing after her sister.

As they rooted around in drawers, Sara motioned Will to come closer.

"Was it really a transformer?" he said in a soft voice.

"Yes, but there might be more to it. Nate is hurt."

"Where, outside?"

"Yes."

Will started for the front door. "I've gotta help him."

"Will, your girls—"

He whipped open the door just as Nate came stumbling into the house with help from Will's neighbor.

"I tried keeping him down until the ambulance came. He wasn't having any of it," the elderly neighbor said.

"What happened?" Will asked.

"I'm fine." Nate collapsed on the couch.

"I'm Sara," she said, extending her hand to the neighbor.

"Oscar Lewis, nice to meet you." They shook hands.

"Yay, more people for the party!" Marissa said, coming out of the kitchen.

Claire took one look at Nate and said, "What happened to Detective Nate?"

"Car clipped me," Nate said.

"Marissa, take the candles. I'll get some ice." Claire unloaded the candles into her sister's arms and disappeared into the kitchen. Sara marveled at how mature the eight-year-old Claire acted in the face of a crisis.

Sirens wailed from the street.

"Oscar, can you tell them I'm in here?" Nate said.

"Sure, police and EMTs?"

"I don't need an ambulance, but the driver of that sedan will."

Oscar left and Sara shut the door. Marissa stood in the corner, lining up candles.

"Hey, baby M, can you help your sister?" Will asked. "We need ice, and warm, wet towels for detective Nate's cuts and bruises."

"Okay, Daddy." Marissa danced off to join her sister in the kitchen.

Sara sat on a coffee table in front of Nate, Will hovering close by. "What really happened?" Sara said to Nate.

"I'm not totally sure. One minute I was texting, the next, a sedan was speeding toward me. I dived out of the way, but he clipped me. I went down, shot at his back tire and he crashed."

"Why would he run you down?" Sara said.

Nate shook his head. "This case is getting stranger by the minute."

A knock sounded at the front door. Will went to open it.

A cute blond woman in her twenties rushed into the living room, spotted Nate and froze. "You're hurt."

"I'm fine," Nate said.

"I heard the call go out and came to see—"

"I'll answer questions for the blog tomorrow, Cassie. This isn't the time."

Sara read more than curiosity on Cassie's face. Sara read true concern.

And Nate was oblivious.

"What happened?" Cassie said, taking a step toward him.

Claire rushed into the room carrying an ice bag wrapped in a towel. "Here's the ice."

"He needs ice?" Cassie said.

"Where do you need it?" Claire asked.

"My knee would be great."

Claire held the ice pack to his knee, and an odd expression crossed Nate's face. "You'll probably get a better story by interviewing the neighbors."

"Really?" Cassie said, her voice laced with sarcasm. Shaking her head, she muttered, "Turkey." She stormed out of the house.

Sara and Will shared a look.

"I saw that," Nate said.

"Who was she?" Sara asked.

"She writes a community blog. I'm her source."

"Yeah, that's one word for it," Will said.

"Focus, guys," Nate said. "Obviously you're not safe here."

"Not a problem," Will said. "I'll call Bree and we'll head over there tonight."

"Head where, Daddy?" Claire said.

"Echo Mountain Resort. We're going to stay there for a while."

Another knock sounded at the door and Will answered. Chief Washburn joined them in the living room. "You okay?" he asked Nate.

"Yeah, but seriously frustrated."

"Well, you're gonna be more frustrated," the chief said. "The driver ran off."

"How is that possible?" Nate said.

"Neighbors saw where he headed. We'll do a search."

"Unbelievable," Nate said. "We lost another one."

"Let's focus on what we do have control over," Will said. "I'll help the girls pack."

Will and the girls were situated at Bree's cottage and fast asleep a few hours later. The girls shared an upstairs bedroom. Sara decided to stay upstairs as well, wanting to be close to protect Will, Claire and Marissa. Will and Nate bunked in the living room for the night.

Even with all the excitement, the girls were up bright and early the next day, ready for church. He asked them to be as quiet as possible so as not to wake Sara, yet she came down for breakfast. Will invited her to church, but she said she needed to focus on changing her looks. He suspected something else kept her from surrendering her troubles to God. That was a discussion for another time.

Officer Ryan McBride escorted Will and the girls to church, and stood guard outside. Nate hung back at the cottage to help Sara and brainstorm angles about the case.

During the service, Will said an extra prayer of thanks that Nate wasn't seriously injured last night.

The theme of the service was having faith during troubling times. Will embraced the message, needing the extra encouragement. He held firm to his faith regarding his abilities to be a good father, and he had faith things would work out for Sara.

Maybe even for Sara and Will?

From a practical standpoint, this relationship wasn't real. It was formed by tense emotions during danger-ous circumstances. Sometimes love and practicality had little to do with one another. He was drawn to Sara, without question. Hopefully, after her case was solved, he could share his feelings. To what end? Her job, her life, was back in Seattle; sure, only three hours away, but it might as well be three thousand miles away. The next woman he married would have to be a good mom for the girls. Parenting wasn't a part-time job.

Parenting? Marriage? Between the excitement of yes-terday and his clients' needs, Will was obviously sleep deprived, apparent in his random thoughts today.

"Go in peace and serve the Lord," Pastor Charles said. "Amen."

"Amen," the congregation repeated.

Will helped the girls on with their jackets, and waited while they buttoned up. Friends smiled and greeted him as they passed down the center aisle. Will offered greet-ings in return, exchanging pleasantries and a brief story or two.

With his girls on either side of him, Will clung to their hands and they made their way toward the exit. Once outside, he spotted Nate. Beside Nate stood a blond woman wearing a red ski cap and sunglasses. She looked like a teenager, and it took him a minute to realize it was Sara. She certainly had changed her looks.

Will led the girls toward Nate and Sara.

"You guys ready to head back to the resort?" Nate said.

"Yeah, they have an indoor pool," Claire said.

"Who's got a pool?" Will's mother-in-law, Mary, said over his shoulder.

"The resort," Claire said.

"Will, may I have a word with you?" Mary said.

"Sure, Mary, what's up?"

"Over here, please." She motioned for Will to join her a few feet away, while his father-in-law entertained the girls with a story.

"Mary?" he questioned.

She stopped, turned around and waved an envelope between them. "It's our official request for custody of the girls."

Will's heart dropped to his knees. "I don't understand."

"I haven't filed these papers, and I won't. Unless you continue to put the girls in harm's way."

"I would never—"

"You're not thinking straight, Will. I heard about last night, about how someone tried to run down Detective Walsh in front of your house. Why was the detective there anyway? Because he was keeping watch over the woman you rescued. Why was she at your house?"

"She was checking to see if I was okay."

"Why wouldn't you be okay?"

He didn't answer.

"Because something else happened that I don't know about." Mary sighed. "I stopped by the house last night and you and the girls were gone. Where did you stay?"

"At the resort."

"In hotel rooms?"

"No, at a friend's cottage."

"Because you were too frightened to stay in your own home. Do you see why I'm concerned?"

"We've got it under control."

"Look—" she hesitated "—you and I often don't see things the same way, but we agree on one thing, and that's the welfare of your girls."

"And?"

"Whatever trouble this woman is in, she's brought it into your life, correct?"

He didn't answer, he couldn't answer. She was right.

"I don't want a court battle, and I don't want to upset Claire and Marissa, but I can't stand the thought of them being put in harm's way because you played the Good Samaritan."

He couldn't believe she was making him feel ashamed about helping a person in trouble.

"Let the girls stay with us until this situation is resolved, and we'll forget about this." Mary slipped the envelope into her purse.

"Will? Everything all right?" Sara said, approaching them.

His mother-in-law narrowed her eyes at Sara, and then glanced at Will. "Please call me by the end of the day and let me know your decision." She passed by Sara and motioned to Ed that they were leaving.

"What was that about?" Sara said.

"She's worried about the girls." He gazed across the parking lot at his daughters, under the protective eye of both Nate and Officer McBride.

"Because of me and the case," Sara said in a flat tone.

"Mary came to the house last night after hearing about the accident. We were gone. She figured out we didn't feel safe at the house. She threatened to take the girls away."

Sara touched his arm. "Will, no."

"Threatened, but she won't. She loves them too much. It would crush them to have us embroiled in a court battle over their welfare."

Marissa started to run off and visit with her friend Addy. Nate blocked her and shifted her closer to the car.

In that moment, looking at his baby girl's disappointed frown as she waved goodbye to her friend, Will realized this was no way for the girls to live—under the watchful eye of an overprotective father and police officers—until the case was solved and Will was out of danger.

It would break his heart to be away from them again, but he had to think of their well-being over his emotional needs.

"I need to talk to Nate."

As he headed toward Nate, Sara walked beside him. "You're a good dad," she said. "Don't ever forget that."

"Thanks." Will nodded at Nate. "Got a sec?"

Sara asked Claire a question about drawing, and both girls offered their advice. Will pulled Nate aside. "I'm thinking it might be easier on all of us, and safer for the girls, if they went away for a few days with their grandparents."

"Are you sure?"

"Yes. I should have suggested it sooner, but was missing them something fierce when I got home from my hiking trip."

"Setting them up at the resort—"

"Doesn't remove them from the potential danger. How safe do you think they'd be with my in-laws?"

"Safer than staying with you, especially if they take them out of town. Also, we could ask Harvey to tag along and play bodyguard. His cop instincts are razor sharp and he's got plenty of time on his hands since he retired from the resort."

"Good idea, thanks." Will gazed at his adorable girls. "I did the right thing by helping Sara, and now I have to do the right thing by keeping Claire and Marissa safe."

"Your in-laws might still be here." Nate craned his neck.

"No, not yet. I want to spend the day with the girls, then if you don't mind, could you take them over to Mary and Ed's?"

"Sounds good. Let's get you back to the resort."

Sara, Will and the girls hung out in Breanna McBride's cottage, drawing, baking and playing games. Sara had tried to isolate herself upstairs in the bedroom, but the girls were having none of it. They demanded she come downstairs and *visit*, as Marissa put it.

They made Christmas cookies, drank hot cocoa and laughed at silly jokes. Sara couldn't remember the last time she'd felt like a part of a family. Then Will told the girls his surprise was that Claire and Marissa were going on an adventure with their grandparents for a few days.

They were excited at first, then disappointed when they found out Will wasn't going. They moaned about missing their dad, and Sara's family moment shattered before her eyes. Rather than blame herself for the situation, Sara was more motivated than ever to wrap up this case so Will could get back to his life, his family.

And Sara could get back to…what?

She wasn't sure anymore. Was there even a job waiting for her back at the bureau? She didn't know. Oddly, she felt resentment toward her job. All of her determination, all of her drive to get the bad guys, had caused Will and his girls to be in danger, and now to be split up for their own protection.

The girls packed their things shortly after dinner and brought their bags down into the main entryway of the cottage.

"You just got home," Claire complained, hugging Will.

Sara looked away, the child's voice ripping at her heart. Marissa watched her big sister's reaction with curiosity, as if she was deciding if she was supposed to complain, as well.

"You girls are going to have fun with Nanny and Papa, okay?" he said to Claire.

"Okay," Claire said. "But no more adventures without you."

Marissa wrapped her arms around Sara's legs. "Bye, Sara."

"Bye, sweetie." She stroked the little girl's hair.

"Practice your drawing," Claire said. She looked at her dad. "Make sure she practices."

Will smiled. "Come on, I'll walk you girls to the car," he said, his voice raspy. "I'll be right back." Will nodded at Sara and escorted his girls out front.

Frustration burned low, and Sara marched into the kitchen. She started to pour herself a cup of coffee. Probably not a good idea to have caffeine at night, then again she wouldn't be able to get much sleep anyway, not until she could guarantee the safety of Will and the girls by putting LaRouche and Harrington away.

How was she going to do that? She wasn't even involved with the investigation, other than being a witness to the murder of David Price. She should be tracking down leads, helping Nate somehow, instead of baking cookies and playing board games with the girls.

She eyed the Christmas cookies, spread out on cooling racks. Little girls' laughter echoed in her mind as her gaze landed on a snowman cookie with green candy eyes and a red nose. Marissa had giggled uncontrollably when her dad had sprinkled powdered sugar on the cookie and called him Rudolph Frosty.

Sara wandered across the kitchen to the cookies and tried remembering a time when she'd made cookies with her dad, yet there was no memory of making Christmas cookies or telling jokes. Sara, her dad and Kenny had seemed to live under a cloud after her mom had randomly gotten sick and died.

"Shake it off," Sara scolded herself.

She left the kitchen and decided to check email in the living room. As she adjusted herself at Breanna's desk, she glanced out the window and spotted Will saying goodbye to the girls. He gave them each a big hug, and had to pry Claire's arms loose from his neck. A ball lodged in Sara's throat.

The girls finally got in the squad car and Will shut the door. When he turned, she saw him swipe at his eyes, and she felt even worse about dragging him into this mess.

There had to be a way to make it up to him.

Sure there was. Remove the threat. She reconsidered distancing herself from him, only they'd established that it wouldn't make a difference. They could get to Sara through Will.

Somehow word had gotten back to LaRouche and Harrington that Sara and Will had grown close, or maybe they knew that he'd saved her life and vice versa.

Whatever the case may be, the only way to keep Will safe was to prove LaRouche and Harrington were the criminals she knew them to be: men who didn't care about killing innocent people for profit.

She refocused on the computer and checked her email. One caught her eye, an email from her boss demanding she call him ASAP. She pulled out her phone and called his cell. It went into voice mail.

"It's Agent Vaughn returning your call. The local police are being very helpful. I look forward to speaking with you." She ended the call, not feeling all that grateful to the man who didn't support her quest to nail LaRouche and Harrington, the man who insinuated to Nate that she'd lost her perspective and maybe, even, was off the rails.

"Bonner," she muttered, and paced the living room. Why did he have to make things so hard? Why didn't he believe her when she showed him the proof of tampering with test results?

This train of thought wasn't going to help her move forward. She'd been stuck in the past on so many levels, that it had almost become habit for her: dig her heels in and hold on like a pit bull with its teeth around an intruder's leg.

She made a mental list of things to discuss with Nate once he returned. In the meantime, the least she could do was be there to support Will. He must feel horrible about separating from his girls again. She wondered what was taking him so long to come back inside.

She went to the front door and hesitated before opening it. Would she find him crying on the front porch? She wasn't sure if she could handle that, nor could she handle the look of resentment in his eyes—resentment toward Sara for causing his life to be turned upside down and sideways.

A car door slammed outside. Nate had already left to take the girls to their grandparents' house, so it couldn't be his car. She opened the door and spotted Officer Carrington headed for the cottage. She scanned the area for Will.

"Wait, did Will end up going with the girls?" she asked, partly hopeful and partly disappointed.

"No, ma'am."

Her heart raced up into her throat. "Then, where is he?"

THIRTEEN

"**W**ill!" Sara called out. She rushed past Officer Carrington to get a better look at the property.

"Ma'am, please get back in the house where it's safe."

"Not until we find him. Will!"

What could have happened? In those few minutes while Sara had been away from the window feeling sorry for herself, had another one of LaRouche and Harrington's men swung by and snatched Will?

"Ma'am, I insist you go inside where it's safe."

Of course, standing here in the open made her a target. If LaRouche and Harrington's men were using Will to lure her out, they had succeeded. She rushed past Officer Carrington, went back into the cottage and called Nate.

"Detective Walsh."

"It's Sara. Are you on speakerphone?"

"Yes."

"Call me after you drop off the girls." She ended the call. The last thing she wanted was to upset Claire and Marissa by announcing their father had gone missing.

She paced the kitchen and eyed the wall phone.

Posted beside it was a list of numbers, including one that read Security. She used Bree's house line to call it.

"Hey, sweet Bree," a man's voice said. "I thought you were helping with the—"

"It's not Breanna. It's Sara, I'm staying in Bree's cottage. Who's this?"

"Scott Becket, security manager for the resort."

"Have you been briefed about my situation?" she asked.

"Yes, Nate told me you're undercover FBI. Is there a problem?"

"Will is missing," she said, trying to sound calm, but failing miserably.

"When did this happen?"

"A few minutes ago. He was saying goodbye to the girls, and then he was gone."

"I'm on it. Stay put."

The line went dead.

"Argh!" she cried. Sliding down the wall, she wrapped her arms around her bent knees, feeling utterly helpless. She buried her face in her arms, brainstorming a way to help them find Will without putting herself in danger.

Suddenly a wet nose nudged her ear. She looked up, and got a big, wet kiss on the cheek from Bree's golden retriever, Fiona.

"What's wrong?" Bree placed a bag of groceries on the kitchen table and kneeled beside Sara.

"It's Will" was all she could get out.

"What about him?"

"He's gone. I don't know where. He disappeared."

"I've got to call Scott."

"Already did."

"Good, then everything will be fine. Scott was an exceptional cop before becoming our security manager. Did you call Nate?"

"He's with the girls. He'll call after he drops them off."

"Then, there's only one thing left to do while we wait." Bree reached out and placed a comforting hand on Sara's shoulder.

And said a prayer.

Sara didn't fight it this time; she was so desperate for Will's safety that she bowed her head and opened her heart. She hoped that God was truly forgiving, that he'd hear Sara's heartfelt prayer and keep Will safe.

"Stop!" Will called.

He'd seen the man hovering on the grounds near the cottage, thanks to the resort's property lights, and Will had called out, demanding the stranger identify himself. Instead, he'd run.

And Will had taken off after him. Maybe not the smartest idea, but the burn of frustration had driven Will out into the night. Frustration about his girls being forced to go away with their grandparents, frustration about Sara being constantly threatened.

"What do you want?" Will called after the guy, who turned a corner. Great, a blind spot. What if he had a gun and was waiting for Will? He stopped and searched the ground for a weapon, a rock or tree branch, something.

This was not Will. He wasn't a violent man by nature.

Yet this stranger might have information to help the authorities with this case. Will couldn't let him get away. He'd do anything to help Nate prove Sara's innocence and the businessmen's culpability in the death of David Price.

He grabbed a rather large branch and hesitated before making the turn.

Took a deep breath.

And flung the branch around the corner. No reaction. Surely the man would have fired off a shot.

Will clicked on the flashlight app on his phone, took a deep breath and peered around the corner. He aimed the light up the trail. The man was gone. Vanished.

How was that possible? The trail took a sharp incline five hundred feet. There was no way the man would have made it to the top, and to the next switchback so quickly.

Then Will noticed something on the ground. He approached a discoloration and kneeled for a better look.

Fresh blood.

The man was wounded, which meant he wouldn't be able to fight very hard against Will once he caught up to him.

Will straightened and started up the trail, using the flashlight to scan left, then right. The blood trail led straight up, then disappeared.

Will pulled out his phone and called Nate.

"Where are you?" Nate said before Will could get off a greeting.

"Are the girls—"

"Just dropped them off. Sara said you disappeared. What happened?"

"I saw a man watching the house so I followed him."

"You what? Get back to the house."

"I'm on a trail leading from the back of the cottage into the mountains. The guy's hurt."

"You found him?"

"Not yet. I found fresh blood and—"

Something slammed against Will's shoulders and he went down, breaking his fall with his hands. He collapsed against the damp earth, the wind knocked from his lungs. The guy would have already shot him if he had a gun, so Will figured he'd stay down and pretend to be unconscious. Depending on how badly the stranger was hurt, Will could detain him until help arrived.

"I've got him," the man said into his phone. "You'll have to come get him. I'm injured."

By the time this man's associates came to get Will, Nate and the local police would be swarming the area. Good, then maybe they'd catch these guys and one of them would confess to working for LaRouche and Harrington.

"Aw, come on, that wasn't the deal," the guy argued.

Will cracked his eyes open and spotted the man's black military boots pacing back and forth. Will also spotted his phone a few inches away. Will snatched it.

The man, clearly agitated, didn't notice Will retrieving his phone. The assailant seemed anxious and frustrated, and definitely not on board with the orders coming from the other end of the phone.

"No, I never signed on for that….Fine, I'll call my brother to help."

A few seconds of silence passed. Will figured they wanted his attacker to move Will's body. To where?

"Bobby, it's Jim. Get out here to Echo Mountain Resort, the trail behind Bree McBride's cottage. I've got a guy I have to keep hidden….Will Rankin….I know. I know! They threatened to tell the police about the morphine I stole from the hospital….I had no choice.

She's in a lot of pain….You'd know if you bothered to stop by, big brother."

As the conversation continued, Will figured out that the criminal businessmen were blackmailing his assailant. Will suddenly remembered where he'd seen those boots before: at the hospital. This was Jim Banks, the security officer who'd helped them look for Sara.

Apparently LaRouche and Harrington were able to get to anyone in town.

"I can't go to jail!" Jim yelled at his brother on the phone.

He had paced a good twenty feet away, as if Jim didn't like to look at what he'd done to Will. Will took the opportunity to flip the situation around. He took a deep breath, stood and aimed the flashlight at his attacker.

"Jim?"

Jim spun around, whipped a knife out of his pocket and pointed it at Will with a trembling hand. Abrasions reddened his cheek, and his right jacket sleeve was soaked with blood.

"I have first-aid training," Will said. "I can help you."

"No, you can't. Come on." He flicked the knife sideways, motioning for Will to lead the way back down.

Which meant they'd be passing right by Bree's cottage. How could this guy think he'd get very far in public? The guy had obviously stopped thinking once he found himself working for LaRouche and Harrington.

Kind of like how Will had stopped thinking clearly when he'd taken off in pursuit of this man.

"I sense you don't want to do this," Will said.

"Stop the psychobabble and walk."

Will realized he'd had enough: enough of hiding out

and enough being bullied. He was definitely done surrendering to violent situations without a fight. It was time to protect the people he cared about.

As he approached Jim, he glanced up ahead at the trail. "You're here!"

Jim instinctively looked to his right.

Will kicked Jim in the side and he fell to his knees. Will grabbed Jim's wrist and twisted until Jim let go of the knife. Will yanked Jim's arm behind his back and the man cried out in pain.

Will shoved him to the ground, pinning him with a knee to his back. "I don't want to hurt you."

Jim groaned in surrender.

"What happened to your arm?" Will said.

"Car accident."

"The accident outside my house last night?"

The guy nodded.

"Will!" Nate called.

Will spotted Nate and Scott jogging toward him, both wearing headlamps.

"How many guys?" Nate called.

"One guy. Jim Banks from the hospital," Will said.

"Found him," Scott said into his cell phone. "He's fine. We'll be back shortly."

"You've obviously got this under control." Nate raised a brow as he motioned for Will to move aside.

Will pushed off the guy, struggling to calm the adrenaline rush. Nate and Scott helped Jim up and he groaned.

"He's bleeding pretty badly," Will offered.

Nate and Scott looked at Will, as if shocked that Will had drawn blood.

"He was the driver who crashed into the pole last night," Will clarified.

"Whoa, okay. I was afraid you lost your temper," Nate said, then looked at Jim. "So what's this about?"

Jim studied the ground.

"Someone's blackmailing him," Will explained. "Something about stealing drugs from the hospital."

"Is that right?" Nate pressed, eyeing his suspect.

"Lawyer," Jim said.

"Sure thing. Right after we book you for attempted murder."

"What! I didn't attempt to kill anyone."

"Did he threaten you with a weapon?" Nate asked Will.

"A knife." He aimed his flashlight at the ground, and went to pick it up.

"I got it." Scott picked up the knife with gloved hands and analyzed it. "Yeah, this could definitely kill someone."

"No, that wasn't the plan. I needed him to come with me."

"Where?" Nate pushed.

"They said…they said to bring him to the water tower on the north side of town."

"For what purpose?" Nate asked.

"I don't know."

"Will!" Sara came racing around the corner, Officer Carrington right behind her.

"I'm sorry, sir," Carrington said to Nate. "Once she heard you'd secured the scene, I couldn't get her to stay put."

"How did she—"

"I called Bree," Scott interrupted Nate.

Sara spotted the knife in Scott's hand and snapped her gaze to Will. Her eyes widened with horror.

"I'm fine," Will said.

"He didn't…"

"He didn't. Let's go." He reached out for her and she hesitated, then took his hand. He didn't like her hesitation, wondering what was behind it.

They headed back down the trail toward the cottage, where two more squad cars were parked.

"Officer Carrington, take Will and Sara inside and keep them there," Nate said. "I'll swing by the hospital with Jim for medical attention." Nate put Jim in the backseat of a patrol car, and pointed at Will and Sara. "Stay inside, hear me?"

"Yes," Will said.

Bree bolted out of the house, her dog right beside her. The golden retriever rushed up to Scott.

"It's okay, girl. We're all okay." Scott scanned the property with a concerned frown, then forced a smile when he looked at Bree. "Let's get inside before Nate locks us up for disobeying orders."

Sara released Will's hand. He wasn't going to let her push him away. He cared about her. A lot.

Will put his arm around Sara's shoulder and pulled her close, whispering in her ear, "Don't push me away."

She shook her head in frustration.

Once they got into the cottage, Bree and Scott headed for the kitchen. "I've got cookies," Bree announced.

"We'll join you in a minute," Will said, leading Sara into a secluded corner of the living room.

He motioned her to a Queen Anne chair, and he shifted onto the footstool in front of her. Her gaze drifted to the hardwood floor.

"What's going on?" He tipped her chin to look at him.

"You could have been killed."

He took her hands in his. "Hey, you didn't make me follow Jim up the trail. That was my decision."

"I'm always involving people in my violent life and they get hurt and I can't seem to fix anything."

"Hold on a second. This isn't about what just happened, is it?"

She didn't answer, but she didn't pull her hands from his, so he pressed on.

"This is about your father?"

Silence stretched between them.

"Sara, you didn't do anything wrong, and you were certainly not responsible for what happened to him. He made the decision to protect you by hiding you in the closet."

Her gaze held his, her eyes tearing. "Why? Why did he do that?"

Will pulled her into a hug and stroked her back. "Because he loved you so very much. It's hard to understand until you have children of your own. You'd literally jump in front of a moving bus to save them. Your dad hid you in a closet so that you would live, and become this strong, tenacious woman who fights for justice."

She sighed against him. "You make that sound like a good thing."

"It *is* a good thing. Think of all the people you've protected. You have sacrificed your life, your happiness to fight for those who can't defend themselves because they're either ignorant of the danger, or don't have the skills to stop the violence. You've become a strong, dedicated woman thanks to your life experiences. God has been watching out for you, Sara, watching you choose the tough cases and fight the hard battles. Embrace what you are instead of thinking it should be different or somehow better. This is better. Here, being here with me."

"You should be holding on to your girls."

"I will, once we resolve this case and everyone is safe. I ache for them, sure, yet as a father I must sacrifice my own needs for theirs. So we're a lot alike, you and I, which is probably why we've connected this way." He continued to stroke her back, liking how it felt when she leaned into him, almost as if…

She needed him.

"I… I don't know what *this* is," she said.

"You don't have to define it, but answer me this. How do you feel, in this moment, here with me?"

"At peace, maybe even…blessed."

"Hold on to that and have faith the rest will work itself out."

Faith. Sara was pretty sure she'd given up on having faith a long time ago. She went to sleep that night with a curious sense of peace, dreaming about possibilities for the future. She'd never really thought about the future before, at least not beyond the next few weeks anyway.

Somehow, through the crises of the past few days, something had awakened inside of her, something akin to hope. Did she dare embrace it?

They had set Will up in a private apartment at the resort for the night, while Sara stayed in Bree's cottage. The resort's security manager, who was Bree's boyfriend, Scott, and Officer Carrington took turns keeping watch over the cottage. They parked two squad cars out front, the strategy being that the police presence would discourage another direct attack.

Sara hated feeling helpless to resolve this situation—her mess of a case—and still felt utterly responsible for bringing the danger to this charming town.

For bringing the danger into Will's life.

Today she would dedicate herself to helping the local authorities with their investigation any way she could.

She went downstairs and spotted Officer Carrington napping on the sofa, while Scott stood guard at the window. Not wanting to awaken the officer, she continued down the hallway into the kitchen.

Will sipped coffee at the kitchen table. He must have sensed her presence because he looked up and cracked a natural smile. "Did you sleep okay?"

He automatically stood and greeted her with a hug.

"Sure, pretty good considering the circumstances."

"Bree left you some scones, and I made a fresh pot of coffee." He turned to grab a mug off the counter.

"I'll get it, thanks."

Her phone vibrated with a call and she answered. "Vaughn."

"It's SSA Bonner, returning your call."

"Good morning, sir." She straightened. "I thought you'd want an update—"

"You're supposed to be on vacation, not chasing a lead I specifically told you was off-limits."

"Sir, I—"

"Do you have any idea what you've done, Agent Vaughn? You've screwed up an eighteen-month investigation."

"I don't understand."

"Another team at the bureau had been working the

David Price angle, trying to get enough leverage on him to make him roll on his partners."

"I had no idea."

"It was above your pay grade. And now Price is dead, and potentially so is your career."

"Wait, what?"

"It isn't always about you and your crusades, Agent Vaughn. I've told you that over and over again. We can't have agents who won't take orders. Therefore, you're suspended until further notice."

The room seemed to close in around her. She glanced at Will, his remarkable green eyes studying her with concern. She wanted to go to him again, be held in his strong, comforting arms. He believed in her. He believed she was an honorable crusader with an altruistic mission to protect people.

And that gave her strength.

"I disagree with this course of action," she said to her boss.

"You can appeal with personnel. But consider what your supervisors will say when asked about working with you, about how you've constantly challenged their authority. I'm not sure you were ever meant to be a part of our team, Agent Vaughn."

"Because I don't give up?" she said, her voice rising in pitch.

Bonner sighed heavily into the phone. "No, Sara." He hesitated. "Because of your tunnel vision. You only see what you're looking at, not anything else, or anyone else around you. If you'd been more aware of the people around you, you would have picked up on the cues that there was something else in the works regarding LHP.

Other agents did, and they backed off, but you couldn't, because you shut out everything else."

"I thought focus made me a good agent."

"It does, to a point. You also have to trust your co-workers and the system, and that's where you disconnect. You don't trust anyone or anything besides your own instincts."

"Which were right in this case. Once I get my phone back, I'll have proof."

"I hope so, for your sake. If there's evidence on the phone and we're able to use it to build a case against LHP, my superiors might reconsider your suspension. Until then, you cannot act on the authority of our office, and I need to ask you to turn in your ID and firearm when you return."

It felt as if she'd been slugged in the gut. He was stripping away her identity.

"I... I'm not sure when I'm coming back," she said, her voice sounding foreign to her.

"Do what's necessary to help the local authorities in the Price homicide as a witness only, not as an agent." Bonner paused. "For what it's worth, I am sorry, and I wish you the best of luck. Goodbye, Sara."

She stared blindly at her phone.

"What is it?" Will touched her arm.

"I've been suspended."

"Oh, honey. I am so sorry."

"He accused me of only thinking about myself, of only seeing what I'm focused on, nothing else around me." She sighed. "He said I can't work with a team."

"Then, he doesn't know you very well."

"It sounds as if the only chance I have of keeping my job is the evidence on my phone."

"Come here." Will pulled her into an embrace.

She felt broken, betrayed, a complete failure. If only they would have told her about the other team investigating LHP she would have dropped it as ordered. But she hadn't because she'd thought they were giving up too easily.

A man cleared his throat, and Will released Sara. Nate hesitated in the doorway of the kitchen.

"She got some bad news," Will said.

"Unfortunately, I've got more bad news." Nate held up Sara's phone as he stepped into the kitchen. Scott also joined them.

"The video file is not retrievable," Nate said. "We can't use it to prove who killed David Price."

There went her job, plus LaRouche and Harrington would get away with murder and pin suspicion on Sara.

"That's unacceptable," she said.

Maybe Bonner thought her determination was a bad thing, yet in this case, it was her best defense.

"Didn't you say you knew a tech?" she asked Will.

"Yes, Zack Carter. He works here at the resort."

"I could get it to him," Scott offered.

"Let's try it, Nate," Will said. "I mean, what have we got to lose?"

"Even if Zack somehow gets the file, we couldn't use that in a court of law," Nate countered.

"LaRouche and Harrington wouldn't need to know that, at least not when you initially question them, right?" Sara offered.

Nate raised an eyebrow. "I suppose not."

"We could still use the recording to our advantage," she said.

The back door opened and Bree came inside with

Fiona. "Oh, hey, everybody. Text alert went out. They're sending K9 teams to search for David Price's body on the east side of Granite Ridge."

"On the east side?" Will questioned.

"Yeah, why?"

"Because I found Sara on the west side of Echo Mountain. You have a map?"

"Sure." Bree went to her pack across the room and pulled a map out of a side pocket.

"What are you thinking?" Nate asked.

"That they're sending SAR teams to the wrong location."

Will spread the map out on the table and pointed to a small lake. "When this is where I found Sara."

"Sara, do you know where you camped the night you and David fell?" Nate questioned.

"We hiked up to Flatrock Overlook, then went west another two miles, so right about here." She pointed. "I fell down this side, and David was hurled off the trail toward the north."

"Which makes sense, because she ended up by the lake," Will said. "But Nate, look at how far away that campsite is from Granite Ridge."

"LaRouche and Harrington are sending search teams on a wild goose chase," Sara said.

"Because they don't want anyone finding the body," Nate offered.

"Which means there might be evidence on the body implicating LaRouche and Harrington," Sara said.

"Or they think David is still alive down there," Nate said.

They all shared a concerned look.

"It's happened before," Bree said. "A hiker has survived a nasty fall."

Nate's phone buzzed on his belt. He ripped it off, studied the message and looked at Sara. "It's my chief. LaRouche and Harrington are in town. They're demanding I lock you up."

FOURTEEN

Instead of locking Sara up, Nate scheduled a meeting with the chief and LaRouche and Harrington.

Then Nate made a call to the search and rescue command officer. "I have a witness who claims David Price fell off the north side of Echo Mountain."

Sara, Will, Bree and Scott anxiously listened in.

"I understand....Uh-huh. Thanks." Nate ended the call with a frustrated groan. "They won't change their plan to search the east side of Granite Ridge."

"Then, they'll never find David Price," Sara protested.

"I'll talk to the chief. Maybe he's got more influence with SAR."

"What about LaRouche and Harrington's demands to lock me up?" Sara asked.

Nate looked at Sara, then Will. "I have no choice."

"Nate, think about this," Will argued.

"No, he's right," Sara said, putting her hand on Will's arm. "Bringing me in for questioning is proper procedure."

"Why do I feel like there's a 'but' at the end of that sentence?" Nate said, crossing his arms over his chest.

"But if you arrest me, and they find out I'm FBI, they'll bury any evidence of wrongdoing. If they cover their tracks, more people will die from the release of their drug, and if SAR searches the wrong area, David Price, our best chance at stopping them, will never be found, and what if he's alive?"

"That's a lot of ifs," Nate said.

Sara released a sigh. "I messed up by going after this on my own, I get it. Let me help you make it right."

"What do you think?" Nate asked Scott, a former cop.

"I guess it depends how badly you want to keep your job versus putting away the elitist jerks."

"You up for a search mission?" Nate asked Will.

"You bet."

"I'm coming," Sara said.

"No, it's not safe—"

"I can show you exactly where David fell," she interrupted Will.

"We need Sara on the team," Nate said. "Scott, you keep an eye on things back here."

"Fiona and I could help if we had something of David Price's so she could catch his scent," Bree offered.

"They have some items at the command center," Nate said. "We'll swing by, then head up into the mountains." Nate glanced at Scott. "If that's okay with you."

"Wait a minute, you're asking his permission to let me go on the mission?" Bree planted her hands on her hips and narrowed her eyes at Nate.

Scott went to her and brushed hair back away from her face in a sweet gesture. "He knows I lie awake nights worrying about you when you're on a mission, and this one has an added element of danger. I have total confidence in your abilities, love, but I don't trust these guys."

"Yeah, and LaRouche and Harrington might have their own guys searching the mountains, too," Sara said.

"Then, we'd better get going and find him first," Bree said with a lift of her chin.

Scott kissed her and looked at Nate. "You heard the woman. You guys better get going."

Three hours later, Sara, Will, Nate and Bree, along with her golden retriever, were closing in on the spot where David Price should have landed after being flung over the mountainside by Victor LaRouche. Sara had taped her ribs so they didn't hurt too much, and kept her wrist close to her stomach for added protection. Nothing was going to stop her from going on this mission— a dangerous mission that might cost Nate his job, and worse. An encounter with thugs out here in the wilderness could be disastrous.

Nate said they had today to work with, then it would be over. He'd have to officially question Sara about David's death, taking into account LaRouche and Harrington's false accusations.

And the chances of finding David Price in one day? Well, she didn't want to think about that. She needed to stay focused.

"Your boss is wrong," Will suddenly said.

Sara eyed him. "Excuse me?"

"You're working with a team right now." He winked.

Warmth filled her chest at the sight of his smile, the teasing wink and the adorable knit hat he wore that made him look young and untouched by the grief she knew he'd survived.

"Stop flirting," Nate said over his shoulder.

"That obvious, huh?" Will answered.

"Nah," Nate said sarcastically.

"Wait, she's got something," Bree said as they approached a thick mass of brush. "Okay, girl, go find him."

Bree released her and the dog took off. The four of them followed.

Will hung back, probably to make sure Sara was okay. As she eyed Nate and Bree in front of them, and Will beside her, she realized the truth to his words: she was part of a team. She liked the feeling.

"I see something!" Bree called.

Nate put out his hand, indicating he'd go first to investigate. The dog barked excitedly and Bree commanded her to heel.

Sara, Will and Bree approached Nate, who stood beside a small cave.

"You think he's in there?" Will asked.

"One way to find out." Nate clicked on his flashlight and headed into the cave. Sara and Will followed, and Bree waited beside the entrance with Fiona.

Heart pounding, Sara hoped, she prayed, that David was still alive. A part of her felt guilty for not being able to stop Vic LaRouche from throwing him off the cliff.

"David? David Price, this is the police," Nate called. "We're here to help."

Nate hesitated and turned to Will and Sara. "That's far enough for you two. Wait here." Nate continued into the cave while Sara and Will waited anxiously for news about David's condition.

Will interlaced his fingers with Sara's. They waited, the passing seconds feeling like hours.

"Get away from me!" a man shouted.

"No, wait—" They heard a grunt and a thud.

Then silence.

"Out, now." Will pushed Sara toward the exit.

She got safely outside and Bree peered around Sara. "Where's Will?"

Sara spun around. "I thought he was right behind me. He must still be in there." Sara instinctively started back inside. Bree grabbed her arm.

"Wait." Bree dug in her pack and pulled out a small black canister. "To defend yourself."

"Pepper spray?"

"Long story."

Sara turned back to the cave.

"We got him!" Will called out.

A minute later, Will and Nate exited the cave, propping up a disoriented David Price.

"He's okay?" Sara said, shocked.

"Dehydrated and out of it," Nate said, rubbing his forehead where a gash dripped blood. "Bree can you get me some gauze or something? And get David some water."

"Sure."

"He hit you?" Sara asked.

"Probably thought I was a bear."

She studied Will.

"I'm fine," he said. "Talked him down so we could bring him out."

They led David out of the cave to a small clearing and sat him on a boulder. "David Price, I'm Detective Walsh of the Echo Mountain PD. Can you tell us what happened?"

Sara remained silent, not wanting to influence David's recollection.

"They came at me." He looked at Nate with wide eyes. "Huge bees!"

Will offered the guy some water and he drank.

"Do you remember how you ended up down here?" Nate asked as he pressed gauze against his own head wound.

"Do you remember going on a mountain excursion?" Sara said, then eyed Nate, hoping she hadn't crossed a line. He was still focused on David.

"You went on a hiking trip with your partners," Nate offered.

"No!" David stood abruptly and swung his arms. Will got behind him and put him in a hold that rendered him immobile.

"Calm down, sir," Nate said. "We're your search and rescue team, remember?"

"Search and rescue," David repeated, and stopped struggling. "Oh, yeah, sorry."

Will released him and David sat on the boulder again.

"Nice hold," Sara said to Will.

He winked. "Gotta be ready for when the girls bring their boyfriends home."

It amazed her that Will could find humor while embroiled in this intense situation.

"Tell us what you remember about your fall," Nate asked David.

"He threw me... My business partner threw me over the edge." He looked at Sara and scrunched his eyebrows. "I know you, don't I?"

"I was on the trail guide team that led you into the mountains."

David nodded, his gaze drifting to his hands.

"She helped us find you, Mr. Price," Nate offered.

David nodded at Sara. "Thank you. I wouldn't have survived another night."

"Can you walk?" Nate asked.

"I think so."

"If not, we've got a litter," Nate offered.

"No, no, I can walk."

"Did you injure yourself in the fall?" Will asked.

"My arm. I may have broken my arm."

Will examined David's arm. "We can splint it temporarily. Should we call for another team to help bring him back?"

"I'd rather do this on our own for now," Nate said.

David suddenly slumped over. Will eased him down to lie the ground.

"You okay to help me carry him down?" Will asked Nate.

"Yeah, I'm fine." Nate rubbed his head.

"Not so fine if you've got a concussion," Will countered. "Call for another team. There aren't enough of us to carry you down if you pass out."

Nate nodded. "I'll call for backup."

"LaRouche and Harrington will find out where we are," Sara said.

"Unofficial backup," Nate explained. "Friends of mine." He yanked his radio off his belt and squinted to see it.

"Blurred vision?" Will asked.

"Take care of David," Nate ordered.

Will and Sara shared a frustrated look as Will continued splinting David's arm.

"It's Nate," he said into his phone. "We found him

where I marked it on the map. He's wounded and we need help carrying him down. Yep....What?... Okay, will do." He looked back at the group. "They'll be here as soon as possible."

David moaned and opened his eyes, blinking as he focused on the towering trees. "I'm still here. I can't be here." He struggled to sit up.

"Hang on, buddy," Will said.

"I have to get back to my family. It's Christmas," he said.

"You've got time. Christmas is two weeks away," Bree offered.

"If you're up to it we can start down," Nate said. "Help is on its way. Chances are we'll run into them and they can carry you the rest of the way."

"I can do it. I can walk," David said.

Will and Nate helped David stand up, and they stayed close, probably worried he'd collapse again. As they hiked down, Bree tried making conversation with Sara, but Sara was more focused on her surroundings. The slightest sound could indicate a potential threat. They were far from safe, and wouldn't be until David had given his official statement.

My business partner threw me over the edge.

Mitigated relief drifted across Sara's shoulders as she considered the significance of David's declaration. It was the proof she needed to clear her name and put an end to LaRouche and Harrington's sinister plan.

And maybe, just maybe, she'd be able to keep her job.

An hour later, a prickling sensation tickled the back of Sara's neck. She'd learned to never question that instinct.

"Everybody down," she ordered, and shoved Will and David down on the ground behind a fallen tree trunk.

A gunshot rang out across the mountain range.

"No!" David cried.

Bree stood there, motionless, the dog barking by her side. Sara dived at Bree, yanking her behind a boulder.

"Tell Fiona to be quiet," Sara said, not wanting the innocent dog to become a target.

Bree looked at Sara with a confused, terrified expression.

"Bree, you're okay," Sara said, squeezing her arm. "Tell the dog to be quiet."

"Fiona, no bark," Bree said.

Fiona nudged Sara's hand so she'd release her grip on Bree. "She's fine, Fiona," Sara said. "Bree, tell her you're fine."

"Good girl," Bree said. "Mama's okay. Right here, honey." The dog settled down beside Bree, who still looked shell-shocked.

"Will, are you okay?" Bree called out.

"David and I are good."

"Nate?" Sara said.

Silence.

"Detective Walsh!" she called out with more force. "Nate!"

Nothing. Sara peered around the boulder and saw Nate's blue jacket. He was down. She took a step to go to him…

Another shot rang out. She darted behind the boulder.

"Sara!" Will shouted.

"I'm fine."

Sara wasn't anxious or panicked. Instead, she suddenly grew calm. She had to protect this group of people who a week ago were strangers, and today meant much more.

Especially Will.

"Everyone stay where you are." Sara turned to Bree. "You're safe back here. Keep Fiona close and quiet, okay?"

Bree nodded.

Sara darted between trees and bushes to get closer to Nate. He lay facedown on the trail. Exposed. "Nate?"

He groaned. "Yeah."

"You need to move. Stay low," she coached from the bushes.

He shifted onto hands and knees, rather one hand, because his other hand clutched his shoulder.

"Come on," she urged.

Nate crouch-ran across the trail to Sara.

A third shot rang out.

Nate ducked, kept running and collapsed beside Sara. He winced as he gripped his shoulder. "Unbelievable."

"How bad?"

"I think through and through."

She pulled a scarf from around her neck. "Move your hand so I can put pressure against the wound."

"Don't worry about me. Take care of the others."

Sara ignored him, pried his hand away from the wound and shoved the scarf in place.

"You have to protect..." Nate's voice trailed off and his head lolled to the side.

Between his head injury and the bullet wound, he was out of it.

"Bree?" she called.

"Yes?"

"I need you to come over here and help Nate."

"Won't they shoot at me?"

"You've got good cover if you stay behind trees and bushes. And stay low."

Bree and Fiona darted to where Sara was tending to Nate. No shots were fired, which confirmed Sara's suspicion that the shooter didn't want to kill all of them, probably just David and Sara.

"Keep pressure on the wound," Sara directed Bree.

"Okay."

Sara grabbed Nate's radio and called in. "Base, this is Sara Vaughn. We have an officer down and we're taking fire. We need backup. Our location is—" She paused. "Will, best guess where we are?"

"About one and a half kilometers north of the resort on Cedar Grove Trail."

She repeated the information into the radio. There was no response.

"Base, do you read me, over?" she said.

When no one responded, she decided to take action.

"Bree, stay with Nate." Sara grabbed Nate's gun and went to check on Will, again staying low. As she scrambled across the damp terrain, a shot cracked through the air.

She dived over the fallen tree trunk and landed beside Will and David. "How's it going over here?"

Will narrowed his eyes. "Just peachy."

"David?" she said, sitting up.

A blank expression creased his features. "We're all going to die."

"Nope, not today."

"What's the plan?" Will asked.

"I'll draw his fire, then you're going to have to use this." She handed Will the gun.

He looked at it. "I don't do guns, and I'm not letting you run out there like a duck at a shooting gallery."

"It's our best option."

"There's got to be another one."

"I'm open for ideas." She placed the gun beside Will and turned to ready herself for the hundred-yard sprint. She wasn't even sure where she was going, yet she had to draw the guy out of hiding.

She felt a hand on her shoulder and she turned to look into Will's warm green eyes.

"Be careful," he said. And he brushed a kiss against her lips.

It was all so surreal: the smell of fresh pine, the kiss and the incredible warmth from his lips that drifted across her shoulders. How could something so beautiful be happening at the same time as something so ugly?

Ugly? She'd never thought of her work as ugly before.

Will broke the kiss. "Try calling for backup again, please?"

She looked beyond him at David, who stared straight ahead at nothing in particular. He looked to be in shock.

She tried the radio again. "Base, we have an officer down, over."

Sara and Will held each other's gazes.

"Base, come in, over." Another few seconds passed. "They can't hear us."

With a sigh, Will closed his eyes. She guessed he was praying. A few seconds later he leaned forward and kissed her cheek, as if to say goodbye.

As if he feared she would be shot and killed.

"Do what you think is best," he said, his voice hoarse.

She hesitated, realizing how deeply he cared about her, and she him.

"This is Chief Washburn. We're sending a team, over."

Sara snapped her gaze from Will's and eyed the radio in shock. "Thanks, Chief," she said. "Nate called for a SAR team to carry down David Price. I'm worried about them being in harm's way, over."

"There are two police officers on that team. We estimate they're only ten minutes out from your location. How bad is Nate hit, over?"

"Shoulder wound. He also suffered a head injury and is currently unconscious, over."

"Doc Spencer is with that first team, plus we have another team of cops headed your way. Stay put and stay safe, over."

"You got it, over."

Another shot rang out. Bree shrieked in fear.

"This is ridiculous." Sara grabbed the gun, ready to go out there and shoot blindly at their tormentor.

Will placed his hand over hers. She hesitated and looked into his eyes.

"Help is on the way," he said. "There's no need for you to put yourself at risk."

"I can't sit here and do nothing while they terrorize us. I refuse to hide anymore." She peered around the tree trunk.

"Sara?" Will said.

Irritated, she turned to him.

"Staying here is not the dishonorable thing to do," he said. "His goal is to draw you out. If you go after him, he wins. He will have taken away the only person in our group with the skills to defend us. We need you, Sara." He hesitated. "I need you."

His emerald eyes, so sincere and compassionate, pinned her in place. She couldn't move if she tried.

"Okay?" he said. "Will you stay and protect us?"

"I... Sure."

He motioned for her to sit beside him.

"No, I'll keep watch, in case he advances on us," she said.

Another shot rang out.

"Really?" she snapped.

Fiona burst into a frantic round of barks.

"What's he shooting at? He can't see us," Will said.

"It's called intimidation," Sara said. "Bree, it's okay, he can't see you. You're safe!"

"I don't feel very safe," she called back.

"I hate this," Sara muttered.

"Then, let's change it," Will offered.

"What are you talking about?"

"If there's one thing I've learned in my thirty-four years, it's that in any given situation we have a choice," Will said. "A choice to be fearful or to feel loved."

"Uh... I know you're religious and all that, but even Jesus wouldn't feel loved if someone was shooting at him."

He cracked a smile. "Probably not. Since we're stuck here until help arrives, and this man's goal is to paralyze us with fear, let's make the choice to feel something else."

And then, Will started singing.

"Joy to the world, the Lord is come!" his deep voice rang out.

Sara felt her jaw drop as she stared at this man with

the peaceful demeanor and beautiful voice, and wondered how she'd ended up here, in the company of such an amazing human being. They were being used as target practice, yet he sang instead of panicking.

Then Bree's voice chimed in, and even David croaked out a few words here and there.

Sara shook her head with wonder. She could only guess what their assailant was thinking—probably that they were all crazy.

"Repeat the sounding joy," Will sang, encouraging her to sing along.

She did, but kept her focus glued to the rugged terrain where the shooter hid, waiting for an opportunity to take one of them out.

"Repeat the sounding joy," she sang softly, her eyes scanning the area.

"This is Officer McBride. We hear you, over," his voice said through the radio.

"Officer McBride, this is Sara Vaughn. Nate's been shot and is unconscious. The shooter is still out there, over."

"Ten-four."

"Who's with you?" she asked.

"Officer Duggins, Doc Spencer and Scott Becket."

She withdrew behind the tree trunk and spoke in a low voice. "We need to flush this guy out of hiding, over."

"We're on it. Keep singing to distract him, over."

She nodded at Will. "You heard them. They want us to keep singing."

Will started "Joy to the World" from the beginning, and the group chimed in. Adjusting her fingers on the gun grip, she aimed around the tree trunk in case the shooter planned one final suicide move to kill David Price.

"Police, put your weapon down!" a voice shouted.

Three shots rang out.

She hoped they didn't kill the attacker, because he could provide more evidence against LaRouche and Harrington if he rolled on them.

She spotted movement behind Bree and Nate.

Sara aimed Nate's weapon…

Scott darted up and over shrubbery and landed beside Bree. He held her in his arms. Sara eased her finger off the trigger.

"Breathe," Will said.

She took a slow breath in.

"I've got to get out of here!" David shouted.

Out of the corner of her eye, Sara spotted David take off.

"No!" Will went after him.

"Will!" Sara shouted.

A shot rang out.

Sara sprung out of their hiding spot.

All she could think was *Will was shot!*

The shooter was heading her way. Totally focused on Will and David, both on the ground.

She aimed her weapon. "Hey!"

The guy turned.

Gotta keep him alive.

She fired, hitting him in the shoulder. He kept coming. She fired again, hitting him in the thigh.

He went down and kept crawling toward David and Will.

She sprinted to the shooter and stepped on his firing hand. Officer McBride and his team raced up to Sara.

Oh, God, Will can't die. You can't let him die.

"Doctor Spencer," Sara said. "Will and David... I think one of them was shot..." She could hear herself stumbling, not making much sense.

"What about Detective Walsh?" Officer McBride asked.

"Over here!" Scott called out.

"Spike, go help Nate." Officer McBride stepped closer to Sara. She couldn't take her eyes off the shooter, or her hand still aiming the gun at his back.

"Agent Vaughn?"

Sara glanced at Officer McBride.

With a nod of respect, he said, "Well-placed shots."

She nodded her thanks. "Was he the only one?"

"Yes, ma'am. We searched the immediate area. It's clear. Do you recognize him?"

"No," Sara said.

The shooter attempted to crawl away.

"Yeah?" Officer McBride dropped and kneeled on his back. He pulled his arms behind his back to cuff him. "Where do you think you're going?"

Sara blinked, seeing the gun still at the end of her extended arm. She was okay. They got the shooter.

But Will... Was he...? She lowered her arm and closed her eyes.

"Sara?"

She opened her eyes to Will's tentative smile. They went into each other's arms.

"Was David Price shot?" Officer McBride asked.

"No. He's suffering from dehydration, a possible concussion and a broken arm," Will said.

"Well put, Doctor Rankin," Dr. Spencer said as he examined David.

"Command, this is Officer McBride," he spoke into his radio. "We've located the injured parties, over." He clicked off the radio. "Scott, how's Nate?"

"I'm fine," Nate called back.

"He needs a litter," Scott countered.

"What are you, my mother?" Nate said.

"And he's belligerent from the head injury," Bree said.

"This is Chief Washburn. Have the assailants been neutralized, over?"

"Yes sir, just one, over," Officer McBride answered.

"Is Will Rankin okay, over?" the chief asked through the radio.

Everyone looked at Will.

"I'm fine," Will said.

"He's fine, over," Officer McBride said.

"A SAR team is on the way to assist. Send Will Rankin down ASAP."

"What, why?" Will said.

"Chief, is there a problem?" Officer McBride prompted.

"His mother-in-law is missing."

FIFTEEN

Will paled. "My girls," he muttered, and headed down the trail.

Sara glanced at Nate for permission to follow Will. After all, she'd shot a man with Nate's gun, and perhaps he wanted her to stay at the scene.

"Go," Nate said.

She took off after Will, but didn't crowd him. She didn't want him to feel smothered.

More like, she didn't want to see his face twisted with panic and emotional turmoil. She wasn't sure she could handle that.

Coward, she scolded herself. He'd spent the past few hours keeping everyone sane and calm, and she didn't have the guts to do the same for him?

If she offered comfort and he pushed her away, she'd ignore the rejection and keep on trying.

"Will," she said, close enough to touch him.

He shook his head. "I can't believe I've put her in danger."

"Hey, hey, let's not assume anything here." She finally touched his arm.

He acted as if he didn't even feel her. She let her hand fall to her side.

"Even if it is related to the case, this is not your fault. You did not willingly put your family in danger. La-Rouche and Harrington are the ones who deserve the blame."

She thought he might have nodded. She'd never seen him like this, so lost and closed off.

"I'm not sure…" His voice trailed off. "I'm not sure how I could live without them."

She darted in front of him and placed her hand against his chest. "Don't talk like that. There's no reason to hurt the girls, even if they have them, which I highly doubt."

He stepped around her. "Didn't know you had an optimistic streak, Agent Vaughn."

"Yeah, I'm full of surprises. Now stop going to those dark places and show me how to pray."

He snapped his attention to her. "What?"

"You heard me. So do I need to fold my hands together or do anything special? Look up to heaven or what?"

"You don't have to do this," he said.

"I want to."

His frown eased a bit. "We could recite the Lord's Prayer, I suppose."

As they made their way back to the resort, they repeated the Lord's Prayer, the words feeling unusually natural as they rolled off her tongue. Color had come back to Will's cheeks, and he had stopped clenching his jaw every few minutes.

For the first time in her life, Sara felt a connection

to God as she helped Will avoid the pitfalls of fear and focus on the guiding light of hope.

Mary's heart raced, pounding against her chest like a jackhammer. Where was she? She slowly blinked her eyes open. White surrounded her. Was she dead?

I'm coming, Megan, I'm coming.

No, Mary couldn't die. Who would take care of the girls? Will was always off on his dangerous adventures, putting his own needs first, before the girls'. And while Edward was a fun grandpa, he wasn't a disciplinarian. Without Mary's influence in their lives, the girls would grow up wild and lost.

She fingered a trail of warm blood trickling down her forehead. No, she wasn't dead. Yet.

She pushed at the billowy white material—the airbag that had saved her life. That was right, she had gone out to get construction paper for Marissa's art project, a project that her father should have helped her finish. But he was too busy saving some strange woman's life—a woman who brought trouble to Echo Mountain. Because of Sara, Mary and Ed were taking the girls out of town tomorrow for a few days.

On the way home from getting construction paper, Mary's tires had lost their grip on the slick road, and she had skidded over an embankment.

She looked left, then right. Surrounded by greenery, trees and bushes, she started to panic.

Then heavy white snow started to fall.

She unbuckled herself and looked over her shoulder. She'd landed at the bottom of a ravine.

In a few hours the car would be covered with snow and no one would even know she was down here. She pushed on the door. It wouldn't budge. She reached across the seat to the other side.

Shoved open the door.

It would only open so far. Not far enough to get her body out. Even if she did, how would she climb up to the street level without help?

Her phone—she had to call for help. Then she remembered leaving it behind because she didn't think she'd be gone that long.

"Somebody help! Help me!" she wailed.

She slammed her blood-smudged palm against the horn three times. Waited. Punched three more times.

She couldn't die this way, withering away, probably starving to death.

Alone.

Mama, I love you, but you're going to die a lonely old woman if you don't start softening your edges with the girls, Megan had lectured.

Mary couldn't help herself. She worried about everything and everyone, especially the girls, since their father seemed to let them do whatever they wanted. That was no way to raise a family.

Yet they adored him. Mary saw it in their eyes every time Claire and Marissa saw their dad after being apart for even a few hours.

Suddenly Mary wondered if all this anger she felt toward Will was really coming from somewhere other than worry. No, she was dizzy from the accident, that was all.

Be honest with yourself, Mary.

She finally admitted that her resentment and anger were born of fear, fear that the girls would forget their mother, Mary's pride and joy. Mary feared Will would bring another woman into their lives, they'd forget about their mom and Grandma would be cast aside like a used paper towel.

"No!" she shouted, gasping for breath as fear smothered her.

She slammed her palms on the horn again, desperate to stay alive, to see her granddaughters, to hold them, to show them she did, in fact, have softer edges.

"I can't die!" she cried, slamming her hands on the horn.

Something thudded against the passenger door. She shrieked.

Will shot her a smile and a casual wave. "Looks as if you took a wrong turn, Nanny."

"Oh, Will!" she sobbed with relief.

Another man came up beside Will, about Will's age with a full beard and jet-black hair. Mary didn't recognize him.

"Is she okay?" the bearded fellow asked.

"She'll be better when we get this door open."

They managed to get the door open. Will reached in and touched her shoulder.

Which only made her cry more.

"Hey, it's okay, Mary," Will said in a gentle voice.

She couldn't stop crying. With relief, with gratitude and maybe even with shame.

Will, of all people, had found her. He'd saved her. She'd been so nasty to him since Megan's death, so judgmental.

"We've located her," Will said into a radio. "She seems okay, a little banged up." He hesitated. "Mary, where are you hurt?"

"Everywhere." She sighed.

"Can you be a little more specific?"

"My head's bleeding and my chest aches. That's about it."

"That's plenty." Will clicked on his radio. "We need a litter and two more guys." He nodded at Mary. "You're going to be fine."

"I can't believe you found me."

"Of course I found you. My girls would be lost without their Nanny. Griff here has got more medical training than me, so we're going to switch spots, okay?"

She squeezed his hand, not wanting to let go. "Could you... Would you be able to... Never mind." She didn't have the gall to ask him to stay close considering the way she'd treated him.

She released Will's hand and he backed out. His partner climbed into the car. "Hi, Mary, I'm Griffin Keane. I'm going to examine your head wound to see how serious it is, okay?"

"Sure." As he reached out to remove hair from the wound, she closed her eyes.

A moment later, she felt Will's hand settle on her shoulder from behind. He'd climbed into the backseat.

She reached up and placed her hand over his. "I get it now," she said. "This is what you do with your time off, rescue little old ladies."

"Little, big, old, young, we don't discriminate," Will said. "We make sure we're ready to go when and where we're needed."

"On call for others," Griffin muttered as he placed a bandage on Mary's forehead.

As understanding opened her heart to compassion, Mary felt more alive than she ever had. She looked over her shoulder at Will. "I'm so sorry."

"Aw, don't worry about it. Ed never liked this car anyway."

"That's not what I meant."

He winked. "I know."

Two hours later, Will waited at the hospital for news about Mary. He had truly felt God's presence when he'd rescued her from the car. It was the first time he'd felt a connection to Mary: a positive, healthy connection.

As they had waited for the second team to assist, Mary had confessed her fears about Will and the girls forgetting Megan. He'd assured her that would *never* happen because he and Mary would remind the girls what a wonderful mother Megan had been.

Will closed his eyes and sighed. Through all the danger and threat of violence over the past few days, he'd come to accept that Megan hadn't pushed Will away because she hadn't had confidence in him as a husband to take care of her. Rather, she had feared for him as a father, a challenging position for even the strongest person. Megan had wanted Will to practice being a single parent while she was still around to advise.

So much sacrifice. So much love.

"How about some tea?"

He opened his eyes to Sara, the determined federal agent he'd somehow fallen in love with.

"Sure," he said, and she handed him the paper cup. He clenched his jaw against the awareness that sparked between them every time they touched.

She sat down next to him. "What aren't you telling me?"

"Excuse me?" He snapped his attention to her.

"That jaw-clench thing usually means trouble."

"No, Mary's good, pretty minor injuries considering. When I first saw the car at the bottom of that ravine…" His voice trailed off.

Sara touched his arm. "But she's okay."

"She is, and I think narrowly escaping death has changed her a bit."

"It usually does." Sara studied her teacup. "Not always for the better."

He guessed she was referring to her father's death.

"Daddy! Daddy!" Claire and Marissa sprinted across the hospital lobby. He put the teacup on the table beside him and opened his arms. They launched themselves at him and he held them close.

"How are my girls?"

"Hey, Will. Thank-you doesn't seem like enough," his father-in-law said.

"I should be thanking you for taking care of my rascals."

Marissa leaned back. "Daddy, I'm not a rascal. Did you really rescue Nanny from a car wreck?"

"I did."

"Does she have a broken nose?" Marissa asked.

"No, what makes you ask that?" Will realized Claire's face was still buried against his shoulder.

"Because Olivia's mother got in a car wreck and her nose was broken, and she wore this big white bandage here." She pressed little-girl fingers on her nose.

"Well, Nanny's nose is fine. She's got some scratches and bruises. She'll be A-OK."

"Hi, Miss Sara." Marissa went in for a hug and Sara hugged back.

Will turned his attention to Claire. "Baby doll?"

She tipped her head and whispered into his ear. "I

know about the guy in the mountains trying to shoot you. I didn't tell Marissa. She'd have nightmares."

His heart sank. He didn't want either of his daughters knowing about the danger. "I'm okay, sweetie," he whispered back. "Miss Sara protected us."

"Mr. Varney," a nurse called from the ER doorway. "Your wife can see you now."

"I'm going, I'm going!" Marissa rushed to her grandfather's side.

"What about you, Claire bear?" Ed asked.

"I need to stay with Daddy," her muffled voice said against his neck.

Ed took Marissa into the examining area.

"I should give you some privacy," Sara said.

"No, wait." Will reached out and grabbed her hand. "Don't leave."

Sara nodded and clung to Will's hand.

Claire sniffled against his neck. She was crying.

Compassion colored Sara's blue eyes as she studied his little girl. She'd make such a great mother some day, a fierce protector. He suspected she would brush off such a suggestion.

She slipped her hand from his and reached out to stroke the back of Claire's head. "Your daddy was so brave. He was never frightened, and he made us all feel safe."

Claire turned her head to look at Sara. "He did?"

"I did?" Will said.

"Yep, and you know how?"

Claire shook her head that she didn't.

"He sang."

"He's a good singer."

When Sara looked at Will, his heart warmed in his chest.

"He's good at many things," Sara said softly.

He sensed someone approach from the left. "Will, where is he? Where's Nate?"

Cassie McBride towered over him.

"He's being patched up in the ER," Will said.

"I'm fine, thank you very much," Bree said, walking up to them.

"Bree, Bree, you're here, too!" Cassie threw her arms around her sister and hugged her tight.

"Yeah, I thought you heard about—"

"Where's Nate?" Cassie broke the hold and looked into her sister's eyes.

"In there." She pointed.

Cassie dashed toward the examining area as Nate was being wheeled out.

"Are you okay?" Cassie said. "Where were you shot? Does it hurt? Where are they taking you?"

"Yes… The shoulder… No, thanks to the pain meds, and I don't know." Nate tipped his head toward the orderly. "Where are you taking me? To Hawaii, I hope."

Cassie narrowed her eyes at Nate. "How much pain medication?"

"I dunno, enough?"

With Claire in his arms, Will walked over to Nate, and Sara followed.

Nate extended his hand and they shook. "Hey, buddy. Hey, Claire. Your daddy's a hero, did you know that?"

Claire nodded. "Miss Sara told me."

Nate nodded at Sara. "You talk to the chief?"

"Not yet. He's taking David's statement."

"I need to get him upstairs so he can rest," the orderly said.

"I'm coming with," Cassie said, tagging alongside the stretcher.

"He said rest, Cassie, not answer twenty-seven questions," Nate said.

"I've never asked that many."

"I'll tell ya what, I'll start counting."

"Why are you being such a wise guy? Do you have a concussion? Have they done an MRI? How'd you get that cut on your forehead?" Her voice softened as they turned the corner.

"She talks too much," Claire said.

"She only talks like that when she's nervous," Will said.

"Why's she nervous?" Claire asked.

"Because she was so worried about Detective Nate."

"Ooh," Claire said. "I get it." She giggled.

"Yeah? What do you get, huh?" Will tickled her tummy as the three of them wandered back to the lounge.

"Sara Vaughn?" Chief Washburn said coming down the hall.

"You ready for my statement?" she asked.

"Yes. I need you to come to the station with me."

Two men turned the corner behind the chief. From Sara's tense reaction, Will assumed they were La-Rouche and Harrington.

"Can't she give it to you here, chief?" Will said.

Chief Washburn approached Sara and Will. "I'm afraid not. David Price has given his statement. He claims Sara shoved him off the trail."

SIXTEEN

Will stood there in shock, devastated by the false accusation. A few hours ago David Price had admitted that Mr. LaRouche shoved him off the mountain, and now he was blaming Sara?

The only thing keeping Will from blowing a gasket was the fact he held Claire in his arms.

Sara touched his shoulder, and Will ripped his attention from LaRouche and Harrington's victorious smirks.

With a resigned expression she said, "It's okay. I'll figure things out from here. Take care of your family." She reached out and brushed her thumb across Claire's cheek. "It was nice seeing you again, sweetie."

"You, too, Miss Sara."

With a sad smile, Sara turned and the chief handcuffed her. Will walked away so that wouldn't be the last image Claire would see of Sara: being led away in cuffs by the chief of police.

Will sensed LaRouche's and Harrington's arrogance, their satisfaction. Somehow they'd convinced David to change his story and accuse Sara of attempted murder. But how?

His father-in-law came out of the examining area with Marissa in tow.

"How's Mary?" Will asked.

"She'll be fine once they get her to a room. She was a little cranky and didn't want the girls seeing her like that—" he squeezed Marissa's hand "—so she asked us to wait out here."

"Would you mind watching the girls for a few minutes? I need to talk to Nate."

"Sure, sure."

Will put Claire down. "Stay close to your sister. I'll be right back."

"Okay, Daddy."

He hugged both his girls and went to see Nate. When he got into the elevator, he wondered if Nate was the right guy to be talking to right now. Will changed his mind and made his way to David Price's room.

Will was unsure what he'd say or how he'd persuade the man to admit the truth. Even if he could, David had given his official statement to the chief about Sara.

As he stepped into David's room, he heard a woman's voice behind the privacy curtain. Will hesitated.

"Send them away? Why would I send them away, David? They were so worried about you when you didn't come home. We all were."

"Listen to me, Beth. It's best for everyone if they spend a little time with their cousins over break. I'm also going to hire security to be with them 24/7."

"Security? Why?"

"Our business is dangerous. I know that now."

"That woman's going to jail. She can't hurt you anymore."

"It's not her I'm worried about," he croaked. "It's my criminal partners."

"David," she said, shocked. "What are you talking about?"

"Abreivtas is dangerous. They knew it and pushed it through anyway. I found out and confronted them. That's when LaRouche shoved me over the cliff."

Will ripped the curtain back. "Then, why are you sending an innocent woman to jail?"

"Who are you and what are you doing here?" David's wife said. "I'm calling security." She reached for the phone.

David grabbed her wrist. "Don't."

She released the phone and waited.

"I owe this man my life," David said, nodding his thanks to Will.

"Then, tell the truth," Will countered.

David sighed. "I can't." He squeezed his wife's hand and shook his head.

"David?" she said.

"I can't risk you having a car accident on the way to Pete's soccer practice, or Julianna's skating lessons or…or someone breaking into the house when I'm out of town," he croaked.

His wife's face paled with shock.

David narrowed his eyes at Will. "Do you have a family, Mr. Rankin?"

"Two girls."

"What would you do if someone threatened them?"

Will remembered the visceral panic that had coursed through him when he'd heard Mary had disappeared and he'd feared the girls were with her.

Will had feared the girls had been taken because of his involvement with Sara.

"Mr. Rankin?" David pushed.

"I'd do whatever was necessary to protect them."

"Then, don't judge me for trying to protect my family."

With a nod, Will left the couple alone. What now? Find Nate? Tell the chief what was going on? Who would believe Will, the man who'd fallen in love with a rogue FBI agent accused of attempted murder?

Will would contact Royce, one of the best attorneys in the county, to make sure she didn't go to jail for a crime she didn't commit. Perhaps Royce could leak damaging information to the proper authorities about Abreivtas.

"Don't get ahead of yourself," he said.

He'd get the girls settled at home and make his calls. Will did whatever was necessary to protect the people he loved, and Sara was now on that list.

Sara flung her arm over her eyes as she stretched out on a cot in Echo Mountain PD lockup.

She hadn't seen Will since the hospital last night. She wondered if he'd given up on her, not that she'd blame him. Anyone involved with Sara would be sucked into a melee of problems, staring with her own traumatic childhood, and violent career. Make that her former career.

She'd failed. Miserably.

It didn't surprise her that David Price had changed his story. LaRouche and Harrington had obviously gotten to him, probably threatening David's kids and lovely wife.

Still, Sara hadn't thought she'd end up being arrested and going to jail. Being an FBI agent had to carry some weight with a jury, and once Nate testified that David had, in fact, claimed LaRouche threw him over the mountainside, well, that should be enough for reasonable doubt.

Unless LaRouche and Harrington were able to buy off the jury. No, she couldn't go there, nor did she want to give up on preventing Abreivtas from being distributed. How was she going to do that from a jail cell?

She had to stop her mind from spinning, and rely on others for help. Nate had stopped by earlier and praised her for how she'd handled herself in the mountains. He'd said he was determined to clear her name, as was Will, although Nate had asked Will to keep his distance from Sara. She agreed with that decision, of course, but missed him all the same.

The door to the cell area creaked open.

"Hello, Sara," Vic LaRouche said.

She sat up and glared at him. Ted Harrington stood right beside him. "You've won," Sara said. "Leave me alone."

"Not quite," LaRouche said. "Proving your innocence can be problematic for us. And we know you don't like problems."

"Neither do you, apparently. What did you do to David, threaten his kids or what?"

"We don't threaten. Threats are a bullying tactic, and infer you never mean to follow through." LaRouche leaned into the bars. "We leverage."

"Don't waste your time on me. I'm not fighting the charges."

"No, but your boyfriend is."

She sighed. "Don't have a boyfriend."

"Will Rankin."

She forced a disinterested look on her face. Psychopaths like LaRouche saw right through it.

"He's already contacted a top defense attorney. We can't have that kind of publicity, can we, Ted?"

"Wouldn't be good for business," Ted Harrington agreed.

"Right, the business of killing people," she snapped.

"We don't kill anyone. We offer approved medications to help people cope with the stresses of life," LaRouche said.

"Whatever. I'm going to jail. What more do you want from me?" she said.

With a maniacal smile, he slipped a photograph through the bars. It dropped to the floor. She glanced down at the smiling faces of Will, Claire and Marissa.

"Since you've been unable to convince Mr. Rankin to distance himself from all this, you leave us no choice. It will be a shame to orphan those adorable girls."

She charged the bars to grab him, but he leaned back, out of reach. "Leave that family alone!"

"Tell you what, we'll do just that on one condition."

She waited, clenching her jaw, wondering how much of this she had to endure.

"You'll take our lovely medication and go to sleep with the comfort of knowing the Rankin family will be safe, and the girls will grow up to live long and happy lives."

She eyed the pill in his hand. Now what? If she didn't take it, they'd probably send another assassin, this time to kill Will. The thought of a world without Will's smiling face and warmhearted laugh was not a world worth living in.

She had no choice. She'd take the pill, and bury it in the side of her mouth.

This was going to be a tough sell, yet she had to do it. If she took the pill and something went wrong…

It would be her last sacrifice.

To save Will and the girls.

"Fine." She motioned with her fingers.

"Oh, no, lovely. Open your mouth."

She hesitated. There was no going back now.

"Or were you going to trick us?" LaRouche raised an eyebrow.

She cracked her mouth open. He reached into the cell and grabbed her hair. With a yank, he tossed the pill down her throat and slammed her jaw shut. Her eyes watered. She had no choice but to swallow.

And she did.

He released her with a jerk and she stumbled back. Her gaze drifted to the photo on the floor. She kneeled and picked it up. This was why she'd taken the risk and set herself up as bait: to protect Will and the girls.

"How long were you hunting us?" LaRouche asked.

She snapped her attention to him and straightened. "What?"

"We know you're FBI. We also know you're unstable, which makes this whole—" he motioned with his hand "—overmedication work seamlessly into our plans."

She swayed, gripping the bars. "You can't—"

"We already have. The drug will be released to the general public next month."

It was having a quicker effect on Sara than she'd expected. She struggled to find her words, make sense of the thoughts going through her brain.

"How did you get it…get it through testing?" she asked.

Her eyelids felt heavy and her legs weakened.

"There she goes," Harrington said.

Collapsing on the floor, she stared up at the bright ceiling lights. A low hum filled her ears. She held the photograph so she could see it.

Will. Will and his emerald eyes.

She would die without telling him she loved him. And more innocent people would die because Sara had failed.

"People will die!" she gasp-shouted.

"Well, you will anyway."

She closed her eyes, wanting them gone, wanting her last few moments on earth to be filled with the image of Will and his girls.

"Sa-ra, oh, Sa-ra," LaRouche said.

"Let's go," Harrington said.

"Wait, I've got to leave this."

"Come on, come on, already," Harrington said.

Sara had no idea what LaRouche had put in the cell and didn't care. She wanted them to leave so she could open her eyes and gaze upon the photograph of a smiling father and his two precious girls.

A door slammed and she opened her eyes. They were gone.

She crawled to the toilet, hoping to make herself throw up. Gray fog blurred her vision. She gasped, gripping the photograph in her hand. Willing herself to focus, she held the photograph close, struggled to see.

"Will," she whispered.

Will couldn't wait any longer. He tracked Nate down at Healthy Eats, where Will demanded to see Sara. Nate seemed worn down, probably from the gunshot wound, and he finally gave in. Will felt bad about pressuring his friend, but he needed to see Sara.

When Will and Nate arrived at the police station, the front office was empty.

"Spike?" Nate said.

Will started toward the cell area and Nate yanked him back. "Hang on a second."

Nate went to the computer and punched a couple of keys. A visual of the cell came up on the screen.

Sara was passed out on the floor.

"We've got to—"

Nate put up his hand to silence Will. Then he rewound the video feed and played it back. There, on the screen, they watched Victor LaRouche shove something into Sara's mouth.

Nate pushed Will aside and went to unlock the door to the cell area.

"Sara," Will said. "Sara, wake up."

Nate unlocked the cell door and called for an ambulance.

"This is Detective Walsh. Send an ambulance to Echo Mountain Police Station immediately. I've got an unconscious female."

Will rushed to Sara's side and felt for a pulse. "Nate, we can't wait for an ambulance." He noticed a pill bottle on the cell floor. "Grab that and follow me," Will ordered.

He picked her up and marched out of the cell. When they got into the front office, Spike came in from the back. He was covered in dirt and carried a fire extinguisher.

"Where were you?" Nate said.

"A car fire out back. I locked up."

"Sit behind this desk and don't move until I tell you to."

"Yes, sir."

Nate opened the door for Will. "Let's get her to the hospital."

Will squeezed his hands together in prayer. *Please, God, please let her wake up. Let her be okay.*

They'd given her a drug to counteract the pill La-Rouche had shoved down her throat, and the doctor said the next twenty-four hours were critical.

So Will sat beside her bed. And prayed.

She'd been still all night, hardly stirring, barely breathing.

He closed his eyes and continued to pray. Will couldn't lose her this way. He couldn't lose her, period. He hadn't felt this kind of connection since Megan.

Who would have thought he'd fall in love with a woman like Sara? The FBI agent was determined first and foremost, and had a protective instinct that would scare off a hardened criminal. Such instincts would come in handy with his precocious daughters. That was, *if* Sara had any interest in a future with Will and the girls.

Was he assuming too much? Was he the only one who felt the dynamic pull between them, the trust growing each and every day they spent together? He hoped he wasn't imagining things.

"You're praying."

He snapped his eyes open. Sara stared at him with a confused frown.

"And you're awake," he said, reaching out to take her hand.

"I'm not dead?" she said, with surprise in her voice.

"We got you to the hospital in time."

"LaRouche and Harrington?"

"The truth is out. Nate's got LaRouche on video, forcing you to take the pill. They thought they'd destroyed it, but Nate had a second feed going to another server, courtesy of Zack Carter, who also retrieved the video off your phone."

"That's great news."

"There's more. David Price decided to tell the truth. He gave the feds evidence against LaRouche and Harrington."

"Wow, all this while I was asleep. Did Nate ever figure out how they got to Petrellis?"

"LaRouche and Harrington tracked him down through employee records and bribed him to kidnap you."

"That poor guy. He was collateral damage."

"The ladies at Echo Mountain Church are planning a fund-raiser to support his wife's care."

"That's awfully nice. Think he'll go to jail?"

"Nate's pushing for community service. But be assured, LaRouche and Harrington are going to jail for a very long time."

"It's over." She sighed. "Finally."

Silence stretched between them. The case may be over, but there was more to discuss.

"Sara—"

"Thanks for stopping by." She pulled her hand from his.

"That sounds like a dismissal."

"You should go."

"Excuse me?"

"Will, I'm in the hospital because I was given an

overdose of a medication that could have killed me. This is what I do for a living. I pursue violent offenders. That kind of ugliness has no place in your life."

"You're going back to the FBI? I thought you were suspended."

"After everything that's happened, especially the lengths I went to to nail LaRouche and Harrington, I think Bonner will offer me my position back."

"Sara, there are other ways to fight for justice that don't involve throwing yourself into the line of fire."

She interlaced her hands together, making it impossible for Will to hold them again. "You don't really know me, Will. You know only a fragment of what I am—the fragile woman who needed to be rescued from the mountains. But I know you. I see the wonderful life you have with two precious girls, and a community that cares about you. You need a woman who will stay home and bake cookies and draw pictures with your daughters. That's not me."

He took a chance. He had to. "How do you know if you've never tried?"

Sara sighed and shook her head. "You should go home, be with your family."

"After you answer me one last question, and I need to know so I don't keep messing things up."

"Okay."

"I wasn't imagining it, was I?" he said, his voice hoarse. "This thing between us?"

"Adrenaline. We were swimming in it most of the time we were together. It's to be expected that you'd confuse it with something else."

"You never felt anything—" he hesitated "—when I did this?"

Leaning forward, he pressed a gentle kiss on her lips. When he pulled back, her eyes watered with unshed tears.

"Of course I felt something," she said. "That's why you need to leave." She turned her back to him. "I wish you and the girls the very best."

Will started to reach out and stopped himself. He couldn't force her to open her heart to the glorious possibilities of love, of making a life with Will and the girls. Yet she'd admitted to feeling something, which meant she loved him, right?

Determined. Wasn't that one of her finest qualities? In this case he sensed she was determined that Will find a better woman than Sara.

There was no better woman than Sara, not for Will anyway. How could he convince her of that?

He pressed a light kiss against her head. "I love you, Sara Vaughn. God bless."

SEVENTEEN

Two days later, Sara was released from the hospital and moved into the Echo Mountain Resort at the request of Detective Walsh. Although the case against LaRouche and Harrington seemed solid, Nate wanted Sara to stay in town until they resolved some issues.

The longer she stayed, the harder it would be to leave, especially because of the gifts Will and the girls dropped off at the front desk for her: chocolates, home-made cookies she assumed were snicker poodles and drawings. There were drawings of Will and the girls, drawings of the mountains and drawings of Will and Sara holding hands.

She sighed. If only…

And why not? Why couldn't you be happy here with Will and the girls?

She grabbed her phone and pressed the number for her boss at the FBI, but didn't hit Send. He'd left her a few messages asking her to call him back and discuss her situation.

A part of her had no interest in whatever he had to say, even if he offered an apology and her job back. After spending the week with the people of Echo Mountain, she saw what true loyalty looked like, loyalty and trust. For whatever reason, she'd never developed that kind of relationship with her peers or supervisors at work. They hadn't even trusted her enough to share critical information about their investigation of David Price—which would have prevented this entire disaster.

The lack of trust was partially her fault. Up to this point in life she rarely trusted anyone, yet if you didn't trust, you couldn't expect people to trust you in return.

Then there was Will.

She placed her phone on the table and gazed out the window.

Who would have thought a man like Will would have helped her see the world differently, taught her to trust and work as a team? She could take that lesson back with her to the FBI, which would make her a better agent.

For some reason, she couldn't make the call.

"What is wrong with you?" she muttered.

A knock sounded at the door. She crossed the hotel room and welcomed Nate. "Hey, come on in."

Nate, arm in a sling, entered her room.

"How's the shoulder?" she asked.

"Less irritating than yesterday."

"And the shooter?"

"Alive, and talking once he heard LaRouche and Harrington had been arrested. He'd been on their payroll for years as an enforcer."

"A drug company needing an enforcer. That says it all." She shook her head. "How's the investigation going?"

Nate noticed her neatly folded clothes in an open suitcase. "Why, you in a hurry to leave town?"

"I guess." She went back to the window. Bree and a young man were putting up Christmas lights along the split rail fence.

Christmas, the holiday she never celebrated because she was alone, because she thought spending it with her little brother would only remind him of everything they'd lost.

"It doesn't work, ya know," Nate said.

She turned to him. "I'm sorry?"

"Running."

"Not sure what you mean."

"I recognize that look in your eye. I used to see it when I looked in the mirror. So I ran, thinking it would go away." He shrugged. "It didn't."

"I'm not sure I know what—"

"Will Rankin."

"What about him?"

"You'll regret it."

She tore her gaze from Nate's and changed the subject. "You think the case is solid against LaRouche and Harrington?"

"One hundred percent. I've gotta ask—what were you thinking swallowing that pill?"

"I'd hoped to fake it, but well, you saw the video. LaRouche got hold of me."

"Why agree to take it in the first place?"

"They threatened to hurt Will and the girls."

"Ah, right, go after the people you love as leverage." Her gaze shot up to meet his.

"I'm a detective, remember?" He winked. "I know Will fell fast and hard, but I wasn't as sure about you—" he hesitated "—until just now. Wish you'd reconsider abandoning him. The guy's been through a lot."

"It's better this way."

"Better for whom?" he challenged.

Her phone rang and she eyed the caller ID. "My boss," she said, to put an end to her conversation with Nate.

"I'll see what I can do about letting you leave town," he said. He opened the door and turned. "Too bad, though. Chief Washburn is retiring and they've offered me his job. I could use a seasoned detective on my team."

"I'm sure you'll have plenty of officers fighting for that spot."

"None with the experience of a federal agent."

Nate left and she went back to the window. Light snow dusted the grounds with the spirit of Christmas. Bree looked up and waved at Sara. Sara waved back and smiled. Then Sara glanced at Claire's and Marissa's drawings on the dining table. Another smile tugged at the corner of her lips. She wasn't used to all this smiling.

Sara fingered one of the drawings and noticed writing on the backside. She turned it over...

And read a Bible quote written in Will's hand: "Hope deferred makes the heart sick, but a longing fulfilled is a tree of life." Proverbs 13:12.

Sara's phone beeped, indicating another missed call. Her boss. Rather than call him back and make a rash decision that would affect the rest of her life, she decided to try something radical, for her anyway.

She kneeled beside the bed, clasped her hands together and opened her heart to God's love, praying for guidance, and maybe even...forgiveness.

Will hadn't seen Sara in the past few days, but he knew she was staying at the resort. His friend, resort manager Aiden McBride, told Will that she rarely left her room.

Will had to stop thinking about her and let nature take its course. Sara must come to peace in her own way, in her own time. When she did, Will hoped, he prayed, she'd find her way back to him.

Tonight, as they waited for the town's Christmas tree to light up, as it would every Saturday through Christmas, he ached for Sara to be here with him and the girls.

"What time is it, Daddy?" Marissa said, smiling as she stared at the tree.

"Almost time, sweetie pie," he said.

Claire squeezed his other hand. "Can we get cider after the tree lighting?"

"Sounds like a great idea."

"And roasted checker nuts?" Marissa asked.

"They're called chestnuts, not checker nuts," Claire said, rolling her eyes.

"I like checker nuts." Marissa pouted.

"So do I," his mother-in-law said, stepping up beside them.

She smiled at Will, actually smiled.

"Hi, Mary," Will said, giving her a hug.

"I like chocolate more than checker—I mean, chestnuts," Claire said.

"We'll get you some of that, too, if you'd like," Mary said.

"Really? You said sugar makes us hyper," Claire said.

"A little sugar at Christmastime won't hurt." Mary smiled at her granddaughters.

"She came, she came to the tree lighting!" Marissa took off into the crowd.

"Wait, Marissa, hang on." Will ran after her, while Mary hung back with Claire.

Eyes on his daughter's bright pink jacket, he didn't even notice what had gotten her all excited until he was face-to-face with Sara.

"Hi, Miss Sara! Merry Christmas!" Marissa said, hugging her. Sara kneeled and hugged Marissa back.

Will was speechless, unsure what to think. She'd kept to herself, locked in her hotel room for the past five days, yet she was here, standing right in front of him.

Sara stood. "Hi," she said to Will.

"Hello."

"Give her a hug, Daddy," Marissa encouraged.

Before he could reach for her, Sara wrapped her arms around his waist and leaned against his chest. He held her then, squeezed her tight so that he could remember this moment forever, because it could be just that, a moment.

He breathed in her scent, a mix of vanilla and cinnamon, and realized he'd always think of Sara at the holidays.

"Claire, Claire, look!" Marissa motioned to her sister.

Will released Sara, who greeted his eldest daughter. "Hi, Claire, it's so good to see you."

"You, too, Miss Sara," Claire said.

"Merry Christmas, Sara," Mary said. "Girls, how about we find Papa at the hot-cocoa table."

"Cocoa! Cocoa! Cocoa!" Marissa clapped, jumping up and down.

"Calm down." Claire rolled her eyes again.

The girls grabbed on to their grandmother's hands and waded through the crowd.

"Wow, your mother-in-law actually wished me a Merry Christmas," Sara said.

"I guess she was impressed that you were willing to die to protect me and the girls."

She looked at him in question.

"Nate told us why you took the drug in the first place."

"Wow, word really gets around."

He shrugged. "Small town."

A moment of uncomfortable silence passed between them, then he asked the question he dreaded hearing the answer to. "When do you go back?"

"To work?"

He nodded.

"I'm not going back."

Could this mean…?

"Why not?" he asked.

"I'm leaving the FBI."

Hope swelled in his chest. "What about catching the bad guys?"

"I can do that from anywhere." She hesitated. "Like here, maybe?"

"You mean…?"

She shrugged. "Echo Mountain, if that's okay with you."

"Really?" he said in disbelief.

"Unless you think it's a bad idea."

"No, it's a great idea. What changed your mind?"

She slipped her hand into his. "A very wise man told me I could fight for justice in ways other than throwing myself into the line of fire."

"Sounds like a brilliant man," he teased.

"I guess that's why I fell in love with him, huh?" She offered a tender smile.

"Aw, honey, I am blessed beyond words," he said,

and kissed her, right there, in front of the entire community of Echo Mountain.

Applause broke out around them, and they both smiled, breaking the kiss. Friends patted him on the back, offering congratulations and warm wishes.

All he could see was Sara, the woman he loved.

The Christmas tree suddenly lit up, bathing the crowd in an array of color. The group burst into song—"Joy to the World."

Will and Sara shared a knowing smile.

"They're playing your song," she teased.

"No, sweetheart, it's our song."

* * * * *

Thick snow squalls blew down the Toronto shoreline of Lake Ontario, turning the city's annual winter wonderland into a haze of sparkling lights. The cold hadn't done much to quell the tourists, though, Detective Liam Bearsmith thought as he methodically trailed his hooded target around the skating rink and through the crowd. Hopefully, the combination of the darkness, heavy flakes and general merriment would keep the jacket-clad criminal he was after from even realizing he was being followed.

The "Sparrow" was a hacker. Just a tiny fish in the criminal pond, but a newly reborn and highly dangerous cyberterrorist group had just placed a pretty hefty bounty on the Sparrow's capture in the hopes it would lead them to a master decipher key that could break any code. If Liam didn't bring in the Sparrow now, terrorists could turn that code breaker into a weapon and the Sparrow could be dead, or worse, by Christmas.

The lone figure hurried up a metal footbridge festooned in white lights. A gust of wind caught the hood of the Sparrow's jacket, tossing it back. Long dark hair flew loose around the Sparrow's slender shoulders.

Liam's world froze as déjà vu flooded his senses. His target was a woman.

What's more, Liam was sure he'd seen her somewhere before.

Liam's strategy had been to capture the Sparrow, question her and use the intel gleaned to locate the criminals he was chasing. His brain freezing at the mere sight of her hadn't exactly been part of the plan. The Sparrow reached up, grabbed her hood and yanked it back down again firmly, but not before Liam caught a glimpse of a delicate jaw that was determinedly set, and how thick flakes clung to her long lashes. For a moment Liam just stood there, his hand on the railing as his mind filled with the name and face of a young woman he'd known and loved a very long time ago.

Kelly Marshall.

Don't miss
Christmas Witness Conspiracy *by Maggie K. Black,*
available wherever Love Inspired Suspense books
and ebooks are sold.

LoveInspired.com

Love Harlequin romance?

DISCOVER.

Be the first to find out about promotions, news and exclusive content!

f Facebook.com/HarlequinBooks

t Twitter.com/HarlequinBooks

⃝ Instagram.com/HarlequinBooks

P Pinterest.com/HarlequinBooks

ReaderService.com

EXPLORE.

Sign up for the Harlequin e-newsletter and download a free book from any series at **TryHarlequin.com**

CONNECT.

Join our Harlequin community to share your thoughts and connect with other romance readers! **Facebook.com/groups/HarlequinConnection**

Get 4 FREE REWARDS!

We'll send you 2 FREE Books plus 2 FREE Mystery Gifts.

Love Inspired books feature uplifting stories where faith helps guide you through life's challenges and discover the promise of a new beginning.

FREE Value Over $20

YES! Please send me 2 FREE Love Inspired Romance novels and my 2 FREE mystery gifts (gifts are worth about $10 retail). After receiving them, if I don't wish to receive any more books, I can return the shipping statement marked "cancel." If I don't cancel, I will receive 6 brand-new novels every month and be billed just $5.24 each for the regular-print edition or $5.99 each for the larger-print edition in the U.S., or $5.74 each for the regular-print edition or $6.24 each for the larger-print edition in Canada. That's a savings of at least 13% off the cover price. It's quite a bargain! Shipping and handling is just 50¢ per book in the U.S. and $1.25 per book in Canada.* I understand that accepting the 2 free books and gifts places me under no obligation to buy anything. I can always return a shipment and cancel at any time. The free books and gifts are mine to keep no matter what I decide.

Choose one: ☐ **Love Inspired Romance Regular-Print** (105/305 IDN GNWC)   ☐ **Love Inspired Romance Larger-Print** (122/322 IDN GNWC)

Name (please print)

Address   Apt. #

City   State/Province   Zip/Postal Code

Email: Please check this box ☐ if you would like to receive newsletters and promotional emails from Harlequin Enterprises ULC and its affiliates. You can unsubscribe anytime.

Mail to the **Reader Service:**
IN U.S.A.: P.O. Box 1341, Buffalo, NY 14240-8531
IN CANADA: P.O. Box 603, Fort Erie, Ontario L2A 5X3

Want to try 2 free books from another series? Call 1-800-873-8635 or visit www.ReaderService.com.
